A ROOKIE READER

PAUL
THE
PITCHER

**Written and Illustrated
By Paul Sharp**

Children's Press®
A Division of Scholastic Inc.
New York • Toronto • London • Auckland • Sydney
Mexico City • New Delhi • Hong Kong
Danbury, Connecticut

Dear Parents/Educators,

Welcome to Rookie Ready to Learn. Each Rookie Reader in this series includes additional age-appropriate Let's Learn Together activity pages that help your young child to be better prepared when starting school. *Paul the Pitcher* offers opportunities for you and your child to talk about the important social/emotional skill of pride in accomplishment.

Here are early-learning skills you and your child will encounter in the *Paul the Pitcher* Let's Learn Together pages:

• Rhyming
• Measurement
• Vocabulary

We hope you enjoy sharing this delightful, enhanced reading experience with your early learner.

Library of Congress Cataloging-in-Publication Data

Sharp, Paul.
 Paul the pitcher / written and illustrated by Paul Sharp.
   p. cm. -- (Rookie ready to learn)
 Summary: Rhymed text describes the different things Paul enjoys when he throws a ball. Includes suggested learning activities.
  ISBN 978-0-531-26426-3 -- ISBN 978-0-531-26651-9 (pbk.)
 [1. Stories in rhyme. 2. Baseball--Fiction.] I. Title. II. Series
  PZ8.3.S532Pau 2011
  [E]--dc22

                                                    2010049996

Pául the pitcher throws a ball.

3

Baseball is the game for Paul.

Paul the pitcher throws a ball.

He throws the ball
from spring till fall.

He throws it to the catcher's mitt,

11

unless the batter gets a hit.

Paul the pitcher loves to throw,

sometimes high,

sometimes low.

18

Paul the pitcher loves to throw,

sometimes fast,

sometimes slow.

To throw the ball is lots of fun,

23

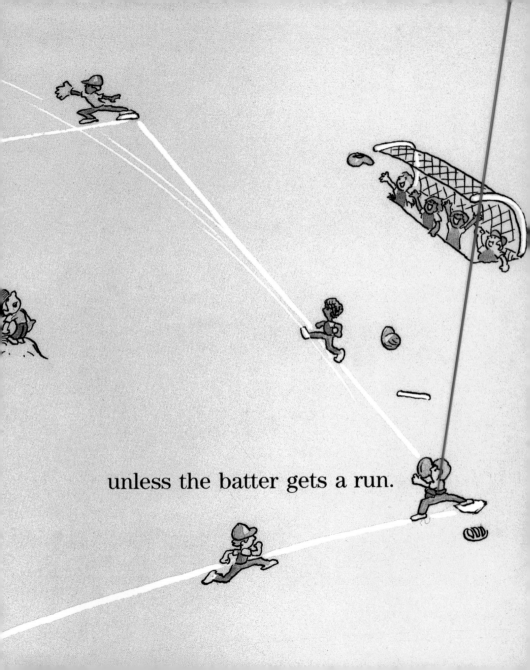

unless the batter gets a run.

Paul the pitcher loves to throw.

Someday he'd like to be a pro.

29

Congratulations!

You just finished reading *Paul the Pitcher* and learned about something Paul likes — baseball.

About the Author/Illustrator

Paul Sharp graduated from the Art Institute of Pittsburgh with a degree in Visual Communications. He has done illustrations for numerous children's books and magazines. This is the fifth book Paul has illustrated for Children's Press. He also wrote it. Paul presently lives, and works as an artist, in Lafayette, Indiana.

Take Me Out to Play Ball

(Sing the song below to the tune of "Take Me Out to the Ball Game.")

Take me out
to the ball game,
Take me out
with the crowd.
I'll show you how
I'm becoming a pro.
It took some time to
perfect my throw.
Let's go, go, go to the
playground,
So I can practice all day.
For it's one, two, three
strikes you're out
And I'll say *hip, hip, hooray*!

PARENT TIP: Paul's favorite activity is baseball. Talk to your child about one of her favorite activities and why it's important to practice. Use fun and encouragement when your child gets frustrated from time to time. Frustration is often a sign that your child is moving to a more challenging level of activity.

Rhyme Time

Many words in *Paul the Pitcher* rhyme, such as *ball* and *fall*. Rhyming words have the same ending sounds.

Look at a picture in the top row. Find and point to the word that rhymes with it in the bottom row.

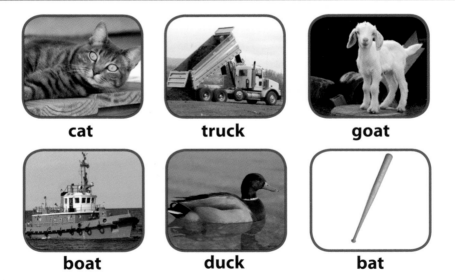

cat	truck	goat
boat	**duck**	**bat**

PARENT TIP: Have more fun rhyming. Challenge your child to see how many other words he can come up with that rhyme with *cat* and *bat*.

Near or Far?

Three batters are on the run. Rulers are used to measure distance. Look at the ruler below. The distance between each number equals one inch. How far did the first batter go? The second? The third?

PARENT TIP: Using the ruler in the book, kids can measure other objects, such as a crayon or a wooden block. You can reinforce the concept of measurement by using words such as *shorter/taller*, *smaller/larger*, *near/far*, etc., in everyday conversations with your child.

You don't have to head outside to practice your baseball swing.

You can do it right at home. Use an empty paper towel tube as the bat. Then make a ball out of aluminum foil. You'll be ready to hit a home run in no time!

PARENT TIP: For children to feel confident, focus on their strength. Make sure you let them know that strengths can come in different forms — characteristics like kindness and generosity; academic, artistic, athletic, or musical skills; or even a sense of humor.

When I Grow Up

Finish this rhyming poem about what you want to be by saying the missing word in each sentence.

When I look to the future,
this is what I see:
A _____
is what I hope to be.

Hard work and
_____are the key
To become the best
possible me!

Paul the Pitcher Word List (38 Words)

a	fun	lots	someday
ball	game	loves	sometimes
baseball	gets	low	spring
batter	he	mitt	the
be	he'd	of	throw(s)
catcher's	high	Paul	till
fall	hit	pitcher	to
fast	is	pro	unless
for	it	run	
from	like	slow	

PARENT TIP: Take this opportunity to point out to your child that the author of the book *Paul the Pitcher* wrote the story with words that rhyme, or have the same ending sound, such as *ball* and *fall*. Find some words in the word list that have the same ending sounds and say them out loud with your child. Your child might enjoy going back through the book to find other words that rhyme.

Fodor's  Maine, Vermont, New Hampshire

Reprinted from *Fodor's New England*

Fodor's Travel Publications, Inc.
New York • Toronto • London • Sydney • Auckland

ISBN 0–679–02579–0

Fodor's Maine, Vermont, New Hampshire

Editors: Jillian L. Magalaner, Scott McNeely
Contributors: Craig Altschul, David Brown, Tara Hamilton, Alison Hoffman, David Laskin, Betty Lowry, Hilary Nangle, Marcy Pritchard, William G. Scheller, Linda K. Schmidt, Peggi Simmons
Creative Director: Fabrizio La Rocca
Cartographer: David Lindroth
Illustrator: Karl Tanner
Cover Photograph: Peter Guttman

Design: Vignelli Associates

Special Sales

Contents

Maps

Foreword

While every care has been taken to ensure the accuracy of the information in this guide, the passage of time will always bring change, and consequently the publisher cannot accept responsibility for errors that may occur.

All prices and opening times quoted here are based on information supplied to us at press time. Hours and admission fees may change, however, and the prudent traveler will avoid inconvenience by calling ahead.

Fodor's wants to hear about your travel experiences, both pleasant and unpleasant. When a hotel or restaurant fails to live up to its billing, let us know and we will investigate the complaint and revise our entries where the facts warrant it. Send your letters to the editors of Fodor's Travel Publications, 201 E. 50th Street, New York, NY 10022.

Highlights and Fodor's Choice

Highlights

Maine   **Commercial train service** will again become a reality in Maine. By 1994, Amtrak is expected to begin service from Boston to Wells, Biddeford-Saco, Old Orchard Beach (in season), and Portland.

Professional baseball is scheduled to begin in April 1994, when the **Sea Dogs,** a minor-league farm team, will man the bases at Hadlock Field in Portland.

The marine creatures of the Gulf of Maine will be the stars of a new **aquarium** at McKown Point in West Boothbay. The facility will open in summer 1994.

Vermont   The **Frog Hollow State Craft Center,** based in Middlebury and with a branch on the Burlington Marketplace, is a highly regarded showcase for traditional and contemporary works from more than 200 Vermont craftspeople. The center received a 1993 grant from the National Endowment for the Arts, which is helping fund an oral-history project documenting Vermont's folk-art past.

The **Catamount Trail,** a 280-mile cross-country ski trail that runs the length of the state, will be skiable end to end by winter 1994. Volunteers dedicated to finishing the trail— which begins in Readsboro, on the Massachusetts border, and winds through the heart of the Green Mountains to North Troy, on the Canadian border—have been working on the project since 1985. The trail is accessible to skiers of all abilities.

The recently expanded **recreation path** in Burlington snakes south along the waterfront for 15 miles, offering walkers, joggers, cyclists, skaters, and cross-country skiers impressive views of Lake Champlain and the Adirondack Mountains. Further additions slated for 1994 will extend the path into South Burlington and Shelburne.

The **golf course** at Manchester's venerable Equinox Hotel has undergone a $3 million restoration by its new management, which also operates the Gleneagles course in Scotland. The improvements, part of a $20 million renovation program at the hotel, involve redesign by golf-course architect Rees Jones, son of Robert Trent Jones.

New Hampshire   In the past, **air travel** to New Hampshire has meant commercial flights to the Manchester or Lebanon. Now Skymaster connects Boston and Newark with New Hampshire's Laconia and Keene regional airports. Business Express also flies to Pease Air Base, in Newington.

Sections of the 250-mile-long **New Hampshire Heritage Trail** have recently been opened, including a 75-mile stretch along the Merrimack River from the Massachusetts border through Nashua and Manchester to Concord, as well as a section in Franconia Notch. The trail may be used for walking, jogging, biking, and cross-country skiing and connects areas of historic and scenic interest. Eventually it will go all the way to Canada.

On December 31, 1993, Concord will open its **Capitol Center for the Arts,** the largest theater in New Hampshire and a notable vaudeville stage of the 1920s. Built around the Old Capitol Theater, formerly a movie house and concert hall, the center will host performances and exhibits in all media.

Fodor's Choice

No two people will agree on what makes a perfect vacation, but it's fun and helpful to know what others think. We hope you'll have a chance to experience some of Fodor's Choices yourself while visiting Maine, Vermont, and New Hampshire. For detailed information about each entry, refer to the appropriate chapters in this guidebook.

Sights

Sunset over Moosehead Lake, from Greenville, ME, during peak foliage

The view from Appalachian Gap on Route 17, VT

Early October on the Kancamagus Highway between Lincoln and Conway, NH

Taste Treats

Lobster at a lobster pound on the Maine coast

Maple syrup right from the sugar house at Morse Farm, Montpelier, VT

A cone of Annabelle's ice cream in Portsmouth, NH

Special Moments

Skiing the first run of the day following a snowstorm at Sugarloaf/USA, ME

Catching a rare glimpse of moose crossing a remote road in VT's Northeastern Kingdom

Whale-watching off Portsmouth, NH

Attractions for Kids

Children's Museum of Maine, Portland, ME

Green Mountain Flyer excursion train, Bellows Falls, VT

Guiding your own "spaceship" during the "Gateway to Infinity" show at the Christa McAuliffe Planetarium in Concord, NH

Shopping

L. L. Bean and the nearby outlet stores, Freeport, ME

Vermont Country Store, Weston, VT

League of New Hampshire Craftsmen shops in Exeter, Concord, Hanover, Lincoln, Manchester, Meredith, North Conway, Sandwich, and Wolfeboro, NH

Ski Resorts

Saddleback, ME, for scenic wilderness views

Killington, VT, for learning to ski

Jay Peak, VT, for the international ambience

Mad River Glen, VT, for challenging terrain

Sugarbush, VT, for an overall great place to ski

Woodstock Inn and Resort at Suicide Six, VT, for lodging

Waterville Valley, NH, for vacation packages

Museums

Maine Maritime Museum, Bath, ME

Shelburne Museum, Shelburne, VT

Hood Museum of Art, Dartmouth College, Hanover, NH

Currier Gallery of Art, Concord, NH

Country Inns and Bed-and-Breakfasts

The John Peters Inn, Blue Hill, ME (*Very Expensive*)

Vermont Marble Inn, Fair Haven (Rutland), VT (*Very Expensive*)

The Rabbit Hill Inn, Lower Waterford, VT (*Moderate–Expensive*)

Martin Hill Inn, Portsmouth, NH (*Moderate*)

Snowvillage Inn, Snowville, NH (*Moderate*)

Places to Eat

Jonathan's, Blue Hill, ME (*Inexpensive–Moderate*)

The Arlington Inn, Arlington, VT (*Expensive*)

Mary's, Bristol, 79 VT (*Moderate–Expensive*)

The Balsams Grand Resort Hotel, Dixville Notch, NH (*Expensive*)

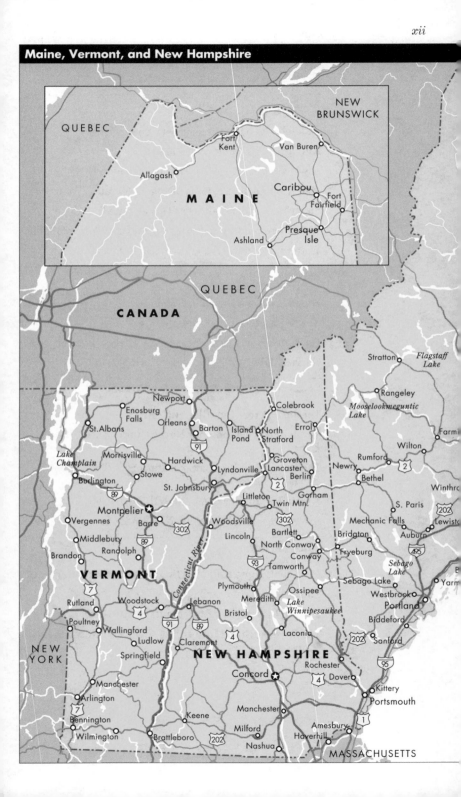

Maine, Vermont, and New Hampshire

QUEBEC

NEW BRUNSWICK

Fort Kent

Van Buren

Allagash

MAINE

Caribou

Fort Fairfield

Presque Isle

Ashland

QUEBEC

CANADA

Stratton

Flagstaff Lake

Rangeley

Enosburg Falls

Newport

Colebrook

Mooselookmeguntic Lake

St.Albans

Orleans

Barton

Island Pond

North Stratford

Errol

Farm

91

Wilton

Lake Champlain

Morrisville

Hardwick

Groveton

Lancaster

Newry

Rumford

2

Burlington

Stowe

Lyndonville

Berlin

Bethel

89

St. Johnsbury

2

Gorham

Winthr

Montpelier

Littleton

Twin Mtn.

S. Paris

202

Vergennes

Barre

302

Woodsville

Mechanic Falls

Lewisto

89

Middlebury

Randolph

Lincoln

Bartlett

Bridgton

Auburn

Brandon

North Conway

Fryeburg

475

VERMONT

Conway

Tamworth

Sebago Lake

7

Plymouth

Ossipee

Sebago Lake

Westbrook

Yarm

Rutland

Woodstock

Lebanon

Meredith

Lake Winnipesaukee

Portland

4

Bristol

Biddeford

Poultney

91

89

Laconia

202

Sanford

Wallingford

Claremont

4

NEW YORK

Ludlow

Springfield

NEW HAMPSHIRE

Rochester

95

Concord

Dover

4

Manchester

Kittery

Arlington

Portsmouth

7

Keene

Manchester

Amesbury

B

Bennington

Milford

1

Wilmington

Brattleboro

202

Haverhill

Nashua

MASSACHUSETTS

Connecticut River

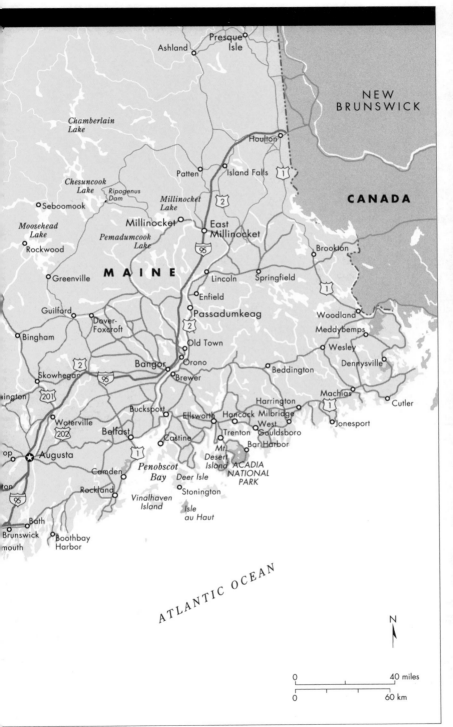

The United States

CANADA

Vancouver
BRITISH COLUMBIA
Calgary
ALBERTA
SASKATCHEWAN
Regina
MANITOBA
Winnipeg

Trans-Canada Hwy.

Seattle
Olympia
WASHINGTON
Columbia R.
Spokane
Great Falls
Missouri R.
MONTANA
Helena
Billings
NORTH DAKOTA
Fargo
Bismarck

Portland
Salem
OREGON
IDAHO
Boise
Snake R.
WYOMING
SOUTH DAKOTA
Pierre
Missouri R.

Carson City
Sacramento
San Francisco
Fresno
NEVADA
Salt Lake City
UTAH
Cheyenne
Denver
NEBRASKA
Lincoln

Las Vegas
Colorado R.
Colorado Springs
COLORADO
KANSAS

CALIFORNIA
Santa Barbara
Los Angeles
San Diego
Flagstaff
ARIZONA
Phoenix
Tucson
Albuquerque
Santa Fe
NEW MEXICO
Amarillo
OKLAHOMA
Oklahoma City

PACIFIC OCEAN

BAJA CALIFORNIA
SONORA
El Paso
CHIHUAHUA
Rio Grande
TEXAS
Austin
San Antonio

RUSSIA
ARCTIC OCEAN
Bering Strait
Bering Sea
Nome
ALASKA
Fairbanks
Anchorage
CANADA
MEXICO
COAHUILA
NUEVO LEON

ALEUTIAN ISLANDS
Juneau

PACIFIC OCEAN

0   400 miles
0   400 km

N

Honolulu
Oahu
Maui
HAWAII
Hawaii
PACIFIC OCEAN

TAM-AULIPAS

ONTARIO
CANADA
QUÉBEC
NEW BRUNSWICK
Québec
Fredericton
Lake Superior
MINNESOTA
Duluth
MICHIGAN
Lake Huron
Lake Ontario
Montréal
Ottawa
Montpelier
N.H.
MAINE
Augusta
Concord
WISCONSIN
St. Paul
Green Bay
NEW YORK
VT.
Boston
Minneapolis
Milwaukee
Lansing
Toronto
Lake Erie
Buffalo
Albany
Hartford
Providence
MASS.
R.I.
CONN.
Madison
Detroit
Cleveland
PENNSYLVANIA
New York
IOWA
Chicago
Pittsburgh
Harrisburg
Trenton
N.J.
Philadelphia
Des Moines
ILLINOIS
INDIANA
OHIO
Columbus
WEST VIRGINIA
Baltimore
MD.
DEL.
Dover
Annapolis
Washington, D.C.
Omaha
Springfield
Indianapolis
Cincinnati
Frankfort
Charleston
Richmond
VIRGINIA
Norfolk
Topeka
St. Louis
Kansas City
Jefferson City
MISSOURI
KENTUCKY
Nashville
Raleigh
NORTH CAROLINA
Tulsa
ARKANSAS
TENNESSEE
Memphis
Columbia
SOUTH CAROLINA
ATLANTIC OCEAN
Little Rock
Birmingham
Atlanta
GEORGIA
Savannah
Dallas
MISSISSIPPI
ALABAMA
Montgomery
Jackson
Mobile
Jacksonville
Tallahassee
FLORIDA
Orlando
Baton Rouge
New Orleans
LOUISIANA
Houston
Gulf of Mexico
Bahama Islands
Miami
Nassau
Lake Michigan
Mississippi R.
Ohio R.
Tennessee R.
Savannah R.
Hudson

N

0   500 miles

0   800 km

AS

Introduction

By David Laskin

Back in the 1940s, photographer Paul Strand took two pictures that capture the essence of northern New England. One photograph, "Susan Thompson, Cape Split, Maine," shows a late-middle-aged woman standing perfectly still at the entrance to her barn. She stands, as if pausing in her work, with her worn hands resting at her sides and her wistful, rather tired eyes just averted from the camera. Susan Thompson has the composure of a person who has lived long and hard in a single place.

The second picture, "Side Porch, New England," is a stark, almost abstract composition. Broad, rough-sawn, white-painted boards frame the porch. A ladder-back chair with a cane seat (unoccupied) stands on the cracked, weathered boards of the porch floor. A broom and a wire rug-beater hang from nails on the wall. The scene is one of poverty, but not of neglect. The broom has obviously swept the porch clean that very morning, and, though the house has not been painted in years, one imagines that the rugs inside receive regular and thorough beatings.

Susan Thompson is gone, and so, most likely, is the old farmhouse with the clean-swept side porch. But even today, you don't have to travel far off the interstates that knife through Maine, Vermont, and New Hampshire before you run across people and houses and landscapes that are hauntingly similar to those Paul Strand photographed nearly 50 years ago. The serenity, the austere beauty, the reverence for humble objects, the unassuming pride in place, the deep connection between man and landscape—all of these remain very much alive in northern New England.

In northern New England, the people and the land (and in Maine, the sea) seem bound by a marriage that has withstood many hardships. The relationship derives its character in part from the harsh climate. Spring withholds its flowers until mid-May, winter blows through in November, and a summer sunny spell is interrupted by rainstorms before it's had time to settle in properly. (There's a saying that there are two seasons in the north country—winter and July.)

There is a heritage here of self-reliance: the hardship of scratching out a living in small farms; the loneliness of sailing onto the cold northern waters to fish. In some places, isolation and hardship breed suspicion and meanness of spirit; in northern New England, they have engendered patience, endurance, a shrewd sardonic humor, and bottomless loyalty.

People sink deep roots in the thin, stony soil. They forgive the climate its cruelty. The north has a way of taking hold of the body and the spirit, as if weaving a kind of spell. It's not just the residents who are susceptible; summer visitors who have endured years of humid, overcast Julys and fog-shrouded Augusts keep coming back.

Distinct as they are in landscape, geology, and feeling, Maine, Vermont, and New Hampshire are linked by their northerness. There is something pure and fine and mystical about the North, just as there is something lush and soft and voluptuous about the South. You can feel the spirit of the North in the very light. The sun seems to burn more sharply and cleanly in the north country: it scours the rocks on the Maine coast, fills Vermont valleys with powdered gold in September, and turns the new snow of January into sapphires and diamonds.

Even more evocative than the light are the sounds of the North: the mournful, five-note whistle of the white-throated sparrow piercing the stillness of a June morning; the slap of lake-water against a sandy shore; or the more insistent murmur of the sea reaching into a cove. At some point in every trip north, I always remind myself to hold my breath, close my eyes, and listen to the silence enfold the land for miles.

The eternal spirit of the region resides in its silence, starkness, light, and birdcalls. But if you seek only the eternal, you miss the crucial role that man has played in shaping northern New England.

The explosions of warfare have not sounded in northern New England since the War of 1812, but throughout the 19th century the explosions of the industrial revolution ripped through the rural quiet in parts of these three states, particularly in southern New Hampshire. But eventually the noise of this revolution subsided. For the first half of the 20th century, the history of northern New England was primarily a history of decline. Mills and quarries were closed. Farms were abandoned. Fishing villages dwindled to a handful of old folks. Fields were overgrown by maple and spruce.

It was only when Americans began to have the time, money, and inclination to travel that the region had a resurgence. Motor courts popped up along Maine's coastal Route 1 during the 1950s. Ski chalets peeked above the pines in Vermont and New Hampshire. Artists, teachers, and urban professionals snatched up the old farmhouses, and hippies set up communes in southern Vermont.

In the 1970s and '80s gentrification began to alter the towns and villages of the North. Second homes and condominiums went up in record numbers on the shores of Lake Winnepesaukee, alongside Maine's Casco and Linekin bays, and throughout the green countryside of southern Vermont.

Gentrification looks lovely compared with some of the other changes that have overtaken northern New England in the past couple of decades. Strip development has swallowed long stretches of Vermont's Route 4, especially around Rutland; and a good deal of southern New Hampshire has a distinctly suburban cast. Factory-outlet fever has reached epidemic proportions in Maine and New Hampshire. It used to be that tourists came to northern New England to buy a jug of maple syrup or a little pillow stuffed with balsam needles—now it's a pair of Bass shoes or Calvin Klein jeans.

Equally distressing are the crowds that have brought urban headaches into the heart of the northern wilderness. An endless caravan of leaf peepers crawls along the Kancamagus Highway in late September. The lift lines at Mount Snow or Bromley can be long enough to make you want to trade skiing for shopping at Manchester's boutiques and outlets. I have found few vacation experiences more depressing than slogging up the long, increasingly steep trail of Vermont's Camel's Hump mountain only to find the summit mobbed with fellow hikers. "Do we seat ourselves, or should we wait for the maitre d'?" one hiker remarked as he surveyed the scores of picnickers who had beat him to the top.

But even in the midst of the changes and crowding of the present, the eternal images, tastes, and experiences of the North endure. The steam of boiling maple sap still rises from sugarhouses all over the Green and White mountains every March. In May, lilacs bloom in fragrant, extravagant mounds beside seemingly every old farmhouse in the North. Loons flapping through the dawn mist rising off a lake, a scarlet-maple branch blazing beside a white church, cows grazing on a lush, green hillside— these images have become clichés, but they are nonetheless stirring and satisfying.

Whenever I feel the first chill of autumn in the air, whenever I see a flock of geese winging north, whenever I come upon a stand of spruce and white pine rising at the end of a freshly mown hay field, I feel the tug of northern New England. The drive north from my home outside New York City is long and dull, and, on the way up, there always comes a moment of doubt: Will it be worth the time and money? Will it have changed? Will it rain or fog the entire time?

Then I see the first ramshackle house with a side porch, the first rough pasture strewn with stones and humps of grass, the first kind, wistful face, and I know it will be all right.

1 Essential Information

Before You Go

Visitor Information

Maine Publicity Bureau, Box 2300, Hallowell, ME 04347, tel. 207/582–9300 or 800/533–9595.
Maine Innkeepers Association, 305 Commercial St., Portland, ME 04101, tel. 207/773–7670.
New Hampshire Office of Travel and Tourism Development, Box 856, Concord, NH 03302, tel. 603/271–2343 or 800/258–3608 for a recorded message about seasonal events.
Vermont Travel Division, 134 State St., Montpelier, VT 05602, tel. 802/828–3236.
Vermont Chamber of Commerce, Department of Travel and Tourism, Box 37, Montpelier, VT 05601, tel. 802/223–3443.

Tours and Packages

Should you buy your travel arrangements to northern New England packaged or do it yourself? There are advantages either way. Buying packaged arrangements saves you money, particularly if you can find a program that includes exactly the features you want. You also get a pretty good idea of what your trip will cost from the outset. You have two options: fully escorted tours and independent packages. Escorted tours mean having limited free time and traveling with strangers. Travel is usually via motorcoach, with a tour director in charge. Your baggage is handled, your time rigorously scheduled, and most meals planned. Escorted tours are usually sold in three categories: deluxe, first-class, and tourist or budget class, the most important difference among them being the level of accommodations. Independent packages, well-suited to the compact New England region, allow plenty of flexibility. They generally include airline travel and hotels, with certain options available, such as sightseeing, car rental, and excursions.

Travel agents are your best source of recommendations for both tours and packages. They will have the largest selection, and the cost to you is the same as buying direct. Whatever program you ultimately choose, be sure to find out exactly what is included: taxes, tips, transfers, meals, baggage handling, ground transportation, entertainment, excursions, sports or recreation (and rental equipment if necessary). Ask about the level of hotel used, its location, the size of its rooms, the kind of beds, and its amenities, such as pool, room service, or programs for children, if they're important to you. Find out the operator's cancellation penalties. Nearly everyone charges them, and the only way to avoid them is to buy trip-cancellation insurance. Also ask about the single supplement, a surcharge assessed to solo travelers. Some operators do not make you pay it if you agree to be matched up with a roommate of the same sex, even if one is not found by departure time. Remember that a program that has features you won't use may not be the most cost-wise choice for you.

Fully Escorted Tours Some operators specialize in one category, while others offer a range. Top operators include **Maupintour** (Box 807, Lawrence, KS 66044, tel. 800/255–4266) and **Tauck Tours** (11 Wilton Rd., Westport, CT 06881, tel. 800/468–2825) in the deluxe category; **Collette Tours** (162 Middle St., Pawtucket, RI 02860, tel. 800/

832–4656), **Domenico Tours** (751 Broadway, Bayonne, NJ 07002, tel. 800/554–8687), **Globus-Gateway** (95-25 Queens Blvd., Rego Park, NY 11374, tel. 800/221–0090), **Gray Line** (275 Tremont St., Boston, MA 02116, 617/426–8805), **Mayflower Tours** (1225 Warren Ave., Downers Grove, IL 60515, tel. 800/ 323–7604 or 708/960–3430), and **New England/Mt. Snow Vacation Tours** (Box 560, West Dover, VT 05356, tel. 800/742–7669), which has 136 programs, in the first-class category.

Independent Packages Independent packages are offered by tour operators who may also do escorted programs, and any number of other companies from large, established firms to small, new entrepreneurs. Airline operators include **American Airlines Fly AAway Vacations** (tel. 800/321–2121), **Continental Airlines's Grand Destinations** (tel. 800/634–5555), and **United Airlines' Vacation Planning Center** (tel. 800/328–6877). Also look into **Americantours International East** (347 Fifth Ave., 3rd floor, New York, NY 10016, tel. 800/800–8942 or 212/683–5337).

These programs come in a wide range of prices based on levels of luxury and options—in addition to hotel and airfare, sightseeing, car rental, transfers, admission to local attractions, and other extras, even breakfasts. Note that when pricing different packages, it sometimes pays to purchase the same arrangements separately, as when a rock-bottom promotional airfare is being offered, for example. Again, base your choice on what's available at your budget for the destinations you want to visit.

Special-Interest Travel Special-interest programs may be fully escorted or independent. Some require a certain amount of expertise, but most are for the average traveler with an interest and are usually hosted by experts in the subject matter. The price range is wide, but the cost is usually higher—sometimes a lot higher—than for ordinary escorted tours and packages, because of the expert guiding and special activities.

Hiking **Hiking Holidays** (Box 750, Bristol, VT 05443, tel. 802/453–4816) and **Hike Inn to Inn** (RR 3, Box 3115, Brandon, VT 05733, tel. 802/247–3300), offer guided walking programs in Vermont; on both programs, lodgings are in country inns.

Shopping **Golden Age Festival** (5501 New Jersey Ave., Wildwood Crest, NJ 08260, tel. 800/257–8920) offers motorcoach trips for senior citizens to the Maine discount outlets.

Tips for British Travelers

Visitor Information Contact the **U.S. Travel and Tourism Administration** (Box 1EN, London W1A 1EN, tel. 071/495–4466).

Passports and Visas You need a valid 10-year passport to enter the United States. A visa is not necessary unless 1) you are planning to stay more than 90 days; 2) your trip is for purposes other than vacation; 3) you have at some time been refused a visa, or refused admission to the United States, or have been required to leave by the U.S. Immigration and Naturalization Service; or 4) you do not have a return or onward ticket. You will need to fill out the Visa Waiver Form, 1–94W, supplied by the airline.

To apply for a visa or for more information, call the U.S. Embassy's Visa Information Line (tel. 0891/200–290; calls cost 48p per minute or 36p per minute cheap rate). If you require a visa, call 0891/234–224 to schedule an interview.

Airports and Airlines Four airlines fly direct to Boston: **British Airways** (tel. 081/897–4000) and **American Airlines** (tel. 0800/010151), departing Heathrow; and **Northwest** (tel. 0345/747800) and **Virgin Atlantic** (tel. 0293/747747) from Gatwick. Northwest also serves Prestwick.

Seven airlines fly direct from Heathrow to New York's JFK or Newark: **British Airways, American Airlines, Virgin Atlantic** (*see above*), **United Airlines** (tel. 0426/915500), **Air India** (tel. 081/759–1818), **Kuwait Airways** (tel. 081/745-7772) and **El Al** (tel. 081/759-9771); BA and Virgin also serve Gatwick, as does **Continental Airlines** (tel. 0293/567977), and Virgin and AA both fly direct to Manchester, too.

Customs
U.S. Customs British visitors age 21 or over may import the following into the United States: 200 cigarettes or 50 cigars or 2 kilograms of tobacco; one U.S. liter of alcohol; gifts to a value of $100. Restricted items include meat products, seeds, plants, and fruit. Never carry illegal drugs.

U.K. Customs From countries outside the EC, such as the United States, you may import duty-free 200 cigarettes, 100 cigarillos, 50 cigars or 250 grams of tobacco; 1 liter of spirits or 2 liters of fortified or sparkling wine; 2 liters of still table wine; 60 millileters of perfume; 250 millileters of toilet water; plus £36 worth of other goods, including gifts and souvenirs.

For further information or a copy of "A Guide for Travellers," which details standard customs procedures as well as what you may bring into the United Kingdom from abroad, contact HM Customs and Excise (New King's Beam House, 22 Upper Ground, London SE1 9PJ, tel. 071/620–1313).

Insurance The **Association of British Insurers,** a trade association representing 450 insurance companies, advises extra medical coverage for visitors to the United States.

For advice by phone or a free booklet, "Holiday Insurance," that sets out what to expect from a holiday-insurance policy and gives price guidelines, contact the Association of British Insurers (51 Gresham St., London EC2V 7HQ, tel. 071/600–3333; 30 Gordon St., Glasgow G1 3PU, tel. 041/226–3905; Scottish Provincial Bldg., Donegall Sq. W, Belfast BT1 6JE, tel. 0232/249176; call for other locations).

Tour Operators Tour packages to northern New England are available from **Bales Worldwide Tours** (Bales House, Junction Rd., Dorking, Surrey RH4 3HB, tel. 0306/76881), in conjunction with Tauck Tours; **Kuoni Travel** (Kuoni House, Dorking, Surrey RH5 4AZ, tel. 0306/76711); and **Serenissima Travel** (21 Dorset Sq., London NW1 5PG, tel. 071/730–9841).

Travelers with Disabilities Main information sources include the **Royal Association for Disability and Rehabilitation** (RADAR, 25 Mortimer St., London W1N 8AB, tel. 071/637–5400), which publishes travel information for the disabled in Britain, and **Mobility International** (228 Borough High St., London SE1 1JX, tel. 071/403–5688), the headquarters of an international membership organization that serves as a clearinghouse of travel information for people with disabilities.

When to Go

Maine, Vermont, and New Hampshire are largely year-round destinations. Although summer is a favored time all over northern New England, fall is balmy and idyllically colorful, and winter's snow makes for great skiing. The only times vacationers might want to stay away are during mud season in April and black-fly season in the last two weeks of May. Note that many country museums and attractions are open only from Memorial Day to mid-October, at other times by appointment only.

Fall is the most colorful season in New England, and many inns and hotels are booked months in advance by foliage-viewing visitors. The first scarlet and gold colors emerge in mid-September in northern areas; "peak" color occurs at different times from year to year. Generally, it is best to visit the northern reaches in early October and then to move southward as the month progresses.

Hotel rates fall as the leaves do, dropping significantly until ski season begins. November and early December are hunting season in much of New England; those who venture into the woods then should wear bright red or orange clothing.

Winter is the time for downhill and cross-country skiing. New England's major ski resorts, having seen dark days in years when snowfall was meager, now have snowmaking equipment.

In spring, despite mud season, maple sugaring goes on in Maine, New Hampshire, and Vermont, and the fragrant scent of lilacs is never far behind.

Climate What follows are average daily maximum and minimum temperatures for some major cities in northern New England.

Portland, ME

Jan.	31F	– 1C	**May**	61F	16C	**Sept.**	68F	20C
	16	– 9		47	8		52	11
Feb.	32F	0C	**June**	72F	22C	**Oct.**	58F	14C
	16	– 9		54	15		43	6
Mar.	40F	4C	**July**	76F	24C	**Nov.**	45F	7C
	27	– 3		61	16		32	0
Apr.	50F	10C	**Aug.**	74F	23C	**Dec.**	34F	1C
	36	2		59	15		22	– 6

Burlington, VT

Jan.	29F	– 2C	**May**	67F	19C	**Sept.**	74F	23C
	11	–12		45	7		50	10
Feb.	31F	– 1C	**June**	77F	25C	**Oct.**	59F	15C
	11	–12		56	13		40	4
Mar.	40F	4C	**July**	83F	28C	**Nov.**	45F	7C
	22	– 6		59	15		31	– 1
Apr.	54F	12C	**Aug.**	79F	26C	**Dec.**	31F	– 1C
	34	1		58	14		16	– 9

Information Sources For current weather conditions for cities in the United States and abroad, plus the local time and helpful travel tips, call the **Weather Channel Connection** (tel. 900/932–8437; 95¢ per minute) from a touch-tone phone.

What to Pack

Airlines generally allow two pieces of check-in luggage and one carry-on piece per passenger. *See also* Luggage in Arriving and Departing, *below.*

Clothing The principal rule on weather in northern New England is that there are no rules. A cold, foggy morning can and often does become a bright, 60-degree afternoon. A summer breeze can suddenly turn chilly, and rain often appears with little warning. Thus, the best advice on how to dress is to layer your clothing so that you can peel off or add garments as needed. Showers are frequent, so pack a raincoat and umbrella. Even in summer you should bring long pants, a sweater or two, and a waterproof windbreaker, for evenings are often chilly and the sea spray can make things cool on boating trips. If you'll be walking in the woods, bring heavy boots and expect to encounter mud. Winter requires heavy clothing, gloves, a hat, warm socks, and waterproof shoes or boots.

Casual sportswear—walking shoes and jeans—will take you almost everywhere, but swimsuits and bare feet will not: Shirts and shoes are required attire at even the most casual venues. Jacket and tie are required in some of the better Kennebunkport, Maine, restaurants and in the occasional, more formal dining room elsewhere.

Miscellaneous Remember to pack an extra pair of glasses, contact lenses, or prescription sunglasses. In summer, bring a hat and sunscreen lotion. If you have a health problem that may require you to purchase a prescription drug, take enough to last the duration of the trip. Pharmacies, especially in rural areas, may be closed on Sunday. Remember also to pack insect repellent—and use it! Recent outbreaks of Lyme disease all over the East Coast make it imperative (even in urban areas) that you protect yourself from ticks from early spring through the summer. And don't forget to pack a list of the addresses of offices that supply refunds for lost or stolen traveler's checks.

Cash Machines

Automated-teller machines (ATMs) are proliferating; many are tied to networks such as **Cirrus** and **Plus.** You can use your bank card at ATMs away from home to withdraw money from your checking account and get cash advances on a credit-card account (providing your card has been programmed with a personal identification number, or PIN). Check in advance on limits on withdrawals and cash advances within specified periods. Remember that finance charges apply on credit-card cash advances from ATMs as well as on those from tellers. And note that transaction fees for ATM withdrawals outside your home turf will probably be higher than for those at home.

For specific locations in the United States, call 800/424-7787 for Cirrus, 800/843-7587 for Plus; and press the area code and first three digits of the number you're calling from or the calling area where you want an ATM.

Traveling with Cameras, Camcorders, and Laptops

About Film and Cameras If your camera is new or if you haven't used it for a while, shoot and develop a few rolls of film before leaving home. Pack some lens tissue and an extra battery for your built-in light meter, and invest in an inexpensive skylight filter, to both protect your lens and provide some definition in hazy shots. Store film in a cool, dry place—never in the car's glove compartment or on the shelf under the rear window.

Films above ISO 400 are more sensitive to damage from airport security X-rays than others; very high speed films, ISO 1,000 and above, are exceedingly vulnerable. To protect your film, carry it with you in a plastic bag and ask for a hand inspection. Such requests are honored at American airports. Don't depend on a lead-lined bag to protect film in checked luggage—the airline may very well turn up the dosage of radiation to see what you've got in there. Airport metal detectors do not harm film, although you'll set off the alarm if you walk through one with a roll in your pocket. Call the Kodak Information Center (tel. 800/242–2424) for details.

About Camcorders Before your trip, put new or long-unused camcorders through their paces, and practice panning and zooming. Invest in a sky-light filter to protect the lens, and check the lithium battery that lights up the LCD (liquid crystal display) modes. As for the rechargeable batteries that power the camera, take along an extra pair, so while you're using your camcorder you'll have one battery ready and another recharging.

About Videotape Unlike still-camera film, videotape is not damaged by X-rays. However, it may well be harmed by the magnetic field of a walk-through metal detector.

About Laptops Security X-rays do not harm hard-disk or floppy-disk storage. Most airlines allow you to use your laptop aloft but request that you turn it off during takeoff and landing so as not to interfere with navigation equipment. Make sure the battery is charged when you arrive at the airport, because you may be asked to turn on the computer at security checkpoints to prove that it is what it appears to be. If you're a heavy computer user, consider traveling with a backup battery.

Traveling with Children

In northern New England, there's no shortage of things to do with your children. Major museums have children's sections, and there are dedicated children's museums in cities large and small. Children love the roadside attractions found in many tourist areas, and miniature golf courses are easy to come by. Special events, such as crafts fairs and food festivals, are fun for youngsters as well. As for restaurants, you don't have to stick with fast food. Family-oriented restaurants that specialize in pizza or pasta, and come equipped with Trivial Pursuit cards, pull toys, fish tanks, and other families traveling with children abound. Friendly's is particularly family-friendly, with its legendary ice cream desserts, and, often, crayons on the tables and a rack of children's books not far from the stack of booster seats. Like many restaurants in the region, Friendly's has a special children's menu and an array of special deals for families. Chain hotels and motels also welcome children, and New England has many family-oriented resorts with lively children's programs. You'll also find family farms that accept guests, and which are lots of fun for children; the Vermont Travel Division (*see above*) publishes a directory. Innkeepers, concierges, and desk clerks can usually recommend baby-sitters or baby-sitting services.

Publications *Family Travel Times,* published 10 times a year by **Travel With**
Newsletter **Your Children** (TWYCH, 45 W. 18th St., 7th Floor Tower, New York, NY 10011, tel. 212/206–0688; annual subscription $55), covers destinations, types of vacations, and modes of travel.

Books *Great Vacations with Your Kids*, by Dorothy Jordon and Marjorie Cohen ($13; Penguin USA, 120 Woodbine St., Bergenfield, NJ 07621, tel. 800/253-6476), and *Traveling with Children—And Enjoying It*, by Arlene K. Butler ($11.95 plus $3 shipping per book; Globe Pequot Press, Box 833, Old Saybrook, CT 06475, tel. 800/243-0495, or 800/962-0973 in CT) help you plan your trip with children, from toddlers to teens. From the same publisher is *Recommended Family Resorts in the United States, Canada, and the Caribbean*, by Jane Wilford with Janet Tice ($12.95).

Tour Operators **GrandTravel** (6900 Wisconsin Ave., Suite 706, Chevy Chase, MD 20815, tel. 301/986-0790 or 800/247-7651) offers international and domestic tours for grandparents traveling with their grandchildren. The catalogue, as charmingly written and illustrated as a children's book, positively invites armchair traveling with lap-sitters aboard. **Rascals in Paradise** (650 5th St., Suite 505, San Francisco, CA 94107, tel. 415/978-9800, or 800/872-7225) specializes in programs for families.

Getting There
Air Fares On domestic flights, children under 2 not occupying a seat travel free, and older children currently travel on the "lowest applicable" adult fare. The adult baggage allowance applies for children paying half or more of the adult fare. Check with the airline for particulars.

Safety Seats The FAA recommends the use of safety seats aloft and details approved models in the free leaflet "**Child/Infant Safety Seats Recommended for Use in Aircraft**" (available from the Federal Aviation Administration, APA-200, 800 Independence Ave. SW, Washington, DC 20591, tel. 202/267-3479). Airline policy varies. U.S. carriers must allow FAA-approved models, but because these seats are strapped into a regular passenger seat, they may require that parents buy a ticket even for an infant under 2 who would otherwise ride free.

Facilities Aloft Airlines do provide other facilities and services for children, such as children's meals and freestanding bassinets (to those sitting in seats on the bulkhead, where there's enough legroom to accommodate them). Make your request when reserving. The annual February/March issue of *Family Travel Times* gives details of the children's services of dozens of airlines. "Kids and Teens in Flight" (free from the U.S. Department of Transportation, tel. 202/366-2220) offers tips for children flying alone.

Hints for Travelers with Disabilities

Newer hotels and restaurants as well as those that have recently been renovated are apt to be equipped for travelers with disabilities; the passage of the Americans with Disabilities Act in 1992 should mean increasing accessibility. The official Vermont state map indicates which public recreation areas at state parks have facilities for travelers using wheelchairs. In addition, both the **Vermont Travel Division** and the **New Hampshire Office of Vacation Travel** (*see above*) publish statewide directories of accessible facilities.

Organizations Several organizations provide travel information for people with disabilities, usually for a membership fee, and some publish newsletters and bulletins. Among them are the **Information Center for Individuals with Disabilities** (Fort Point Pl., 27-

43 Wormwood St., Boston, MA 02210, tel. 617/727–5540 or 800/462–5015 in MA between 11 and 4, or leave message; TDD/TTY tel. 617/345–9743); **Mobility International USA** (Box 3551, Eugene, OR 97403, voice and TDD tel. 503/343–1284), the U.S. branch of an international organization based in Britain and present in 30 countries; **MossRehab Hospital Travel Information Service** (1200 W. Tabor Rd., Philadelphia, PA 19141, tel. 215/456–9603, TDD tel. 215/456–9602); the **Society for the Advancement of Travel for the Handicapped** (SATH, 347 5th Ave., Suite 610, New York, NY 10016, tel. 212/447–7284, fax 212/725–8253); the **Travel Industry and Disabled Exchange** (TIDE, 5435 Donna Ave., Tarzana, CA 91356, tel. 818/368–5648); and **Travelin' Talk** (Box 3534, Clarksville, TN 37043, tel. 615/552–6670).

Travel Agencies and Tour Operators **Directions Unlimited** (720 N. Bedford Rd., Bedford Hills, NY 10507, tel. 914/241–1700), a travel agency, has expertise in tours and cruises for the disabled. **Evergreen Travel Service** (4114 198th St. SW, Suite 13, Lynnwood, WA 98036, tel. 206/776–1184 or 800/435–2288) operates Wings on Wheels Tours for those in wheelchairs, White Cane Tours for the blind and tours for the deaf, and makes group and independent arrangements for travelers with any disability. **Flying Wheels Travel** (143 W. Bridge St., Box 382, Owatonna, MN 55060, tel. 800/535–6790 or 800/722–9351 in MN), a tour operator and travel agency, arranges international tours, cruises, and independent travel itineraries for people with mobility disabilities. **Nautilus**, at the same address as TIDE (*see above*), packages tours for the disabled internationally.

Publications In addition to the fact sheets, newsletters, and books mentioned above are several free publications available from the Consumer Information Center (Pueblo, CO 81009): "New Horizons for the Air Traveler with a Disability," a U.S. Department of Transportation booklet describing changes resulting from the 1986 Air Carrier Access Act and those still to come from the 1990 Americans with Disabilities Act (include Department 608Y in the address), and the Airport Operators Council's *Access Travel: Airports* (Dept. 5804), which describes facilities and services for the disabled at more than 500 airports worldwide.

Twin Peaks Press (Box 129, Vancouver, WA 98666, tel. 206/694–2462 or 800/637–2256) publishes the *Directory of Travel Agencies for the Disabled* ($19.95), listing more than 370 agencies worldwide; *Travel for the Disabled* ($19.95), listing some 500 access guides and accessible places worldwide; the *Directory of Accessible Van Rentals* ($9.95) for campers and RV travelers worldwide; and *Wheelchair Vagabond* ($14.95), a collection of personal travel tips. Add $2 per book for shipping. The Sierra Club publishes *Easy Access to National Parks* ($16 plus $3 shipping; 730 Polk St., San Francisco, CA 94109, tel. 415/776–2211).

Hints for Older Travelers

In Hotels Notify country-innkeepers in advance if you want a room on the ground floor, a room with a shower, or a room with bathing facilities other than a Victorian clawfoot tub, which requires climbing in and out.

Organizations The **American Association of Retired Persons** (AARP, 601 E St. NW, Washington, DC 20049, tel. 202/434–2277) provides independent travelers the Purchase Privilege Program, which offers discounts on hotels, car rentals, and sightseeing, and the AARP Motoring Plan, provided by Amoco, which furnishes domestic trip-routing information and emergency road-service aid for an annual fee of $39.95 per person or couple ($59.95 for a premium version). AARP also arranges group tours, cruises, and apartment living through AARP Travel Experience from American Express (400 Pinnacle Way, Suite 450, Norcross, GA 30071, tel. 800/927–0111); these can be booked through travel agents, except for the cruises, which must be booked directly (tel. 800/745–4567). AARP membership is open to those 50 and over; annual dues are $8 per person or couple.

Two other membership organizations offer discounts on lodgings, car rentals, and other travel products, along with such nontravel perks as magazines and newsletters. The **National Council of Senior Citizens** (1331 F St. NW, Washington, DC 20004, tel. 202/347–8800) is a nonprofit advocacy group with some 5,000 local clubs across the United States; membership costs $12 per person or couple annually. **Mature Outlook** (6001 N. Clark St., Chicago, IL 60660, tel. 800/336–6330), a Sears Roebuck & Co. subsidiary with 800,000 members, charges $9.95 for an annual membership.

Note: When using any senior-citizen identification card for reduced hotel rates, mention it when booking, not when checking out. At restaurants, show your card before you're seated; discounts may be limited to certain menus, days, or hours. If you are renting a car, ask about promotional rates that might improve on your senior-citizen discount.

Educational Travel **Elderhostel** (75 Federal St., 3rd floor, Boston, MA 02110, tel. 617/426–7788) is a nonprofit organization that has offered inexpensive study programs for people 60 and older since 1975. Programs take place at more than 1,800 educational institutions in the United States, Canada, and 45 other countries; courses cover everything from marine science to Greek myths and cowboy poetry. Participants generally attend lectures in the morning and spend the afternoon sightseeing or on field trips; they live in dorms on the host campuses. Fees for programs in the United States and Canada, which usually last one week, run about $300, not including transportation.

Tour Operators **Saga International Holidays** (222 Berkeley St., Boston, MA 02116, tel. 800/343–0273), which specializes in group travel for people over 60, offers a selection of variously priced tours and cruises covering five continents.

Further Reading

New England has been home to some of America's classic authors, including Herman Melville, Henry David Thoreau, Edith Wharton, Robert Frost, and Emily Dickinson. Thoreau wrote about Maine in *Maine Woods. The Country of the Pointed Firs*, by Sarah Orne Jewett, is a collection of sketches about the Maine coast at the turn of the century.

Maine, A Guide Downeast, edited by Dorris A. Isaacson, and *Maine: An Explorer's Guide*, by Christina Tree and Mimi

Steadman, are useful guides to sights, hotels, and restaurants throughout Maine. Among books written about the Maine Islands are Philip Conkling's *Islands in Time*, Bill Caldwell's *Islands of Maine*, and Charlotte Fardelmann's *Islands Down East*. Kennebunk resident Kenneth Roberts set a series of historical novels, beginning with *Arundel*, in the coastal Kennebunk region during the Revolutionary War. Carolyn Chute's *The Beans of Egypt, Maine* offers a fictional glimpse of the hardships of contemporary rural life in that state.

Vermont: An Explorers Guide, by Christina Tree and Peter Jennison, is a comprehensive guide to virtually every back road, event, attraction, town, and recreational opportunity in Vermont. Charles Morrissey's *Vermont: A History* delivers just what the title promises. Peter S. Jennison's *Roadside History of Vermont* travels the most popular highways and gives historical background on points along the way. *Without a Farmhouse Near*, by Deborah Rawson, describes the impact of change on small Vermont communities. *Real Vermonters Don't Milk Goats*, by Frank Bryan and Bill Mares, looks at the lighter side of life in the Green Mountain state.

Visitors to New Hampshire may enjoy *New Hampshire Beautiful*, by Wallace Nutting; *The White Mountains: Their Legends, Landscape, and Poetry*, by Starr King; and *The Great Stone Face and Other Tales of the White Mountains*, by Nathaniel Hawthorne. New Hampshire was also blessed with the poet Robert Frost, whose first books, *A Boy's Way* and *North of Boston*, are set here. It's commonly accepted that the Grover's Corners of Thornton Wilder's *Our Town* is the real-life Peterborough, New Hampshire.

Arriving and Departing

By Plane

Flights are either nonstop, direct, or connecting. A **nonstop** flight requires no change of plane and makes no stops. A **direct** flight stops at least once and can involve a change of plane, although the flight number remains the same; if the first leg is late, the second waits. This is not the case with a **connecting** flight, which involves a different plane and a different flight number.

Airports   **Burlington International Airport** in Vermont, **Manchester Airport** in New Hampshire, and **Portland International Jetport** and **Bangor International Airport** in Maine are the major airports in northern New England. **Logan International Airport,** in Boston, the largest airport in New England, is served by most major carriers. **Theodore Francis Green State Airport,** just outside of Providence, Rhode Island, is another major New England airport.

Luggage   Free baggage allowances depend on the airline, route, and
Regulations   class of your ticket. In general, you are entitled to check two bags—neither exceeding 62 inches, or 158 centimeters (length + width + height), or weighing more than 70 pounds (32 kilograms). A third piece may be brought aboard as a carryon; its total dimensions are generally limited to less than 45 inches (114 centimeters), so it will fit easily under the seat in front of you or in the overhead compartment.

Safeguarding Your Before leaving home, itemize your bags' contents and their
Luggage worth, then tag them inside and out with your name, address,
and phone number. (If you use your home address, cover it so
that potential thieves can't see it.) At check-in, make sure that
the tag attached by baggage handlers bears the correct three-
letter code for your destination. If your bags do not arrive with
you, or if you detect damage, do not leave the airport until
you've filed a written report with the airline.

Smoking Since February 1990, smoking has been banned on all domestic
flights of less than six hours duration; the ban also applies to
domestic segments of international flights aboard U.S. and foreign carriers.

By Car

Because the three northern New England states form a relatively compact region with an effective network of interstate
highways and other good roads linking the many cities, towns,
and recreational and shopping areas that attract visitors, a car
is the most convenient means of travel. Yet driving is not without its frustrations; traffic can be heavy on coastal routes on
weekends and in midsummer. Each of the states makes available, free on request, an official state map that has directories,
mileage, and other useful information in addition to routings.
The speed limit in most of New England is 65 miles per hour (55
in more populated areas).

Car Rentals

All major car-rental companies are represented in New England, including **Avis** (tel. 800/331–1212, 800/879–2847 in Canada); **Budget** (tel. 800/527–0700); **Dollar** (tel. 800/800–4000);
Hertz (tel. 800/654–3131, 800/263-0600 in Canada); **National**
(tel. 800/227–7368), and **Thrifty** (tel. 800/367–2277). Rates vary
wildly according to the season, but, in general, economy car
rentals cost $30–$45 per day and $210–$230 per week. This
does not include tax, which varies from state to state.

Extra Charges Picking up the car in one city and leaving it in another may en-
tail drop-off charges or one-way service fees, which can be substantial. The cost of a collision or loss-damage waiver (*see
below*) can be high, also.

Cutting Costs If you know you will want a car for more than a day or two, you
can save by planning ahead. Major companies have programs
that discount their standard rates by 15%–30% if you make the
reservation before departure (anywhere from two to 14 days),
rent for a minimum number of days (typically three or four),
and prepay the rental. Ask about these advance-purchase
schemes when you call for information. More economical rentals are those that come as part of fly/drive or other packages,
even those as bare-bones as the rental plus an airline ticket (*see*
Tours and Packages, *above*).

Other sources of savings are companies that operate as whole-
salers—companies that do not own their own fleets but rent in
bulk from those that do and offer advantageous rates to their
customers. Among them is **Auto Europe** (Box 1097, Camden,
ME 04843, tel. 207/236–8235 or 800/223–5555, 800/458–9503 in
Canada). Rentals through such companies must be arranged
and paid for in advance. Ask whether unlimited mileage is

available and find out about any deposits, cancellation penalties, and drop-off charges, and confirm the cost of the CDW.

One last tip: Remember to fill the tank when you turn in the vehicle, to avoid being charged for refueling at what you'll swear is the most expensive pump in town.

Insurance and Collision Damage Waiver The standard rental contract includes liability coverage (for damage to public property, injury to pedestrians, etc.) and coverage for the car against fire, theft (not included in certain countries), and collision damage with a deductible—most commonly $2,000–$3,000, occasionally more. In the case of an accident, you are responsible for the deductible amount unless you've purchased the collision damage waiver (CDW), which costs an average $12 a day, although this varies depending on what you've rented, where, and from whom.

Because this adds up quickly, you may be inclined to say "no thanks"—and that's certainly your option, although the rental agent may not tell you so. Note before you decline that deductibles are occasionally high enough that totaling a car would make you responsible for its full value. Planning ahead will help you make the right decision. By all means, find out if your own insurance covers damage to a rental car while traveling (not simply a car to drive when yours is in for repairs). And check whether charging car rentals to any of your credit cards will get you a CDW at no charge. In many other states, laws mandate that renters be told what the CDW costs, that it's optional, and that their own auto insurance may provide the same protection.

By Train

Amtrak (tel. 800/872–7245) offers service to northern New England on the *Montrealer*, which crosses Massachusetts and makes stops in New Hampshire and Vermont on its overnight run between Washington and Montréal.

Maine's only passenger rail service is offered by Canada's **VIA Rail** (tel. 800/361–3677), which crosses the state on its service between Montréal and Halifax, stopping at Sackman, Greenville, Brownville Junction, Mattawankeag, Danforth, and Vancebolo.

By Bus

Greyhound Lines (tel. 800/231–2222) provides bus service to major cities and towns in northern New England.

Staying in Maine, Vermont, and New Hampshire

Shopping

Antiques, crafts, maple syrup and sugar, fresh produce, and the greatly varied offerings of the factory outlets lure shoppers to northern New England's outlet stores, flea markets, shopping malls, bazaars, yard sales, country stores, and farmers' markets. In Maine the factory outlet area runs along the coast, in Freeport, Kennebunkport, Wells, Searsport, and Bridgton; in New Hampshire the largest outlet concentration is in North Conway.

Local newspapers and the bulletin boards of country stores carry notices of flea markets, shows, and sales that can be lots of fun—and a source of bargains as well. The **Vermont Antiques Dealers Association** will mail a directory of its members to anyone who sends a stamped, self-addressed envelope to Murial McKirryher, 55 Allen St., Rutland, VT 05701. A directory of **Vermont Hand Crafters** (Box 9385, South Burlington, VT 05403) is available for a stamped, self-addressed envelope.

Opportunities abound for obtaining fresh farm produce from the source; some farms allow you to pick your own strawberries, raspberries, and blueberries, and there are maple-syrup producers who demonstrate the processes to visitors. The **New Hampshire Department of Agriculture** (Box 2042, Concord, NH 03301) publishes lists of maple-syrup producers and farmers' markets in New Hampshire.

Sales Tax   Vermont sales tax is 8%; Maine, 6%; and New Hampshire has no sales tax.

Sports and Outdoor Activities

Biking   A favorite area for bicycling is the New Hampshire lakes region. Biking in Maine is especially scenic in and around Kennebunkport, Camden, and Deer Isle; the carriage paths in Acadia National Park are ideal. Free information is available from the Maine Publicity Bureau and the Vermont Travel Division; for more on their respective areas, contact **Maine Coast Cyclers** (Camden, tel. 207/236–8608), and **Bicycle Holidays** (RD 3, Box 2394-CD, Middlebury, VT 05753, tel. 802/388–2453).

Boating and   In most lakeside and coastal resorts, sailboats and powerboats
Sailing   can be rented at a local marina. Penobscot Bay in Maine has fine cruising grounds. Lakes in New Hampshire and Vermont are splendid for all kinds of boating.

Camping   Many state parks have campgrounds. Contact the **Vermont Association of Private Campground Owners and Operators** (Pine Valley Resort Campground, 40 Woodstock Rd., White River Junction, VT 05001), the **New Hampshire Campground Owners** (Box 320, Twin Mountain, NH 03595, tel. 603/846–5511), and the **Maine Campground Owners Association** (655 Main St., Lewiston, ME 04240, tel. 207/782–5874).

Hiking   The most famous trails are the 255-mile **Long Trail,** which runs north–south through the center of Vermont, and the Maine-to-Georgia **Appalachian Trail,** which runs through New England on both private and public land (contact the Appalachian Mountain Club, Box 298, Gorham, NH 03581, tel. 603/466–2725, and the White Mountains National Forest, Box 638, Laconia, NH 03247, tel. 603/528–8721). You'll find good hiking in many state parks throughout the region, and New Hampshire's White Mountains are crisscrossed by trails. **Road's End Farm Hiking Center** (Jackson Hill Rd., Chesterfield, NH 03443, tel. 603/363–4703) is open from May through December, and the **Audubon Society of New Hampshire** (Box 528–B, Concord, NH 03302, tel. 603/224–9909) maintains marked trails for hikers.

Hunting and Maine's north woods are loaded with moose, bear, deer, and
Fishing game birds. Elsewhere, deer and small-game hunting are big in
the fall. Anglers will find surf-casting along the shore, deep-
sea fishing in the Atlantic on party and charter boats, fishing
for trout in rivers, and angling for bass, landlocked salmon, and
other fish in freshwater lakes. Sporting goods stores and bait-
and-tackle shops are reliable sources for licenses, necessary in
fresh waters, and for leads to the nearest hotspots. Also contact the **Maine Department of Inland Fisheries and Wildlife** (284
State St., Statehouse Station 41, Augusta, ME 04333, tel. 207/
289–2043); the **New Hampshire Fish and Game Department**
(Drawer TP, 2 Hazen Dr., Concord, NH 03301, tel. 603/271–
3421); or the **Vermont Fish and Wildlife Department** (103 S.
Main St., Waterbury, VT 05676, tel. 802/244–7331).

Beaches

Long, wide beaches edge the northern New England coast; the
most popular are in the Kennebunk area of Maine and the coastal region of New Hampshire. Many state and town beaches in
northern New England have lifeguards on duty and many have
picnic facilities. The waters are at their warmest in August,
though they're cold even at the height of summer along much of
the Maine coast. Inland, there are small lake beaches, most
notably in New Hampshire and Vermont.

National and State Parks and Forests

For more information on any of these parks, contact the state
tourism offices (*see* Visitor Information, in Before You Go,
above).

Maine **Acadia National Park** (Box 177, Bar Harbor 04609, tel. 207/288–
National Park 3338), which preserves fine stretches of shoreline and the highest mountains along the East Coast, covers much of Mount De-
sert Island and more than half of Isle au Haut and Schoodic
Point on the mainland. Camping is permitted at designated
campgrounds; hiking, biking, and boat cruises are the most
popular activities.

National Forest **White Mountain National Forest** (Evans Notch Ranger District, RFD 2, Box 2270, Bethel 04217, tel. 207/824–2134) has
camping areas in rugged mountain locations, hiking trails, and
picnic areas.

State Parks **Baxter State Park** (64 Balsam Dr., Millinocket 04462, tel. 207/
723–5140) comprises more than 200,000 acres of wilderness
surrounding Katahdin, Maine's highest mountain. Campgrounds are at sites near the park's dirt road and in remote
backcountry sections; reservations are strongly recommended. Hiking and moose-watching are major activities at
Baxter. The **Allagash Wilderness Waterway** (Maine Department of Conservation, Bureau of Parks and Recreation, State
House Station 22, Augusta 04333, tel. 207/289–3821 May–Oct.;
207/723–8518 Nov.–Apr.) is a 92-mile corridor of lakes and rivers surrounded by vast commercial forest property. Canoeing
the Allagash is a highly demanding activity that requires advance planning and the ability to handle white water. Guides
are recommended for novice canoers. Other major state parks
in Maine include **Camden Hills State Park** (tel. 207/236–3109),
with hiking and camping; **Crescent Beach State Park** (Rte. 77,

Cape Elizabeth, tel. 207/767–3625), with a good sand beach and picnic area; **Grafton Notch State Park** (north of Bethel), with spectacular White Mountain scenery, hiking, and picnic area; **Lamoine State Park** (Rte. 184, 8 mi from Ellsworth), with camping and swimming on Blue Hill Bay near Acadia; **Lily Bay State Park** (Moosehead Lake, tel. 207/695–2700), with lakeside camping, boat ramps, and a hiking trail; **Popham Beach State Park** (Rte. 209 near Phippsburg, tel. 207/389–1335), with a sand beach and picnic area; **Rangeley Lake State Park** (tel. 207/864–3858), with lakeside camping, boat ramps, showers, and swimming beach; **Reid State Park** (Rte. 127, tel. 207/371–2303), with a large sand swimming beach; and **Sebago Lake State Park** (Rte. 302, Naples, tel. 207/693–6613), with nature trails, boat ramp, sand beach, and camping.

Vermont National Forests The 275,000-acre **Green Mountain National Forest** (Box 519, Rutland, VT 05702, tel. 802/773–0300) extends south from the center of the state to the Massachusetts border. Hikers, canoeists, campers, and anglers find plenty to keep them happy. Among the most popular spots are the Falls of Lana near Middlebury; Hapgood Pond between Manchester and Peru; Silver Lake near Middlebury; and Chittenden Brook near Rochester. There are six wilderness areas. The **Green Mountain Club** (RR1, Box 650, Route 100, Waterbury Center, VT 05677 tel. 802/244–7037) publishes a number of helpful maps and guides.

State Parks The 40 parks owned and maintained by the state contain 45 recreational areas that may include hiking trails, campsites, swimming, boating facilities, nature trails (some have an onsite naturalist), and fishing. The official state map details the facilities available at each. The **Department of Forests, Parks, and Recreation** (tel. 802/244-8711) provides park information.

New Hampshire National Forest The **White Mountains National Forest** (Box 63, Laconia, NH 03247, tel. 603/528-8721) covers 770,000 acres of northern New Hampshire.

State Parks New Hampshire parklands vary widely, even within a region. Major recreation parks are at Franconia Notch, Crawford Notch, and Mt. Sunapee. Rhododendron State Park (Monadnock) has a singular collection of wild rhododendrons; Mt. Washington Park (White Mountains) is on top of the highest mountain in the northeast. In addition, 23 state recreation areas provide vacation facilities that include camping, picnicking, hiking, boating, fishing, swimming, bike trails, winter sports, and food services. The **Division of Parks and Recreation** (Box 856, Concord 03302, tel. 603/271–3254) provides information.

Dining

Seafood is king throughout New England. Clams, quahogs, lobster, and scrod are prepared here in an infinite number of ways, some fancy and expensive, others simple and moderately priced. One of the best ways to enjoy seafood is "in the rough," off paper plates on a picnic table at a real New England clamboil or clambake—or at one of the many shacklike eating places along the coast, where you can smell the salt air!

At inland resorts and inns, traditional fare—rack of lamb, game birds, familiar specialties from other cultures—dominates the menu. Among the quintessentially New England dishes are Indian pudding, clam chowder, fried clams, and cranberry anything. You can also find multicultural variations on old themes, such as Portuguese *chouricco* (a spicy red sausage that transforms a clamboil into something heavenly) and the mincemeat pie made with pork in the tradition of the French Canadians who populate the northern regions.

Lodging

Hotel and motel chains provide standard rooms and amenities in major cities and at or near traditional vacation destinations. Otherwise you'll stay at small inns where each room is different and the amenities vary in number and quality. Price isn't always a reliable indicator here; fortunately, when you call to make reservations, most hosts will be happy to give all manner of details about their properties, down to the color scheme of the handmade quilts—so ask all your questions before you book. Don't expect telephone, TV, or honor bar in your room; you might even have to share a bathroom. Most inns offer breakfast—hence the name bed-and-breakfast—yet this formula varies, too; at one B&B you may be served muffins and coffee, at another a multicourse feast with fresh flowers on the table. Many inns prohibit smoking, and some are wary of children. Almost all say no to pets.

At many larger resorts and inns with restaurants, the Modified American Plan (MAP), in which rates include breakfast and dinner, is an option or even standard policy during peak summer season. Other resorts may give guests a dinner credit.

Inexpensive accommodations are hard to find in the desirable resort areas, especially during high season, but packages for weekend getaways, local sports, or cultural events are frequently available; it can pay to ask about them.

Home Exchange This is obviously an inexpensive solution to the lodging problem, because house-swapping means living rent-free. You find a house, apartment, or other vacation property to exchange for your own by becoming a member of a home-exchange organization, which then sends you its annual directories listing available exchanges and includes your own listing in at least one of them. Arrangements for the actual exchange are made by the two parties to it, not by the organization. Principal clearinghouses include **Intervac U.S./International Home Exchange** (Box 590504, San Francisco, CA 94159, tel. 415/435–3497), the oldest, with thousands of foreign and domestic homes for exchange in its three annual directories; membership is $62, or $72 if you want to receive the directories but remain unlisted. The **Vacation Exchange Club** (Box 650, Key West, FL 33041, tel. 800/638–3841), also with thousands of foreign and domestic listings, publishes four annual directories plus updates; the $50 membership includes your listing in one book. **Loan-a-Home** (2 Park La., Apt. 6E, Mount Vernon, NY 10552, tel. 914/664–7640) specializes in long-term exchanges; there is no charge to list your home, but the directories cost $35 or $45 depending on the number you receive.

Apartment and Villa Rentals If you want a home base that's roomy enough for a family and comes with cooking facilities, a furnished rental may be the solution. It's generally cost-wise, too, although not always—some rentals are luxury properties (economical only when your party is large). Home-exchange directories do list rentals—often second homes owned by prospective house swappers—and there are services that not only look for a house or apartment for you (even a castle if that's your fancy) but also handle the paperwork. Some send an illustrated catalogue and others send photographs of specific properties, sometimes at a charge; up-front registration fees may apply.

Among the companies are **Interhome Inc.** (124 Little Falls Rd., Fairfield, NJ 07004, tel. 201/882–6864), **Rent a Home International** (7200 34th Ave. NW, Seattle, WA 98117, tel. 206/789–9377 or 800/488–7368), and **Vacation Home Rentals Worldwide** (235 Kensington Ave., Norwood, NJ 07648, tel. 201/767–9393 or 800/633–3284). **Hideaways International** (15 Goldsmith St., Box 1270, Littleton, MA 01460, tel. 508/486–8955 or 800/843–4433) functions as a travel club. Membership ($79 yearly per person or family at the same address) includes two annual guides plus quarterly newsletters; rentals are arranged directly between members, not by the club staff.

Credit Cards

The following credit card abbreviations have been used: AE, American Express; D, Discover; DC, Diners Club; MC, MasterCard; V, Visa. It's always a good idea to call ahead and confirm an establishment's credit card policy.

Great Itineraries

The following recommended itineraries, arranged by theme, are offered as a guide in planning individual travel.

Scenic Coastal Tour

Maine's coastline is a picturesque succession of rocky headlands, sand-rimmed coves, and small towns built around shipbuilding, fishing, and other seaside trades. For more detailed information, follow in the Maine chapter the tours noted as "The Coast."

Length of Trip Three to four days

The Main Route **Two to three nights:** Swing through the Kennebunks and Portland to the small towns and islands around Penobscot Bay.

Factory Outlet Shopping

While this tour generally follows the same coastline as the preceding tour, its focus is on the challenge of finding bargains at Maine's wealth of factory outlet stores.

Length of Trip Three days

The Main Route **Two nights:** Head up the coast for the Maine towns of Kittery, Freeport, Wells, and Searsport, where outlet shopping abounds.

Kancamagus Trail

This circuit takes in some of the most spectacular parts of the White and Green Mountains, along with the upper Connecticut River Valley. In this area the antiques hunting is exemplary and the traffic is often almost nonexistent. The scenery evokes the spirit of Currier & Ives—or at least the opening sequence of the *Newhart* TV series.

Length of Trip   Three to six days

The Main Route   **One to three days:** From the New Hampshire coast, head northwest to Wolfeboro, perhaps detouring to explore around Lake Winnipesaukee. Take Route 16 north to Conway, then follow Route 112 west along the scenic Kancamagus Pass through the White Mountains to the Vermont border.

One to two days: Head south on Route 10 along the Connecticut River, past scenic Hanover, New Hampshire, home of Dartmouth College. At White River Junction, cross into Vermont. You may want to follow Route 4 through the lovely town of Woodstock to Killington, then along Route 100 and I–89 to complete the loop back to White River Junction. Otherwise, simply proceed south along I–91, with stops at such pleasant Vermont towns as Putney and Brattleboro.

One to two days: Take Route 119 east to Rhododendron State Park in Fitzwilliam, New Hampshire. Nearby is Mount Monadnock, the most-climbed mountain in the United States; in Jaffrey take the trail to the top. Dawdle along back roads to visit the preserved villages of Harrisville, Dublin, and Hancock, then continue east along Route 101 to return to the coast.

2 Skiing

Updated by Craig Altschul and Peggi Simmons

For close to 100 years the softly rounded peaks of New England have attracted people who want to ski. When blanketed with snow, these mountains generate a quiet beauty that lingers in the mind long after one has left them.

Ski lifts made the sport widely accessible, and the manufacturing and treating of snow when nature falls short has made skiing less dependent on weather conditions. The costs of these facilities—and those of safety features and insurance—are borne by the skier in the price of the lift ticket.

Lift Tickets Most people (including the media) make the mistake of listing the single-day, weekend-holiday adult lift pass as the "guidepost." It is always the highest price, and astute skiers look for package rates, multiple days, stretch weekends (a weekend that usually includes a Monday or Friday), frequent-skier programs, season-ticket plans, and off-site purchase locations to save their skiing dollars. The newest bargains are specially priced Sunday full and half-day rates for families.

Single-day adult lift tickets throughout New England range from about $20 to $42. The bigger and more famous the resort, the higher the lift ticket. Be sure to check for senior discounts (over-70s usually ski free) and junior pricing.

Skiing remains one of the more inexpensive sports, even at resorts that demand top-of-the-line rates. Divide six hours of skiing time into $40 (for a high-end full-day lift ticket), and the price is $6.66 per hour. Considering the costs of the lifts and the snow farming (making snow and grooming it), skiing remains a sports bargain . . . even though it doesn't seem that way anymore.

Equipment Rental Rental equipment is available at all ski areas, at ski shops around resorts, and even in cities distant from ski areas. Shop personnel will advise customers on the appropriate equipment for an individual's size and ability and on how to operate the equipment. Good skiers should ask to "demo" or test premium equipment.

At the ski area, beginners should ask about special packages that include basic equipment (rental skis with bindings, ski boots, ski poles), a lesson lasting one hour or more, and a lift ticket that may be valid only on the beginners' slopes.

Trail Rating Ski areas have devised fairly accurate standards for rating and marking trails and slopes. Trails are rated: Easier (green circle), More Difficult (blue square), Most Difficult (black diamond), and Expert (double diamond). Keep in mind that trail difficulty is measured relative to other trails *at the same ski area*, not those of an area down the road or in another state. Yet the trail-marking system throughout New England is remarkably consistent and reliable.

Lessons The Professional Ski Instructors of America (PSIA) have a progressive teaching system that is used with relatively little variation at most ski schools. This allows skiers to take lessons at ski schools in different ski areas and still improve. Lessons usually last 1½–2 hours and are limited to 10 participants.

Most ski schools have adopted the PSIA teaching system for children, and many also use SKIwee, which awards progress cards and applies other standardized teaching approaches. Classes for children are normally formed according to age and

Maine, Vermont, and New Hampshire Ski Areas

Vermont
Bolton Valley Resort, **4**
Bromley Mountain, **12**
Burke Mountain, **5**
Jay Peak, **1**
Killington, **9**
Mad River Glen, **7**
Mt. Snow–Haystack, **14**
Okemo Mountain, **11**
Pico Ski Resort, **8**
Smugglers' Notch Resort, **3**
Stowe Mountain Resort, **2**
Stratton, **13**
Sugarbush, **6**
Suicide Six, **10**

New Hampshire
Attitash, **21**
Balsams-Wilderness, **15**
Black Mountain, **19**
Bretton Woods, **16**
Cannon Mountain, **18**
Gunstock, **24**
Loon Mountain, **20**
Mt. Cranmore, **22**
Mt. Sunapee, **25**
Waterville Valley, **23**
Wildcat Mountain, **17**

Maine
Big Squaw Mountain, **26**
Saddleback Ski and Summer Lake Preserve, **28**
Sugarloaf/USA, **27**
Sunday River, **29**

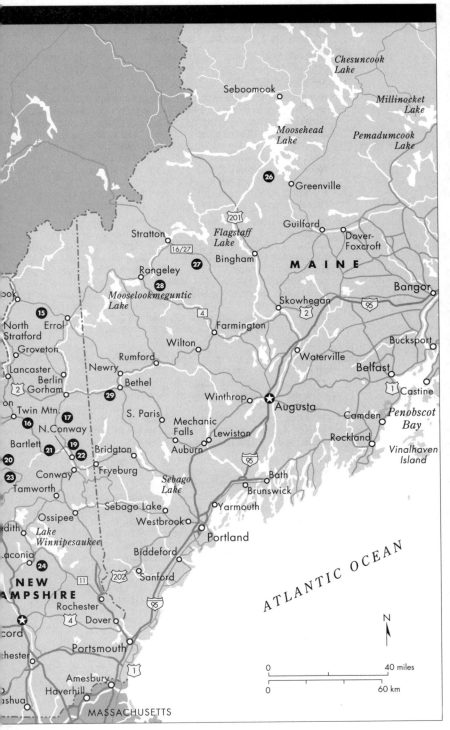

ability. Many ski schools offer half-day or full-day sessions in which children ski together with an instructor, eat together, and take their breaks together.

Child Care Nurseries can be found at virtually all ski areas, and some accept children as young as 6 weeks and as old as 6 years. Reservations are advisable.

Safety A few words about safety: The image of a person with a leg in a cast lounging before a fireplace at a ski resort is a picture many nonskiers associate with the sport. That image is a carryover from the days of stiff skis, soft boots, and nonreleasing bindings, aggravated by icy slopes and a thin snow-cover. Equipment and facilities have improved even in the last 10 years; according to statistics, skiing today is no more hazardous than most other participant sports. Yet accidents occur and people are hurt. All ski areas in the United States have trained Ski Patrolers ready to come to the aid of injured skiers.

Other Activities There is outlet or factory-direct shopping developing in or near northern New England's ski country. Hundreds of outlets are located in the Mt. Washington Valley, New Hampshire, and at Manchester Center, Vermont. In Maine, be sure to stop at Kittery and Freeport (L.L. Bean) on the way in or out. Shopping villages can be found at some of the larger resorts, such as Waterville Valley, New Hampshire; Sugarloaf, Maine; and Stratton, Vermont. Nonskiers might also enjoy sports centers at major ski areas (for activities such as tennis, racquetball, and swimming), and there's usually a cross-country ski touring center nearby.

Lodging Lodging is among the most important considerations for skiers who plan more than a day trip. While some of the ski areas described here are small and draw only day trippers, most ski areas offer a variety of accommodations—lodges, condominiums, hotels, motels, inns, bed-and-breakfasts—close to or a short distance from the action. Because of the general state of the New England economy the past few years, some prices have tended to drop a bit to lure skiers back to the hills.

Weekend accommodations can be arranged easily by telephone; for a longer vacation, one should request and study the resort area's accommodations brochure. For stays of three days or more, a package rate may offer the best deal. Packages vary in composition, price, and availability throughout the season; their components may include a room, meals, lift tickets, ski lessons, rental equipment, transfers to the mountain, parties, races, and use of a sports center. Tips and taxes may also be included. Most packages require a deposit upon making the reservation, and a penalty for cancellation usually applies.

The following rate categories apply to the hotels and inns described in this chapter. Usually, Very Expensive lodging is slopeside—often a convenience that's worth the money.

Category	Cost*
Very Expensive	over $150
Expensive	$100–$150

Moderate	$60–$100
Inexpensive	under $60

*All prices are for a standard double room during peak season, with no meals unless noted, and excluding any service charge and local taxes.

Maine Skiing

Maine sometimes has snow when other New England states do not, and vice versa. In recent years ski areas in Maine have embraced snowmaking with a vengeance, and they now have the capacity to cover mountains. In turn, more skiers have discovered Maine skiing, yet in most cases this has not resulted in crowds, hassles, or lines. The exception is Sunday River, which has become a huge, well-managed attraction and one of New England's most popular ski destinations.

Maine ski areas are building more and better lodging, and skiers generally find lower prices here for practically every component of a ski vacation or a day's outing: lift tickets, accommodations, lessons, equipment, and meals. Nightlife activities at most resorts center on the ski areas and hotel bars and restaurants.

Big Squaw Mountain (Moosehead Resort)
Box D, Greenville 04441
Tel. 207/695–2272

Remote but pretty, Moosehead Resort and Ski Area at Big Squaw is an attractive place for family ski vacations and one that offers appealing package rates. A hotel at the base of the mountain, integrated into the main base lodge, has a restaurant, bar, and other services and offers ski packages.

Downhill Skiing Trails are laid out according to difficulty, with the easy slopes toward the bottom, intermediate trails weaving from midpoint, and steeper runs high up off the 1,750-vertical-foot peak. The 17 trails are served by one triple and one double chair lift and one surface lift.

Other Activities Moosehead Lake and other ponds and streams provide fishing, sailing, canoeing, swimming, and lake-boat cruising in summer. At the mountain there are two tennis courts, hiking, and lawn games. A recreation program for children functions midweek in summer.

Child Care The nursery takes children from infants through age 6 and provides skiing lessons for those who want them. The ski school has daily lessons and racing classes for children of all ages and abilities.

Lodging **Big Squaw Mountain Moosehead Resort.** From the door of the resort you can ski to the slopes and to cross-country trails. The motel-style units and dorm rooms have picture windows opening onto the woods or the slopes, and Katahdin and Moosehead Lake (6 miles away) can be seen from the lawn. The restaurant serves hearty family meals. Live entertainment is often offered on the weekends. American Plan and ski packages are available. *Rte. 15, Greenville 04441, tel. 207/695–2272 or 800/ 348–6743 in ME. 58 rooms with bath. Facilities: restaurant,*

cafeteria, ski shop, ski school, nursery, playground, volley-
ball, 2 all-weather tennis courts. AE, MC, V. Inexpensive.

Saddleback Ski and Summer Lake Preserve
Box 490, Rangeley 04970
Tel. 207/864–5671; snow conditions, 207/864–3380; reserva-
tions, 207/864–5364

A down-home, laid-back atmosphere prevails for families that
come to Saddleback, where the quiet and the absence of
crowds, even on busy weekends, draw return visitors. The base
area has the feeling of a small community for the guests at
trailside homes and condominiums. Midweek lift tickets and
packages come at attractively low rates. With recent expansion
and plans for more, Saddleback is becoming a major resort.

Downhill Skiing The expert terrain is short and concentrated at the top of the
mountain, and an upper lift makes the trails easily accessible
for skiers who want to stick with them. The middle of the mountain is mainly intermediate, with a few meandering easy trails,
while the beginner or novice slopes are located toward the bottom. Two double chair lifts and three T-bars (usually without
lines) carry skiers to the 40 trails on the 1,830 feet of vertical.

Cross-Country Skiing Forty kilometers (25 miles) of groomed cross-country trails
spread out from the base area and circle Saddleback Lake and
several ponds and rivers.

Other Activities More than 100 miles of maintained snowmobile trails in the
Rangeley Region, along with ice skating, sledding, and to-
boganning, are available in winter.

Child Care The nursery takes children ages 6 weeks through 8 years. For
those who are new to skiing, Snoopy classes offer a half day or
full day of lessons for children 4–7. The goal at Saddleback is to
get children into the Junior Masters Program: Levels One and
Two are for 5-year-olds and up with beginning and intermediate skiing skills; the Ski Meisters is for 9-year-olds and up
who can ski in control. A Junior Racing Program serves three
age groups: 9–11, 12–14, and 15 and up.

Lodging **Country Club Inn.** Cathedral ceilings, two fieldstone fireplaces, sitting areas, games tables, and views of the mountains
and lake from the 2,000-foot elevation enhance a stay at this
contemporary inn. Dining in the restaurant provides another
opportunity to enjoy the spectacular view. MAP rates are
available. *Box 680F, Country Club Dr., Rangeley 04970, tel.
207/864–3831. 20 rooms with bath during peak season, 10 during off-peak season. Facilities: restaurant, bar/lounge, pool table. AE, MC, V. Closed Apr., Nov. Expensive.*
Rangeley Inn and Motor Lodge. From Main Street you see only
the massive, three-story, blue inn building (circa 1907), but behind it the newer motel wing commands Haley Pond, a lawn,
and a garden. The traditional lobby and a smaller parlor have
12-foot ceilings, a jumble of rocking and easy chairs, and polished wood. Sizable guest rooms boast iron and brass beds,
subdued wallpaper, and a clawfoot tub in the bath. Motel units
contain Queen Anne reproduction furniture, velvet chairs, and
a whirlpool bath. Gourmet meals are served in the spacious dining room with the Williamsburg brass chandeliers. Modified
American Plan is available. *Main St., Rangeley 04970, tel. 207/
864–3341 or 800/666–3687. 36 rooms with bath, 15 motel units*

with bath. *Facilities: dining room, bar, conference and meeting room. AE, MC, V. Inexpensive–Moderate.*

Town & Lake Motel. This complex of efficiencies, motel units, and cottages alongside the highway and on Rangeley Lake is just down the road from the shops and restaurants of downtown Rangeley. Two-bedroom cottages with well-equipped kitchens are farther from the highway, and some face Saddleback. Pets are welcome. *Rte. 16, Rangeley 04970, tel. 207/864–3755. 16 motel units with bath, 9 cottages. Facilities: swimming, canoes, boat rental in summer. AE, MC, V. Inexpensive–Moderate.*

Sugarloaf/USA
Kingfield 04947
Tel. 207/237–2000; snow conditions, 207/237–2000

Sugarloaf emerged as a major ski resort in the 1980s, with two sizable hotels, a condominum complex, and a cluster of shops, restaurants, and meeting facilities. Sugarloaf/USA refers to itself as the "Snowplace of the East" because of the abundance of natural snow it usually receives, plus its newly acquired ability to manufacture 20 tons of snow per minute. Plenty of special packages and activities are offered at this sophisticated ski resort.

Downhill Skiing The vertical of Sugarloaf, 2,837 feet, makes it taller than any other New England ski peak, except Killington, Vermont. The advanced terrain begins with the steep snowfields on top, wide open and treeless. Coming down the face of the mountain, there are black-diamond runs everywhere, often blending into easier terrain. A number of intermediate trails can be found down the front face, and a couple more come off the summit. Easier runs are predominantly toward the bottom, with a few long, winding runs that twist and turn from higher elevations. The 91 trails are served by Maine's only gondola, two quads, one triple, eight double chair lifts, and a T-bar.

Cross-Country Skiing The Sugarloaf Ski Touring Center has 85 kilometers (53 miles) of cross-country trails that loop and wind through the valley.

Other Activities The Sugartree Sports and Fitness Club features an indoor pool, six indoor and outdoor hot pools, racquetball courts, weightlifting equipment, aerobics machines, saunas, steam rooms, a massage room, and a beauty salon. Use of club facilities is included in all lodging packages. For summer, there is an 18-hole golf course and six tennis courts.

Child Care A nursery takes children from 6 weeks through 6 years. Once they reach 3, children are provided with free ski equipment if they are interested in trying the sport. A night nursery is open on Wednesday and Saturday, 6–10 PM by reservation. Mountain Magic provides instruction for ages 4–6 on a half-day or full-day basis; and Mountain Adventure, with half-day and full-day instruction, is offered to ages 7–14. Nightly activities are free.

Lodging **Sugarloaf Inn Resort.** This lodge provides ski-on access to Sugarloaf/USA, a complete health club, and rooms that range from king size on the fourth floor to dorm style (bunk beds) on the ground floor. A greenhouse section of the Seasons restaurant affords views of the slopes and offers "Ski-in" lunches. At breakfast the sunlight pours in the dining room, and at dinner you can watch the snow-grooming machines prepare your favorite run. *RR 1, Box 5000, Kingfield 04947, tel. 207/237–*

2000 or 800/843–5623. 37 rooms with bath, 5 dorm rooms. Facilities: restaurant, lounge, health club, sauna, Jacuzzi, aerobics classes, video arcade, conference facilities. Also included are adult alpine or nordic midweek lessons. AE, MC, V. Moderate–Very Expensive.

Sugarloaf Mountain Hotel. This six-story brick structure at the base of the lifts on Sugarloaf combines a New England ambience with full hotel service in the European manner. Oak and redwood paneling in the main rooms is enhanced by contemporary furnishings. Valet parking, ski tuning, lockers, and mountain guides are available through the concierge. *RR 1, Box 2299, Carrabassett Valley 04947, tel. 207/237–2222 or 800/527–9879. 90 rooms with bath, 26 suites. Facilities: restaurant, pub, spa, 2 hot tubs, sauna, tanning booth, massage concierge. AE, MC, V. Moderate–Very Expensive.*

Lumberjack Lodge. Located on the access road, ½ mile from Sugarloaf, this informal lodge is the closest accommodation to the mountain. The Tyrolean-style building contains eight efficiency units, each with living and dining area, kitchenette, full bath, bedroom, and no phone or TV. Units sleep up to eight people. A free shuttle to the lifts operates during the peak season. Restaurants nearby serve those who may not want to prepare their own meals. *Rte. 27, Carrabassett 04947, tel. 207/237–2141. 8 units. Facilities: recreation room with fireplace and cable TV, video games, ping-pong, bumper pool, sauna. AE, MC, V. Closed May–Sept. Inexpensive.*

Sunday River
Box 450, Bethel 04217
Tel. 207/824–3000; snow conditions, 207/824–6400; reservations, 800/543–2SKI

From a sleepy little ski area with minimal facilities, Sunday River came on in the 1980s like gangbusters. Today it is among the best managed ski areas in the East. Sunday River recently expanded to a new mountain peak with its own quad chair lift, nine new trails, and the Snow Cap Inn. Spread throughout the valley are three base areas, trail-side condominiums, town houses, and a ski dorm. Imaginatively packaged ski weeks are geared toward a variety of interested groups, including college students, Canadians, and disabled skiers, among others. Beginners are offered a program that guarantees they will learn the basics of skiing in one day or their money will be refunded.

Downhill Skiing Billed as the steepest, longest, widest lift-served trail in the East, White Heat is the latest in a line of trails opened at Sunday River in recent years. At present the area has more than 72 trails, the majority in the intermediate range. Expert and advanced runs are grouped from the peaks, and most beginner slopes are located near the base of the area. Some trails representing all difficulty levels spread down from five peaks (the tallest with a vertical drop of 2,001 feet) that are served by six quads, five triples, and one double chair lift. Each spring the area holds a "Bust n' Burn" mogul skiing contest on White Heat.

Other Activities Within the housing complexes are indoor pools, outdoor heated pools, saunas, and Jacuzzis for winter and summer. For summer, there are two tennis courts, a volleyball court, and mountain biking.

Child Care   The nursery takes children ages 6 weeks through 2 years; the Day Care Center takes them from 2 through 6 years. The SKIwee program accommodates children 4–6, and Mogul Meister is available for ages 7–12. Both programs are available in half- or full-day sessions.

Lodging   **Bethel Inn and Country Club.** Bethel's grandest accommodation is a full-service resort with a health club, conference facilities, and lodgings ranging from old-fashioned inn rooms to new condos on the fairway. Guest rooms in the main inn, furnished with Colonial reproductions and George Washington bedspreads, are the most desirable; choice rooms have fireplaces and face the mountains over the golf course. Four cottages on the town common have plain rooms, and the condos echo the inn's Colonial decor. The dining room, done in lemon yellow with pewter accents, serves elaborate dinners. *Village Common, Box 49, Bethel 04217, tel. 207/824–2175 or 800/654–0125, fax 207/824–2233. 57 rooms with bath, 40 two-bedroom condo units. Facilities: restaurant, tavern with weekend entertainment, all-weather tennis court, golf course, health club, conference center. AE, D, DC, MC, V. Rates are EP, meal packages available. Moderate–Very Expensive.*

Summit Hotel and Conference Center. Opened Christmas 1992, the condominium hotel was an instant hit with skiers. There are 140 slopeside rooms, most featuring complete kitchens and entertainment centers. Conference facilities give a great excuse to combine business and skiing for groups of 10–400. *Summit Hotel and Conference Center, Bethel , 04217. Tel. 207/824–3000; 800/543–2SKI. Facilities: restaurant, lounge, valet parking, child care, heated outdoor Olympic-size pool, tennis courts, health club with sauna and steam room. AE, D, MC, V. Moderate–Expensive.*

Sunday River Inn. Located at the base of the Sunday River ski area, this modern chalet offers private rooms for families and dorm rooms (bring your sleeping bag) for groups and students, but all within easy access of the slopes. Hearty meals are served buffet-style, and the comfy living room is dominated by a stone hearth. *Sunday River Rd., RFD 2, Box 1688, Bethel 04217, tel. 207/824–2410. 12 rooms, 5 dorms, 1 apartment chalet with 4 rooms. Facilities: cross-country skiing, Finnish sauna. AE, MC, V. Rates are MAP. Closed Apr.–Thanksgiving. Inexpensive.*

Vermont Skiing

The Green Mountains run through the middle of Vermont like a bumpy spine, visible from almost every point in the state, and generous accumulations of snow make the mountains an ideal site for skiing. Today Vermont has 20 Alpine ski resorts with nearly 900 trails and some 4,000 acres of skiable terrain. Together, the resorts offer 175 lifts and have the capacity to carry a total of nearly 200,000 skiers per hour. In addition, the area offers a wide variety of accommodations and dining options, from inexpensive dormitories to luxurious inns, at the base of most ski mountains or within an easy drive. While grooming is sophisticated at all Vermont areas, conditions usually range from hard pack to icy, with powder a rare luxury.

Vermont's major resorts are Stowe, Jay Peak, Sugarbush, Killington, Okemo, Mt. Snow, and Stratton. Midsize, less hectic areas to consider include Bromley, Bolton Valley, Smugglers' Notch, Pico, Mad River Glen, and Burke Mountain. All have less- and more-expensive packages.

Bolton Valley Resort
Box 300, Bolton 05477
Tel. 802/434–2131 or 800/451–3220

Although some skiers come for the day, most people who visit Bolton Valley stay at one of the hotels or condominium complexes at the base of the mountain, all within an easy walk of the ski lifts. Because of this proximity and the relatively gentle skiing, Bolton attracts more family groups and beginners than singles. The mood is easygoing, the dress and atmosphere casual. Package vacation plans, a specialty at Bolton Valley, range from the All-Frills Vacation for two to five days to a Super Saver low-season package that provides accommodations, lift tickets and sports-club membership.

Downhill Skiing Most of the 44 interconnecting trails on Bolton's two mountains, each with a vertical drop of 1,600 feet, are intermediate and novice in difficulty. Timberline Peak trail network, with a vertical of 1,000 feet, offers more challenging terrain and wider slopes. Top-to-bottom trails are lit for night skiing 4–10 PM every evening except Sunday.

Cross-Country Skiing Bolton Valley has 100 kilometers (62 miles) of cross-country trails. Lessons and rentals (including telemark) are available.

Other Activities The sports center has an indoor pool, Jacuzzi, sauna, one indoor tennis court, and an exercise room. Weekly events and activities include sleigh rides, parties, races, and special family programs. In summer there are eight outdoor tennis courts and a nature center offering guided tours of the region.

Child Care The HoneyBear day-care center offers supervised play and games, indoors and outdoors, for infants and children up to 6 years old. Child care is also available three nights per week. For children who want to learn to ski, there's a Bolton Cubs program for ages 5–7, and Bolton Bears for ages 6–12.

Lodging **Bolton Valley Resort.** Like the ski area, this self-contained resort is geared to families. Hotel units have either a fireplace or a kitchenette, and there are condominium units with as many as four bedrooms. *Bolton Valley 05477, tel. 802/434–2131. 146 rooms with bath. Facilities: 5 restaurants, deli, pub, fitness center, 9 tennis courts, indoor and outdoor pools, sauna, whirlpool. AE, D, DC, MC, V. Moderate.*
Black Bear Inn. Within the walls of this modern, two-level ski lodge are 24 guest rooms, each with special touches such as quilts made by the innkeeper, in-room movies (a different one each night), and you guessed it—bears! Be sure to ask for a room with a balcony—many of which overlook the Green Mountains and cross-country ski trails. *Mountain Rd., Bolton Valley 05477, tel. 802/434–2126 or 802/434–2920. 24 rooms with bath. Facilities: restaurant, access to sports club, cable TV, outdoor pool. MC, V. Inexpensive–Moderate.*

Nightlife The Bolton Valley Resort's **James Moore Tavern** (tel. 802/434–2131) has live entertainment, and the **Sports Center** (tel. 802/434–2131) organizes social activities and tournament games.

Bromley Mountain
Box 1130, Manchester Center 05255
Tel. 802/824–5522

Venerable Bromley, whose first trails were cut in 1936, is where thousands of skiers learned to ski and learned to love the sport. Today, Bromley attracts families who enjoy its low-key atmosphere as well as experienced skiers who seek their skiing roots. The area has a comfortable red-clapboard base lodge with a large ski shop and a condominium village adjacent to the slopes.

Downhill Skiing Bromley ski areas face south and east, making it one of the warmer spots to ski in New England. The bulk of its 35 trails are beginner (35%) and intermediate (34%), with some surprisingly good advanced–expert terrain (31%) serviced by the Blue Ribbon quad chair on the east side. The vertical drop is 1,334 feet. Six double chair lifts, one quad lift, a J-bar, and two surface lifts for beginners provide transportation. A reduced-price, two-day lift pass is available. Kids up to age 14 ski free with a paying adult on non-holiday weekdays.

Other Activities Snowboarding and telemark skiing lessons are offered by the ski school. On weekends the area holds a variety of ski races. In summer an Alpine slide with mountain rides is a major attraction for adults and children, and the Bromley Village condominiums have a heated outdoor pool and tennis courts.

Child Care Bromley was one of the first ski areas to have a nursery, and it remains one of the region's best places to bring children. Besides a nursery for children from one month to age 6 with half-day and all-day sessions, there is ski instruction in the Mighty Moose Club for children ages 3–5. Children 6–14 can attend the All-Day Mountain Club, which includes lunch.

Lodging The town of Manchester, a center of activity for the resorts of Bromley Mountain and Stratton, offers a large variety of accommodations; additional selections will be found under Manchester Lodging and Newfane Lodging in the Southern Vermont section of the Vermont chapter.

Barrows House. A long-time favorite with Bromley skiers who want to escape the commercial hustle of Manchester, is Jim and Linda McGinniss' 200-year-old inn, located about 8 miles away in nearby Dorset. Superb dining. *Rte. 30, Dorset 05251, tel. 802/867–4455. 28 rooms and 8 cottages with bath. Facilities: restaurant, tavern, sauna, outdoor pool, tennis courts, summer music festival. MC, V. Rates are MAP. Expensive.*
The Highland House. "No request is too big" could be the credo of innkeepers Michael and Laurie Gayda and the staff of this 1842 country inn, situated 10 minutes by car from Bromley Mountain, on 32 private acres. The 17 individually decorated rooms contain reproduction furniture, dried-flower wall ornaments, bed quilts, and other country details. Included in the room rate is a hearty New England–style breakfast; in the evenings the six-table dining area becomes a candlelit room. *Rte. 100, Londonderry 05148, tel. 802/824–3019. 9 rooms in main house, 8 in additional building overlooking pool; all with bath. Facilities: restaurant, 5 km of cross-country ski trails on premises, tennis court, outdoor heated pool. AE, MC, V. Rates include full breakfast; package rates available. Moderate.*
Johnny Seasaw's. In the central living room of this Adirondack-style shingled cottage are a circular fireplace, a games room

with pool table, and a raised alcove dubbed the "seducerie." Rooms vary from dormitory-style to individual cottages with working fireplaces. The inn retains the flavor of the legendary roadhouse it once was. *Rte. 11/30, Peru 05152, tel. 802/824–5533. 25 rooms with bath. Facilities: restaurant, tennis court, outdoor pool. MC, V. Closed Apr.–mid-May, late Oct.–Thanksgiving. Moderate.*

Nightlife Après-ski action is largely located in Manchester. **Park Bench Cafe** (tel. 802/362–2557) has live jazz on Friday and Saturday nights; **Mulligan's Pub & Restaurant** (tel. 802/362–3663) has a DJ on Friday and Saturday nights. The **Marsh Tavern** (tel. 802/362–4700) at the Equinox Hotel has more subdued pop and cabaret music.(Also, *see* Nightlife in Stratton, *below*.)

Burke Mountain
Box 247, East Burke 05832
Tel. 802/626–3305; reservations, 800/541–5480; snow conditions, 800/922–BURK

Burke has a reputation for being a low-key, family mountain that draws most of its skiers from Massachusetts and Connecticut. In addition to having plenty of terrain for tenderfeet, intermediate skiers, experts, and racers, Burke also has slopeside lodging and vacation packages, many of which are significantly less expensive than those at other Vermont areas.

Downhill Skiing With a 2,000-foot vertical drop, Burke is something of a sleeper among the larger eastern ski areas. Although there is limited snowmaking (35%), the mountain's northern location and exposure assure plenty of natural snow. It has one quad, one double chair lift, and three surface lifts. Lift lines, even on weekends and holidays, are light to non-existent.

Cross-Country Skiing Burke Mountain Ski Touring Center has more than 60 kilometers (37 miles) of groomed trails, some leading to high points with scenic views of the countryside.

Child Care The nursery here takes children ages 6 weeks to 6 years. SKIwee lessons through the ski school are available to children ages 4–8. Bear Chasers is for ages 9–12, and Ski Max is for ages 13–16.

Lodging **Burke Mountain Resort.** A variety of accommodations are available at this resort, from economical to luxurious, fully furnished slopeside studios and one-, two-, three-, and four-bedroom town houses and condominiums. Some have fireplaces, others wood-burning stoves. *Box 247, East Burke 05832, tel. 800/541–5480. AE, MC, V. Open year-round. Two-night minimum required. Moderate.*
Old Cutter Inn. Only ½ mile from the Burke Mountain base lodge is this small converted farmhouse with a two-bedroom apartment in a separate building. The restaurant features superb Continental cuisine. *RR 1, Box 62, East Burke 05832, tel. 802/626–5152. 9 rooms, 5 with bath. Facilities: restaurant, lounge, outdoor pool. MC, V. MAP available. Closed Apr., Nov. Inexpensive.*

Nightlife **Burke Mountain Resort** (tel. 802/626–3305) restaurant and lounge is open most nights, has weekend entertainment, and serves American favorites and selected specialty fare. In nearby Lyndenville, **Gumby's** (tel. 802/626–3064) and **The Packing House** (tel. 802/626–8777) have live music.

Jay Peak
Rte. 242, Jay 05859
Tel. 802/988-2611 or 800/451-4449

Jay Peak boasts the most natural snow of any ski area in the East. Sticking up out of the flat farmland, Jay catches an abundance of precipitation from the Maritime provinces of Canada. Its proximity to Québec gives an international flavor to the area—French-speaking and English-speaking skiers mix on the slopes, in the base lodges, at the Hotel Jay, and at the adjacent Jay Peak condominiums. Although Jay is a popular weekend outing for Montréalers, its distance from metropolitan centers along the Eastern seaboard has led to the availability of bargain midweek packages designed to entice skiers to drive the extra hour beyond other northern Vermont areas. In January, for instance, guests of the Hotel Jay ski free Monday through Friday.

Downhill Skiing Jay Peak is in fact two mountains, the highest reaching nearly 4,000 feet with a vertical drop of 2,153 feet, served by a 60-passenger tram. The area also has a quad, a triple, and a double chair lift and two T-bars. The smaller mountain has more straight-fall-line, expert terrain, while the tram-side peak has many curving and meandering trails perfectly suited for intermediate and beginning skiers. Every morning at 9 AM the ski school offers a free tour, from the tram down one trail.

Cross-Country Skiing A touring center at the base of the mountain has 40 kilometers (25 miles) of cross-country trails.

Child Care An indoor nursery for youngsters 2–7 is open from 9 to 4 at the mountain Child Care Center. Guests of Hotel Jay or the Jay Peak condominiums get this nursery care free, as well as evening care and supervised dining at the hotel. Children 5–12 can participate in an all-day SKIwee program, which includes lunch.

Lodging **Hotel Jay.** Ski-lodge simplicity sets the tone here, with wood paneling in the rooms, built-in headboards, and vinyl wallpaper in the bathroom. The hotel is located right at the lifts, so it's very convenient for people who plan to spend most of their time on the slopes. Rooms on the southwest side have a view of Jay Peak, those on the north overlook the valley, and upper floors have balconies. Summer rates are very low. *Rte. 242, Jay 05859, tel. 802/988-2611 or 800/451-4449. 48 rooms with bath. Facilities: restaurant, bar, 4 tennis courts, outdoor pool, games room, satellite TV, sauna, whirlpool. AE, D, DC, MC, V. Rates are MAP and include lift tickets. Expensive.*

Jay Peak Condominiums. The 84 condominiums have fully equipped 1–3 bedrooms with modern kitchens, washers-dryers, and spacious living areas with fireplaces. Most are slopeside. All condo packages include lodging and lift tickets. *Rte. 242, Jay 05859, tel. 802/988-2611 or 800/451-4449 outside VT. 84 units. Facilities: TV, washer-dryer, fireplace. AE, D, DC, MC, V. Packages including lift tickets and meal plans are available. Expensive.*

Snowline. One side of the hallway in this small lodge used to be a building exterior before it was enclosed, and the decor includes hooked-rug wall hangings. Most important, this retreat is convenient to the lifts. The small restaurant offers steaks and burgers. *Rte. 242, Jay 05859, tel. 802/988-2822. 10 rooms with* *bath. Facilities: restaurant, lounge, TV in public area. AE, D, MC, V. Inexpensive–Moderate.*

Nightlife The **International** restaurant at the Hotel Jay (tel. 802/988–2611) has a rock band and dancing on Saturday night during ski season, and there's often a pianist in the hotel's **Sports Lounge.**

Killington
400 Killington Rd., Killington 05751
Tel. 802/773–1330; snow conditions, 802/422–3261

"Megamountain," "Beast of the East," and just plain "big" are appropriate descriptions of Killington. This is the largest ski resort in the East, the one with the most slopes and the greatest number of skiers. Killington manages its crowds well, if somewhat impersonally, but despite its extensive facilities and terrain, lift lines on weekends—especially holiday weekends—can be long, but they move quickly. It has the longest ski season in the East and some of the best package plans anywhere. With a single telephone call, skiers can select price, date, and type of ski week they want; choose accommodations; book air or railroad transportation; and arrange for rental equipment and ski lessons. More than 100 lodging establishments serve the Killington region (including Pico and Rutland), though only a few of them are within walking distance of the lifts. On the Bear Mountain side, there are slopeside condominiums in the Sunrise Mountain Village. Some lodges have free shuttles to the area, and there is a scheduled mountain bus service. Five base lodges serve the mountains, and there's a cafeteria-style restaurant on Killington Peak.

Downhill Skiing It would probably take a skier a week to test all 107 trails on the six mountains of the Killington complex, even though everything interconnects. About 75% of the 827 acres of skiing can be covered with machine-made snow, and that's still more snowmaking than any other area in the world can manage. Transporting skiers to the peaks of this complex are a 3 ½-mile gondola plus seven quads, four triples, and five double chair lifts, as well as two surface lifts. That's a total of 19 ski lifts, a few of which reach the area's highest elevation, at 4,220 feet off Killington Peak, and a vertical drop of 3,175 feet to the base of the gondola. The range of skiing includes everything from Outer Limits, one of the steepest and most challenging trails anywhere in the country, to the 10-mile-long, super-gentle Juggernaut Trail.

Other Activities Killington proper is for skiing, but elsewhere in the region—up and down the access road—there are health clubs, indoor tennis and racquetball courts, ski touring centers, ice skating, and sleigh rides. In summer, Killington has an 18-hole golf course adjacent to a condominium complex; outdoor tennis courts and a tennis school; a concert series; and ballet, theater, and chamber music performances. There is a lift-accessed 33-mile mountain bike trail system as well. Rutland is one of Vermont's largest and least charming cities, but it's handy, with several malls and movie theaters.

Child Care Nursery care is available for children from infants to 8 years old. For youngsters 3–8, the First Tracks program provides an hour of instruction in the morning or afternoon. The Superstars Program for children 6–12 has all-day skiing, with a break for lunch.

Lodging **Summit Lodge.** Located just 3 miles from Killington Peak on an access road is this rambling, rustic two-story country lodge that caters to a varied crowd of ski enthusiasts. Country decor and antiques blend with modern conveniences to create a relaxed atmosphere. Two restaurants allow formal and informal dining. *Killington Rd., Killington 05751, tel. 802/422–3535 or 800/635–6343, fax 802/422–3536. 45 rooms with bath, 2 suites. Facilities: 2 restaurants, indoor racquetball courts, saunas, Jacuzzi, massage, recreation rooms, fireplace lounge, live entertainment, ice-skating pond. AE, DC, MC, V. Very Expensive.*

The Inn at Long Trail. This 1938 inn, with a Gaelic charm (Guinness beer is on tap at the pub) is situated just ¼ mile from the Pico ski slopes. The unusual decor consisting of boulders inside and outside, makes nature a prevailing theme. *Rte. 4, Box 267, Killington 05751, tel. 802/775–7181 or 800/325–2540. 16 country bedrooms, 6 suites with fireplaces. Facilities: restaurant, bar. MC, V. Closed June, mid-Oct.–Thanksgiving. Expensive–Very Expensive.*

Cortina Inn. The large luxury lodge and miniresort features small-scale exhibits by local artists and diverse activities. About two-thirds of the rooms have private balconies, but the views aren't spectacular. However, the inn is very comfortable and the location is prime—providing easy access to either Killington or Pico. *Rte. 4, Mendon 05751, tel. 802/773–3331 or 800/451–6108. 98 rooms with bath. Facilities: restaurant, lounge, shuttle service to slopes, 8 tennis courts, indoor pool, fitness center with whirlpools, saunas. AE, D, DC, MC, V. Expensive.*

Killington Village Inn. A fieldstone fireplace dominates the lobby of the chalet-style ski lodge. There's a complimentary shuttle to the base lodge. *Killington Rd., Killington 05751, tel. 802/422–3301 or 800/451–4105. 29 rooms with bath. Facilities: restaurant, pub, tennis court, Jacuzzi, cable TV, and movies in rooms. AE, D, DC, MC, V. Rates include full breakfast. Expensive.*

Mountain Inn. This may be a ski lodge, but it has the feeling of a small luxury resort, and it's within walking distance of Killington's lifts. *RR 1, Box 2850, Killington 05751, tel. 802/422–3595 or 800/842–8909. 50 rooms with bath. Facilities: restaurant, lounge, outdoor pool, whirlpool, sauna, steam room, games room. AE, DC, MC, V. Closed mid-Apr.–late June, mid-Oct.–Thanksgiving. Moderate–Expensive.*

Additional accommodations sections will be found under Rutland Lodging in the Central Vermont section of the Vermont chapter.

Nightlife Try the hot, spicy chicken wings to warm up after skiing at **Casey's Caboose** (tel. 802/422–3792). Among the many music-oriented night spots on Killington Road are the **Pickle Barrel** (tel. 802/422–3035), which specializes in big rock bands; the **Wobbly Barn** (tel. 802/422–3392), with dancing to blues and rock during ski season; and the **Nightspot** (tel. 802/422–9885), a singles-oriented dance club. Near Pico, the lounge at the **Inn at Long Trail** (tel. 802/775–7181) features Irish music on weekends.

Mad River Glen

Rte. 17, Waitsfield 05673
Tel. 802/496–3551; snow conditions, 802/496–2001 or 800/696–2001

Mad River Glen was developed in the late 1940s and has changed relatively little since then; the single chair lift may be the only lift of its vintage still carrying skiers. There is an unkempt aura about this place that for 40 years has attracted core groups of skiers from among wealthy families in the East as well as rugged individualists looking for a less-polished terrain. Remember that most of Mad River's trails are covered only by natural snow (85%) . . . when there is natural snow. The apt area motto is "Ski It If You Can."

Downhill Skiing Mad River is steep. Terrain changes constantly on 33 interactive trails, of which 75% are intermediate to superexpert. Intermediate and novice terrain are regularly groomed. Three chairs (including the famed single) service the mountain's 2,000-foot vertical.

Child Care The Cricket Club nursery (tel. 802/496–2123) takes children 3 weeks to 5 years while the ski school has classes for children 4–12. Junior Racing is available weekends and during holiday periods.

Lodging and Nightlife For more information, *see* Lodging and Nightlife in Sugarbush, *below*.

Mt. Snow–Haystack

400 Mountain Rd., Mt. Snow 05356
Tel. 802/464–3333 or 802/464–8501; snow conditions, 802/464–2151; lodging, 800/245–SNOW

Established in the 1950s, Mt. Snow was a place where ordinary people could be comfortable and confident and have a good time skiing. The resort was unpretentious, and its atmosphere made visitors feel that they had become part of the skiing community. Although the area's ownership and management have changed—in 1977 it was purchased by SKI, Ltd., the owners of Killington—Mt. Snow still retains that aura. Recently, Mt. Snow and financially troubled next-door neighbor Haystack entered into a "trial marriage." The big mountain has leased the smaller ski area for three years and is now marketing the two as Mt. Snow–Haystack. There is a free shuttle over the 2 ½ miles between areas, and the trail count for the complex is now 127.

At Mt. Snow, both the bustling Main Base Lodge and the Sundance Base Lodge have food service and other amenities. The Carinthia Base Lodge (site of the old Carinthia ski area, absorbed by Mt. Snow in 1986) is usually the least crowded and most easily accessible from the parking lot. Mt. Snow attracts a good mix of families and single skiers, and it often holds theme weeks for special groups such as college students and families. One of the most popular is the "Teddy Bear Ski Week" for kids. A hotel and several condominiums are within walking distance of the lifts.

Haystack—the southernmost ski area in Vermont—is much smaller than Mt. Snow, but offers a more personal atmosphere, and relatively inexpensive packages are available for families and students. There is a modern, new base lodge close to the lifts, and a condominium village at the base of the mountain and three condo complexes around the golf course provide on-site accommodations; a free shuttle connects skiers to all services. Because of the joint marketing effort with Mt. Snow, the once serene atmosphere may change, but splitting the crowds could help everyone and the change could ultimately save the smaller area from extinction.

Downhill Skiing Mt. Snow is a remarkably well-formed mountain. From its 1,700-foot vertical summit, most of the trails down the face are intermediate, wide, and sunny. Toward the bottom and in the Carinthia section are the beginner slopes; most of the expert terrain is on the North Face. In all, there are 84 trails, of which about two-thirds are intermediate. The trails are served by two quad, six triple, and eight double chair lifts and two surface lifts. The ski school's EXCL instruction program is designed to help advanced and expert skiers. On the Lower Exhibition trail, skiers can be videotaped and critiqued free of charge; they can then take a 45-minute class with one or two other skiers who need the same type of instruction.

Most of the 43 trails at Haystack are pleasantly wide with bumps and rolls and straight fall lines—good cruising, intermediate runs. There's also a section with three double black-diamond trails—very steep but short. A beginner section, safely tucked below the main-mountain trails, provides a haven for lessons and slow skiing. Three triple and two double chair lifts and one T-bar service Haystack's 1,400 vertical feet.

Cross-Country Skiing Four cross-country trail areas within 4 miles of the resort provide more than 100 kilometers (62 miles) of varied terrain.

Other Activities Sleigh rides and winter nature walks head the list of nonskiing winter activities at Mt. Snow. In summer, Mt. Snow has an 18-hole golf course and from May through September the resort holds a golf school. The area also conducts a mountain-biking instruction program and rents bikes for use on its trails.

Child Care The Pumkin Patch nursery takes children ages 6 weeks through 8 years and provides indoor and outdoor supervised play. Reservations are required. The ski school offers SKIwee programs, with full-day or half-day sessions for ages 4–12.

Lodging **Inn at Sawmill Farm.** This Williams family's small, aristocratic country inn is a touch on the formal side: The decor has the country look one finds in the glossy magazines, and men must wear jackets in public areas after 6 PM. The 10 outside rooms are the largest and have working fireplaces. The dining room's menu and extensive wine list are renowned in New England. *Rte. 100, West Dover 05356, tel. 802/464–8131. 21 rooms with bath. Facilities: outdoor pool, tennis court. No credit cards. MAP only. Very Expensive.*
The White House of Wilmington. The grand staircase in this Federal-style mansion leads to spacious rooms that are individually decorated and have antique bathrooms, brass wall sconces, mah-jongg sets, and in some cases the home's original wallpaper. The newer section has more contemporary plumbing; some rooms have fireplaces and lofts. The inn is set back from busy Route 9, so road noise is no problem. A description of the public rooms—heavy velvet drapes, tufted leather wingchairs—suggests formality, yet the atmosphere here is casual and comfortable. Although it's just a short drive to the downhill skiing of Mt. Snow–Haystack, the White House is pri-

marily a cross-country ski touring center, with a rental shop and extensive trails. Instruction is also available. *Rte. 9, Wilmington 05363, tel. 802/464–2135 or 800/541–2135. 12 rooms with bath. Facilities: restaurant, lounge, Jacuzzi, sauna, indoor and outdoor pools. AE, DC, MC, V. Rates are MAP. Very Expensive.*

The Hermitage. Everywhere you look there is evidence of the owner Jim McGovern's passion for decoys, wine, and Michel Delacroix prints. The duck pond and the roaming game birds make staying at this 19th-century estate like visiting the country during the hunt season. Rooms are in two buildings—the Wine House is the newest, built 13 years ago; the Brookbound Inn, which has the most modest rooms, is about ½ mile down the road. *Coldbrook Rd., Box 457, Wilmington 05363, tel. 802/464–3511. 15 rooms with bath in the main inn, 14 rooms with bath at Brookbound. Facilities: 50 km (31 mi) of cross-country touring tracks, rental equipment, lessons, restaurant, lounge, sauna, tennis court. AE, DC, MC, V. Rates are MAP. Expensive–Very Expensive.*

Nutmeg Inn. This cozy inn has all the Colonial touches appropriate to a two-centuries-old farmhouse: an old butter churn, antique dressers, rag rugs, mason jars with dried flowers, and hand-hewn beams in the low-ceiling living room. Added touches are fresh quilts on the brass beds and thick carpeting. Three suites in the barn are larger and get less road noise, and the king suite has a private balcony with a terrific view of Haystack Mountain. *Rte. 9 W, Wilmington 05363, tel. 802/464–3351. 13 rooms. AE, MC, V. Rates include full breakfast. Moderate–Expensive.*

Nightlife The **Snow Barn** (tel. 802/464–3333), near the base of Mt. Snow, has live entertainment weekends during the season; a little farther down Route 100, **Deacon's Den Tavern** (tel. 802/464–9361) and the **Sitzmark** (tel. 802/464–3384) have live bands on weekends. In nearby Wilmington, **Poncho's Wreck** (tel. 802/464–9320) is lively during the season. For a quieter après-ski experience, there's **Le Petit Chef** (tel. 802/464–8437) or the **Dover Forge** (tel. 802/464–9361).

Okemo Mountain
RFD 1, Ludlow 05149
Tel. 802/228–4041 or 802/228–5571; snow conditions, 802/228–5222

Okemo has evolved and emerged in recent years as a major resort and an almost ideal ski area for families with children. The main attraction is a long, broad, gentle slope with two beginner lifts just above the base lodge. All the facilities at the bottom of the mountain are close together, so family members can regroup easily during the ski day. Condominium housing is located at the base and along some of the lower trails. The net effect is efficient and attractive. It even boasts today's obligatory clock tower.

Downhill Skiing Above the broad beginner's slope at the base, the upper part of Okemo has a varied network of trails: long, winding, easy trails for beginners, straight fall-line runs for experts, and curving cruising slopes for intermediates. The 71 trails are served by five quads, three triple chair lifts, two surface lifts, and 95% are covered by snowmaking. From the summit to the base lodge, the vertical drop is 2,150 feet. The ski school offers a complimentary Ski Tip Station, where intermediate or better skiers can get an evaluation and a free run with an instructor.

Child Care The area's nursery, for children 1–8 years of age, has a broad range of indoor activities plus supervised outings. Children 3 and up can get brief introduction-to-skiing lessons. All-day or half-day SKIwee (ages 4–8) lessons are available.

Lodging **Okemo Mountain Lodge.** The three-story, brown-clapboard building has balconies and fireplaces in all guest rooms, and the one-bedroom condominiums clustered around the base of the ski lifts are close to restaurants, shops, and the resort's clock tower. Also available are Kettlebrook and Winterplace slope-side condominiums, run by Okemo Mountain Lodging Service. *Rte. 100, RFD 1, Ludlow 05149, tel. 802/228–5571 or 802/228–4041. 76 rooms with bath. Facilities: restaurant, lounge, cable TV, shuttle bus to Ludlow. AE, MC, V. Expensive.*

Nightlife **Priority's** (tel. 802/228–2800), at the base of the mountain, has entertainers; **Dadd's** (tel. 802/228–9820) has electronic games and weekend bands for a little harder rocking.

Pico Ski Resort
2 Sherburne Pass, Rutland 05701
Tel. 802/775–4346; snow conditions, 802/775–4345 or 800/848–7325

Although it's only 5 miles down the road from Killington, Pico has long been an underground favorite among people looking for uncrowded, low-key skiing. When modern lifts were installed and a village square was constructed at the base, some feared that friendly patina would be threatened, but the new condo-hotel, restaurants, and shops have not altered the essential nature of Pico.

Downhill Skiing From the area's 4,000-foot summit, most of the trails are advanced to expert, with two intermediate bail-out trails for the timid. The rest of the mountain's 2,000 feet of vertical terrain is mostly intermediate or easier. The lifts for these slopes and trails are two high-speed quads, two triples, and three double chairs, plus two surface lifts.

Other Activities A sports center at the base of the mountain has fitness facilities, a 75-foot pool, aerobics section, Jacuzzi, saunas, a nursery, and a massage room.

Child Care The nursery takes children from 6 months through 6 years old and provides indoor activities, outdoor play, and optional ski instruction. The ski school has an Explorer's instruction program for children 3–6 and Mountaineers classes for ages 6–12; either can be taken for full- or half-day periods.

Lodging **Pico Resort Hotel.** This resort at the base of Pico Mountain, a stone's throw from the ski lift, offers condominiums with hotel services. Condos have full kitchen, modern bath, fireplace, daily maid service, and use of the sports center. Two restaurants serve American and Italian cuisine, and there's a convenience store on the premises. Live entertainment is scheduled daily in the late afternoon in the base lodge. *Sherburne Pass 05701, tel. 802/747–3000 or 800/848–7325, fax 802/775–4703. 150 units. Facilities: 2 restaurants, base lodge food service, indoor pool, sports center, Jacuzzi, sauna, TV lounge. D, MC, V. Moderate–Expensive.*

Additional accommodations selections will be found under Rutland Lodging in the Central Vermont section of the Vermont chapter.

Nightlife *See* Nightlife in Killington, *above.*

Smugglers' Notch Resort
Smugglers' Notch 05464
Tel. 802/644–8851 or 800/451–8752

This resort complex has condominiums, restaurants, a grocery store, sports shops, meeting and convention facilities, and even a post office at the base of the lifts. Most skiers stay at the resort, and a large majority take advantage of the reasonably priced package plans that include lift tickets and daily lessons. Smugglers' has long been respected for its family programs and, therefore, attracts such clientele.

Downhill Skiing Smugglers' is made up of three mountains. The highest, Madonna, with a vertical drop of 2,610 feet, is in the center and connects with a trail network to Sterling (1,500-foot vertical). The third mountain, Morse (1,150-foot vertical), is more remote, but you can visit all three without removing your skis. The tops of each of the mountains have expert terrain—a couple of double black diamonds make Madonna memorable—while intermediate trails fill the lower sections. Morse specializes in beginner trails. The 56 trails are served by only four double chair lifts and one surface lift—something of a shortcoming. The area has improved its grooming and snowmaking capabilities in recent years and has added a 6.5-million-gallon reservoir and 4 miles of additional snowmaking pipe. There is now top-to-bottom snowmaking on all three mountains.

Cross-Country Skiing Thirty-seven groomed and tracked kilometers (23 miles) of cross-country trails have been laid out.

Other Activities Management committed itself to developing an activities center long before the concept was adopted by other ski resorts. The self-contained village has ice skating, sleigh rides, and horseback riding. For indoor sports, there are hot tubs, tennis courts, and a pool. In summer, Smugglers' offers a water playground, miniature golf, shuffleboard, outdoor tennis courts, and an outdoor pool.

Child Care The Alice's Wonderland Child Care Center is a spacious facility that takes children from 6 weeks through 6 years old. The Discovery Ski Camp gives children 3–6 lessons, movies, games, and story-time entertainment. Adventure Ski Camp for ages 7–12 has all-day skiing and other activities. For teens ages 13–17 there's The Explorer Program, which runs daily, beginning at noon.

Lodging **The Village at Smugglers' Notch.** The large year-round resort complex offers condos—some with fireplaces and decks—with contemporary furnishings. Most guests stay several nights as part of a ski- or tennis-package plan. *Rte. 108, Jeffersonville 05464, tel. 802/644–8851 or 800/451–8752. 331 condo units. Facilities: 3 restaurants, lounge, 2 indoor and 8 outdoor tennis courts, hot tub, indoor pool, exercise equipment, tanning machines, saunas, outdoor ice rink, child-care center, games room, 3 water slides. AE, DC, MC, V, Expensive–Very Expensive.*

The Highlander Motel. On the access road, 2½ miles from Smugglers' Village, the Highlander has 15 motel units and three "inn" rooms facing the mountain. Fireside dining for breakfast and dinner. *Rte. 108 S, Jeffersonville 05464, tel. 802/644-2725 or 800/367-6471. 18 rooms. Facilities: restaurant, cable TV, games room. MC, V. Packages. Moderate.*

Nightlife Most après-ski action centers in Smugglers' Village, where there are afternoon bonfires and nightly live entertainment in the **Meeting House** (tel. 802/644–8851) or **Smugglers' Lounge** (Village Restaurant, tel. 802/644–2291). Sleigh rides, fireworks, and torch-light parades occur twice weekly. **The Brewski** (tel. 802/644–5432), on Route 108 just outside the village, has occasional entertainment. Good dining is available nearby at **Cafe Banditos** (tel. 802/644-8884), **Three Mountain Lodge** (tel. 802/644-5736), and **Le Cheval D'Or** (tel. 802/644-5556).

Stowe Mountain Resort

5781 Mountain Rd., Stowe 05672
Tel. 802/253–3000 or 800/247–8693; snow conditions, 802/253–2222

To be precise, the name of the village is Stowe, the name of the mountain is Mt. Mansfield, but to generations of skiers the area, the complex, and the region are just plain Stowe. This classic resort, steeped in tradition, dates to the 1930s, when the sport of skiing was a pup. Even today the area's mystique attracts more serious skiers than social skiers. In recent years, on-mountain lodging; free shuttle buses that gather skiers from lodges, inn, and motels along the Mountain Road; improved snowmaking; and new lifts have added convenience to the Stowe experience. Yet the traditions remain: the Winter Carnival in January, the Sugar Slalom in April, ski weeks all winter. So committed is the ski school to improvements that even noninstruction package plans include one free ski lesson. Three base lodges provide plenty of essentials plus two on-mountain restaurants.

Downhill Skiing Mt. Mansfield, with a vertical drop of 2,360 feet, is one of the giants among Eastern ski mountains. Its symmetrical shape allows skiers of all abilities long, satisfying runs from the summit. The famous Front Four runs (National, Liftline, Starr, and Goat) are the intimidating centerpieces for tough, expert runs, yet there is plenty of mellow intermediate skiing and one long beginner trail from the top that ends at the Toll House, where there is easier terrain. Mansfield's satellite sector is a network of intermediate and one expert trail off a basin served by a gondola. Spruce Peak, separate from the main mountain, is a teaching hill and a pleasant experience for intermediates and beginners. In addition to the new high-speed, eight-passenger gondola, Stowe has one quad, one triple, and six double chair lifts plus one handle tow, to service its 45 trails. Night skiing has been added on a three-year trial basis and trails are accessed by the gondola.

Cross-Country Skiing The resort has 35 kilometers (20 miles) of groomed cross-country trails and 40 kilometers (24 miles) of back-country trails. There are four interconnecting cross-country ski areas with over 100 km of groomed trails within the town of Stowe, including the famed Trapp Family Lodge.

Other Activities In addition to sleighing and tobogganing facilities, Stowe boasts a public ice-skating rink with rental skates.

Child Care The Kanga's Pocket infant care center takes children ages 2 months through 3 years; Pooh's Corner day-care center takes ages 3–12. The ski school has two instruction programs: Minimeisters for ages 3–7; and Stowemeisters for children 6 and over who have skiing experience are eligible for all-day skiing with an instructor in the Mountain Adventure program.

Lodging **Stowe Mountain Resort.** This is the lodging closest to the lifts, owned and operated by the same company that built the ski operation. The resort includes an inn, townhouses, and 35 individual lodge-condominums. The inn, which was converted from a motel in the 1960s and recently renovated, has folk-art prints to enhance the decor; some units have balconies. *5781 Mountain Rd., Stowe 05672, tel. 802/253–3000 or 800/253–4754. 77 rooms with bath. Facilities: restaurant, tavern, tennis court, golf course, outdoor swimming pool, cable TV, exercise equipment, whirlpool, sauna, trout pond. AE, DC, MC, V. Rates are MAP. Very Expensive.*

Topnotch at Stowe. The 26-year-old resort is one of the state's most posh. Floor-to-ceiling windows, a freestanding circular stone fireplace, and cathedral ceilings make the lobby an imposing setting, appropriate for the afternoon tea served from a rolling cart. Rooms have thick rust-color carpeting, a small shelf of books, and perhaps a barnboard wall or an Italian print. The restaurant is renowned, and there's a health spa. *Mountain Rd., Stowe 05672, tel. 802/253–8585 or 800/451–8686. 92 rooms with bath, 8 suites. Facilities: 2 restaurants, lounge, 4 indoor tennis courts, 8 outdoor tennis courts, indoor and outdoor pools, cable TV, room service, riding stables. AE, MC, V. Very Expensive.*

The Gables. The converted farmhouse is a rabbit warren of charming, antiques-filled rooms. The four rooms in the carriage house have cathedral ceilings, fireplaces, TVs, whirlpool tub, and are open year-round. There is a porch with white Adirondack chairs on which you can enjoy the view of Mt. Mansfield. The tiny plant-filled sunroom is fine for lazy mornings, and the innkeepers are known for generous breakfasts. *Mountain Rd., Stowe 05672, tel. 802/253–7730 or 800/422–5371. 17 rooms with bath. Facilities: cable TV in public area, hot tub, outdoor pool, disabled-equipped room. AE, MC, V. Closed late Apr.–May. Rates are MAP. Expensive–Very Expensive.*

Green Mountain Inn. The two-story Colonial-style inn built in 1833 attracts skiers of all ages. Its communal living room and library provide a comfortable atmosphere for relaxing before dining in one of the two house restaurants. MAP rates are optional; both formal dining and bistro fare are available. *Box 60, Main St., Stowe 05672, tel. 802/253–7301 or 800/445–6629 (out of state only). 50 rooms with bath, 4 suites. Facilities: 2 restaurants, conference rooms, living room, library, health club. AE, MC, V. Moderate–Expensive.*

The classic Trapp Family Lodge (yes, from the book and movie *Sound of Music*) and additional nearby accommodations are described under Stowe Lodging in the Northern Vermont section of the Vermont chapter.

Nightlife The **Matterhorn Night Club** (tel. 802/253–8198) has music for dancing. The **Rusty Nail Saloon** (tel. 802/253–9444) and **BK**

Clark's (tel. 802/253–9300) also provide live music. Other options include the lounges at **Topnotch at Stowe** (tel. 802/253–8585) and the less-expensive **Stoweflake Inn** (tel. 802/253–7355).

Stratton

Stratton Mountain 05155
Tel. 802/297–2200 or 800/843–6867; snow conditions, 802/297–4211

Since its creation in 1961, Stratton has undergone several physical transformations and upgrades, yet the area's sophisticated character has been retained. It has been the special province of well-to-do families and, more recently, young professionals from the New York–southern Connecticut corridor. In recent years an entire village, with a covered parking structure for 700 cars, has arisen at the base of the mountain. Adjacent to the base lodge are a condo-hotel, restaurants, and about 25 shops lining a minimall. Beyond that complex are many ski-in, ski-out villas and several condominiums and town houses minutes away from the slopes. Across the main road and accessible by shuttle are three more good-size hotel-inns. Package plans are available, and conventions and meetings can be accommodated. Stratton is a self-contained center 4 miles up its own access road off Route 30 in Bondville.

Downhill Skiing   Stratton's skiing comprises three sectors. The first is the lower mountain directly in front of the base lodge-village-condo complex; a number of lifts reach mid-mountain from this entry point, and practically all skiing is beginner or low-intermediate. Above that, the upper mountain, with a vertical drop of 2,000 feet, is graced with a high-speed, 12-passenger gondola, *Starship XII.* Down the face are the expert trails, while on either side are intermediate cruising runs with a smattering of wide beginner slopes. The third sector, the Sun Bowl, is off to one side with two quad chair lifts and two new expert trails, a full base lodge, and a lot of intermediate terrain. This is where the new Japanese ownership (it also owns Breckenridge in Colorado) pins its hopes for the future. In all, Stratton has 92 slopes and trails served by the gondola and four quad, one triple, and six double chair lifts.

Cross-Country   The Stratton area has 32 kilometers (20 miles) of cross-country
Skiing   skiing on the golf course.

Other Activities   The area's sports center has two indoor tennis courts, three racquetball courts, a 25-meter indoor swimming pool, a Jacuzzi, steam room, a fitness facility with Nautilus equipment, and a restaurant. The summertime facilities include 15 additional outdoor tennis courts, 27 holes of golf, horseback riding, and mountain biking. Instruction programs in tennis and golf are offered. The area hosts a summer entertainment series and is home of the LPGA classic and Women's Hardcourt Tennis Championships.

Child Care   The day-care center takes children ages 6 weeks through 5 years for indoor activities and outdoor excursions in mild weather. The ski school has a Little Cub program for ages 4–6 and Big Cub for 7–12; both are daylong programs with lunch. SKIwee instruction programs are also available for ages 4–12. A junior racing program and special instruction groups are aimed at more-experienced junior skiers.

Lodging The town of Manchester, a center of activity for the resorts of Stratton and Bromley Mountain, offers a large variety of accommodations; additional selections will be found under Manchester Lodging and Newfane Lodging in the Southern Vermont section of the Vermont chapter.

Windham Hill Inn. In the converted, turn-of-the-century dairy barn, two rooms share an enormous deck that overlooks the West River Valley. Rooms in the main building (some have a balcony) are more formal. Personal touches abound; the innkeeper's fascination with antique shoes is evident everywhere, and the antiques-filled rooms might be decorated with a child's white dress or a chenille bedspread. Guests can choose to be seated at a communal table for dinner. *West Townshend 05359, tel. 802/874-4080. 15 rooms with bath. Facilities: restaurant, lounge, phones, fireplaces in common areas, skating pond. Closed in early spring, Nov. 1–Thanksgiving. AE, MC, V. MAP only. Very Expensive.*

Stratton Mountain Inn and Village Lodge. The complex includes a 125-room inn—the largest on the mountain—and a 91-room lodge built in 1985, which has studio units. Ski packages that include lift tickets bring down room rates. *Stratton Mountain Rd., Stratton Mountain 05155, tel. 802/297-2500 or 800/ 777-1700. 216 rooms with bath. Facilities: 2 restaurants, golf course, outdoor pool, 2 racquetball courts, 2 tennis courts, sauna, 2 Jacuzzis, cable TV. AE, D, DC, MC, V. Expensive–Very Expensive.*

Nightlife One of the better lounges at Stratton Mountain is **Mulligan's** (tel. 802/297-9293), which has three bars on three floors, American cuisine, and dancing to DJs and live bands. **Haig's** (tel. 802/297-1300) in Bondville, 5 miles from Stratton, has live entertainment and dancing year-round. **The Red Fox Inn** (tel. 802/297-2488), 5 miles from the ski area, has a DJ and occasional live music in the tavern. (*See also* Nightlife in Bromley, *above.*)

Sugarbush
RR Box 350, Warren 05674
Tel. 802/583-2381; snow conditions, 802/583-7669; lodging, 800/53-SUGAR

In the early 1960s Sugarbush had the reputation of being an outpost of an affluent and sophisticated crowd from New York. While that reputation has faded, Sugarbush has maintained a with-it aura for the smart set—not that anyone would feel uncomfortable here. The base of the mountain has a village of condominiums, restaurants, shops, bars, and a sports center, and just down the road is the Sugarbush Inn, recently acquired by the ski area.

Downhill Skiing Sugarbush is two distinct mountain complexes. Sugarbush South area is what old-timers recall as Sugarbush Mountain: With a vertical of 2,400 feet it is known for formidable steeps toward the top and in front of the main base lodge. In recent years, intermediate trails that twist and turn off most of the lifts have been widened and regraded to make them more inviting. This sector has three triple and four double chair lifts and two surface lifts. The Sugarbush North peak offers what the South side has in short supply—beginner runs. North also has steep fall-line pitches and intermediate cruisers off its 2,600 vertical feet. This mountain has three quads (including a high-speed version), two double chair lifts, and two surface lifts. There are plans to connect the two mountains with a series of lifts and trails, but for the present a shuttle bus takes skiers back and forth. Top-level racers seem to spew out of the Green Mountain Academy in Waitsfield.

Cross-Country Skiing More than 25 kilometers (15 miles) of marked cross-country trails are adjacent to the Sugarbush Inn.

Other Activities Two sports centers near the ski lifts have Nautilus and Universal equipment; indoor and outdoor tennis, squash, and racquetball courts; Jacuzzi, sauna, and steam rooms; an indoor pool; and outdoor skating. In summer there are 36 outdoor tennis courts, 9 outdoor pools, and an 18-hole golf course on the Sugarbush property.

Child Care The Sugarbush Day School accepts children ages 6 weeks through 6 years; older children have indoor play and outdoor excursions. The Minibear Program introduces children ages 4–5 to skiing as an adjunct to the nursery. For children 6–11 years, the Sugarbear instruction program operates half days or full days.

Lodging **Sugarbush Inn.** This yellow-clapboard country inn is the centerpiece of the resort, with activities to interest all family members. The plant-filled public areas are spacious, and bedrooms have been remodeled recently. The large enclosed porch is used as a dining area. *Warren 05674, tel. 800/53–SUGAR. 46 rooms with bath. Facilities: 3 restaurants, 11 tennis courts, 18-hole golf course, weight room, games room, complete sports pavilion with indoor swimming pool. D, DC, MC, V. Moderate–Very Expensive.*

PowderHound Resort. Most of the rooms in this farmhouse-turned-inn that dates back more than 100 years are two-room suites that have living area, bath, and kitchenette. *Rte. 100, Box 369, Warren 05674, tel. 802/496–5100 or 800/548–4022. 44 rooms with bath. Facilities: restaurant, lounge, tennis court, volleyball, croquet, cable TV, shuttle to lifts. MC, V. Moderate–Expensive.*

Christmas Tree Inn. A modern country-style inn 3 miles from Sugarbush and 7 miles from Mad River, the Christmas Tree attracts couples and families. In addition to the 12 country-yet-contemporary rooms in the inn, on the grounds are 29 condos, each with one or three bedrooms, fireplace, cable TV, full kitchen, and telephones. Antiques and Laura Ashley accents set the tone throughout. Breakfast is served in the inn's dining room. Handmade jigsaw puzzles are set out around the large fireplace in the main room to challenge guests. *Sugarbush Access Rd., Warren 05674, tel. 802/583–2211 or 800/535–5622. 12 rooms with bath, 29 condos. Facilities: outdoor pool and tennis courts in summer. AE, MC, V. Rates include breakfast for inn guests only. Inexpensive–Moderate.*

Golden Lion. At the base of the road to the Sugarbush ski area, this small, riverside family motel is guarded by a golden chainsaw–carved lion. The fireside lobby, where Continental breakfast is served, is cozy; rooms are standard motel decor. *Rte. 100 at Access Rd., Box 336, Warren 05674, tel. 802/496–3084. 12 rooms with bath; 1 efficiency; 1 apartment. Facilities: cable TV, riverside beach. AE, D, MC, V. Rates include breakfast. Inexpensive–Moderate.*

Nightlife In Sugarbush Village, **Chez Henri** (tel. 802/583–2600) boasts of being the only disco in the Mad River Valley. The **Blue Tooth** (tel. 802/583–2656) has a variety of live entertainment and dancing during ski season and is popular with the singles crowd; it's on the access road to Sugarbush.

Suicide Six
Woodstock 05091
Tel. 802/457–1666; snow conditions, 802/457–1622

Suicide Six is a tail wagging a dog, the canine being the Woodstock Inn, owner of the ski resort. The inn, located 3 miles from the ski area in Woodstock village, offers package plans that are remarkably inexpensive, considering the high quality of the accommodations. In addition to skiers interested in exploring Woodstock, the area attracts students and racers from nearby Dartmouth College.

Downhill Skiing Despite Suicide Six's short vertical of only 650 feet, the area offers challenging skiing. There are several steep runs down the mountain's face and intermediate trails that wind around the hill. Beginner terrain is mostly toward the bottom. The 19 trails are serviced by two double chair lifts and one surface lift.

Cross-Country Skiing The ski touring center has 60 kilometers (37 miles) of trails. Equipment and lessons are available.

Other Activities A sports center at the Woodstock Inn has an indoor lap pool; indoor tennis, squash, and racquetball courts; whirlpool, steam, sauna, and massage rooms; and exercise and aerobics rooms. Outdoor tennis courts, lighted paddle courts, croquet space, and an 18-hole golf course are available in the summer.

Child Care Although the ski area has no nursery, baby-sitting can be arranged. Lessons for children are given by the ski-school staff.

Lodging **Woodstock Inn and Resort.** The present facility is the latest in a series of Woodstock Inns that have presided over the village green since 1793. The hotel's floor-to-ceiling fieldstone fireplace, with its massive wood-beam mantel, has a distinctive New England character, and it comes as no surprise to learn that the resort is owned by the Rockefeller family, which has been instrumental in preserving the town's charm. In the guest rooms the modern ash furnishings are enlivened by patchwork quilts on the beds and original art that depicts bucolic Vermont scenes. Some rooms have fireplaces. *Rte. 4, Woodstock 05091, tel. 802/457–1100 or 800/448–7900. 146 rooms with bath. Facilities: restaurant, lounge, conference rooms, indoor and outdoor pools, 2 indoor and 10 outdoor tennis courts, sports center with fitness equipment, 2 squash courts, 2 racquetball courts, whirlpool, saunas, 18-hole Robert Trent Jones golf course, gift shop, cable TV. AE, MC, V. Expensive–Very Expensive.*

Additional accommodations selections will be found under Quechee Lodging and Woodstock Lodging in the Central Vermont section of the Vermont chapter.

Nightlife **Bentley's** (tel. 802/457–3232) in Woodstock has a DJ and dancing on weekends. There is often live entertainment in **Richardson's Tavern** at the **Woodstock Inn and Resort** (tel. 802/457–1100).

New Hampshire Skiing

Magnificent Mt. Washington, which looms like a beacon over the White Mountains, may have been the original attraction in the northern region of New Hampshire. Scandinavian settlers who came to the high, handsome, rugged peaks in the late 1800s brought their skis with them. But skiing got its modern start in the Granite State in the 1920s, with the cutting of trails on Cannon Mountain.

Today there are 28 ski areas in New Hampshire, ranging from the old, established slopes (Cannon, Cranmore, Wildcat) to the most contemporary (Attitash, Loon, Waterville Valley). Whatever the age of the area, traditional activities—carnivals, races, ski instruction, family services—are important aspects of the skiing experience. On the slopes, skiers encounter some of the toughest runs in the country alongside some of the gentlest, and the middle range is a wide one.

The New Hampshire ski areas participate in a number of promotional packages allowing a sampling of different resorts. There's Ski 93 (referring to resorts along I–93), Ski the White Mountains, Ski the Mt. Washington Valley, and more.

Attitash
Rte. 302, Bartlett 03812
Tel. 603/374–2369

In the 1980s a new, young management at Attitash directed the resort's appeal to active young people and families. Keeping a high and busy profile, the area hosts many activities, race camps, and demo equipment days. Lodging at the base of the mountain is available in condominiums and motel-style units a bit away from the hustle of North Conway. Several pass plans are available. In 1992 Attitash installed Ski Data, a European computerized ticket system where skiers may purchase as many or as few runs as they wish. Tickets may be shared and are good for two years.

Downhill Skiing Enhanced with massive snowmaking, the trails and lifts have expanded significantly in recent years. There are expert pitches at the top of the mountain (try Idiot's Option, for example), but the bulk of the skiing is geared to advanced-intermediates and below, with wide fall-line runs from mid-mountain. Beginners have a share of good terrain on the lower mountain. Serving the 22 miles of trails and the 1,750-foot vertical drop are two triple and four double chair lifts.

Other Activities Attitash has two Alpine slides and five water slides in summertime; and concerts, stock theater, rodeo, and a horse show are held on premises. There's also horseback and pony riding, a golf driving range, and a scenic chair-lift ride to the new White Mountain observation tower.

Child Care Attitots Clubhouse takes children, ages 6 weeks through 5 years. Children's programs are: Attitots Plus (3 years of age), Mini Attiteam (4–5 years of age), Attiteam (6–8 years of age), Attidudes (9–12 years of age), and Attiteens (13–16 years of age). Children's programs are all housed at the Attitash Children's Center.

Lodging **Attitash Mountain Village & Conference Center.** This condo-motel complex, opened in 1989, has a glass-enclosed pool and units that will accommodate 2–14 people. Some quarters with fireplaces and kitchenettes are especially good for families. The style is Alpine-contemporary; the staff, young and enthusiastic. *Rte. 302, Bartlett 03812, tel. 603/374–6501 or 800/862–1600. 250 rooms with bath. Facilities: restaurant, pub, games room, indoor pool, sauna, whirlpool. AE, D, MC, V. Expensive.*

Best Western Storybook Resort Inn. This family-owned, family-run motor inn is well suited to families, especially the larger rooms on the hillside. Copperfield's Restaurant has gingerbread, sticky buns, farmer's omelets, and a special children's menu. *Box 129, Glen Junction 03838, tel. 603/383–6800 or 800/528–1234. 78 rooms with bath. Facilities: restaurant, indoor and outdoor pool, sauna, cable TV. No pets. AE, DC, MC, V. Inexpensive–Moderate.*

More than 100 hotels, lodges, and motels are located in the Mt. Washington Valley. Many can be reached through the Attitash Travel and Lodging Bureau, tel. 800/223–SNOW.

Nightlife   *See* Nightlife in Mt. Cranmore and Wildcat, *below.*

Balsams/Wilderness
Dixville Notch 03576
Tel. 603/255–3400 or 800/255–0600; in NH, 800/255–0800; snow conditions, 603/255–3951

Maintaining the tradition of a grand resort hotel is the primary goal at Balsams/Wilderness. Skiing was originally provided as an amenity for hotel guests, but the area has since become popular with day trippers as well. Restoration and renovation of the large, sprawling structure that dates to 1866 has been continuous since the early 1970s. Guests will find many nice touches: valet parking, gourmet meals, dancing and entertainment nightly, cooking demonstrations, and other organized recreational activities.

Downhill Skiing   Sanguinary, Umbagog, Magalloway—the slope names sound tough, but they are only moderately difficult, leaning toward intermediate. There are trails from the top of the 1,000-foot vertical drop for every skill level. One double chair lift and two T-bars carry skiers up the mountain.

Cross-Country Skiing   Balsams/Wilderness has 70 kilometers (45 miles) of cross-country skiing, tracked and also groomed for skating (a cross-country ski technique), with natural-history markers annotating some trails.

Other Activities   In winter, the area offers ice skating, hayrides, sleigh rides, snowshoeing, and snowmobiling. In summer, the resort has 27 holes of golf; six tennis courts; two trap fields; a heated outdoor pool; boating, swimming, and fly fishing on Lake Gloriette; and trails for hiking and climbing.

Child Care   The nursery takes children up to age 6 at no charge to hotel guests, however, there is a fee for day trippers. Wind Whistle lessons are designed to introduce skiing to children 3–5 years old. For those 5 and up, group lessons are available.

Lodging   **Balsams Grand Resort Hotel.** The famous full-service retreat with 15,000 acres of outdoor facilities and wilderness leaves nothing undone—and there's no reason to leave the grounds! "Ladies and gentlemen serving ladies and gentlemen" is the motto of the staff, numbering in the hundreds. Dinner in the dining room requires jackets for men, but other meals are informal. Trivia collectors will enjoy knowing that Balsams is where the first votes are counted in each presidential election. *Dixville Notch 03576, tel. 603/255–3400 or 800/255–0600. 232 rooms with bath. Facilities: dining room, billiard room, children's program, day nursery, dancing, movie theater, heated outdoor pool in summer, skating, skiing, sleigh rides, snowmobiling. AE, D, MC, V. Rates are MAP in winter and AP in summer and include all activities. Handicapped accessible. Moderate–Very Expensive.*

Additional accommodations selections will be found under Lodging in the White Mountains section of the New Hampshire chapter.

Black Mountain
Rte. 16B, Jackson 03846
Tel. 603/383–4490; in NH, 800/698–4490

The setting is 1950s, the atmosphere is friendly and informal, and skiers have fun here. There's a country feeling at the big base building, which resembles an old farmhouse, and at the skiing facilities, which generally have no lines. Black has the essentials for families and singles who want a low-key skiing holiday. The Valley Pass and One Pass lift tickets are available. Black is part of the Mt. Washington Valley ticket programs and has made a comeback as a popular ski destination in this region.

Downhill Skiing The bulk of the terrain is easy to middling, with intermediate trails that wander over the 1,100-vertical-foot mountain. Devil's Elbow on the Black Beauty trail—once a real zinger—has been expanded and is no longer as difficult as it once was to ski. The lifts are a triple and a double chair lift and two surface tows. Most of the skiing is user-friendly, particularly for beginners. The southern exposure adds to the warm atmosphere.

Child Care The nursery takes children up to 1 year old. For children up to 6 years, full day sessions with ski equipment are available. Reservations are required. The ski school offers Penguin Peak Skiing Nursery for ages 3–6, and the 1st Mountain Division for ages 6–12.

Lodging **Nordic Village.** The light wood and white walls of these deluxe condos are as Scandinavian as the snowy views. The Club House has a pool and spa, and there is a nightly bonfire at Nordic Falls. Fireplaces, full kitchens, and Jacuzzis can be found in the larger units; some economy cottages have wood stoves and kitchenettes. *Rte. 26, Jackson 03846, tel. 603/383–9101 or 800/472–5207. 135 apartments. Facilities: heated indoor and outdoor pools, therapy spa, steam room, skating area, sleigh rides, whirlpool, Jacuzzi. AE, MC, V. Moderate–Very Expensive.*

Whitneys' Village Inn. The Bowman family brings 30 years of inn-keeping experience to this classic country inn at the base of Black Mountain. You'll find antiques in the living room, period pieces in the one-of-a-kind bedrooms (some with sitting area), and suites that can take the bang of ski-week families. The windows of the dining room look out onto the slopes. *Box W, Jackson 03846, tel. 603/383–8916 or 800/677-5737. 28 rooms with bath, 2 cottages. Facilities: restaurant, games room, pond. No pets. AE, DC, MC, V. Rates are MAP. Moderate–Expensive.*

Additional accommodations selections will be found under Lodging in the White Mountains section of the New Hampshire chapter.

Nightlife The **Shovel Handle Pub** in Whitneys' Village Inn (tel. 603/383-8916) is the après-ski bar nearest the slopes.

Bretton Woods

Rte. 302, Bretton Woods 03575
Tel. 603/278-5000; information, 800/232-2972; lodging, 603/278-1000

Bretton Woods offers comfort and convenience in the attractive three-level open-space base lodge, the drop-off area, the easy parking, and the uncrowded setting that make skiing a pleasant experience for families. On-mountain town houses are available with reasonably priced packages through the resort. The spectacular views of Mt. Washington alone are worth the visit.

Downhill Skiing The skiing is mostly gentle, with some intermediate pitches near the top of the 1,500-foot vertical. Among the 30 trails are a few expert runs. One quad, one triple, and two double chair lifts, and one T-bar service the trails. The area has night skiing Friday and Saturday, and a limited lift-ticket policy helps keep lines short.

Cross-Country Skiing A short distance from the base of the mountain is a large cross-country center with 86 kilometers (51 miles) of groomed and double-track trails.

Other Activities A recreation center has racquetball, saunas and whirlpools, indoor swimming, an exercise room, and a games room. In summer, 27 holes of golf, 12 tennis courts, an outdoor pool, fly fishing, and hiking are available at the Mount Washington Hotel.

Child Care The nursery takes children ages 2 months through 3 years. The Hobbit Ski School, for ages 4–12, uses progressive instructional techniques. The all-day program includes lifts, lessons, equipment, lunch, and supervised play.

Lodging **Bretton Arms.** Built in 1896, this restored historic inn predates even the grande dame Mount Washington Hotel across the way, so you *know* that the trendsetters of the last century stayed here. Reservations are required in the dining room and should be made on arrival. Guests are invited to use the facilities of the historic Mount Washington Hotel during the summer and the Lodge at Bretton Woods year-round. *Rte. 302, Bretton Woods 03575, tel. 603/278-1000 or 800/258-0330. 34 rooms with bath. Facilities: restaurant, lounge, color TV, free shuttle service. MC, V. Rates are EP. Expensive.*
Lodge at Bretton Woods. Rooms have contemporary furnishings, a balcony, and views of the Presidential Range. Darby's Restaurant serves Continental cuisine around a circular fireplace, and the bar is a hangout for après skiers. The lodge, across the road from the Mount Washington Hotel, shares its facilities in summer. *Rte. 302, Bretton Woods 03575, tel. 603/278-1000 or 800/258-0330. 50 rooms. Facilities: restaurant, indoor pool, spa pool, sauna, whirlpool, games room, lounge. No pets. MC, V. Moderate.*

Additional accommodations selections will be found under Lodging in the White Mountains section of the New Hampshire chapter.

Cannon Mountain
Franconia Notch State Park, Franconia 03580
Tel. 603/823–5563; snow conditions, 603/823–7771 or 800/552–1234

Nowhere is the granite of the Granite State more pronounced than at Cannon Mountain, where you'll find the essentials for feeling the thrill of downhill. One of the first ski areas in the United States, the massif has retained the basic qualities that make the sport unique—the camaraderie of young people who are there for challenge and family fun. The New England Ski Museum is located adjacent to the base of the tramway, and at the site you can purchase the One Pass lift ticket. Cannon is owned and run by the state, and as a result, greater attention is being paid to skier services, family programs, snowmaking, and grooming.

Downhill Skiing The Peabody slopes, cut in the 1960s, were regarded as too easy for Cannon's diehards when at most ski areas the slopes would have been considered tough enough. The tone of this mountain's skiing is reflected in the narrow, steep pitches off the peak of the 2,146 feet of vertical rise. Some trails marked intermediate may seem more difficult because of the sidehill slant of the slopes (rather than the steepness). Under a new fall of snow, Cannon has challenge not often found at modern ski areas. There is an 80-passenger tramway to the top, one quad, one triple, and two double chair lifts, and one surface lift.

Cross-Country Skiing The Cannon Mountain area has 50 kilometers (31 miles) of cross-country trails.

Child Care Cannon's Peabody Base Lodge takes children 1 year and older. All-day and half-day SKIwee programs are available for children 4–12, and season-long instruction can be arranged.

Lodging **Indian Head Resort.** Views of Indian Head Rock, the GreatStone Face, and the Franconia Mountains are available across the 180 acres of this resort-motel. Take Exit 33 from I–93, then Route 3 north. *Rte. 3, North Lincoln 03251, tel. 603/745–8000 or 800/343–8000. 98 rooms with bath. Facilities: restaurant, games room, outdoor pool, indoor pool, sauna, cable TV, whirlpool, 2 tennis courts. AE, D, DC, MC, V. Moderate–Expensive.*

Horse and Hound Inn. Off the beaten path and yet convenient to the Cannon Mountain tram 2¾ miles away, is this traditional inn set on 8 acres surrounded by the White Mountain National Forest. Antiques and assorted collectibles offer guests a cheery atmosphere, and on the grounds are 10 kilometers (6 miles) of cross-country ski trails. *205 Wells Rd., Franconia 03580, tel. 603/823–5501. 10 rooms, 8 with bath; 2 suites. Facilities: restaurant, bar, lounge, pool table, videos. AE, DC, MC, V. Closed Apr. Rates include breakfast. Moderate.*

Additional accommodations will be found under Lodging in the White Mountains section of the New Hampshire chapter.

Nightlife There's live nightly entertainment in the **Thunderbird Lounge** at the Indian Head Resort (tel. 603/745–8000). **Hillwinds** (tel.

603/823–5551), on Main Street in Franconia, offers live entertainment weekends.

Gunstock
Box 1307, Laconia 03247
Tel. 603/293–4341 or 800/GUNSTOCK; snow conditions, 603/293–4345

High above Lake Winnipesaukee, the pleasant, all-purpose ski area of Gunstock attracts some skiers for overnight stays and others—many from Boston and its suburbs—for the day's skiing. Gunstock allows skiers to return lift tickets for a cash refund for any reason—weather, snow conditions, health, equipment problems. That policy plus a staff of customer-service people give a bit of class to an old-time ski area; Gunstock dates to the 1930s.

Downhill Skiing Some clever trail cutting, summer grooming, and surface sculpting have made this otherwise pedestrian mountain an interesting place for intermediates. That's how most of the 39 trails are rated, with designated sections for slow skiers and learners. The 1,400 feet of vertical has one quad, two triple, and two double chair lifts and two surface tows.

Cross-Country Skiing The Gunstock ski area offers 32 kilometers (19 miles) of cross-country trails.

Child Care The nursery takes children from infants up. The ski school teaches the SKIwee system to children 3–12.

Lodging **B. Mae's Resort Inn.** All the rooms in this resort complex and conference center are large; some one-bedroom condominiums have kitchens. *Rte. 11A, Gilford 03246, tel. 603/293–7526 or 800/458–3877. 82 rooms with bath. Facilities: restaurant, lounge, games room, exercise room, indoor pool, cable TV, whirlpool. No pets. AE, D, DC, MC, V. Moderate–Expensive.*
Gunstock Inn and Health Club. This country-style resort and motor inn about a minute's drive from the Gunstock recreation area has rooms of various sizes furnished with American antiques, with views of the mountains and Lake Winnipesaukee. *580 Cherry Valley Rd. (Rte. 11A), Gilford 03246, tel. 603/293–2021 or 800/654–0180. 27 rooms with bath. Facilities: restaurant, health club, indoor pool, spa, cable TV. No pets. AE, D, MC, V. Moderate–Expensive.*

Loon Mountain
Kancamagus Hwy., Lincoln 03251
Tel. 603/745–8111; snow conditions, 603/745–8100; lodging, 800/229–STAY

On the Kancamagus Highway and the Pemigewasset River is the modern Loon Mountain resort. Loon opened in the 1960s, and saw serious development in the 1980s, when more mountain facilities, base lodges, and a large hotel near the main lifts at the bottom of the mountain were added. The result attracts a broad cross-section of skiers. In the base lodge, on the mountain, and around the area are a large number of food services and lounge facilities. The first-rate Mountain Club hotel has guest rooms within walking distance of the lifts, and there are on-slope and nearby condominium complexes.

Downhill Skiing Wide, straight, and consistent intermediate trails prevail at Loon, which makes it ideal for plain fun or for advancing one's skills. Beginner trails and slopes are set apart, so faster skiers won't interfere. Most advanced runs are grouped on the North Peak section farther from the main mountain. The vertical is 2,100 feet; a four-passenger gondola, two triple and five double chair lifts, and one surface lift serve the 41 trails and slopes.

Cross-Country Skiing The touring center has 35 kilometers (22 miles) of cross-country trails.

Other Activities The Mountain Club has a fitness center with a whirlpool, lap pool, saunas, steam rooms, an exercise room, and racquetball and squash courts. Massages and aerobics classes are available. An outdoor pool, tennis courts, horseback riding, archery, in-line skating, skeet shooting, mountain biking, and the gondola Skyride to the summit are available in summer.

Child Care The Honeybear nursery takes children as young as 6 weeks. Nonintensive ski instruction is offered to youngsters of nursery age. The ski school has a Mountain Explorers program for children 9–12 and SKIwee for ages 3–8. Children 5 and under ski free every day, while those 6–12 ski free midweek during nonholiday periods when parents participate in a five-day ski week.

Lodging **The Mountain Club on Loon.** A recently built slopeside resort hotel has a full range of activities, including live entertainment five nights a week in the lounge. Suites sleep as many as eight; some are studios with Murphy beds; 70 have kitchens. Take Exit 32 from I–93 (Kancamagus Hwy.). *Rte. 112, Lincoln 03251, tel. 603/745–8111 or 800/433–3413. 234 rooms with bath. Facilities: restaurant, lounge, deli, convenience store, fitness center, garage, indoor pool, racquetball court, squash court, sauna, cable TV. AE, D, DC, MC, V. Moderate–Very Expensive.*

Mill House Inn. This hotel on the western edge of the Kancamagus Highway offers country-inn style along with free transportation to Loon and Waterville Valley during ski season. Nonskiers will have plenty to do, too: shopping, a four-screen cinema, and the North Country Center for the Performing Arts are nearby. *Box 696, Lincoln 03251, tel. 603/745–6261 or 800/654–6183. 96 rooms with bath, including 24 suites. Facilities: restaurant, nightclub, exercise room, outdoor pool, indoor pool, sauna, tennis court, whirlpools. AE, D, DC, MC, V. Moderate–Expensive.*

Additional accommodations will be found under Lodging in the White Mountains section of the New Hampshire chapter.

Nightlife Après-ski activity will be found at the **Granite Bar** at the Mountain Club (tel. 603/745–8111), and there's dancing at the **Loon Saloon** at the ski area. **Dickens** (tel. 603/745–2278), in the Village of Loon, has live musical entertainment.

Mt. Cranmore
Box 1640, North Conway, 03860
Tel. 603/356–5543; snow conditions, 800/786–6754; lodging, 800/543–9206

The ski area at Mt. Cranmore, on the outskirts of North Conway, came into existence in 1938 when local residents saw an opportunity to make the most of their mountain. One early innovation, the clankety-clank Simobile lift, has sadly been put out to museum pastures and no longer operates. An aggressive mountain-improvement program has been under way for several years, with new grooming equipment, a triple chair, expanded terrain, and base-restaurant services. A fitness center completes the "new" Cranmore.

Downhill Skiing The mountain and trail system at Cranmore is well laid out and fun to ski. Most of the runs are naturally formed intermediates that weave in and out of glades. Beginners have several slopes and routes from the 1,200-foot summit, while experts must be content with a few short but steep pitches. One triple and four double chair lifts carry skiers to the top. There is night skiing Thursday through Saturday and nightly during holiday periods.

Cross-Country Skiing Sixty-five kilometers (40 miles) of groomed cross-country trails weave through North Conway and the countryside.

Other Activities Mt. Cranmore Recreation Center contains four indoor tennis courts, exercise equipment, an indoor pool, aerobics workout space, and a 48-foot indoor climbing wall. There is outdoor skating and, in summer, four outdoor tennis courts.

Child Care The nursery takes children 1 year and up. For children 4–12, the SKIwee program offers all-day skiing and instruction. The Rattlesnake Youth Development Program gives season-long ski instruction for children in the same age range.

Lodging **Best Western Fox Ridge.** One mile from North Conway Village on a 300-acre resort estate you can find Fox Ridge, with its family rooms with loft sleeping areas, and suites that have a kitchen and a living room with a convertible couch. *Box 990, White Mountain Hwy., North Conway 03860, tel. 603/356–3151 or 800/343–1804. 136 rooms with bath. Facilities: restaurant, lounge, exercise room, games room, indoor pool, saunas, cable TV, Jacuzzi, cross-country ski trails. No pets. AE, D, DC, MC, V. Moderate–Expensive.*

Eastern Slope Inn Resort and Conference Center. Although this has been an operating inn for more than a century, recent restoration and refurbishing have updated its image and its facilities. The resort has the ambience of a historic site along with such modern amenities as an enclosed pool. Jackson Square, the inn restaurant, serves traditional American fare in a glassed-in courtyard. Nightly entertainment. *Main St., North Conway 03860, tel. 603/356–6321 or 800/258–4708. 125 rooms with bath. Facilities: restaurant, pub, games room, indoor pool, sauna, whirlpool. AE, D, MC, V. Moderate.*

Additional accommodations will be found under Lodging in the White Mountains section of the New Hampshire chapter.

Nightlife For lively weekend entertainment go to **Barnaby's** (tel. 603/356–5781) or the **Cranmore Pub** (tel. 603/356–2472) in North Conway. **Fox Ridge** (tel. 603/356–3151) offers music and dancing on weekends, as does the **Darby Field Inn** (tel. 603/447–2181). The **Red Jacket Mountain View Inn** (tel. 603/356–5411) has weekend and holiday entertainment. *See also* Nightlife for Wildcat Mountain, *above.*

Mt. Sunapee

Mt. Sunapee State Park, Rte. 103, Mt. Sunapee 03772
Tel. 603/763–2356; snow conditions, 800/322–3300; lodging, 603/763–2145 or 800/258–3530

Without glitz or glamour, state-run Sunapee remains popular among local residents and skiers from Boston, Hartford, and the coast for its low-key atmosphere and easy skiing. Two base lodges supply the essentials.

Downhill Skiing This mountain of 1,510 vertical feet, the highest in southern New Hampshire, has 19 miles of gentle-to-moderate terrain with a couple of pitches that could be called steep. A nice beginner's section is located beyond the base facilities, well away and well protected from other trails. Three triple and three double chair lifts and one surface lift transport skiers.

Child Care The Duckling Nursery takes children from 12 months through 5 years of age. Little Indians ski instruction gives ages 3 and 4 a taste of skiing, while SKIwee lessons are available for ages 5–12.

Lodging **Bradford Inn.** This delightfully old-fashioned country inn in the village of Bradford has two common rooms and a popular restaurant, J. Albert's, which features New England cooking. Rooms have details circa 1898, and there are family suites. Senior citizen discounts and facilities for the disabled are available. *Main St., Bradford 03221, tel. 603/938-5309 or 800/669-5309. 14 rooms with bath. Facilities: restaurant, outdoor pool, tennis court. MC, V. Rates include full breakfast. Moderate.*

Additional accommodations will be found under Lodging in the Dartmouth-Lake Sunapee section of the New Hampshire chapter.

Waterville Valley
Waterville Valley 03215
Tel. 603/236-8311; snow conditions, 603/236-4144; lodging, 800/468-2553

Most everything in the valley belongs to or is licensed by the mountain company, effectively making the area an enclave, of sorts. There are inns, lodges, and condominiums; restaurants, taverns, small cafés; shops, boutiques, and a grocery store; conference facilities; a post office; and a sports center. Everything has been built with taste and regard for the New England sensibility, and the resort attracts skiers from Boston and environs. An array of three- to five-day vacation packages is available.

Downhill Skiing Mt. Tecumseh, a short shuttle ride from the Town Square and accommodations, has been laid out with great care and attention to detail. A good selection of the 53 trails offers most advanced skiers an adequate challenge, and there are slopes and trails for beginners, too. Yet the bulk of the skiing is intermediate: straight down the fall line, wide, and agreeably long. The variety is great enough that no one will be bored on a weekend visit. The lifts serving the 2,020 feet of vertical rise include one high-speed, detachable quad; three triple and five double chair lifts; and four surface lifts. A second mountain, Snow's, about 2 miles away, is open on weekends and takes some of the overflow; it has five fairly easy trails and one double chair lift off a 580-foot vertical. You might spot some of the Kennedy clan on the Waterville slopes. This ski area has hosted more World Cup races than any other in the nation.

Cross-Country Skiing The cross-country network, with the ski center in the Town Square, has 105 kilometers (62 miles) of trails, 70 of them groomed.

Other Activities An ice skating arena is adjacent to the Town Square. The Sports Center has tennis, racquetball, and squash courts; a 25-meter indoor pool; jogging track; exercise equipment and classes; whirlpools, saunas, and steam rooms; massage service; and a games room. In summer, there is an outdoor pool, 18 tennis courts, nine holes of golf, biking, horseback riding, in-line skating, and water sports on Corcoran's Pond.

Child Care The nursery takes children 6 weeks through 4 years old. Children ages 6–12 who want to ski have a choice of group lessons or half-day or full-day SKIwee lessons. Petite SKIwee is designed for children 3–5, SKIweek is for ages 6–8, and Grand SKIwee is for ages 9–12. The Kinderpark, a children's slope, has a slow-running lift and special props to hold children's attention. Children 5 and under ski free anytime; midweek, those 12 and under ski and stay free with a parent on multiday packages. Evening child care is available for ages 6 weeks through 12 years.

Lodging **Black Bear Lodge.** The all-suite hotel has one- and two-bedroom units with full kitchens, heated indoor and outdoor pools, a sauna, a steam room, and bus service to the slopes. *Snow's Brook Rd., Box 357, Waterville Valley 03215, tel. 603/236–4501 or 800/468–2553. 107 suites. Facilities: indoor and outdoor pools, access to sports center, cable TV, saunas, steam room. No pets. AE, D, DC, MC, V. Expensive–Very Expensive.*

Golden Eagle Lodge. Waterville's premier lodging property, is reminiscent of the grand hotels of an earlier era. There are 139 condominium suites in this four-year-old complex, with a two-story lobby and a front desk staff that provides all the services you'd find in a hotel. *Waterville Valley Co., Inc., 03215, tel. 603/236–8311. 139 condominium suites. Facilities: kitchen, living/dining area, cable TV, indoor pool, whirlpools, saunas, game room, shuttle to the slopes. AE, D, DC, MC, V. Expensive–Very Expensive.*

Snowy Owl Inn. The inn is cozy and intimate, and offers a variety of setups: The fourth-floor bunk-bed loft are rooms ideal for families; the first-floor rooms are suitable for couples who want a quiet getaway. Among the attractive features are a three-story-high central fieldstone fireplace (one of seven fireplaces), a surrounding atrium supported by single-log posts, and lots of prints and watercolors of snowy owls. Four restaurants are within walking distance. *Box 407, Snow's Brook Rd., Waterville Valley 03215, tel. 603/236–8383 or 800/468–2553. 80 rooms with bath. Facilities: indoor pool, saunas, sports center access, cable TV, whirlpool. No pets. AE, D, DC, MC, V. Rates include breakfast. Moderate–Expensive.*

Nightlife The valley has a number of popular lounges, taverns, and cafés. **The Yacht Club** (tel. 603/236–8885), overlooking Corcoran's Pond, has live entertainment. Weekend and holiday entertainment can be found at **Legends 1291** (tel. 603/236–4678), Waterville's only year-round disco, and **Brookside Bistro** (tel. 603/236–4309).

Wildcat Mountain
Pinkham Notch, Rte. 16, Jackson 03846
Tel. 603/466–3326; snow conditions, 617/965–7991 or 800/552–8952

Wildcat has been working hard to live down its reputation of being a difficult mountain and has adopted the motto: "As tough as Cannon, as easy as Bretton Woods." But if you're looking for it, the tough stuff is here. The area is a favorite of local residents, and attractive pricing (junior lift tickets extend to 15-year-olds instead of the usual 12-year age limit) has made it ideal for families. Races and special events for ski clubs and also set Wildcat apart from other nearby mountains. The area has weekend, three-day, and five-day packages at reasonable rates. Wildcat is part of Mt. Washington Valley promotional programs.

Downhill Skiing Wildcat's expert trails deserve their designations and then some. Intermediates have newly widened mid-mountain-to-base trails, and beginners will find gentle terrain and a broad teaching slope. The 30 runs with a 2,100-foot vertical drop are served by a two-passenger gondola and one double and four triple chair lifts. On a clear day, from the 4,000-foot summit, views of nearby Mt. Washington and the infamous Tuckerman's Ravine are spectacular.

Child Care The Kitten Club Child Care Center takes children 18 months and up. All-day SKIwee instruction is offered to children 5–12. A separate slope is used for teaching children to ski.

Lodging **Eagle Mountain Resort.** When this country estate of 1879 was restored and modernized in 1986, it became a showplace and is now run by Colony Resorts. The public rooms are rustic-palatial, in keeping with the period of tycoon roughing-it; the bedrooms are large and furnished with period pieces. *Carter Notch Rd., Jackson 03846, tel. 603/333–9111 or 800/527–5022; reservations through Colony, tel. 800/777–1700. 94 rooms with bath. Facilities: restaurant, health club, outdoor pool, saunas, whirlpool. No pets. AE, D, MC, V. Moderate.*

Wildcat Inn & Tavern. Located in the center of Jackson Village, the restaurant in this small 19th-century inn is a lodestone for skiers in nearby condos and bed-and-breakfasts. The fragrance of home-baking permeates into guest rooms, which are full of interesting furniture and knickknacks. *Rte. 16A, Jackson 03846, tel. 603/383–4245. 12 rooms, 10 with bath. Facilities: restaurant. AE, MC, V. Rates include breakfast. Inexpensive–Moderate.*

Nightlife The **Wildcat Inn & Tavern** (tel. 603/383–4245) has weekend entertainment. In Glen, the **Bernhof Inn** (tel. 603/383–4414) is the setting for an evening of fondue and soft music by the fireside, and the **Red Parka Club** (tel. 603/383–4344) is nearby. *See* Nightlife in Mt. Cranmore, *above,* for additional information.

3 Maine

*By David Laskin
with an
introduction by
William G.
Scheller*

*The travel writings
of David Laskin
have appeared in
the New York
Times and Travel
and Leisure, and
1990 saw
publication of his
book Eastern
Islands: Accessible
Islands of the East
Coast.*

*Updated by Hilary
Nangle*

If any two individuals can be associated directly with the disparate images evoked by the very mention of the state of Maine, they are George Bush and Carolyn Chute.

Former president George Bush is the most famous summer resident of Kennebunkport, where he and his family vacation in his grandfather's rambling seaside mansion. Having so recently had a summer White House on the Maine coast reminds Americans that this craggy, wildly irregular stretch of shoreline has long enjoyed an aristocratic cachet: Here Nelson Rockefeller was born in the millionaires' enclave at Bar Harbor; here the Brahmin historian Samuel Eliot Morison sailed the cold waters of Frenchman Bay. In those times, anyone living on the coast of Maine who wasn't rich, famous, or powerful was almost certainly an old-stock yeoman, probably someone with a lobster boat.

Carolyn Chute is the novelist who wrote *The Beans of Egypt, Maine.* Chute's fictional Egypt and its inhabitants are a reminder that Appalachia stretches far to the north of the Cumberland Gap and that not far inland from the famous rockbound coast there are places where rusting house trailers are far more common than white Federalist sea captains' mansions.

In fact, neither stereotype (and both have strong foundations in fact) makes a serious dent in the task of defining or explaining Maine. Reality in most of the state resembles neither a cross between a Ralph Lauren ad and a Winslow Homer painting nor a milieu in which modern history dates from the day they began renting videos at the gas station.

Maine is by far the largest state in New England. At its extremes it measures 300 miles north to south and 200 miles across; all five other New England states could fit within its perimeters. There is an expansiveness to Maine, a sense of real distance between places that hardly exists elsewhere in the region, and along with the sheer size and spread of the place there is a tremendous variety of terrain. One speaks of "coastal" Maine and "inland" Maine, as though the state could be summed up under the twin emblems of lobsters and pine trees. Yet the state's topography and character are a good deal more complicated.

Even the coast is several places in one. South of the rapidly gentrifying city of Portland, such resort towns as Ogunquit, Kennebunkport, and Old Orchard Beach (sometimes called the Québec Riviera because of its popularity with French Canadians) predominate along a reasonably smooth shoreline. Development has been considerable; north of Portland and Casco Bay, secondary roads turn south off Route 1 onto so many oddly chiseled peninsulas that it's possible to drive for days without retracing your route and to conclude that motels, discount outlets, and fried-clam stands are taking over the domain of presidents and lobstermen. Freeport is an entity unto itself, a place where a bewildering assortment of off-price, name-brand outlets has sprung up around the famous outfitter L. L. Bean (no relation to the Egypt clan).

Inland Maine likewise defies characterization. For one thing, a good part of it is virtually uninhabited. This is the land Henry David Thoreau wrote about in *Maine Woods* nearly 150 years ago; aside from having been logged over several times, much of it hasn't changed since Thoreau and his Native American

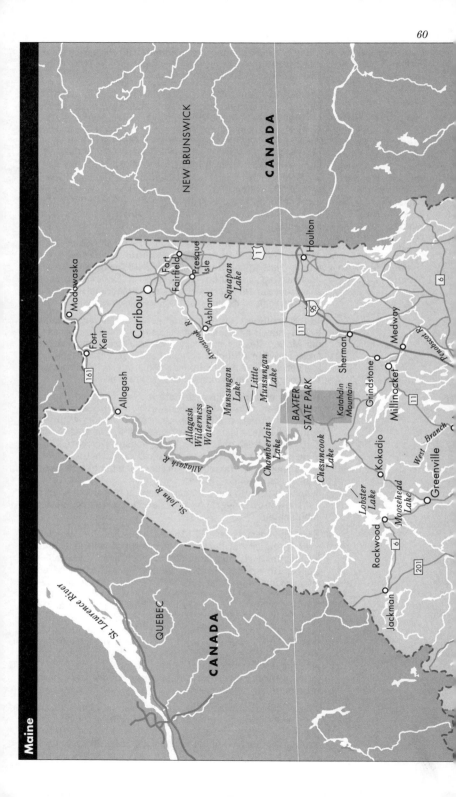

Maine

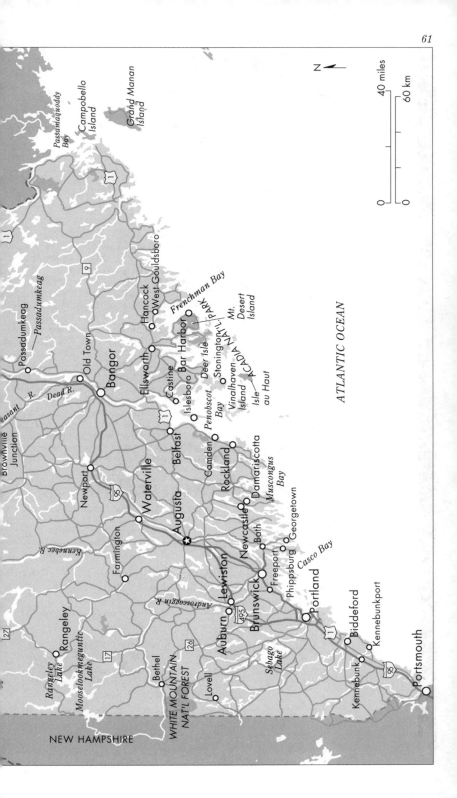

guides passed through. Ownership of vast portions of northern Maine by forest-products corporations has kept out subdivision and development; many of the roads here are private, open to travel only by permit. The north woods' day of reckoning may be coming, however, for the paper companies plan to sell off millions of acres in a forested belt that reaches all the way to the Adirondacks in New York State. In the 1990s state governments and environmental organizations are working to preserve as much as possible of the great silent expanses of pine.

Logging the north created the culture of the mill towns, the Rumfords, Skowhegans, and Bangors that lay at the end of the old river drives. The logs arrive by truck today, but Maine's harvested wilderness still feeds the mills and the nation's hunger for paper.

Our hunger for potatoes has given rise to an entirely different Maine culture, in one of the most isolated agricultural regions of the country. Northeastern Aroostook County is where the Maine potatoes come from, and this place, too, is changing. In what was once called the Potato Empire, farmers are as pressed between high costs and low prices as any of their counterparts in the Midwest; add to the bleak economic picture a growing national preference for Idaho baking potatoes rather than the traditional small, round Maine boiling potatoes, and Aroostook's troubles are compounded. The visitor seeking an untouched fishing village with locals gathered around a potbellied stove in the general store may be sadly disappointed; that innocent age has passed in all but the most remote of villages. Tourism has supplanted fishing, logging, and potato farming as Maine's number one industry, and most areas are well equipped to receive the annual onslaught of visitors. But whether you are stepping outside a motel room for an evening walk or watching a boat rock at its anchor, you can sense the infinity of the natural world. Wilderness is always nearby, growing to the edges of the most urbanized spots.

Essential Information

Visitor Information

Maine Publicity Bureau (Box 2300, Hallowell 04347, tel. 207/582–9300 or 800/533–9595).

Maine Innkeepers Association (305 Commercial St., Portland 04101, tel. 207/773–7670) publishes a statewide lodging and dining guide.

Tour Groups

Golden Age Festival (5501 New Jersey Ave., Wildwood Crest, NJ 08260, tel. 609/522–6316 or 800/257–8920) offers a four-night bus tour geared to senior citizens, with shopping at Kittery outlets and L. L. Bean, a Boothbay Harbor boat cruise, and stops at Kennebunkport, Pemaquid Point, Mt. Battie, and Acadia National Park.

Festivals and Seasonal Events

Mid-Feb.: Western Mountain Winter Wonderland Week at Sunday River Resort in Bethel has hot-air balloons, sleigh rides, and dog sledding. *Tel. 207/824–2187.*

Early Mar.: Ice-Fishing Tournament on Moosehead Lake near Rockwood begins the first Saturday. Tel. 207/534–2261.

Mid-Mar.: Rangeley Lake Sled Dog Races attracts more than 100 teams from throughout the Northeast and Canada. *Tel. 207/864–5364.*

Late Mar.: On **Maine Maple Sunday,** the fourth Sunday in March, maple sugarhouses open their doors to visitors. *Tel. 207/289–3491.*

Late Apr.: Boothbay Harbor Fishermen's Festival. *Tel. 207/633–4008 or 633–4834.*

Late June: Boothbay Harbor Windjammer Days, starts the high season for the boating set. *Tel. 207/633–2353.*

Late June: Maine Storytellers Festival gathers the tallest tale tellers at the Rockport Opera House on the last weekend in June. *Tel. 207/773–4909.*

July 4th weekend: Bath Heritage Days features four days of concerts, family entertainment, an art show, a parade, and fireworks. *Tel. 207/443–9751.*

Mid-July–mid-Aug.: Bar Harbor Music Festival hosts classical and popular music concerts. *Tel. 212/222–1026 or 207/288–5744.*

Late July: Camden Garden House Tour, on the third Thursday, shows fine houses and gardens in Camden and Rockport. *Tel. 207/236–4404.*

July–Aug.: Bangor State Fair, a true country fair, fills Bass Park from the last weekend in July through the first week in August. *Tel. 207/942–9000.*

Early Aug.: Bluegrass Festival is a three-day affair at Thomas Point Beach in Brunswick. *Tel. 207/725–6009.*

Early Aug.: The Maine Festival, Portland's premier fair, brings together musicians, artists, dancers, and farmers. *Tel. 207/772–9012.*

Early Aug.: Maine Lobster Festival, Rockland, is a public feast held on the first weekend of the month. *Tel. 207/596–0376.*

Mid-Aug.: Maine Antiques Festival, with more than 350 dealers, is held at the Union Fair Grounds. *Tel. 207/563–1013.*

Late Aug.: Rangeley Lakes Blueberry Festival takes place on the Rangeley Inn Green on the third Thursday of the month. *Tel. 207/864–2972.*

Early Sept.: Blue Hill Fair—horse races, rides, auctions—is Labor Day weekend at the fairgrounds. *Tel. 207/374–9976.*

Mid-Sept.: International Seaplane Fly-In Weekend sets Moosehead Lake buzzing on the weekend after Labor Day. *Tel. 207/695–2702.*

Late Sept.: Common Ground Country Fair in Windsor is an organic farmer's delight, including livestock shows, a pie contest, and contra dancing. *Tel. 207/623–5115.*

Late Sept.: Tour D'Acadia, a 24-mile bike race through the park, begins in Bar Harbor on the last Sunday. *Tel. 207/288–3511.*

Late Sept.–Early Oct.: Fryeburg Fair offers agricultural exhibits, harness racing, an iron-skillet-throwing contest, and a pig scramble. *Tel. 207/935–3268.*

Arriving and Departing

By Plane Maine's major airports are **Portland International Jetport** (tel. 207/774–7301) and **Bangor International Airport** (tel. 207/947–0384); each has scheduled daily flights by major U.S. carriers.

Hancock County Airport (tel. 207/667–7329), 8 miles northwest of the city, is served by Continental Express (tel. 207/667–7171 or 800/525–0280).

Knox County Regional Airport (tel. 207/594–4131), 3 miles south of Rockland, has flights by Continental Express Regional.

By Car Interstate 95 is the fastest route to and through the state from coastal New Hampshire and points south, turning inland at Brunswick and going on to Bangor and the Canadian border. Route 1, more leisurely and more scenic, is the principal coastal highway from New Hampshire to Canada.

By Train Canada's **VIA Rail** (Box 8116, 2 Place Ville-Marie, Montréal, Québec, tel. 800/361–3677) provides Maine's only passenger rail service. The run between Montréal and Halifax crosses the center of the state, stopping at Jackman, Greenville, Brownville Junction, Mattawamkeag, Danforth, and Vanceboro.

By Bus **Vermont Transit** (tel. 207/772–6587), a subsidiary of **Greyhound Lines,** connects towns in southwestern Maine with cities in New England and throughout the United States.

By Boat **Marine Atlantic** (tel. 207/288–3395 or 800/341–7981) operates ferry service between Yarmouth, Nova Scotia, and Bar Harbor; **Prince of Fundy Cruises** (tel. 800/341–7540) operates ferry service between Yarmouth and Portland (May–October only).

Getting Around Maine

By Plane Regional flying services, operating from the regional and municipal airports, provide access to remote lakes and wilderness areas.

By Car In many areas of the state a car is the only practical means of travel. The Maine Map and Guide, available for $1 from offices of the Maine Publicity Bureau, is useful for driving throughout the state; it has directories, mileage charts, and enlarged maps of city areas.

By Boat **Casco Bay Lines** (tel. 207/774–7871) provides ferry service from Portland to the islands of Casco Bay, and **Maine State Ferry Service** (tel. 207/596–2202 or 800/521–3939 in Maine) provides ferry service from Rockland to Penobscot Bay.

Dining

For most visitors Maine means lobster, and lobster can be found on the menus of a majority of Maine restaurants. As a general rule, the closer you are to a working harbor, the fresher your lobster will be. Aficionados eschew ordering lobster in restaurants, preferring to eat them "in the rough" at classic lobster pounds, where you select your lobster swimming in a pool and enjoy it at a waterside picnic table. Shrimp and crab are also caught in the cold waters off Maine, and the better restaurants in Portland and the coastal resort towns prepare the shellfish in creative combinations with lobster, haddock, salmon, and swordfish. Blueberries are grown commercially in Maine, and Maine cooks use them generously in pancakes, muffins, pies, and cobblers. Full country breakfasts of fruit, eggs, breakfast meats, pancakes, and muffins are commonly served at inns and bed-and-breakfasts.

Highly recommended restaurants in each price category are indicated by a star ★.

Category	Cost*
Very Expensive	over $35
Expensive	$25–$35
Moderate	$15–$25
Inexpensive	under $15

average cost of a three-course dinner, per person, excluding drinks, service, and 7% sales tax

Lodging

Bed-and-breakfasts and Victorian inns furnished with lace, chintz, and mahogany have joined the family-oriented motels of Ogunquit, Boothbay Harbor, Bar Harbor, and the Camden region. Two world-class resorts with good health club and sports facilities are on the coast near Portland and on Penobscot Bay. Although accommodations tend to be more rustic away from the coast, Bethel, Center Lovell, and Rangeley offer sophisticated hotels and inns. In the far north the best alternative to camping is to stay in a rustic wilderness camp, several of which serve hearty meals. For a list of camps, write to the **Maine Sporting Camp Association** (Box 89, Jay 04239).

At many of Maine's larger hotels and inns with restaurants, Modified American Plan (includes breakfast and dinner) is either an option or required during the peak summer season. In general, when MAP is optional, hotels give dinner credits of $20 per guest.

Highly recommended lodgings in each price category are indicated by a star ★.

Category	Cost*
Very Expensive	over $100
Expensive	$80–$100
Moderate	$60–$80
Inexpensive	under $60

All prices are for a standard double room for two during peak season, with no meals unless noted and excluding 7% sales tax.

The Coast: North from Kittery

Maine's southernmost coastal towns won't give you the rugged, windbitten "downeast" experience, but they offer all the amenities, they are easy to drive to from the south, and most have the sand beaches that all but vanish beyond Portland.

Kittery, which lacks a large sand beach, hosts a complex of factory outlets. North of Kittery the Maine coast has long stretches of hard-packed white-sand beach, closely crowded by nearly unbroken ranks of beach cottages, motels, and oceanfront restaurants. The summer colonies of York Beach, Ogunquit, and Wells Beach have the crowds and the ticky-tacky shorefront overdevelopment. Farther inland, York's historic district is on the National Register.

More than any other region south of Portland, the Kennebunks—and especially Kennebunkport—offer the complete Maine coast experience: classic townscapes where perfectly proportioned white-clapboard houses rise from manicured lawns and gardens; rocky shorelines punctuated by sandy beaches, beach motels, and cottages; quaint downtown districts packed with gift shops, ice-cream stands, and tourists; harbors where lobster boats bob alongside yachts; lobster pounds and well-appointed dining rooms. The range of accommodations includes rambling Victorian-era hotels, beachside family motels, and inns.

Important Addresses and Numbers

Visitor Information **Kennebunk–Kennebunkport Chamber of Commerce** (Cooper's Corner, Rtes. 9 and 35, tel. 207/967–0857).

Kittery–Eliot Chamber of Commerce (Box 526, 3-B Government St., Kittery, tel. 207/439–7545).

Maine Tourist Information Center (Rte. 1 and I–95, tel. 207/439–1319).

Ogunquit Chamber of Commerce (Box 2289, Ogunquit, tel. 207/646–2939 or 207/646–5533, mid-May–mid-October).

Wells Chamber of Commerce (Box 356, Wells 04090, tel. 207/646–2451).

The Yorks Chamber of Commerce (Box 417, York, tel. 207/363–4422).

Emergencies **Maine State Police** (Scarborough, tel. 207/793–4500 or 800/482–0730).

Kennebunk Walk-in Clinic (Rte. 1 N, tel. 207/985–6027).

Southern Maine Medical Center (1 Mountain Rd., Biddeford, tel. 207/283–3663).

Getting Around North from Kittery

By Car Route 1 from Kittery is the shopper's route north, while other roads hug the coastline. I–95 should be faster for travelers headed for specific towns. The exit numbers can be confusing: As you go north from Portsmouth, Exits 1–3 lead to Kittery and Exit 4 leads to the Yorks. After the tollbooth in York, the Maine Turnpike begins, and the numbers start over again, with Exit 2 for Wells and Ogunquit and Exit 3 (and Route 35) for Kennebunk and Kennebunkport. Route 9 goes from Kennebunkport to Cape Porpoise and Goose Rocks.

By Trolley A trolley circulates among the Yorks, June to Labor Day. Eight trolleys serve the major tourist areas and beaches of Ogunquit, including four that connect with Wells, mid-May through mid-October. The trolley from Dock Square in Kennebunkport to Kennebunk Beach runs from late June to Labor Day.

Exploring North from Kittery

Numbers in the margin correspond to points of interest on the Southern Maine Coast map.

❶ Our tour of the Maine coast begins at **Kittery,** just across the New Hampshire border, off I–95 on Route 1. Kittery will be of most interest to shoppers headed for its factory outlet stores.

❷ Beyond Kittery, Route 1 heads north to **the Yorks,** and a right onto Route 1A (York Street) leads to the **York Village Historic District,** where a number of 18th- and 19th-century buildings have been restored and maintained by the Old York Historical Society. Most of the buildings are clustered along York Street and Lindsay Road, and you can buy an admission ticket for all the buildings at the Jefferds Tavern (Rte. 1A and Lindsay Rd.), a restored late-18th-century inn. Other historic buildings open to the public include the Old York Gaol (1720), once the King's Prison for the Province of Maine, which has dungeons, cells, and jailer's quarters; and the Elizabeth Perkins House (1731), with Victorian-era furniture that reflects the style of its last occupants, the prominent Perkins family. The district offers tours with guides in period costumes, crafts workshops, and special programs in summer. *Tel. 207/363–4974. Admission: $6 adults, $2.50 children 6–16, $16 family. Open mid-June–Sept., Tues.–Sat. 10–4.*

Complete your tour of the Yorks by driving down Nubble Road (turn right off Route 1A) to the end of Cape Neddick, where you can park and gaze out at the Nubble Light (1879), which sits on a tiny island just offshore. The keeper's house is a tidy Victorian cottage with pretty gingerbread woodwork and a red roof.

Shore Road to Ogunquit passes the 100-foot Bald Head Cliff, which allows a view up and down the coast; on a stormy day the surf can be quite wild here. Shore Road will take you right into **❸** **Ogunquit,** a coastal village that became a resort in the 1880s and gained fame as an artists' colony, though few artists or actors can afford the condos and seaside cottages that now dominate the Ogunquit seascape.

On Shore Road, the **Ogunquit Museum of Art,** a low-lying concrete building overlooking the ocean and set amid a 3-acre sculpture garden, shows works by Henry Strater, Marsden Hartley, William Bailey, Gaston Lachaise, Walt Kuhn, and Reginald Marsh. The huge windows of the sculpture court command a view of cliffs and ocean. *Shore Rd., tel. 207/646–4909. Admission free. Open July–mid-Sept., Mon.–Sat. 10:30–5, Sun. 2–5.*

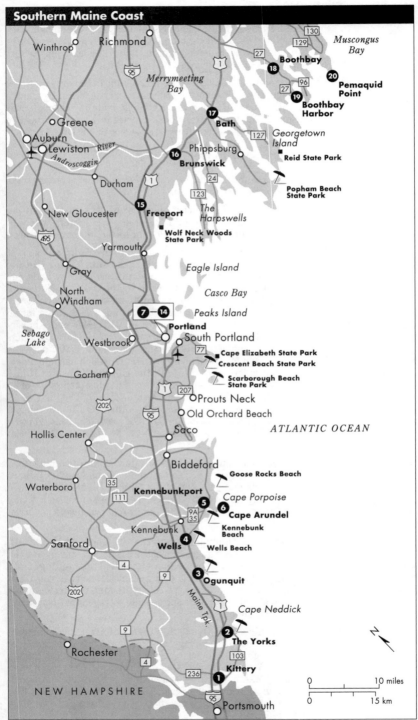

Southern Maine Coast

Winthrop
Richmond
Greene
Auburn
Lewiston
Androscoggin River
Durham
New Gloucester
Yarmouth
Gray
North Windham
Sebago Lake
Westbrook
Gorham
Hollis Center
Waterboro
Sanford
Rochester

NEW HAMPSHIRE
Portsmouth

Merrymeeting Bay
16 Brunswick
Phippsburg
15 Freeport
The Harpswells
■ Wolf Neck Woods State Park
Eagle Island
Casco Bay
Peaks Island
7–14 Portland
South Portland
■ Cape Elizabeth State Park
Crescent Beach State Park
Scarborough Beach State Park
Prouts Neck
Old Orchard Beach
Saco
Biddeford
ATLANTIC OCEAN
Goose Rocks Beach
Kennebunkport
Cape Porpoise
5
6 Cape Arundel
Kennebunk
Kennebunk Beach
4 Wells
Wells Beach
3 Ogunquit
Cape Neddick
2 The Yorks
Maine Tpk.
1 Kittery

17 Bath
Georgetown Island
■ Reid State Park
Popham Beach State Park
Muscongus Bay
Boothbay
18
20 Pemaquid Point
19 Boothbay Harbor

0   10 miles
0   15 km

Perkins Cove, a neck of land connected to the mainland by a pedestrian drawbridge, is ½ mile from the art museum. "Quaint"
is the only word for this jumble of sea-beaten fish houses transformed by the tide of tourism to shops and restaurants. When
you've had your fill of browsing and jostling the crowds at Perkins Cove, stroll out along the Marginal Way, a mile-long foot-
path that hugs the shore of a rocky promontory known as
Israel's Head.

❹ Follow Route 1 north to **Wells,** a family-oriented beach community consisting of several densely populated summer communities along 7 miles of shore. The 1,600-acre Wells Reserve at
Laudholm Farm consists of meadows, orchards, fields, salt
marshes, and an extensive trail network, as well as two river
estuaries and 9 miles of seashore. The Visitor Center features
an introductory slide show and five rooms of exhibits. *Laudholm Farm Rd., tel. 207/646–1555. Admission free. Grounds
open daily 8–5; Visitor Center open May–Oct., Mon.–Sat.
10–4, Sun. noon–4; closed weekends Nov.–Apr.*

Five miles north of Wells, Route 1 becomes Main Street in
Kennebunk. For a sense of the area's history and architecture,
begin here at the **Brick Store Museum.** The cornerstone of this
block-long preservation of early 19th-century commercial
buildings is William Lord's Brick Store, built as a dry-goods
store in 1825 in the Federal style, with an open-work balus-
trade across the roof line, granite lintels over the windows, and
paired chimneys. Walking tours of Kennebunk's National Historic Register District depart from the museum on Friday at 1
and on Wednesday at 10, June through October. *117 Main St.,
tel. 207/985–4802. Admission: $2 adults, $1 children 6–16.
Open Tues.–Sat. 10–4:30.*

❺ While heading for **Kennebunkport** on Summer Street (Route
35), keep an eye out for the **Wedding Cake House** about a mile
along on the left. The legend behind this confection in fancy
wood fretwork is that its sea-captain builder was forced to set
sail in the middle of his wedding, and the house was his bride's
consolation for the lack of a wedding cake. The home, built in
1826, is not open to the public but there is a gift shop in the attached carriage house.

Route 35 takes you right into Kennebunkport's **Dock Square,**
the busy town center, which is lined with shops and galleries
and draws crowds in the summer. Parking is tight in Kennebunkport in peak season. One possibility is the municipal lot
next to the Congregational Church ($2/hour, May–Oct.); an-
other is the Consolidated School on School Street (free, June
25–Labor Day).

When you stroll the square, walk onto the drawbridge to admire the tidal Kennebunk River. Then turn around and head up
Spring Street two blocks to Maine Street and the very grand
Nott House, known also as White Columns, an imposing Greek
Revival mansion with Doric columns that rise the height of the
house. The Nott House is the gathering place for village walking tours on Tuesday and Friday mornings in July and August.
*Maine St., tel. 207/967–2751. Admission: $2. Open mid-Apr.–
late Oct., Wed.–Fri. 1–4.*

Return to your car for a leisurely drive on Ocean Avenue, which
follows the Kennebunk River to the sea and then winds around
❻ the peninsula of **Cape Arundel.** Parson's Way, a small and tran-

quil stretch of rocky shoreline, is open to all. As you round Cape Arundel, look to the right for the entrance to George Bush's summer home at Walker's Point.

The **Seashore Trolley Museum,** on Log Cabin Road about 3 miles from Dock Square, shows transport from classic Victorian-era horsecars to vintage 1960s streetcars and includes exhibits about the Atlantic Shore Railway, which once ran a trolley from Boston to Dock Square. Best of all, you can take a trolley ride for nearly 3½ miles through woods and fields and past the museum restoration shop. *Log Cabin Rd., tel. 207/ 967–2800. Admission: $5.50 adults, $4.50 senior citizens, $3.50 children 6–16. Open June–mid-Sept., daily 10–5, reduced hours in spring and fall.*

North from Kittery for Free

Ogunquit Museum of Art, Ogunquit.
St. Anthony Monastery and Shrine (Kennebunkport, tel. 207/ 967–2011), a Tudor-style Franciscan monastery, has gardens and quiet walks along the river.
Wells Reserve at Laudholm Farm, Wells.

What to See and Do with Children

Maine Aquarium. Live sharks, seals, penguins, a petting zoo, a tidal pool, snack bar, and gift shop make a busy stop on a rainy day. *Rte. 1, Saco, tel. 207/284–4511. Admission: $6.50 adults, $5.50 senior citizens, $4.50 children 5–12, $2.50 children 2–4. Open June–mid-Sept., daily 9–9; mid-Sept.–May, daily 9–5.*
Wells Auto Museum. A must for motor fanatics as well as youngsters, the museum has 70 vintage cars, antique coin games, and a restored Model T you can ride in. *Rte. 1, tel. 207/646–9064. Admission: $3 adults, $2 children 6–12. Open mid-June–mid-Sept., daily 10–5; Memorial Day–mid-June and Oct.–Columbus Day, weekends 10–5.*

Off the Beaten Track

Old Orchard Beach, a 3-mile strip of sand beach with an amusement park reminiscent of Coney Island, is only a few miles north of Biddeford on Route 9. Despite the summertime crowds and fried-food odors, the carnival atmosphere can be infectious. **Palace Playland** (tel. 207/934–2001) on Old Orchard Street has an array of rides and booths, including a 1906 carousel and a Ferris wheel with dizzying ocean views. There is no free parking anywhere in town. *Open June–Labor Day.*

Shopping

Several factory outlet stores along Route 1 in Kittery and Wells offer clothing, shoes, glassware, and other products from top-of-the-line manufacturers. As an outgrowth of its long-established art community, Ogunquit has numerous galleries, many on Shore Road. Perkins Cove in Ogunquit and Dock Square in Kennebunkport have seasonal gift shops, boutiques, and galleries.

Antiques **J. J. Keating** (Rte. 1, tel. 207/985–2097) deals in antiques, re-
Kennebunk productions, and auctions.
Meadowside Farm Antiques (1803 Alewive Rd., tel. 207/985–

4387) sells American country furniture, accessories, and folk art, in a 1753 house.

Kennebunkport **Old Fort Inn and Antiques** (Old Fort Ave., tel. 207/967–5353) stocks a small but choice selection of primitives, china, and country furniture in a converted barn adjoining an inn.

Wells **Kenneth & Ida Manko** (Seabreeze St., tel. 207/646–2595) shows folk art, primitives, paintings, and a large selection of 19th-century weather vanes. (Turn right on Eldridge Road off Route 1, and after ½ mile turn left on Seabreeze Street.)
R. Jorgensen (Rte. 1, tel. 207/646–9444) features an eclectic selection of 18th- and 19th-century formal and country period antiques from the British Isles, Europe, and the United States.

Books **Kennebunk Book Port** (10 Dock Sq., tel. 207/967–3815), housed
Kennebunkport in a rum warehouse built in 1775, has a wide selection of titles and specializes in local and maritime subjects.

Wells **Douglas N. Harding Rare Books** (Rte. 1, tel. 207/646–8785) has a huge stock of old books, maps, and prints.

Crafts **Marlows Artisans Gallery** (109 Lafayette Center, tel. 207/985–
Kennebunk 2931) features wood, glass, weaving, and pottery crafts.

Kennebunkport **The Wedding Cake Studio** (104 Summer St., tel. 207/985–2818) offers faux finishes, trompe l'oeil, decorative painting, and hand-painted clothing.

Women's Clothing **Chadwick's** (10 Main St., tel. 207/985–7042) carries a selection
Kennebunk of women's casual clothing, beachwear, and evening gowns.

Ogunquit **The Shoe String** (Rte. 1, tel. 207/646–3533) has a range of shoes and handbags, from the sporty to the dressy.

Sports and Outdoor Activities

Biking **Cape-Able Bike Shop** (Townhouse Corners, Kennebunkport, tel. 207/967–4382) has bicycles for rent.

Bird-Watching **Biddeford Pool East Sanctuary** (Rte. 9, Biddeford) is a nature preserve where shorebirds congregate.

Rachel Carson National Wildlife Refuge (Rte. 9, Wells) is a mile-long loop through a salt marsh bordering the Little River and a white pine forest.

Boat Trips **Finestkind** (Perkins Cove, Ogunquit, tel. 207/646–5227) has cruises to Nubble Lighthouse, cocktail cruises, and lobstering trips.

Chick's Marina (Ocean Ave., Kennebunkport, tel. 207/967–2782) offers sightseeing and whale-watching cruises for up to six people.

Canoeing The **Maine Audubon Society** (tel. 207/781–2330 or 207/883–5100 June–Labor Day) offers daily guided canoe trips in **Scarborough Marsh** (Rte. 9, Scarborough), the largest salt marsh in Maine.

Deep-Sea Fishing *Cape Arundel Cruises* (Arundel Wharf, Rte. 9, Kennebunkport, tel. 207/967–5595) has full-day trips.

Elizabeth II (Arundel Boatyard, Kennebunkport, tel. 207/967–5595) carries passengers on 1½-hour narrated cruises down the Kennebunk River and out to Cape Porpoise. The *Nau-*

tilus, run by the same outfit, goes on whale-watching cruises from May through October, daily at 10 AM.

Ugly Anne (Perkins Cove, tel. 207/646–7202) offers half- and full-day trips.

Whale-Watching *Indian* (Arundel Wharf, Rte. 9, Kennebunkport, tel. 207/967–5912) offers full-day trips.

Beaches

Maine's sand beaches tend to be rather hard-packed and built up with beach cottages and motels. Yet the water is clean (and cold), the surf usually gentle, and the crowds manageable except on the hottest summer weekends.

Kennebunk Beach. Gooch's Beach, Middle Beach, and Kennebunk Beach (also called Mother's Beach) are the three areas of Kennebunk Beach. Beach Road with its cottages and old Victorian boardinghouses runs right behind them. For parking permits, go to the Kennebunk Town Office (1 Summer St., tel. 207/985–3675 or 985–2102 in summer). Gooch's and Middle beaches attract lots of teenagers; Mother's Beach, which has a small playground and tidal puddles for splashing, is popular with moms and kids.

Kennebunkport. Goose Rocks, a few minutes' drive north of town, is the largest in the Kennebunk area and the favorite of families with small children. For a parking permit, go to the Kennebunkport Town Office (Elm St., tel. 207/967–4244).

Ogunquit. The 3 miles of sand beach have snack bars, boardwalk, rest rooms, and changing areas at the Beach Street entrance. The less crowded section to the north is accessible by footbridge and has rest rooms, all-day paid parking, and trolley service. The ocean beach is backed by the Ogunquit River, which is ideal for children because it is sheltered and waveless. There is a parking fee.

York. York's Long Sands Beach has free parking and Route 1A running right behind it; the smaller Short Sands beach has meter parking. Both beaches have commercial development.

Dining and Lodging

Kennebunks **White Barn Inn.** The rustic but elegant dining room of this inn
Dining serves regional New England cuisine. The menu changes weekly and may include steamed Maine lobster nestled on fresh fettuccine with carrots and ginger in a Thai-inspired honey and sherry vinegar sauce or grilled veal chop with baby carrots, wild rice cakes, sorrel, and lemon grass scented with curry sauce; or roasted breast of free range chicken with aromatic vegetables Brunoise, fried herbs, olive oil, smashed potatoes, and a thyme-infused consommé. *Beach St., tel. 207/967–2321. Reservations advised. Jacket and tie advised. AE, D, MC, V. Expensive–Very Expensive.*
Windows on the Water. This restaurant overlooks Dock Square and the working harbor of Kennebunkport. Try the California lobster ravioli or the Brazilian-style filet mignon. The "A Night on the Town" special, a five-course dinner for two, including wine, tax, and gratuity, for $69, is a good value if you have a healthy appetite; reservations are required. *Chase Hill*

Rd., tel. 207/967–3313. Reservations advised. Dress: casual. AE, D, DC, MC, V. Expensive–Very Expensive.

★ **Cape Arundel Inn.** Were it not for the rocky shore beyond the picture windows, the pillared porch with wicker chairs, and the cozy parlor, with fireplace and backgammon boards, which you just passed through, you might well think you were dining at a major Boston restaurant. The lobster bisque is creamy, with just a bit of cognac. Entrées include marlin with sorrel butter; coho salmon with mushrooms, white wine, and lemon; rack of lamb; and pecan chicken with peaches and crème fraîche. The inn has 13 guest rooms, seven in the Victorian-era converted "cottage" and six in a motel facility adjoining. There's also a carriage-house apartment. *Ocean Ave., tel. 207/967–2125. Reservations advised. Dress: neat but casual. AE, MC, V. Closed mid-Oct.–mid-May. No lunch. Expensive.*

Olde Grist Mill. The bar and lounge area occupy a restored grist mill, with original equipment and fixtures intact; the dining room is a spare, modern space with white linen, china, and picture windows on the Kennebunk River. The Continental menu features sole in papillote with seafood stuffing; sirloin steak au poivre; and a classic shore dinner. The baked Indian pudding is a local legend. *1 Mill La., Kennebunkport, tel. 207/967–4781. Reservations accepted. Dress: neat but casual. AE, DC, MC, V. Closed Mon. mid-Apr.–July 4 and Labor Day–Oct.; closed Nov.–mid-Apr. No lunch. Expensive.*

Lodging **Old Fort Inn.** This inn at the crest of a hill on a quiet road off
★ Ocean Avenue has a secluded, countryish feel and the welcome sense of being just a touch above the Kennebunkport action. The front half of the former barn is now an antiques shop (specializing in Early American pieces); the rest of the barn is the reception area and a large parlor decorated with grandfather clocks, antique tools, and funny old canes. To get to the guest rooms, you cross a lawn, skirt the bright flower beds that set off the ample pool (a rarity at an inn), and enter the long, low fieldstone and stucco carriage house, which has been artfully converted to lodgings. Although the rooms are not large, their decor reflects the innkeepers' witty and creative way with design and antiques: There are quilts on the four-poster beds; wreaths, primitive portraits, and framed antique bodices hang on the walls; the loveseats are richly upholstered, some with blue-and-white ticking. Some rooms have hand stenciling, and several of the beds have fishnet canopies. Numbers 2 and 12 have choice corner locations. Number 1 is one of the smaller rooms. *Box M, Kennebunkport 04046, tel. 207/967–5353. 16 double rooms with bath, 2 suites. Facilities: phones, TV, and wet bars in rooms; laundry facilities; pool; tennis court; bikes for rent. AE, D, MC, V. Rates include buffet breakfast. Closed mid-Dec.–mid-Apr. Very Expensive.*

Breakwater Inn. Kennebunkport has few accommodations that are elegantly old-fashioned in decor, located right on the water, and well suited to families with young children, and this inn is all three. Overlooking Kennebunk Beach from the breakwater, rooms have stained-pine four-poster beds and hand stenciling or wallpaper. The Riverside building next door offers spacious, airy rooms with sliding glass doors facing the water. *Box 1160, Ocean Ave., Kennebunkport 04046, tel. 207/967–3118. 20 rooms with bath, 2 suites. Facilities: dining room, small playground. AE, MC, V. Closed Dec. 15–Jan. 15. Expensive–Very Expensive.*

Bufflehead Cove. Situated on the Kennebunk River at the end of a winding dirt road, the friendly gray-shingle bed-and-breakfast affords the quiet of country fields and apple trees only five minutes from Dock Square. The small guest rooms are dollhouse pretty, with white wicker and flowers painted on the walls. *Box 499, 04046, tel. 207/967-3879. 4 rooms with bath, 1 suite. Facilities: private dock. No smoking. AE, MC, V. Closed Jan.-Feb. Expensive-Very Expensive.*

Captain Jefferds Inn. The three-story white-clapboard sea captain's home with black shutters, built in 1804, has been restored and filled with the innkeeper's collections of majolica, American art pottery, Venetian glass, and Sienese pottery. Most rooms are done in Laura Ashley fabrics and wallpapers, and many have been furnished with English curly maple chests, marbletop dressers, old books, and paintings. Pets are welcome. A hearty breakfast is included. *Pearl St., Box 691, Kennebunkport 04046, tel. 207/967-2311. 12 rooms with bath; 3 suites in the carriage house. Facilities: croquet. MC, V. Closed early Dec.-Apr. Expensive-Very Expensive.*

The Captain Lord Mansion. A long and distinguished history, a three-story elliptical staircase, and a cupola with widow's walk make this something more than the standard bed-and-breakfast. The rooms, named for clipper ships, are mostly large and stately—11 have a fireplace—though the style relaxes as one ascends from the ground-floor rooms (damask and mahogany) to the country-style third-floor accommodations (pine furniture and leafy views). *Box 800, Kennebunkport 04046, tel. 207/967-3141. 16 rooms with bath. D, MC, V. Expensive-Very Expensive.*

Inn at Harbor Head. The 100-year-old shingled farmhouse on the harbor at Cape Porpoise has become a tiny bed-and-breakfast full of antiques, paintings, and heirlooms. The Harbor Room upstairs has murals; the Greenery downstairs boasts a whirlpool tub and a garden view. The Summer suite and the Garden room have the best water views. The grounds are bright with flower beds. *RR 2, Box 1180, Kennebunkport 04046, tel. 207/967-5564. 4 rooms with bath, 1 suite. Facilities: private dock. No smoking. MC, V. Expensive-Very Expensive.*

The Seaside. The modern motel units, all with sliding glass doors opening onto private decks or patios, half of them with ocean views, are appropriate for families; so are the cottages, which have from one to four bedrooms, and where well-behaved pets are accepted. The four bedrooms in the inn, furnished with antiques, are more suitable for adults. A small breakfast is included in the inn and motel-room price. *Gooch's Beach, Kennebunkport 04046, tel. 207/967-4461 or 207/967-4282. 26 rooms with bath, 10 cottages. Facilities: private beach, laundry, playground. MC, V. Inn rooms closed Labor Day-June; cottages closed Nov.-Apr. Expensive-Very Expensive.*

Kittery
Dining

Warren's Lobster House. A local institution, this waterfront restaurant offers reasonably priced boiled lobster, first-rate scrod, a raw bar, and a huge salad bar. *Rte. 1, tel. 207/439-1630. Reservations advised. Dress: casual. AE, MC, V. Moderate.*

Lodging

Deep Water Landing. This comfortable, turn-of-the-century New Englander welcomes guests to the three rooms on its third floor. Fruit trees and flower beds border the lawns, and the breakfast room offers harbor views. *92 Whipple Rd., 03904, tel.*

207/439–0824. 3 rooms with shared bath. Facilities: breakfast room. No pets. No credit cards. Inexpensive.

Ogunquit **Arrows.** Elegant simplicity is the hallmark of this 18th-century
Dining farmhouse, 2 miles up a back road. The menu changes frequent-
★ ly, offering such entrées as filet of beef glistening in red and
yellow sauces, grilled salmon and radicchio with marinated
fennel and baked polenta, and Chinese-style duck glazed with
molasses. Appetizers (Maine crabmeat mousse or lobster
risotta) and desserts (strawberry shortcake with Chantilly
cream or steamed chocolate pudding) are also beautifully exe-
cuted and presented. *Berwick Rd., tel. 207/361–1100. Reservations advised. Jacket and tie advised. Closed day after
Thanksgiving–May; spring and fall, Mon.–Wed. MC, V. Expensive–Very Expensive.*

★ **Hurricane.** Don't let its weather-beaten exterior deter you—
this small, comfortable seafood bar and grill offers first-rate
cooking and spectacular views of the crashing surf. Start with
lobster gazpacho or bouillabaisse, crab Rangoon, or the house
salad (assorted greens with pistachio nuts and roasted shallots). Entrées include charbroiled swordfish with three sauces,
veal braised with wild mushrooms, and shrimp scampi served
over fresh pasta. Be sure to save room for the classic crème
brûlée or white chocolate torte. *Perkins Cove, tel. 207/646–
6348. Dress: casual. AE, MC, V. Moderate–Expensive.*

Ogunquit Lobster Pound. Select your lobster live, then dine under the trees or in the rustic dining room of the log cabin. The
menu includes steamed clams, steak, and chicken; and there is
a special children's menu. *Rte. 1, tel. 207/646–2516. No reservations. Dress: casual. AE, MC, V. Closed late Oct.–mid-May.
Moderate.*

Lodging **Colonial Inn.** This complex of accommodations in the middle of
Ogunquit includes a large white Victorian inn building, modern motel units, and efficiency apartments. Inn rooms have
flowered wallpaper, Colonial reproduction furniture, and
white ruffle curtains. Efficiencies are popular with families.
Two-thirds of the rooms have water views. *Shore Rd., Box 895,
03907, tel. 207/646–5191. 80 units, 54 with bath; 26 suites. Facilities: restaurant, heated outdoor pool, laundromat, grills,
Jacuzzi, playground, shuffleboard. AE, D, MC, V. Closed
Nov.–Apr. Moderate–Very Expensive.*

Seafair Inn. A century-old white-clapboard house set back behind shrubs and lawn in the center of town, the Seafair has a
homey atmosphere and proximity to the beach. Rooms are furnished with odds and ends of country furniture; the Continental breakfast is served on an enclosed sun porch. *Box 1221,
03907, tel. 207/646–2181. 18 units, 14 with bath; 4 efficiency
suites. MC, V. Closed Nov.–Mar. Moderate–Expensive.*

Prouts Neck **Black Point Inn.** At the tip of the peninsula that juts into the
Lodging ocean at Prouts Neck, 12 miles south of Portland, stands one of
★ the great old-time resorts of Maine. The sun porch has wicker
and plants, the music room—in the English country-house
style—has wing chairs, silk flowers, Chinese prints, and a
grand piano. In the guest rooms are rock maple bedsteads,
Martha Washington bedspreads, and white-ruffle Priscilla curtains. Older guests prefer the main inn; families choose from
the three cottages. The extensive grounds offer beaches, hiking, a bird sanctuary, and sports. The dining room, done in pale
Renaissance-style wallpaper and water-stained pine paneling,

has a menu strong in seafood. *510 Black Point Rd., Scarborough 04074, tel. 207/883–4126 or 800/258–0003. 80 rooms with bath, 6 suites. Facilities: restaurant, bar, entertainment; 14 tennis courts, 18-hole golf course, outdoor saltwater pool and Jacuzzi, indoor freshwater pool and Jacuzzi, volleyball, putting green, bicycles, sailboats, fishing boats. MC, V. Closed Nov.–Apr. Very Expensive.*

Wells **The Gray Gull.** This rambling old beach house offers views of
Dining sea walls and rocks on which seals like to sun themselves. In the evening, choose from scallops baked with coconut milk, citrus, pineapple juices, and dark rum; chicken breast rolled in walnuts and baked with maple syrup, Yankee pot roast, and softshell crabs almandine. Breakfast is popular here in the summer: Blueberry pancakes, ham and cheese strata, or eggs McGull served on crabcakes with hollandaise sauce are good choices. *321 Webhannet Dr., at Moody Point, tel. 207/646–7501. Reservations advised. Dress: casual. AE, MC, V. Moderate–Expensive.*

Billy's Chowder House. As the crowded parking lot suggests, this simple restaurant in a salt marsh is popular with locals and tourists alike. For a generous lobster roll or haddock sandwich (not to mention chowders), Billy's is hard to beat. *Mile Rd., tel. 207/646–9064. Dress: casual. MC, V. Closed 1 month in winter. Moderate.*

The Yorks **York Harbor Inn.** The dining room of this inn has country charm
Dining and great ocean views. In the past, Frank Jones, king of New
★ England alemakers, patronized the inn; nowadays you might spot local resident and poet May Sarton enjoying a meal here. Shrimp-stuffed avocado or mussels provençale make excellent lunch choices; for dinner, start with escargot and brie in puff pastry, the special Mediterranean salad, or a creamy seafood chowder, and then try the veal and shrimp Niçoise or beef tenderloin garnished with fresh asparagus and crabmeat. Just save room for the black-bottom cheesecake or any of the other wonderful desserts. *Rte. 1A (Box 573), York Harbor 03911, tel. 207/363–5119. Reservations advised. Dress: casual. AE, DC, MC, V. Expensive.*

Cape Neddick Inn. This restaurant and art gallery has an airy ambience, with tables set well apart, lots of windows, and art everywhere. The new American menu has offered lobster macadamia tart (shelled lobster sautéed with shallots, macadamia nuts, sherry, and cream and served in pastry); breaded pork tenderloin; and such appetizers as spicy sesame chicken dumplings and gravlax with Russian pepper vodka. Duckling flamed in brandy is always on the menu. *Rte. 1, Cape Neddick, tel. 207/ 363–2899. Reservations advised. Dress: casual. AE, MC, V. Closed Mon.–Tues. Columbus Day–May 31. No lunch. Moderate–Expensive.*

Dockside Dining Room. The seclusion, the gardens, and the water views are the attractions of the inn dining room on a private island in York Harbor. Entrées may include scallop-stuffed shrimp Casino; broiled salmon; steak au poivre with brandied mushroom sauce; and roast stuffed duckling. There's also a children's menu. *York Harbor off Rte. 103, tel. 207/363–2722. Reservations advised on weekends. Dress: neat but casual. MC, V. Closed Mon. Closed late Oct.–Memorial Day. Moderate.*

Lodging **Dockside Guest Quarters.** Situated on a private island 8 acres large in the middle of York Harbor, the Dockside promises water views, seclusion, and quiet. Rooms in the Maine house, the oldest structure on the site, are furnished with Early American antiques, marine artifacts, and nautical paintings and prints. Four modern cottages tucked among the trees have less character but bigger windows on the water, and many have kitchenettes. *Box 205, York 03909, tel. 207/363–2868. 22 rooms, 20 with bath; 5 suites. Facilities: private dock, dining rooms, small motorboat, croquet, badminton. MC, V. (limit $100). Closed late Oct.–Apr. Moderate–Very Expensive.*

The Arts

Music **Hamilton House** (Vaughan's La., South Berwick, tel. 207/384–5269), the Georgian home featured in Sarah Orne Jewett's *The Tory Lover*, presents "Sundays in the Garden," a series of free summer concerts. Concerts begin at 3; the grounds are open noon until 5 for picnicking.

Theater **Ogunquit Playhouse** (Rte. 1, tel. 207/646–5511), one of America's oldest summer theaters, mounts plays and musicals from late June to Labor Day.

The Coast: Portland to Pemaquid Point

Maine's largest city, yet small enough to be seen with ease in a day or two, Portland is undergoing a cultural and economic renaissance. New hotels and a bright new performing arts center have joined the neighborhoods of historic homes; the Old Port Exchange, perhaps the finest urban renovation project on the East Coast, balances modern commercial enterprise with a salty waterfront character in an area bustling with restaurants, shops, and galleries. The piers of Commercial Street abound with opportunities for water tours of the harbor and excursions to the Calendar Islands.

Freeport, north of Portland, is a town made famous by the L. L. Bean store, whose success led to the opening of scores of other clothing stores and outlets. Brunswick is best known for Bowdoin College; Bath has been a shipbuilding center since 1607, and the Maine Maritime Museum preserves its history.

The Boothbays—the coastal areas of Boothbay Harbor, East Boothbay, Linekin Neck, Southport Island, and the inland town of Boothbay—attract hordes of vacationing families and flotillas of pleasure craft. The Pemaquid peninsula juts into the Atlantic south of Damariscotta and just east of the Boothbays, and near Pemaquid Beach one can view the objects unearthed at the Colonial Pemaquid Restoration.

Important Addresses and Numbers

Visitor Information **Convention and Visitors Bureau of Greater Portland** (305 Commercial St., tel. 207/772–5800).

Boothbay Harbor Region Chamber of Commerce (Box 356, Boothbay Harbor, tel. 207/633–2353).

Brunswick Area Chamber of Commerce (59 Pleasant St., Brunswick, tel. 207/725–8797).

Bath Area Chamber of Commerce (45 Front St., Bath, tel. 207/443–9751).

Freeport Merchants Association (Box 452, Freeport, tel. 207/865–1212).

Greater Portland Chamber of Commerce (145 Middle St., Portland, tel. 207/772–2811).

Getting Around Portland to Pemaquid Point

By Car The Congress Street exit from I–295 will take you into the heart of Portland. Numerous city parking lots have hourly rates of 50¢ to 85¢; the Gateway Garage on High Street, off Congress, is a convenient place to leave your car while exploring downtown. North of Portland, I–95 takes you to Exit 20 and Route 1, Freeport's Main Street, which continues on to Brunswick and Bath. East of Wiscasset you can take Route 27 south to the Boothbays, where Route 96 is a good choice for further exploration.

By Bus Portland's **Metro** (tel. 207/774–0351) runs seven bus routes in Portland, South Portland, and Westbrook. The fare is $1 for adults and 50¢ for senior citizens, people with disabilities, and children; exact change is required. Buses operate from 5:30 AM to 11:45 PM.

Exploring Portland

Numbers in the margin correspond to points of interest on the Southern Maine Coast and Portland maps.

❼ Congress Street, **Portland**'s main street, runs the length of the peninsular city from the Western Promenade in the southwest to the Eastern Promenade in the northeast, passing through the small downtown area. A few blocks southeast of downtown, the bustling Old Port Exchange sprawls along the waterfront.

❽ One of the notable homes on Congress Street is the **Neal Dow Memorial,** a brick mansion built in 1829 in the late Federal style by General Neal Dow, a zealous abolitionist and prohibitionist. The library has fine ornamental ironwork, and the furnishings include the family china, silver, and portraits. Don't miss the grandfather clocks and the original deed granted by James II. *714 Congress St., tel. 207/773–7773. Admission free. Open for tours weekdays 11–4. Closed holidays.*

❾ Just off Congress Street, the distinguished **Portland Museum of Art** has a strong collection of seascapes and landscapes by such masters as Winslow Homer, John Marin, Andrew Wyeth, and Marsden Hartley. Homer's *Pulling the Dory* and *Weatherbeaten,* two quintessential Maine coast images, are here. The Joan Whitney Payson Collection includes works by Monet, Picasso, and Renoir. The strikingly modern Charles Shipman Payson wing was designed by Harry N. Cobb, an associate of I. M. Pei, in 1983. *7 Congress Sq., tel. 207/775–6148 or 773–2787 for recorded information. Admission: $5 adults, $4 senior citizens and students, $2.50 children 6–18, free Sat. 10–noon. Open Tues.–Sat. 10–5, Thurs. 10–9, Sun. noon–5.*

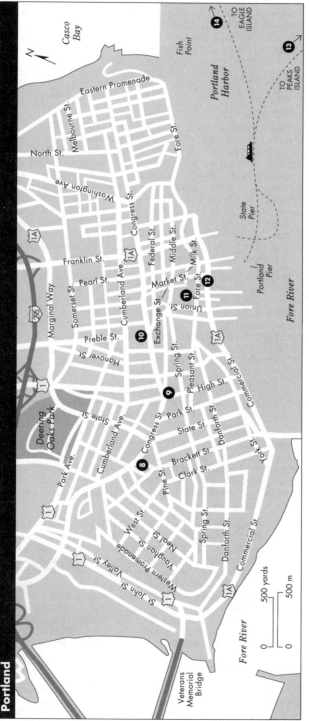

Eagle Island, **14**
Mariner's Church, **12**
Neal Dow Memorial, **8**
Old Port Exchange, **11**

Peaks Island, **13**
Portland Museum of
Art, **9**
Wadsworth Longfellow
House, **10**

⑩ Walk east on Congress Street to the **Wadsworth Longfellow House** of 1785, the boyhood home of the poet and the first brick house in Portland. The late Colonial-style structure sits well back from the street and has a small portico over its entrance and four chimneys surmounting the hip roof. Most of the furnishings are original to the house. *485 Congress St., tel. 207/ 772–1807 or 207/774–1822. Admission: $3 adults, $1 children. Open June–Columbus Day weekend, Tues.–Sat. 10–4. Closed July 4. Garden open daily 9–5.*

⑪ Although you can walk from downtown to the **Old Port Exchange,** you're better off driving and parking your car either at the city garage on Fore Street (between Exchange and Union streets) or opposite the U.S. Customs House at the corner of Fore and Pearl streets. Like the Customs House, the brick buildings and warehouses of the Old Port Exchange were built following the Great Fire of 1866 and were intended to last for ages. When the city's economy slumped in the middle of the present century, however, the Old Port declined and seemed slated for demolition. Then artists and craftspeople began opening shops here in the late 1960s, and in time restaurants, chic boutiques, bookstores, and gift shops followed.

The Old Port is best explored on foot. Allow a couple of hours to wander at leisure on Market, Exchange, Middle, and Fore

⑫ streets. The **Mariner's Church** (376 Fore St.) has a fine facade of granite columns, and the Elias Thomas Block on Commercial Street demonstrates the graceful use of bricks in commercial architecture. Inevitably the salty smell of the sea will draw you to one of the wharves off Commercial Street; Custom House Wharf retains some of the older, rougher waterfront atmosphere.

Island Excursions The brightly painted ferries of **Casco Bay Lines** (tel. 207/774–7871) are the lifeline to the Calendar Islands of Casco Bay, which number about 136, depending on the tides and how one defines an island.

⑬ **Peaks Island,** nearest Portland, is the most developed, and some residents commute to work in Portland. Yet you can still commune with the wind and the sea on Peaks, explore an old fort, and ramble along the alternately rocky and sandy shore. One bed-and-breakfast has overnight accommodations (*see* Peaks Island Lodging, *below*).

⑭ The 17-acre **Eagle Island,** owned by the State of Maine and open to the public for day trips in summer, was the home of Admiral Robert E. Peary, the American explorer of the North Pole. Peary built a stone and wood house on the island as a summer retreat in 1904, then made it his permanent residence. The house remains as it was when Peary was here with his stuffed Arctic birds and the quartz he brought home set into the fieldstone fireplace. The *Kristy K.*, departing from Long Wharf, makes a four-hour narrated tour. *Long Wharf, tel. 207/774–6498. Excursion tour: $15 adults, $12 senior citizens, $9 children 5–9. Departures mid-June–Labor Day, daily 10.*

Exploring North of Portland

⑮ **Freeport,** on Route 1, 15 miles northeast of Portland, has charming back streets lined with old clapboard houses and even a small harbor on the Harraseeket River, but the overwhelming majority of visitors come to shop, and L. L. Bean is the store that put Freeport on the map. Founded in 1912 as a small mail-order merchandiser of products for hunters, guides, and fisherfolk, L. L. Bean now attracts some 3.5 million shoppers a year to its giant store in the heart of Freeport's shopping district on Route 1. Here you can still find the original hunting boots, along with cotton, wool, and silk sweaters; camping and ski equipment; comforters; and hundreds of other items for the home, car, boat, or campsite. Across the street from the main store, a Bean factory outlet has seconds and discontinued merchandise at marked-down prices. *Rte. 1, Freeport, tel. 800/341–4341. Open 24 hrs.*

All around L. L. Bean, like seedlings under a mighty spruce, some 70 outlets have sprouted, offering designer clothes, shoes, housewares, and toys at marked-down prices (*see* Shopping, *below*).

16 It's 9 miles northeast on Route 1 from Freeport to **Brunswick.** Follow the signs to the Brunswick business district, Pleasant Street, and—at the end of Pleasant Street—Maine Street, which claims to be the widest (198 feet across) in the state. Friday from May through October sees a fine farmer's market on the town mall, between Maine Street and Park Row.

Maine Street takes you to the 110-acre campus of **Bowdoin College,** an enclave of distinguished architecture, gardens, and grassy quadrangles in the middle of the city. Campus tours (tel. 207/725–3000) depart weekdays from Moulton Union. Among the historic buildings are Massachusetts Hall, a stout, sober, hip-roofed brick structure that dates from 1802, and Hubbard Hall, an imposing 1902 neo-Gothic building that houses **The Peary-MacMillan Arctic Museum.** The museum contains photographs, navigational instruments, and artifacts from the first successful expedition to the North Pole, in 1909, by two of Bowdoin's most famous alumni, Admiral Robert E. Peary and Donald B. MacMillan. *Tel. 207/725–3416. Admission free. Open Tues.–Sat. 10–5, Sun. 2–5. Closed holidays.*

Don't miss the **Bowdoin College Museum of Art,** a splendid limestone, brick, and granite structure in a Renaissance Revival style, with three galleries upstairs, and five more downstairs, radiating from a rotunda. Designed in 1894 by Charles F. McKim, the building stands on a rise, its facade adorned with classical statues and the entrance set off by a triumphal arch. The collections encompass Assyrian and Classical art and that of the Dutch and Italian old masters, including Pieter Brueghel's *Alpine Landscape*; a superb gathering of Colonial and Federal paintings, notably the Gilbert Stuart portraits of Madison and Jefferson; and paintings and drawings by Winslow Homer, Mary Cassatt, John Sloan, Rockwell Kent, Jim Dine, and Robert Rauschenberg. *Walker Art Bldg., tel. 207/725–3275. Admission free. Open Tues.–Sat. 10–5, Sun. 2–5. Closed holidays.*

Before going on to Bath, you may elect to drive down Route 123 or Route 24 to the peninsulas and islands known collectively as the **Harpswells.** The numerous small coves along Harpswell Neck shelter the boats of local lobstermen, and summer cottages are tucked away amid the birch and spruce trees.

17 **Bath,** 7 miles east of Brunswick on Route 1, has been a shipbuilding center since 1607. Today the Bath Iron Works turns out guided-missile frigates for the U.S. Navy and merchant container ships.

The **Maine Maritime Museum** in Bath (take the Bath Business District exit from Route 1, turn right on Washington Street, and follow the signs) has ship models, journals, photographs, and other artifacts to stir the nautical dreams of old salts and young. The 142-foot Grand Banks fishing schooner *Sherman Zwicker*, one of the last of its kind, is on display when in port. You can watch apprentice boatbuilders wield their tools on classic Maine boats at the restored Percy & Small Shipyard and Apprentice Shop. The outdoor shipyard is closed in winter, but the indoor exhibits, videos, and activities are enhanced. *243 Washington St., tel. 207/443-1316. Admission: $6 adults, $5.40 senior citizens, $2.50 children 6-15. Open daily 9:30-5. Closed Thanksgiving, Dec. 25, Jan. 1.*

From Bath it's 10 miles northeast on Route 1 to Wiscasset, where the huge rotting hulls of the schooners *Hester* and *Luther Little* rest, testaments to the town's once-busy harbor. Those who appreciate both music and antiques will enjoy a visit to the **Musical Wonder House** to see and hear the vast collection of antique music boxes from around the world. *18 High St., tel. 207/882-7163. Admission free. 1-hr tour of main floor: $8 adults ($15 for 2), $6 children under 12 and senior citizens; 3-hr tour of entire house: $25 ($40 for 2). Open May 15-Oct. 15, daily 10-6. 1-hr tours given Sept.-Oct. 15 at 11, 1, and 3; May 15-Aug., whenever enough people; 3-hr tours by appointment. Closed Oct. 16-May 14.*

Across the river, drive south on Route 27 to reach the **Boothbay** ⑱ **Railway Village,** about a mile north of **Boothbay,** where you can ride 1½ miles on a narrow-gauge steam train through a re-creation of a turn-of-the-century New England village. Among the 24 village buildings is a museum with more than 50 antique automobiles and trucks. *Rte. 27, Boothbay, tel. 207/633-4727. Admission: $5 adults, $2.50 children 2-12. Open mid-June–mid-Oct., daily 9:30-5.*

Continue south on Route 27 into Boothbay Harbor, bear right on Oak Street, and follow it to the waterfront parking lots. ⑲ **Boothbay Harbor** is a town to wander through: Commercial Street, Wharf Street, the By-Way, and Townsend Avenue are lined with shops, galleries, and ice-cream parlors. Excursion boats (*see* Sports and Outdoor Activities, *below*) leave from the piers off Commercial Street.

Time Out The **P&P Pastry Shoppe** (6 McKown St.) is a welcome stop for a sandwich or a pastry.

Having explored Boothbay Harbor, return to Route 27 and head north again to Route 1. Proceed north to Business Route 1, and follow it through Damariscotta, an appealing shipbuilding town on the Damariscotta River. Bear right on the Bristol Road (Route 129/130), and when the highway splits, stay on ⑳ Route 130, which leads to Bristol and terminates at **Pemaquid Point.**

About 5 miles south of Bristol you'll come to New Harbor, where a right turn will take you to Pemaquid Beach and the **Colonial Pemaquid Restoration.** Here, on a small peninsula jutting into the Pemaquid River, English mariners established a fishing and trading settlement in the early 17th century. The excavations at Pemaquid Beach, begun in the mid-1960s, have turned up thousands of artifacts from the Colonial settlement, including the remains of an old customs house, tavern, jail, forge, and homes, and from even earlier Native American settlements. The State of Maine operates a museum displaying many of the artifacts. *Rte. 130, Pemaquid Point, tel. 207/677–2423. Admission: $1.50 adults, 50¢ children 6–12. Open Memorial Day–Labor Day, daily 9:30–5.*

Route 130 terminates at the **Pemaquid Point Light,** which looks as though it sprouted from the ragged, tilted chunk of granite that it commands. The former lighthouse keeper's cottage is now the **Fishermen's Museum,** with photographs, models, and artifacts that explore commercial fishing in Maine. Here, too, is the Pemaquid Art Gallery, which mounts changing exhibitions from July 1 through Labor Day. *Rte. 130, tel. 207/677–2494. Museum admission by contribution. Open Memorial Day–Columbus Day, Mon.–Sat. 10–5, Sun. 11–5.*

Portland to Pemaquid Point for Free

Bowdoin College Museum of Art, Brunswick
Neal Dow Memorial, Portland
The Peary-MacMillan Arctic Museum, Brunswick

What to See and Do with Children

Boothbay Railway Village, Boothbay
Children's Museum of Maine. Touching is okay at this museum where little ones can pretend they are lobstermen, shopkeepers, or computer experts. *142 Free St., Portland, tel. 207/797–5483. Admission: $2.50 adults, $2 senior citizens and children over 1, ½ price Wed. Open daily 9:30–4:30.*

Off the Beaten Track

Stroudwater Village, 3 miles west of Portland, was spared the devastation of the fire of 1866 and thus contains some of the best examples of 18th- and early 19th-century architecture in the region. Here are the remains of mills, canals, and historic homes, including the Tate House, built in 1755 with paneling from England. It overlooks the old mastyard where George Tate, Mast Agent to the King, prepared tall pines for the ships of the Royal Navy. The furnishings date to the late 18th century. *Tate House, 1270 Westbrook St., tel. 207/774–9781. Admission: $3 adults, $1 children. Open July–Sept. 15, Tues.–Sat. 10–4, Sun. 1–4.*

Shopping

The best shopping in Portland is at the Old Port Exchange, where many shops are concentrated along Fore and Exchange streets. Freeport's name is almost synonymous with shopping, and shopping in Freeport means **L. L. Bean** and the 70 factory outlets that opened during the 1980s. Outlet stores are located in the Fashion Outlet Mall (2 Depot St.) and the Freeport Crossing (200 Lower Main St.), and many others crowd Main Street and Bow Street. The *Freeport Visitors Guide* (Freeport Merchants Association, Box 452, Freeport 04032, tel. 207/865–

1212) has a complete listing. Boothbay Harbor, and Commercial Street in particular, is chockablock with gift shops, T-shirt shops, and other seasonal emporia catering to visitors.

Antiques
Portland

F. O. Bailey Antiquarians (141 Middle St., tel. 207/774–1479), Portland's largest retail showroom, features antique and reproduction furniture; jewelry, paintings, rugs, and china.
Mary Alice Reilley Antiques (83 India St., tel. 207/773–8815) carries china, glass, tins, primitives, and a large selection of English and Irish country pine furniture.

Boothbay Harbor

Maine Trading Post (Commercial St., tel. 800/788–2760) sells antiques and quilts, as well as period restorations and reproductions that include rolltop desks able to accommodate personal computers.

Freeport

Harrington House Gallery Store (45 Main St., tel. 207/865–0477) is a restored 19th-century merchant's home owned by the Freeport Historical Society; all the period reproductions that furnish the rooms are for sale. In addition, you can buy wallpaper, crafts, Shaker items, toys, and kitchen utensils.

Books and Maps
Portland

Carlson and Turner (241 Congress St., tel. 207/773–4200) is an antiquarian book dealer with an estimated 40,000 titles.
Raffles Cafe Bookstore (555 Congress St., tel. 207/761–3930) presents an impressive selection of fiction and nonfiction. Coffee and a light lunch are served, and there are frequent readings and literary gatherings.

Freeport

DeLorme's Map Store (Rte. 1, tel. 207/865–4171) carries an exceptional selection of maps and atlases of Maine and New England, nautical charts, and travel books.

Clothing
Portland

A. H. Benoit (188 Middle St., tel. 207/773–6421) sells quality men's clothing from sportswear to evening attire.
Joseph's (410 Fore St., tel. 207/773–1274) has elegant tailored designer clothing for men and women.

Boothbay Harbor

House of Logan (Townsend Ave., tel. 207/633–2293) has specialty clothing for men and women, plus children's togs next door at the Village Store.

Crafts
Edgecomb

Edgecomb Potters (Rte. 27, tel. 207/882–6802) sells glazed porcelain pottery and other crafts.
Sheepscot River Pottery (Rte. 2, tel. 207/882–9410) has original hand-painted pottery as well as a large collection of American-made crafts including jewelry, kitchenware, furniture, and home accessories.

Galleries
Portland

Abacus (44 Exchange St., tel. 207/772–4880) has unusual gift items in glass, wood, and textiles, plus fine modern jewelry.
The Pine Tree Shop & Bayview Gallery (75 Market St., tel. 207/773–3007 or 800/244–3007) has original art and prints by prominent Maine painters.
Stein Glass Gallery (20 Milk St., tel. 207/772–9072) specializes in contemporary glass, both decorative and utilitarian.

Sports and Outdoor Activities

Boat Trips
Portland

For tours of the harbor, Casco Bay, and the nearby islands, try **Bay View Cruises** (Fisherman's Wharf, tel. 207/761–0496), **The Buccaneer** (Long Wharf, tel. 207/799–8188), **Casco Bay Lines** (Maine State Pier, tel. 207/774–7871), **Eagle Tours** (Long

Wharf, tel. 207/774–6498), or **Old Port Mariner Fleet** (Long Wharf, tel. 207/775–0727).

Boothbay Harbor   ***Appledore*** (tel. 207/633–6598), a 66-foot windjammer, departs from Pier 6 at 9, noon, 3, and 6 for voyages to the outer islands.

Argo Cruises (tel. 207/633–2500) runs the *Islander* for morning cruises, Bath Hellgate cruises, supper sails, and whale watching; the ***Islander II*** for 1½-hour trips to Seal Rocks; the *Miss Boothbay*, a licensed lobster boat, for lobster-trap hauling trips. Biweekly evening cruises feature R&B or reggae. Departures are from Pier 6.

Balmy Days II (tel. 207/633–2284) leaves from Pier 8 for its day trips to Monhegan Island; the ***Maranbo II,*** operated by the same company, tours the harbor and nearby lighthouses.

Bay Lady (tel. 207/633–6990), a 31-foot Friendship sloop, offers sailing trips of under two hours from Fisherman's Wharf.

Cap'n Fish's Boat Trips (tel. 207/633–3244) offers sightseeing cruises throughout the region, including puffin cruises, trips to Damariscove Harbor, Pemaquid Point, and up the Kennebec River to Bath, departing from Pier 1.

Eastward (tel. 207/633–4780) is a Friendship sloop with six-passenger capacity that departs from Ocean Point Road in East Boothbay for one-day or half-day sailing trips. Itineraries vary with passengers' desires and the weather.

Deep-Sea Fishing   Half-day and full-day fishing charter boats operating out of Portland include ***Anjin-San*** (tel. 207/772–7168) and ***Devils Den*** (DeMillo's Marina, tel. 207/761–4466).

Operating out of Boothbay Harbor, **Cap'n Fish's Deep Sea Fishing** (tel. 207/633–3244) schedules daylong and half-day trips, departing from Pier 1, and **Lucky Star Charters** (tel. 207/633–4624) runs full-day and half-day charters for up to six people, with departures from Pier 8.

Nature Walks   **Wolfe's Neck Woods State Park** has self-guided trails along Casco Bay, the Harraseeket River, and a fringe salt marsh, as well as walks led by naturalists. Picnic tables and grills are available, but there's no camping. Follow Bow Street opposite L. L. Bean off Route 1. *Wolfe's Neck Rd., tel. 207/865–4465. Open Memorial Day–Labor Day.*

Beaches

Crescent Beach State Park (Rte. 77, Cape Elizabeth, tel. 207/767–3625), about 8 miles from Portland, has a sand beach, picnic tables, seasonal snack bar, and bathhouse.

Scarborough Beach State Park (Rte. 207, off Rte. 1 in Scarborough, tel. 207/883–2416) has a long stretch of sand beach with good surf. Parking is limited.

Popham Beach State Park, at the end of Route 209, south of Bath, has a good sand beach, a marsh area, and picnic tables. *Phippsburg, tel. 207/389–1335. Admission: $1.50 adults, 50¢ children, late Apr.–mid-Oct.*

Reid State Park, on Georgetown Island, off Route 127, has 1½ miles of sand on three beaches. Facilities include bathhouses, picnic tables, fireplaces, and snack bar. Parking lots fill by 11 AM on summer Sundays and holidays. *Georgetown, tel. 207/371–2303. Admission: $2 adults, 50¢ children, late Apr.–mid-Oct.*

Dining and Lodging

Many of Portland's best restaurants are in the Old Port Exchange district. Casual dress is the rule in restaurants throughout the area except where noted.

Bath **Kristina's Restaurant & Bakery.** This frame house turned res-
Dining taurant, with a front deck built around a huge oak tree, turns out some of the finest pies, pastries, and cakes on the coast. A satisfying dinner menu features new American cuisine, including fresh seafood and grilled meats. Pastries can be packed to go. *160 Centre St., tel. 207/442–8577. Reservations accepted. D, MC, V. Closed Mon. No dinner Sun. Inexpensive–Moderate.*

Lodging **Fairhaven Inn.** This cedar-shingle house built in 1790 is set on 27 acres of pine woods and meadows sloping down to the Kennebec River. Guest rooms are furnished with handmade quilts and mahogany pineapple four-poster beds. The home-cooked breakfast offers such treats as peach soup, blintzes, and apple upside-down French toast. *RR 2, Box 85, N. Bath, 04530, tel. 207/443–4391. 7 rooms, 5 with bath. Facilities: hiking and cross-country ski trails. Children welcome by prior arrangement. AE, MC, V. Rates include breakfast. Moderate.*

Boothbay **Kenniston Hill Inn.** The white-clapboard house with columned
Lodging porch offers comfortably old-fashioned accommodations in a country setting only minutes from Boothbay Harbor. Four guest rooms have fireplaces, some have four-poster beds, rocking chairs, and gilt mirrors. Full breakfasts are served family-style at a large wood table. *Box 125, 04537, tel. 207/633–2159. 10 rooms with bath. No pets. No smoking. MC, V. Expensive.*

Boothbay Harbor **Black Orchid.** The classic Italian fare includes fettuccine Al-
Dining fredo with fresh lobster and mushrooms, and *petit filet à la diabolo* (fillets of Angus steak with Marsala sauce). The upstairs and downstairs dining rooms sport a Roman-trattoria ambience, with frilly leaves and fruit hanging from the rafters and little else in the way of decor. In the summer there is a raw bar outdoors. *5 By-Way, tel. 207/633–6659. AE, MC, V. Closed Nov.–Apr. No lunch. Moderate–Expensive.*
Andrew's Harborside. The seafood menu is typical of the area—lobster, fried clams and oysters, haddock with seafood stuffing—but the harbor view makes it memorable. Lunch features lobster and crab rolls; children's and seniors' menus are available. You can dine outdoors on a harborside deck during the summer. *8 Bridge St., tel. 207/633–4074. Dinner reservations accepted for 5 or more. MC, V. Closed mid-Oct.–mid-May. Moderate.*

Lodging **Fisherman's Wharf Inn.** All rooms overlook the water at this modern motel-style facility built 200 feet out over the harbor. The large dining room has floor-to-ceiling windows, and several day-trip cruises leave from this location. *40 Commercial St., 04538, tel. 207/633–5090 or 800/628–6872. 54 rooms with bath. Facilities: restaurant. AE, D, DC, MC, V. Closed Nov.–mid-May. Moderate–Very Expensive.*
The Pines. Families seeking a secluded setting with lots of room for little ones to run will be interested in this motel on a

hillside a mile from town. Rooms have sliding glass doors opening onto private decks, two double beds, and small refrigerators. Cribs are free. *Sunset Rd., Box 693, 04538, tel. 207/633–4555. 29 rooms with bath. Facilities: all-weather tennis court, heated outdoor pool, playground. MC, V. Closed mid-Oct.–early May. Moderate.*

Brunswick **The Great Impasta.** This small, storefront restaurant is a great
Dining spot for lunch, tea, or dinner. Try the seafood lasagna, or match your favorite pasta and sauce to create your own dish. *42 Maine St., tel. 207/729–5858. No reservations. AE, D, DC, MC, V. Closed Sun. Inexpensive–Moderate.*

Lodging **Captain Daniel Stone Inn.** One of only two Someplace Different select hostelries in the United States, this Federal-style inn overlooks the Androscoggin River. While no two rooms are furnished identically, all offer executive-style comforts and many have whirlpool baths and pullout sofas in addition to queen-size beds. A guest parlor, 24-hour breakfast room, and excellent service in the Narcissa Stone Restaurant make this an upscale escape from college-town funk. *10 Water St., 04011, tel. 207/725–9898. Facilities: air-conditioning, cable TV, complimentary Continental breakfast, movies. No pets. No smoking. AE, DC, MC, V. Expensive.*

Freeport **Harraseeket Inn.** The formal, no-smoking dining room upstairs
Dining is a simply appointed, light and airy space with picture windows facing the inn's garden courtyard. The New England/Continental cuisine emphasizes fresh, local ingredients. Downstairs, the Broad Arrow Tavern appears to have been furnished by L. L. Bean, with fly rods, snowshoes, moose heads, and other hunting-lodge trappings. The fare is hearty, with less formal lunches and snacks and dinners of charbroiled skewered shrimp and scallops, ribs, burgers, pasta, or lobster. *162 Main St., tel. 207/865–9377 or 800/342–6423. Reservations advised. Collared shirt at dinner. AE, D, DC, MC, V. Expensive–Very Expensive.*

Harraseeket Lunch & Lobster Co. This no-frills, bare-bones, genuine lobster pound and fried seafood place is located beside the town landing in South Freeport. Seafood baskets and lobster dinners are what it's all about; there are picnic tables outside and a dining room inside. *Main St., South Freeport, tel. 207/865–4888. No reservations. No credit cards. Inexpensive.*

Lodging **Harraseeket Inn.** When two white-clapboard houses, one a fine Greek Revival home of 1850, found themselves two blocks from the biggest retailing explosion ever to hit Maine, the innkeepers added a four-story building that looks like an old New England inn—white clapboard with green shutters—and is in fact a steel and concrete structure with elevators and Jacuzzis. The Harraseeket strives to achieve the country inn experience, with afternoon tea in the mahogany drawing room and fireplaces throughout. Guest rooms (vintage 1989) have reproductions of Federal-period canopy beds and bright, coordinated fabrics. The full breakfast is served buffet-style in an airy upstairs formal dining room facing the garden. *162 Main St., 04032, tel. 207/865–9377 or 800/342–6423. 54 rooms with bath, including 6 suites. Facilities: restaurant, tavern, room service until 11 PM, croquet, some rooms have a working fireplace. AE, D, DC, MC, V. Very Expensive.*

Georgetown **The Osprey.** Located in a marina on the way to Reid State Park,
Dining this gourmet restaurant may be reached both by land and sea.
The appetizers alone are worth the stop: homemade garlic and
Sicilian sausages; artichoke strudel with three cheeses; and
warm braised duck salad with Oriental vegetables in rice paper. Entrées might include such classics as saltimbocca or such
originals as salmon en papillote with julienne leeks, carrots,
and fresh herbs. The wine list is excellent. The glassed-in porch
offers water views and breezes. *6 mi down Rte. 127, turn left at
restaurant sign on Robinhood Rd., tel. 207/371–2530. Reservations advised. MC, V. Open daily June–Labor Day; call for
schedule rest of year. Moderate–Expensive.*

Newcastle **Newcastle Inn.** The white-clapboard house, vintage mid-19th
Lodging century, has a homey living room with a red velvet sofa, books,
★ family photos on the mantel, and a sun porch with white wicker
furniture and ice-cream parlor chairs. Guest rooms are not
large, but they have been carefully appointed with old spool
beds, toys, and Victorian velvet sofas, minimizing clutter and
maximizing the light and the river views. Guests choose between bed-and-breakfast (a full gourmet meal, perhaps scrambled eggs with caviar in puff pastry, ricotta cheese pie, or
frittata) and Modified American Plan. *River Rd., 04553, tel.
207/563–5685 or 800/83–BUNNY. 15 rooms with bath. Facilities: dining room. No smoking. MC, V. Expensive.*

Peaks Island **Keller's B&B.** This turn-of-the-century home offers rustic ac-
Lodging commodations with deck views of Casco Bay and the Portland
skyline. The beach is only steps away from your room. *20 Island Ave., tel. 207/766–2441. 4 rooms with bath. MC, V. Moderate.*

Pemaquid Point **The Bradley Inn.** Within walking distance of the Pemaquid
Dining and Lodging Point lighthouse, beach, and fort, the 1900 Bradley Inn began
as a rooming house for summer rusticators and alternated be-
tween abandonment and operation as a B&B until its complete
renovation in the early 1990s. Rooms are comfortable and un-
cluttered; ask for one of the cathedral-ceilinged, waterside
rooms on the third floor, which offer breathtaking views of the
sun setting over the water. The Ship's Restaurant offers such
entrées as Moroccan chicken, filet mignon, and seafood alfredo;
there's light entertainment in the pub on weekends. *Rte. 130,
HC 61, 361 Pemaquid Point, New Harbor 04454, tel. 207/677–
2105. 12 rooms with bath, 1 cottage. Facilities: restaurant, pub,
cable TV and phones in rooms, croquet, bicycles, light entertainment on weekends. Continental breakfast included in rate.
AE, MC, V. Expensive–Very Expensive.*

Portland **The Back Bay Grill.** Mellow jazz, a mural of Portland, an im-
Dining pressive wine list, and wonderful, carefully prepared food
★ make this simple, elegant restaurant a popular spot. Appetizers such as pizza with capicola, three cheeses, peppers, and
shallots, and mixed greens with caramelized pecans in a gor-
gonzola-balsamic vinaigrette are followed by grilled chicken,
halibut, oysters, salmon, trout, pork chops, or steak. *65 Portland St., tel. 207/772–8833. Reservations advised. Jacket
advised. Closed Sun. AE, D, MC, V. Expensive–Very
Expensive.*
Alberta's. Small, bright, casual, and friendly, Alberta's specializes in what one waiter described as "electric American" cuisine: dishes like London broil spiced with garlic, cumin, and
lime; pan-blackened rib-eye steak with sour cream and scal-

lions; and Atlantic salmon fillet with orange-ginger sauce, grilled red cabbage, and apple salad. The two-tier dining room has photos mounted on salmon-hued walls, and the music ranges from country to classical. *21 Pleasant St., tel. 207/774-0016. No reservations. AE, DC, MC, V. Beer and wine only. Closed Thanksgiving, Dec. 25. No lunch weekends. Moderate-Expensive.*

★ **Cafe Always.** White linen tablecloths, candles, and Victorian-style murals by local artists set the mood for innovative cuisine. Begin with Pemaquid Point oysters seasoned with pink peppercorns and champagne, or chicken and wild rice in a nori roll, before choosing from vegetarian dishes, pasta, or more substantial entrées, such as grilled tuna with a fiery Japanese sauce or leg of lamb with goat cheese and sweet peppers. *47 Middle St., tel. 207/774-9399. Reservations advised. Dress: neat but casual. AE, MC, V. Closed Mon. Moderate-Expensive.*

Seamen's Club. Built just after Portland's Great Fire of 1866, and an actual sailors' club in the 1940s, this restaurant has become an Old Port Exchange landmark, with its Gothic windows and carved medallions. Seafood is an understandable favorite—moist, blackened tuna, salmon and swordfish prepared differently each day, and lobster fettuccini are among the highlights. *375 Fore St., tel. 207/772-7311. Reservations advised. Dress: neat but casual. AE, DC, MC, V. Moderate-Expensive.*

Katahdin. Somehow, the painted tables, flea-market decor, mismatched dinnerware, and faux-stone bar work together here. The cuisine, large portions of home-cooked New England fare, is equally unpretentious and fun: Try the chicken pot pie, fried trout, crab cakes, or the nightly Blue Plate special—and save room for a fruit-crisp for dessert. *108 Spring St., tel. 207/774-1740. No reservations. MC, V. Moderate.*

★ **Street & Co.** If the secret of a restaurant's success can be "keep it simple," Street & Co., the best seafood restaurant in Maine, goes one step further—"keep it small." You enter through the kitchen, with all its wonderful aromas, and dine amid dried herbs and shelves of staples on one of a dozen copper-topped tables (so your waiter can place a skillet of steaming seafood directly in front of you). Begin with lobster bisque or diavolo for two, crab sautéed with Oriental mushrooms and watercress, or grilled eggplant—vegetarian dishes are the only alternatives to fish. Choose from an array of superb entrées, ranging from calamari, clams, mussels, or shrimp served over linguine, to blackened, broiled, or grilled seafood. The desserts are top-notch. *33 Wharf St., tel. 207/775-0887. Reservations advised. AE, MC, V. No lunch. Inexpensive-Moderate.*

Lodging **Pomegranate Inn.** Clever touches such as faux marbling on the moldings and mustard-colored rag-rolling in the hallways give this bed-and-breakfast a bright, postmodern air. Most guest rooms are spacious and bright, accented with original paintings on floral and tropical motifs; the location on a quiet street in the city's Victorian Western Promenade district ensures serenity. Telephones and televisions, rare in an inn, make this a good choice for businesspeople. *49 Neal St., 04102, tel. 207/772-1006 or 800/356-0408. 7 rooms with bath, 1 suite. AE, DC, MC, V. Expensive-Very Expensive.*

★ **Portland Regency Inn.** The only major hotel in the center of the Old Port Exchange, the Regency building was Portland's armory in the late 19th century and is now the city's most luxurious, most distinctive hotel. The bright, plush, airy rooms have four-poster beds, tall standing mirrors, floral curtains, and loveseats. The health club, the best in the city, offers massage and has an aerobics studio, free weights, Nautilus equipment, a large Jacuzzi, dry sauna, and steam room. 20 Milk St., 04101, tel. 207/774–4200 or 800/727–3436. *95 rooms with bath, 8 suites. Facilities: restaurant, health club, nightclub, banquet and convention rooms. AE, D, DC, MC, V. Expensive.*

Sonesta Hotel. Across the street from the art museum and in the heart of the downtown business district, the 12-story brick building, vintage 1927, looks a bit dowdy today. Rooms in the tower section (added in 1961) have floor-to-ceiling windows, and the higher floors have harbor views. The small health club offers Universal gym equipment, rowing machines, stationary bikes, and a sauna. *157 High St., 04101, tel. 207/775–5411 or 800/777–6246. 202 rooms with bath. Facilities: 2 restaurants, 2 bars, health club, banquet and convention rooms. AE, D, DC, MC, V. Moderate–Expensive.*

The Arts

Center for the Arts at the Chocolate Church (804 Washington St., tel. 207/422–8455) offers changing exhibits by Maine artists such as Douglas Alvord and Dahlov Ipcar, as well as performances by Marion McPartland, Livingston Taylor, a children's orchestra, and repertory theater groups. There is also a classic film series, classes, and workshops.

Portland Performing Arts Center (25A Forest Ave., Portland, tel. 207/761–0591) hosts music, dance, and theater performances.

Dance **Ram Island Dance Company** (25A Forest Ave., Portland, tel. 207/773–2562), the city's resident modern dance troupe, appears at the Portland Performing Arts Center.

Music **Bowdoin Summer Music Festival** (Bowdoin College, Brunswick, tel. 207/725–3322 Sept.–May or 914/664–5957 June–Aug.) is a six-week concert series featuring performances by students, faculty, and prestigious guest artists.

Carousel Music Theater ("The Meadows," Boothbay Harbor, tel. 207/633–5297) mounts musical revues from Memorial Day to Columbus Day.

Cumberland County Civic Center (1 Civic Center Sq., Portland, tel. 207/775–3458) hosts concerts, sporting events, and family shows in a 9,000-seat auditorium.

Portland Symphony Orchestra (30 Myrtle St., Portland, tel. 207/773–8191) gives concerts October through August.

Theater **Mad Horse Theatre Company** (955 Forest Ave., Portland, tel. 207/797–3338) performs contemporary and original works.

Maine State Music Theater (Pickard Theater, Bowdoin College, Brunswick, tel. 207/725–8769 or 800/698–8769) stages musicals from mid-June through August.

Portland Stage Company (25A Forest Ave., Portland, tel. 207/774–0465), a producer of national reputation, mounts six productions, from November through April, at the Portland Performing Arts Center.

Theater Project of Brunswick (14 School St., Brunswick, tel. 207/729–8584) performs from late June through August.

Nightlife

Bars and Lounges Cafe No (20 Danforth St., Portland, tel. 207/772–8114) transports guests back to the '50s with coffeehouse poetry readings, beat music, and Middle Eastern food. There's live jazz Thursday through Saturday, with open jam sessions on Sunday from 4 until 8. *Closed Monday.*

Gritty McDuff's Brew Pub (396 Fore St., Portland, tel. 207/772–2739) attracts the young, the lively, and connoisseurs of the ales and bitters brewed on the premises. Steak and kidney pie and fish and chips are served.

Three Dollar Dewey's (446 Fore St., Portland, tel. 207/772–3310), long a popular Portland night spot, is an English-style ale house.

Top of the East (Sonesta Hotel, 157 High St., Portland, tel. 207/775–5411) has a view of the city and live entertainment—jazz, piano, and comedy.

Music McSeagull's Gulf Dock (Boothbay Harbor, tel. 207/633–4041) draws young singles with live music and a loud bar scene.

Raoul's Roadside Attraction (865 Forest Ave., tel. 207/775–2494), southern Maine's hippest nightclub/restaurant, books both local and name bands, especially R&B, jazz, and reggae groups.

The Coast: Penobscot Bay

Purists hold that the Maine coast begins at Penobscot Bay, where the vistas over the water are wider and bluer, the shore a jumble of broken granite boulders, cobblestones, and gravel punctuated by small sand beaches, and the water numbingly cold. Port Clyde in the southwest and Stonington in the southeast are the outer limits of Maine's largest bay, 35 miles apart across the bay waters but separated by a drive of almost 100 miles on scenic but slow two-lane highways.

Rockland, the largest town on the bay, is Maine's major lobster distribution center and the port of departure to several bay islands. The Camden Hills, looming green over Camden's fashionable waterfront, turn bluer and fainter as one moves on to Castine, the elegant small town across the bay. Deer Isle is connected to the mainland by a slender, high-arching bridge, but Isle au Haut, accessible from Deer Isle's fishing town of Stonington, may be reached by passenger ferry only: More than half of this steep, wooded island is wilderness, the most remote section of Acadia National Park.

Important Addresses and Numbers

Visitor Information Blue Hill Chamber of Commerce (Box 520, Blue Hill, 04614).

Castine Town Office (tel. 207/326–4502).

Deer Isle–Stonington Chamber of Commerce (Rte. 15, Little Deer Isle; Box 268, Stonington, 04681, tel. 207/348–6124).

Rockland–Thomaston Area Chamber of Commerce (Harbor Park, Box 508, Rockland, 04841, tel. 207/596–0376).

Rockport–Camden–Lincolnville Chamber of Commerce (Box 919, Camden, 04843, tel. 207/236–4404).

Searsport Chamber of Commerce (Box 468, Searsport, 04974, tel. 207/548–6510).

Emergencies **Island Medical Center** (Airport Rd., Stonington, tel. 207/367–2311).

Penobscot Bay Medical Center (Rte. 1, Rockland, tel. 207/596–8000).

Arriving and Departing by Plane

Bangor International Airport (tel. 207/947–0384), north of Penobscot Bay, has daily flights by major U.S. carriers.

Knox County Regional Airport (tel. 207/594–4131), 3 miles south of Rockland, has frequent flights to Boston.

Getting Around Penobscot Bay

By Car Route 1 follows the west coast of Penobscot Bay, linking Rockland, Camden, Belfast, and Searsport. On the east side of the bay, Route 175 (south from Route 1) takes you to Route 166A (for Castine) and Route 15 (for Blue Hill, Deer Isle, and Stonington). A car is essential for exploring the bay area.

Exploring Penobscot Bay

Numbers in the margin correspond to points of interest on the Penobscot Bay map.

From Pemaquid Point at the western extremity of Muscongus Bay to Port Clyde at its eastern extent, it's less than 15 miles across the water, but it's 50 miles for the motorist who must return north to Route 1 to reach the far shore.

Travelers on Route 1 can make an easy detour south through Tenants Harbor and Port Clyde before reaching Rockland. Turn onto Route 131 at Thomaston, 5 miles west of Rockland, and follow the winding road past waterside fields, spruce woods, ramshackle barns, and trim houses. **Tenants Harbor,** 7 miles from Thomaston, is a quintessential Maine fishing town, its harbor dominated by squat, serviceable lobster boats, its shores rocky and slippery, its town a scattering of clapboard houses, a church, a general store. The fictional Dunnet Landing of Sarah Orne Jewett's classic sketches of Maine coastal life, *The Country of the Pointed Firs*, is based on this region.

Route 131 ends at Port Clyde, a fishing town that is the point of departure for the *Laura B.* (tel. 207/372–8848 for schedules), the mailboat that serves Monhegan Island. Tiny, remote **Monhegan Island** with its high cliffs fronting the open sea was known to Basque, Portuguese, and Breton fishermen well before Columbus "discovered" America. About a century ago Monhegan was discovered again by some of America's finest painters, including Rockwell Kent, Robert Henri, and Edward Hopper, who sailed out to paint the savage cliffs, the meadows, the wild ocean views, and the shacks of fisherfolk. Tourists fol-

Penobscot Bay

lowed, and today Monhegan is overrun with visitors in summer.

Returning north to Route 1, you have less than 5 miles to go to
❸ **Rockland** on Penobscot Bay. This large fishing port is the commercial hub of the coast, with working boats moored alongside growing flotilla of cruise schooners. Although a number of boutiques and restaurants have emerged in recent years, the town has retained its working-class flavor—you are more likely to find rusting hardware than ice-cream shops at the water's edge.

The outer harbor is bisected by a nearly mile-long breakwater, which begins on Waldo Avenue and ends with a lighthouse that was built in 1888. Next to the breakwater is **The Samoset Resort** (Warrenton St., tel. 207/594–2511 or 800/341–1650), a sprawling oceanside resort featuring an 18-hole golf course, indoor and outdoor swimming pools, tennis, racquetball, restaurant, and health club.

Also in Rockland is the **William A. Farnsworth Library and Art Museum.** Here are oil and watercolor landscapes of the coastal lands you have just seen, among them Andrew Wyeth's *Eight Bells* and N.C. Wyeth's *Her Room.* Jamie Wyeth is also represented in the collections, as are Winslow Homer, Rockwell Kent, and the sculptor Louise Nevelson. *19 Elm St., tel. 207/ 596–6457. Admission free. Open Mon.–Sat. 10–5, Sun. 1–5. Closed Mon. Oct.–May.*

❹ From Rockland it's 8 miles north on Route 1 to **Camden,** "Where the mountains meet the sea"—an apt description, as you will discover when you step out of your car and look up from the harbor. Camden is famous not only for geography but for the nation's largest windjammer fleet; at just about any hour during the warmer months you're likely to see at least one windjammer tied up in the harbor, and windjammer cruises are a superb way to explore the ports and islands of Penobscot Bay.

Time Out **Ayer's Fish Market** on Main Street has the best fish chowder in town; take a cup to the pleasant park at the head of the harbor when you're ready for a break from the shops on Bayview and Main streets.

The entrance to the 6,000-acre **Camden Hills State Park** (tel. 207/236–3109) is 2 miles north of Camden on Route 1. If you're accustomed to the Rockies or the Alps, you may not be impressed with heights of not much more than 1,000 feet, yet the Camden Hills are landmarks for miles along the vast, flat reaches of the Maine coast. The park contains 25 miles of trails, including an easy trail up Mount Megunticook, the highest of the group. The 112-site camping area, open May through November, has flush toilets and hot showers. Admission to the trails or the auto road up Mount Battie is $1.50 per person.

❺ Farther north on Route 1, **Searsport**—Maine's second-largest deepwater port (after Portland)—claims to be the antiques capital of Maine. The town's stretch of Route 1 hosts a seasonal weekend flea market in addition to its antiques shops.

Searsport preserves a rich nautical history at the **Penobscot Marine Museum,** whose seven buildings display portraits of 284 sea captains, artifacts of the whaling industry (lots of scrimshaw), paintings and models of famous ships, navigational instruments, and treasures that seafarers collected. *Church St., tel. 207/548–2529. Admission: $4 adults, $3.50 senior citizens, $1.50 children 7–15. Open June–mid-Oct., Mon.–Sat. 9:30–5, Sun. 1–5.*

⑥ Historic **Castine,** over which the French, the British, and the Americans fought from the 17th century to the War of 1812, has two museums and the ruins of a British fort, but the finest thing about Castine is the town itself: the lively, welcoming town landing, the serene Federal and Greek Revival houses, and the town common. Castine invites strolling, and you would do well to start at the town landing, where you can park your car, and walk up Main Street past the two inns and on to the white Trinitarian Federated Church with its tapering spire.

Turn right on Court Street and walk to the town common, which is ringed by a collection of white-clapboard buildings that includes the Ives House (once the summer home of the poet Robert Lowell), the Abbott School, and the Unitarian Church, capped by a whimsical belfry that suggests a gazebo.

From Castine, take Route 166 north to Route 199 and follow the **⑦** signs to **Blue Hill.** Castine may have the edge over Blue Hill in charm, for its Main Street is not a major thoroughfare and it claims a more dramatic perch over its harbor, yet Blue Hill is certainly appealing and boasts a better selection of shops and galleries. Blue Hill is renowned for its pottery, and two good shops are right in town.

The scenic Route 15 south from Blue Hill passes through Brooksville and on to the graceful suspension bridge that **⑧** crosses Eggemoggin Reach to **Deer Isle.** The turnout and picnic area at Caterpillar Hill, 1 mile south of the junction of Routes 15 and 175, commands a fabulous view of Penobscot Bay, the hundreds of dark green islands, and the Camden Hills across the bay, which from this perspective look like a range of mountains dwarfed and faded by an immense distance—yet they are less than 25 miles away.

Route 15 continues the length of Deer Isle—a sparsely settled landscape of thick woods opening to tidal coves, shingled houses with lobster traps stacked in the yards, and dirt roads **⑨** that lead to summer cottages—to **Stonington,** an emphatically ungentrified community that tolerates summer visitors but makes no effort to cater to them. Main Street has gift shops and galleries, but this is a working port town, and the principal activity is at the waterfront, where fishing boats arrive with the day's catch. The high, sloped island that rises beyond the archipelago of Merchants Row is Isle au Haut, accessible by mailboat from Stonington, which contains sections of Acadia National Park.

Island Excursions **Islesboro,** accessible by car-and-passenger ferry from Lin-**⑩** colnville Beach north of Rockland (Maine State Ferry Service, tel. 207/789–5611), has been a retreat of wealthy, very private families for more than a century. The long, narrow, mostly wooded island has no real town to speak of; there are scatterings of mansions as well as humbler homes at Dark Harbor and at Pripet near the north end. Since the amenities on Islesboro are quite spread out, you don't want to come on foot. If you plan to spend the night on Islesboro, you should make a reservation well in advance (*see* Islesboro Lodging, *below*).

Time Out **Dark Harbor Shop** (tel. 207/734–8878) on Islesboro is an old-fashioned ice-cream parlor where tourists, locals, and summer folk gather for sandwiches, newspapers, gossip, and gifts. Open June through August.

⑪ **Isle au Haut** thrusts its steeply ridged back out of the sea 7 miles south of Stonington. Accessible only by passenger ferry (tel. 207/367–5193), the island is worth visiting for the ferry ride alone, a half-hour cruise amid the tiny, pink-shore islands of Merchants Row, where you may see terns, guillemots, and harbor seals. More than half the island is part of Acadia National Park; 17½ miles of trails extend through quiet spruce and birch woods, along cobble beaches and seaside cliffs, and over the spine of the central mountain ridge. From late June to mid-September, the mailboat docks at Duck Harbor within the park. The small campground here, with five Adirondack-type lean-tos (open mid-May to mid-October), fills up quickly; reservations are essential, and they can be made only by writing to Acadia National Park (Box 177, Bar Harbor 04609).

Penobscot Bay for Free

Maine Coast Artists Gallery (Russell Ave., Rockport, tel. 207/236–2875) shows the work of Maine artists from June through September; lectures and classes are also scheduled.

Shore Village Museum exhibits U.S. Coast Guard memorabilia and artifacts, including lighthouse lenses, lifesaving gear, ship models, Civil War uniforms, and dolls. *104 Limerock St., Rockland, tel. 207/594–0311. Open June–mid-Oct., daily 10–4.*

What to See and Do with Children

Owls Head Transportation Museum, 2 miles south of Rockland on Route 73, shows antique aircraft, cars, and engines and stages weekend air shows. *Rte. 73, Owls Head, tel. 207/594–4418. Admission: $4 adults, $3.50 senior citizens, $2.50 children 5–12. Open May–Oct., daily 10–5; Nov.–Apr., weekdays 10–4, weekends 10–3.*

Off the Beaten Track

The Haystack Mountain School of Crafts, on Deer Isle, attracts an internationally renowned group of glassblowers, potters, sculptors, jewelers, and weavers to its summer institute. You can attend evening lectures or visit the studios of artisans at work (by appointment only). *South of Deer Isle Village on Route 15, turn left at Gulf gas station and follow signs for 6 miles, tel. 207/348–2306. Admission free. Open June–Sept.*

Shopping

The most promising shopping streets are Main and Bayview streets in Camden and Main Street in Stonington. Antiques shops are scattered around the outskirts of villages, in farmhouses and barns; yard sales abound in summertime.

Antiques **Creative Antiques** (Rte. 175, tel. 207/359–8525) features
Brooklin painted furniture, hooked rugs, and prints.

Deer Isle Village **Old Deer Isle Parish House** (Rte. 15, tel. 207/367–2455) is a place for poking around in the jumbles of old kitchenware, glassware, books, and linen.

Sargentville **Old Cove Antiques** (Rte. 15, tel. 207/359–2031) has folk art, quilts, hooked rugs, and folk carvings.

Searsport Billing itself the antiques capital of Maine, Searsport hosts a massive weekend flea market on Route 1 during the summer months. Indoor shops, most of them in old houses and barns, are also located on Route 1, in Lincolnville Beach as well as Searsport. Shops are open daily during the summer months, by chance or by appointment from mid-October through the end of May.

Art Galleries **Gallery 68** (68 Main St., tel. 207/338–1558) carries contempo-
Belfast rary art in all media.

Blue Hill **Leighton Gallery** (Parker Point Rd., tel. 207/374–5001) shows oil paintings, lithographs, watercolors, and other contemporary art in the gallery, and sculpture in its garden.

Deer Isle Village **Blue Heron Gallery & Studio** (Church St., tel. 207/348–6051) features the work of the Haystack Mountain School of Crafts faculty (*see* Off the Beaten Track, *above*).
Deer Isle Artist Association (Rte. 15, no tel.) has group exhibits of prints, drawings, and sculpture from mid-June through September.

Lincolnville **Maine's Massachusetts House Galleries** (Rte. 1, tel. 207/789–5705) offers a broad selection of northern art, including bronzes, carvings, sculptures, and landscapes and seascapes in pencil, oil, and watercolor.

Books and Gifts **Fertile Mind Bookshop** (13 Main St., tel. 207/338–2498) sells a
Belfast thoughtfully chosen selection of books, records, maps, and cards, including Maine-published works.

Crafts and Pottery **Handworks Gallery** (Main St., tel. 207/374–5613) carries un-
Blue Hill usual crafts, jewelry, and clothing.
Rackliffe Pottery (Rte. 172, tel. 207/374–2297) is famous for its vivid blue pottery, including plates, tea and coffee sets, casseroles, and canisters.
Rowantrees Pottery (Union St., tel. 207/374–5535) has an extensive selection of styles and patterns in dinnerware, tea sets, vases, and decorative items.

South Penobscot **North Country Textiles** (Rte. 175, tel. 207/326–4131) is worth the detour for fine woven shawls, placemats, throws, and pillows in subtle patterns and color schemes.

Furniture **The Windsor Chairmakers** (Rte. 1, tel. 207/789–5188) sells cus-
Lincolnville tom-made, handcrafted beds, chests, china cabinets, dining tables, and highboys.

Sports and Outdoor Activities

Boat Trips Windjammers create a stir whenever they sail into Camden harbor, and a voyage around the bay on one of them, whether for an afternoon or a week, is unforgettable. The season for the excursions is June through September.

Camden ***Angelique*** (Yankee Packet Co., Box 736, tel. 207/236–8873 or 800/282–9989) makes three- and six-day trips. ***Appledore*** (0 Lilly Pond Dr., tel. 207/236–8353) offers day sails as well as private charters. **Maine Windjammer Cruises** (Box 617CC, tel. 207/236–2938 or 800/736–7981) has three two-masted schooners making three- and six-day trips along the coast and to the islands. The Schooner *Roseway* (Box 696, tel. 207/236–4449 or 800/255–4449) takes three- and six-day cruises.

Rockland The **Vessels of Windjammer Wharf** (Box 1050, tel. 207/236–3520 or 800/999–7352) organizes three- and six-day cruises on the *Pauline*, a 12-passenger yacht, and the *Stephen Taber*, a windjammer.

Rockport **Timberwind** (Box 247, tel. 207/236–0801 or 800/759–9250) sails out of Rockport harbor.

Stonington **Palmer Day IV** (Stonington Harbor, tel. 207/367–2207) cruises Penobscot Bay in July and August, stopping at North Haven and Vinalhaven.

Biking **Maine Sport** (Rte. 1, Rockport, tel. 207/236–8797) rents bikes, canoes and kayaks, and camping gear.

Hiking **Country Walkers** (RR 2, Box 754, Waterbury, VT 05676–9754, tel. 802/244–1347) leads nature-oriented walking vacations from Blue Hill through Castine and the Schoodic Peninsula, from mid-May to mid-October.

Deep-Sea Fishing **Bay Island Yacht Charters** (Box 639, Camden, tel. 207/236–2776 or 800/421–2492) has charters by the day, week, and month.

Water Sports Eggemoggin Reach is a famous cruising ground for yachts, as are the coves and inlets around Deer Isle and the Penobscot Bay waters between Castine and Islesboro. For island camping and inn-to-inn tours, try **Indian Island Kayak** (16 Mountain St., Camden, tel. 207/236–4088). **Maine Sport** (Rte. 1, Rockport, tel. 207/236–8797) offers sea kayaking expeditions, starting at the store.

State Parks

Camden Hills State Park (*see* Exploring Penobscot Bay, *above*).

Holbrook Island Sanctuary (on Penobscot Bay in Brooksville, tel. 207/326–4012) has a gravelly beach with a splendid view; hiking trails through meadow and forest; no camping facilities.

Dining and Lodging

Camden has the greatest variety of restaurants and inns in the region.

Blue Hill **Jonathan's.** The older downstairs room has captain's chairs, *Dining* blue tablecloths, and local art; in the post-and-beam upstairs, ★ there's wood everywhere, candles with hurricane globes, and high-back chairs. The menu may include chicken breast in a fennel sauce with peppers, garlic, rosemary, and shallots; shrimp scorpio (shrimp served on linguine with a touch of ouzo and feta cheese); and grilled strip steak. Chocolate bourbon pecan cake makes a compelling finale. The wine list has 250 selections from French and California vineyards. *Main St., tel. 207/ 374–5226. Reservations advised in summer. Dress: casual. MC, V. Closed Mon. Jan.–Apr. Inexpensive–Moderate.*

Lodging **The John Peters Inn.** The John Peters is unsurpassed for the ★ privacy of its location and the good taste in the decor of its guest rooms. The living room has two fireplaces, books and games, baby grand piano, and Empire furniture. Oriental rugs are everywhere. Huge breakfasts in the light and airy dining rooms include the famous lobster omelet, served complete with lobster-claw shells as decoration. The Surry Room, one of the best rooms (all are nice), has a king-size bed, a fireplace, curly-maple chest, gilt mirror, and six windows with delicate lace curtains. The Honeymoon Suite is immense, with wet bar and minifridge, white furniture, deck, and a view of Blue Hill Bay. The large rooms in the carriage house, a stone's throw down the hill from the inn, have dining areas, cherry floors and woodwork, wicker and brass accents, and a modern feel. Four have decks, kitchens, and fireplaces, a real plus here. *Peters Point, Box 916, Blue Hill, 04614, tel. 207/374–2116. 7 rooms with bath, 1 suite in inn; 6 rooms with bath in carriage house. Facilities: phones in carriage house rooms, fireplaces in 9 bedrooms; swimming pool, canoe, sailboats, pond, 2 moorings. No pets. MC, V. Closed Nov.–Apr. Very Expensive.*

Camden
Dining
★

The Belmont. Round tables are set well apart in this dining room with smoke-colored walls and soft classical music or jazz. The changing menu of new American cuisine might include sautéed scallops with Pernod leek cream; grilled pheasant with cranberry; chicken with a tomato coconut curry; or braised lamb shanks. *6 Belmont Ave., tel. 207/236–8053. Reservations advised. Dress: casual. MC, V. Closed Jan.–Apr., Mon. May–Columbus Day, Mon.–Wed. Columbus Day–Dec. Dinner only. Expensive.*

The Waterfront Restaurant. A ringside seat on Camden Harbor can be had here; the best view is from the outdoor deck, open in warm weather. The fare is seafood: boiled lobster, scallops, bouillabaisse, steamed mussels, Cajun barbecued shrimp. Lunchtime features are lobster salad, crabmeat salad, lobster and crab rolls, tuna niçoise, turkey melt, and burgers. *Bayview St., tel. 207/236–3747. No reservations. Dress: casual. MC, V. Moderate.*

Cappy's Chowder House. Lobster traps, a moosehead, and a barbershop pole decorate this lively but cozy tavern; the Crow's Nest dining room upstairs is quieter and has a harbor view. Simple fare is the rule here: burgers, sandwiches, seafood, and, of course, chowder. A bakery downstairs sells breads, cookies, and filled croissants to go. *1 Main St., tel. 207/236–2254. No reservations. MC, V. Inexpensive–Moderate.*

Dining and Lodging

Whitehall Inn. Camden's best-known inn, just north of town on Route 1, boasts a central white-clapboard, wide-porch ship captain's home of 1843 connected to a turn-of-the-century wing. Just off the comfortable main lobby with its faded Oriental rugs, the Millay Room preserves memorabilia of the poet Edna St. Vincent Millay, who grew up in Rockland. Rooms are sparsely furnished, with dark wood bedsteads, white bedspreads, and clawfoot bathtubs. Some rooms have ocean views. The dining room is open to the public for dinner and breakfast, offering traditional and creative American cuisine. Dinner entrées include Eastern salmon in puff pastry, swordfish grilled with roast red pepper sauce, and lamb tenderloin. *Box 558, 04843, tel. 207/236–3391. 50 rooms, 42 with bath. Facilities: restaurant, all-weather tennis court, shuffleboard, motorboat, golf privileges. AE, MC, V. Closed mid-Oct.–mid-May. Rates are MAP. Very Expensive.*

Lodging **Norumbega.** The stone castle amid Camden's elegant clapboard houses, built in 1886 by Joseph B. Stearns, the inventor of duplex telegraphy, was obviously the fulfillment of a fantasy. The public rooms boast gleaming parquet floors, oak and mahogany paneling, richly carved wood mantels over four fireplaces on the first floor alone, gilt mirrors, and Empire furnishings. At the back of the house, several decks and balconies overlook the garden, the gazebo, and the bay. The view improves as you ascend; the newly completed penthouse suite features a small deck, private bar, and a skylight in the bedroom. *61 High St., 04843, tel. 207/236–4646. 13 rooms with bath. AE, MC, V. Very Expensive.*

Windward House. A choice bed-and-breakfast, this Greek Revival house of 1854, situated at the edge of town, features rooms furnished with fishnet lace canopy beds, cherry highboys, curly-maple bedsteads, and clawfoot mahogany dressers. Guests are welcome to use any of three sitting rooms, including the Wicker Room with its glass-topped white wicker table where morning coffee is served. A small deck overlooks the back garden. Breakfasts may include quiche, apple puff pancakes, peaches-and-cream French toast, or soufflés. *6 High St., 04843, tel. 207/236–9656. 6 rooms with bath, 1 efficiency. MC, V. Expensive–Very Expensive.*

Castine **Gilley's Seafood.** This unpretentious harborside restaurant has
Dining just the kind of traditional dishes Downeasters love: a variety of chowders, lobster stew, subs, and tiny Maine shrimp or fresh clams. *Water St., tel. 207/326–4001. Reservations accepted. Dress: casual. MC, V. Closed Tues. off-season. Inexpensive.*

Dining and Lodging **The Pentagoet.** A recent renovation of the rambling, pale yellow Pentagoet gave each room a bath, enlarged the dining room, and opened up the public rooms. The porch wraps around three sides of the inn. Guest rooms are warmer, more flowery, more feminine than those of the Castine Inn across the street; they have hooked rugs, a mix of Victorian antiques, and floral wallpapers. Dinner in the deep rose and cream formal dining room (open to the public on a limited basis) is an elaborate affair; entrées might include lobster (usually prepared two different ways), grilled salmon with Dijon sauce, and pork loin braised in apple cider. Inn guests can expect a hearty breakfast. *Main St., 04421, tel. 207/326–8616. 16 rooms with bath. MC, V. Closed Nov.–Apr. Rates are MAP. Very Expensive.*

★ **The Castine Inn.** Dark wood pineapple four-poster beds, white upholstered easy chairs, and oil paintings are typical of the room furnishings here. The third floor has the best views: the harbor over the back garden on one side, Main Street on the other. The dining room, decorated with whimsical murals, is open to the public for breakfast and dinner; the menu features traditional New England fare—Maine lobster, crabmeat cakes with mustard sauce, roast leg of lamb, and chicken and leek pot pie. A snug, old-fashioned pub off the lobby has small tables and antique spirit jars over the mantel. *Main St., 04421, tel. 207/326–4365. 27 rooms with bath, 3 suites. Facilities: restaurant, pub. MC, V. Closed Nov.–mid-Apr. Rates include full breakfast. Moderate–Expensive.*

Deer Isle **Fisherman's Friend Restaurant.** Fresh salmon, halibut,
Dining monkfish, lobster, and even prime rib and chicken are on the
★ menu here. Friday is fish-fry day: free seconds on fried haddock for $5.99. *School St., Stonington, tel. 207/367–2442. Res-*

ervations advised. Dress: casual. No credit cards. BYOB. Closed mid-Nov.–mid-Mar.; closed Mon. after Columbus Day. Inexpensive.

Lodging **Goose Cove Lodge.** The heavily wooded property at the end of a back road has 2,500 feet of ocean frontage, two sandy beaches, a long sandbar that leads to the Barred Island nature preserve, nature trails, and sailboats for rent nearby. Some cottages and suites are in secluded woodlands, some on the shore, some attached, some with a single large room, others with one or two bedrooms. All but two units have fireplaces. In July and August the minimum stay is one week. *Box 40, Sunset 04683, tel. 207/348-2508. 11 cottages, 10 suites. Facilities: rowboat, canoe, volleyball, horseshoes. No credit cards. Closed mid-Oct.– Apr. Rates are MAP. Moderate–Expensive.*

Pilgrim's Inn. The bright red, four-story, gambrel-roof house dating from about 1793 overlooks a mill pond and harbor at the center of Deer Isle. The library has wing chairs and Oriental rugs; a downstairs taproom has pine furniture, braided rugs, and parson's benches. Guest rooms, each with its own character, sport Laura Ashley fabrics and select antiques. The dining room in the attached barn, an open space both rustic and elegant, has farm implements, French oil lamps, and tiny windows. The single-entrée menu changes nightly; it might include rack of lamb or fresh local seafood; scallop bisque; asparagus and smoked salmon; and poached pear tart for dessert. *Deer Isle 04627, tel. 207/348-6615. 13 rooms, 8 with bath, 1 cottage. Facilities: restaurant. No credit cards. Closed mid-Oct.–mid-May. Rates are MAP or bed-and-breakfast. Moderate–Expensive.*

Captain's Quarters Inn and Motel. Accommodations, as plain and unadorned as Stonington itself, are in the middle of town, a two-minute walk from the Isle au Haut mailboat. You have your choice of motel-type rooms and suites or efficiencies, and you can take your breakfast muffins and coffee to the sunny deck on the water. *Main St., Box 83, Stonington, 04681, tel. 207/367-2420. 13 units, 11 with bath. AE, MC, V. Inexpensive–Moderate.*

Isle au Haut **Keeper's House.** This converted lighthouse-keeper's house, set
Lodging on a rock ledge surrounded by thick spruce forest, has no electricity and limited access by road; guests dine by candlelight on seafood or chicken and read in the evening by kerosene lantern. Trails link the inn with the park trail network, and you can walk to the village, a collection of simple houses, a church, a tiny school, and a general store. The five guest rooms are spacious, airy, and simply decorated with painted wood furniture and local crafts. A separate cottage, the Oil House, has no indoor plumbing. *Box 26, Isle au Haut 04645, tel. 207/367-2261. 5 rooms with shared bath, 1 cottage. Facilities: dock. No credit cards. Closed Nov.–Apr. Rates include 3 meals. Expensive– Very Expensive.*

Islesboro **Dark Harbor House.** The yellow-clapboard, neo-Georgian sum-
Lodging mer "cottage" of 1896 has a stately portico and a hilltop setting. Inside, an elegant double staircase curves from the ground floor to the bedrooms, which are spacious, some with balconies, half with fireplaces, one with an 18th-century four-poster bed. The dining room, open to the public for prix-fixe dinners, features seafood and West Indian specialties. *Box 185, 04848, tel.*

207/734-6669. 10 rooms with bath. Facilities: restaurant. MC, V. Closed mid-Oct.–mid-May. Very Expensive.

Lincolnville **Chez Michel.** This tiny restaurant, serving up a fine rabbit
Dining pâté, mussels marinière, steak au poivre, and poached salmon, might easily be on the Riveria instead of Ducktrap Beach. Chef Michel Hetuin creates bouillabaisse as deftly as New England chowder, and he welcomes special requests. *Rte. 1, tel. 207/ 789-5600. Reservations accepted for 6 or more. Dress: casual. MC, V. Closed Mon. off-season. Inexpensive–Moderate.*

North Brooklin **The Lookout.** The stately white-clapboard building stands in a
Lodging wide field at the tip of Flye Point, with a superb view of the water and the mountains of Mount Desert Island. Although the floors slope and a century of damp has left a certain mustiness, the rustic rooms are nicely furnished with country antiques original to the house and newer matching pieces. The larger south-facing rooms command the view. Six cottages have from one to four bedrooms each. With the dining room expanded onto the porch, seven tables enjoy a view of the outdoors. Entrées could include filet mignon, grilled salmon, and shrimp and scallops provençale; Wednesday night is the lobster cookout. *North Brooklin, 04661, tel. 207/359-2188. 6 rooms with shared bath, 6 cottages. Facilities: restaurant. MC, V. Closed mid-Oct.–mid-Apr. Moderate.*

Spruce Head **The Craignair Inn.** Built in the 1930s as a boardinghouse for
Dining and Lodging stonecutters and converted to an inn a decade later, the Craignair commands a coastal view of rocky shore and lobster boats. Inside the three-story gambrel-roof house you'll find country clutter, books, and cut glass in the parlor; braided rugs, brass beds, and dowdy dressers in the guest rooms. In 1986 the owners converted a church dating from the 1890s into another accommodation with six rooms—each with bath—that have a more modern feel. The waterside dining room, decorated with Delft and Staffordshire plates, serves such fare as bouillabaisse; lemon pepper seafood kebab; rabbit with tarragon and wine; and those New England standards: shore dinner, prime rib, and scampi. A bourbon pecan tart and crème brûlée are the dessert headliners. *Clark Island Rd., 04859, tel. 207/ 594-7644. 23 rooms, 8 with bath. Facilities: restaurant. AE, MC, V. Closed Feb. Moderate–Expensive.*

Tenants Harbor **East Wind Inn & Meeting House.** On Route 131, 10 miles off
Dining and Lodging Route 1 and set on a knob of land overlooking the harbor and the islands, the inn offers simple hospitality, a wraparound porch, and unadorned but comfortable guest rooms furnished with an iron bedstead, flowered wallpaper, and heritage bedspread. The dining room has a rustic decor; the dinner menu features duck with black currant sauce; seafood stew with scallops, shrimp, mussels, and grilled sausage; boiled lobster; and baked stuffed haddock. *Box 149, 04860, tel. 207/372-6366. 26 rooms, 12 with bath. Facilities: sailboat cruises in season. AE, MC, V. Moderate–Expensive.*

The Arts

Music **Bay Chamber Concerts** (Rockport Opera House, Rockport, tel. 207/236-2823) offers chamber music Thursday and Friday nights during July and August; concerts are given once a month October through May.

Kneisel Hall Chamber Music Festival (Box 648, Blue Hill, tel. 207/374–2811) has concerts Sunday and Friday in summer.

Theater **Cold Comfort Productions** (Box 259, Castine, no tel.), a community theater, mounts plays in July and August.

Nightlife

Bars and Lounges **Dennett's Wharf** (Sea St., Castine, tel. 207/326–9045) has a long bar that can become rowdy after dark. Open May through October.

Peter Ott's Tavern (16 Bayview St., Camden, tel. 207/236–4032) is a steakhouse with a lively bar scene.

Thirsty Whale Tavern (Camden Harbour Inn, 83 Bayview St., Camden, tel. 207/236–4200) is a popular local drinking spot.

The Coast: Acadia

East of Penobscot Bay, Acadia is the informal name for the area that includes Mount Desert Island (pronounced dessert) and its surroundings: Blue Hill Bay; Frenchman Bay; and Ellsworth, Hancock, and other mainland towns. Mount Desert, 13 miles across, is Maine's largest island, and it harbors most of Acadia National Park, Maine's principal tourist attraction with more than 4 million visitors a year. The 34,000 acres of woods and mountains, lake and shore, footpaths, carriage paths, and hiking trails that make up the park extend as well to other islands and some of the mainland. Outside the park, on Mount Desert's east shore, an upper-class resort town of the 19th century has become a busy tourist town of the 20th century in Bar Harbor, which services the park with a variety of inns, motels, and restaurants.

Important Addresses and Numbers

Visitor Information **Acadia National Park** (Box 177, Bar Harbor 04609, tel. 207/288–3338).

Bar Harbor Chamber of Commerce (Box BC, Cottage St., Bar Harbor 04609, tel. 207/288–3393, 207/288–5103, or 800/288–5103).

Getting Around Acadia

By Car North of Bar Harbor the scenic 27-mile Park Loop Road takes leave of Route 3 to circle the eastern quarter of Mount Desert Island, with one-way traffic from Sieur de Monts Spring to Seal Harbor and two-way traffic between Seal Harbor and Hulls Cove. Route 102, which serves the western half of Mount Desert, is reached from Route 3 just after it crosses onto the island or from Route 233 west from Bar Harbor. All these island roads pass in, out, and through the precincts of Acadia National Park.

Guided Tours

Acadia Taxi and Tours (tel. 207/ATT–4020) conducts half-day historic and scenic tours of the area.

National Park Tours (tel. 207/288–3327) offers a 2½-hour bus tour of Acadia National Park, narrated by a park naturalist, which departs twice daily across from Testa's Restaurant on Main Street in Bar Harbor.

Acadia Air (tel. 207/667–5534), on Route 3 between Ellsworth and Bar Harbor at Hancock County Airport, offers aircraft rentals and aerial whale-watching trips.

Exploring Acadia

Numbers in the margin correspond to points of interest on the Acadia map.

Coastal Route 1 passes through Ellsworth, where Route 3 turns south to Mount Desert Island and takes you into the busy **❶** town of **Bar Harbor.** Although most of Bar Harbor's grand mansions were destroyed in the fire of 1947 and replaced by modern motels, the town retains the beauty of a commanding location on Frenchman Bay. Shops, restaurants, and hotels are clustered along Main, Mount Desert, and Cottage streets.

❷ The **Hulls Cove** approach to Acadia National Park is 4 miles northwest of Bar Harbor on Route 3. Even though it is often clogged with traffic in summer, the Park Loop Road provides the best introduction to Acadia National Park. At the start of the loop at Hulls Cove, the visitor center shows a free 15-minute orientation film and has maps of the hiking trails and carriage paths in the park.

❸ Follow the road to the parking area for **Sand Beach,** a small stretch of pink sand backed by the mountains of Acadia and the odd lump of rock known as the Beehive. The **Ocean Trail,** which parallels the Park Loop Road from Sand Beach to the Otter Point parking area, is a popular and easily accessible walk with some of the most spectacular scenery in Maine: huge slabs of pink granite heaped at the ocean's edge, ocean views unobstructed to the horizon, and Thunder Hole, a natural seaside cave in which the ocean rushes and roars.

Those who want a mountaintop experience without the effort **❹** of hiking can drive to the summit of **Cadillac Mountain,** at 1,523 feet the highest point along the eastern coast. From the smooth, bald summit you have a 360-degree view of the ocean, the islands, the jagged coast, and the woods and lakes of Acadia and its surroundings.

On completing the 27-mile Park Loop, you can continue your auto tour of the island by heading west on Route 233 for the villages on Somes Sound—a true fjord—the only one on the East **❺** Coast—which almost bisects Mount Desert Island. **Somesville,** the oldest settlement on the island (1621), is a carefully preserved New England village of white-clapboard houses and churches, neat green lawns, and bits of blue water visible behind them.

❻ Route 102 south from Somesville takes you to **Southwest Harbor,** which combines the rough, salty character of a working port with the refinements of a summer resort community. From the town's Main Street along Route 102, turn left onto Clark Point Road to reach the harbor.

Acadia

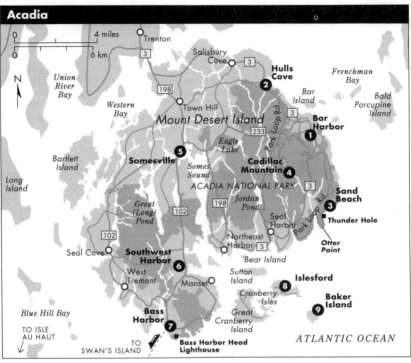

Time Out At the end of Clark Point Road in Southwest Harbor, **Beal's Lobster Pier** serves lobsters, clams, and crab rolls in season at dockside picnic tables.

Those who want to tour more of the island will continue south on Route 102, following Route 102A where the road forks, and passing through the communities of Manset and Seawall. The Bass Harbor Head lighthouse, which clings to a cliff at the eastern entrance to Blue Hill Bay, was built in 1858. The tiny lobstering village of **Bass Harbor** has cottages for rent, a gift shop, and a car-and-passenger ferry to Swans Island.

Island Excursions Situated off the southeast shore of Mount Desert Island at the entrance to Somes Sound, the five Cranberry Isles—Great Cranberry, Islesford (or Little Cranberry), Baker Island, Sutton Island, and Bear Island—escape the hubbub that engulfs Acadia National Park in summer. Great Cranberry and Islesford are served by the Beal & Bunker passenger ferry (tel. 207/244–3575) from Northeast Harbor; Baker Island is reached by the summer cruise boats of the Islesford Ferry Company (tel. 207/276–3717); Sutton and Bear islands are privately owned.

Islesford comes closest to having a village: a collection of houses, a church, a fishermen's co-op, a market, and a post office near the ferry dock. The Islesford Historical Museum, run by the national park, has displays of tools, documents relating to the island's history, and books and manuscripts of the writer Rachel Field (1894–1942), who summered on Sutton Island.

Puddles on the Water (tel. 207/244–3177), on the Islesford Dock, serves three meals a day from June through September.

❾ The 123-acre **Baker Island,** the most remote of the group, looks almost black from a distance because of its thick spruce forest. The cruise boat from Northeast Harbor makes a 4½-hour narrated tour, in the course of which you are likely to see ospreys nesting on a sea stack off Sutton Island, harbor seals hauled out on ledges, and cormorants flying low over the water. Because Baker Island has no natural harbor, the tour boat ties up offshore and you take a fishing dory to reach the island.

Acadia for Free

Bar Harbor Historical Society Museum displays photographs of Bar Harbor from the days when it catered to the very rich. Other exhibits document the great fire of 1947, in which many of the Gilded Age cottages were destroyed. *34 Mt. Desert St., tel. 207/288–4245. Admission free. Open mid-June–Oct., Mon.– Sat. 1–4; by appointment in other seasons.*

What to See and Do with Children

Acadia Zoo, a 30-acre preserve and petting zoo, has pastures, streams, woods, and wild and domestic animals. *Rte. 3, Trenton, tel. 207/667–3244. Open May–Columbus Day.*
Mount Desert Oceanarium has exhibits in three locations on the fishing and sea life of the Gulf of Maine, as well as hands-on "touch tanks." *Clark Point Rd., Southwest Harbor, tel. 207/ 244–7330; Rte. 3, Bar Harbor, tel. 207/288–5005; Lobster Hatchery at Municipal Pier, Bar Harbor, tel. 207/288–2344. Call for admission fees. Open mid-May–mid-Oct., Mon.–Sat. 9–5; Lobster Hatchery open evenings July–Aug.*

Off the Beaten Track

Bartlett Maine Estate Winery offers tours, tastings, and gift packs. Wines are produced from locally grown apples, blueberries, raspberries, and other fruit. *Rte. 1 in Gouldsboro, north of Bar Harbor, tel. 207/546–2408. Open June–Oct., Tues.– Sun. 10–5.*
Jackson Laboratory, a center for research in mammalian genetics, studies cancer, diabetes, and heart disease. *Rte. 3, 3½ mi south of Bar Harbor, tel. 207/288–3371. Audiovisual presentations mid-June–Aug., Tues. and Thurs. at 2.*

Shopping

Bar Harbor in the summer is a good place for browsing for gifts, T-shirts, and novelty items; for bargains, head for the outlets that line Route 3 in Ellsworth, which have good discounts on shoes.

Antiques
Bernard **E. and L. Higgins** (tel. 207/244–3983) has a good stock of wicker, along with pine and oak country furniture.

Southwest Harbor **Marianne Clark Fine Antiques** (Main St., tel. 207/244–9247) has an eclectic stock of formal and country furniture, American paintings, and accessories from the 18th and 19th centuries.

Crafts
Bar Harbor **Acadia Shops** (inside the park at Cadillac Mountain summit; Thunder Hole on Ocean Dr.; Jordan Pond House on Park Loop Rd.; and 85 Main St.) sell crafts and Maine foods.
Island Artisans (99 Main St., tel. 207/288–4214) is a crafts cooperative.
The Next Egg Gift Gallery (12 Mt. Desert St., tel. 207/288–9048) carries upscale, handcrafted baubles.

Sports and Outdoor Activities

Biking, Jogging,
Cross-Country
Skiing The network of carriage paths that wind through the woods and fields of Acadia National Park is ideal for biking and jogging when the ground is dry and for cross-country skiing in winter. Hulls Cove visitor center has a carriage-paths map.

Bikes for hire can be found at **Acadia Bike & Canoe** (48 Cottage St., Bar Harbor, tel. 207/288–9605); **Bar Harbor Bicycle Shop** (141 Cottage St., tel. 207/288–3886); and **Southwest Cycle** (Main St., Southwest Harbor, tel. 207/244–5856).

Boat Trips
Bar Harbor **Acadia Boat Tours & Charters** (West St., tel. 207/288–9505) embarks on 1½-hour lobster fishing trips in summer. **Acadian Whale Watcher** (Golden Anchor Pier, tel. 207/288–9794) runs 2½-hour whale-watching cruises in summer. *Natalie Todd* (Inn Pier, tel. 207/288–4585) offers weekend windjammer cruises from mid-May through mid-October.

Northeast Harbor **Blackjack** (Town Dock, tel. 207/276–5043 or 207/288–3056), a 33-foot Friendship sloop, makes four trips daily, May through October, Monday through Saturday. *Sunrise* (Sea St. Pier, tel. 207/276–5352) does lobster fishing tours in the summer months.

Camping The two campgrounds in Acadia National Park (tel. 207/288–3338)—**Blackwoods,** open year-round, and **Seawall,** open late May to late September—fill up quickly during the summer season. Off Mount Desert Island, but convenient to it, the campground at **Lamoine State Park** (tel. 207/667–4778) is open mid-May to mid-October; the 55-acre park has a great location on Frenchman Bay.

Canoeing and
Kayaking For canoe rentals and guided kayak tours, see **Acadia Bike & Canoe,** or **National Park Canoe Rentals** (Rte. 102, 2 mi west of Somesville, at the head of Long Pond, tel. 207/244–5854).

Hiking Acadia National Park maintains nearly 200 miles of foot and carriage paths, ranging from easy strolls along flatlands to rigorous climbs that involve ladders and handholds on rock faces. Among the more rewarding hikes are the Precipice Trail to Champlain Mountain, the Great Head Loop, the Gorham Mountain Trail, and the path around Eagle Lake. The National Park visitor center has a trail guide and map.

Sailing
Bar Harbor **Harbor Boat Rentals** (Harbor Pl., 1 West St., tel. 207/288–3757) has 13-foot and 17-foot Boston whalers and some sailboats.

Southwest Harbor **Manset Boat Rental** (Manset Boatyard, just south of Southwest Harbor, tel. 207/244–9233) rents sailboats.

Dining and Lodging

Bar Harbor has the greatest concentration of accommodations on Mount Desert Island. Much of this lodging has been converted from elaborate 19th-century summer cottages. A number of fine restaurants are also tucked away in these old homes and inns.

Bar Harbor
Dining
★

George's. Candles, flowers, and linens grace the tables in four small dining rooms in an old house. The menu shows a distinct Mediterranean influence in the lobster streudel wrapped in phyllo, and in the sautéed veal; fresh chargrilled salmon and swordfish stand on their own. Couples tend to linger in the romantic setting. Jazz piano may be heard nightly July 4–Labor Day. *7 Stephen's La., tel. 207/288–4505. Reservations advised. Dress: casual. AE, D, DC, MC, V. Closed late Oct.–mid-June. Dinner only. Moderate–Expensive.*

Jordan Pond House. Oversize popovers and tea are a warm tradition at this rustic restaurant in the park, where in fine weather you can sit on the terrace or the lawn and admire the views of Jordan Pond and the mountains. The dinner menu offers lobster stew, seafood thermidor, and fisherman's stew. *Park Loop Rd., tel. 207/276–3316. Reservations one day in advance advised in summer. Dress: casual. AE, D, MC, V. Closed late Oct.–late May. Moderate.*

★ **124 Cottage Street.** The four dining rooms of the cheerful, flower-filled restaurant have the feel of a country inn, and the back room has an extra treat—a sliding glass door to a small garden and woods. The fare is seafood and pasta dishes with an Oriental twist: Szechuan shrimp; pasta primavera with pea pods and broccoli; seafood pasta with mussels, shrimp, and scallops in tomato sauce; broiled swordfish, salmon, haddock. *124 Cottage St., tel. 207/288–4383. Reservations advised. Dress: casual. MC, V. Closed late Oct.–mid-June. Dinner only. Moderate.*

Lodging
Holbrook House. Built in 1876 as a boardinghouse with a wraparound porch for rocking and big shuttered windows to catch the breeze, the lemon-yellow Holbrook House sits right on Mount Desert Street, the main access route through Bar Harbor. In 1876 it was no doubt pleasant to listen to the horses clip-clop past, but today, the traffic noise can be annoying, especially from the porch. The Holbrook House offers a far more restrained (and more authentic) approach to Victorian interior design than the Cleftstone Manor (*see below*). The downstairs public rooms include a lovely, formal sitting room with bright, summery chintz on chairs and windows and a Duncan Phyfe sofa upholstered in white silk damask. A full breakfast is served on china and crystal in the sunny, glassed-in porch. The guest rooms are furnished with lovingly handled family pieces in the same refined taste as the public rooms. Room 6, on the second floor, has a corner location with four big windows, a four-poster bed, and oil paintings. Room 11, though smaller, is the quietest room, and has a snug, country feel with Laura Ashley fabrics. Right in town, Holbrook House is a short walk to the shops and restaurants of Bar Harbor. A stay at the Holbrook House is like a visit with your most proper (but by no means stuffy) relatives, the ones who inherited all the best furniture and have kept it in impeccable condition. *74 Mt. Desert St., Bar Harbor 04609, tel. 207/288–4970. 10 rooms with bath in inn, 2 rooms share 1 bath and living room in Lupine Cottage, 2 rooms share 1 bath and living room in Fern Cottage. Facilities: cable TV in library and cottages; croquet. Rates include full breakfast. MC, V. Closed mid-Oct.–May. Very Expensive.*

Cleftstone Manor. Attention, lovers of Victoriana! This inn was made in high Victorian heaven expressly for you. Ignore the fact that it is set amid sterile motels just off Route 3, the road along which traffic roars into Bar Harbor. Do not be put off by the unpromising, rambling, green-shuttered exterior. Inside, a deeply plush, mahogany and lace world of Victorian splendor awaits you. The parlor is cool and richly furnished with red velvet and brocade trimmed sofas with white doilies, grandfather and mantel clocks, and oil paintings hanging on powder-blue walls. In the imposingly formal dining room, Joseph Pulitzer's library table extends for seemingly miles beneath a crystal chandelier. Of the guest rooms, the prize chamber (especially for honeymooners) is the immense Romeo and Juliet, once a section of the ballroom, which now has a pillow-decked sofa; blue velvet Victorian chairs; a lace-canopy bed; and a massive, ornately carved Irish buffet that takes up most of one wall. *Rte. 3, Eden St., 04609, tel. 207/288-4951 or 800/962-9762. 14 rooms with bath, 2 suites. Facilities: 6 rooms with fireplaces. Rates include full breakfast. D, MC, V. Closed Nov.–Apr. Expensive–Very Expensive.*

Mira Monte. Built as a summer home in 1864, the Mira Monte bespeaks Victorian leisure, with columned verandas, latticed bay windows, and landscaped grounds for strolling and sunning; and the inn is set back far enough from the road to assure quiet and seclusion. The guest rooms have brass or four-poster beds, white wicker, hooked rugs, lace curtains, and oil paintings in gilt frames. The quieter, rear-facing rooms offer sunny garden views. Some rooms have porches, fireplaces, and separate entrances. *69 Mt. Desert St., 04609, tel. 207/288-4263 or 800/553-5109. 11 rooms with bath. AE, MC, V. Closed Nov.–Apr. Expensive–Very Expensive.*

Wonder View Motor Lodge. While the rooms are standard motel accommodations, with two double beds and nondescript furniture, this establishment is distinguished by its extensive grounds, the view of Frenchman Bay, and a location opposite the Bluenose ferry terminal. The woods muffle the sounds of traffic on Route 3. Pets are accepted, and the dining room has picture windows. *Rte. 3, Box 25, 04609, tel. 207/288-3358 or 800/427-3358. 80 rooms with bath. Facilities: dining room, outdoor pool. AE, MC, V. Closed late Oct.–mid-May. Inexpensive–Expensive.*

Hancock
Dining
★

Le Domaine. On a rural stretch of Route 1, 9 miles east of Ellsworth, a French chef prepares *lapin pruneaux* (rabbit in a rich brown sauce); sweetbreads with lemon and capers; and coquilles St. Jacques. The elegant but not intimidating dining room has polished wood floors, copper pots hanging from the mantel, and silver, crystal, and linen on the tables. *Rte. 1, tel. 207/422-3395 or 422-3916. Reservations advised. Dress: neat but casual. AE, D, MC, V. Dinner only. Closed Nov.–Apr. Expensive.*

Lodging
Le Domaine. The seven smallish rooms in the inn are done in French country style, with chintz and wicker, simple desks, and sofas near the windows. Four rooms have balconies or porches over the gardens. The 100-acre property offers paths for walking and badminton on the lawn. *Box 496, 04640, tel. 207/422-3395 or 207/422-3916. 7 rooms with bath. Facilities: restaurant. AE, D, MC, V. Closed Nov.–Apr. Rates are MAP. Very Expensive.*

Hulls Cove
Lodging
Inn at Canoe Point. Seclusion and privacy are bywords of this snug, 100-year-old Tudor-style house on the water at Hulls

Cove, 2 miles from Bar Harbor. The Master Suite, a large room with a fireplace, is a favorite for its size and the French doors opening onto a waterside deck. The inn's large living room has huge windows on the water, a fieldstone fireplace, and, just outside, a deck that hangs over the water. *Box 216, Rte. 3, 04609, tel. 207/288–9511. 3 rooms with bath, 2 suites. No credit cards. Very Expensive.*

Northeast Harbor
Dining

Asticou Inn. At night guests of the inn trade topsiders and polo shirts for jackets and ties to dine in the stately formal dining room, which is open to the public for a prix-fixe dinner by reservation only. A recent menu featured swordfish with orange mustard glaze; lobster; seared catfish; and chicken in a lemon cream and mushroom sauce. *Tel. 207/276–3344. Reservations required. Jacket and tie required. Closed mid-Sept.–mid-June. Expensive.*

Lodging

Asticou Inn. This grand turn-of-the-century inn at the head of exclusive Northeast Harbor serves a loyal clientele. Guest rooms in the main building have a country feel, with bright fabrics, white lace curtains, and white painted furniture. The more modern cottages scattered around the grounds afford greater privacy; among them, the decks and picture windows make the Topsider Cottages particularly attractive. A stay at the inn includes breakfast and dinner, but the cottages and the Victorian-style Cranberry Lodge across the street operate on a bed-and-breakfast policy from mid-May to mid-June and from mid-September to January 1. *Northeast Harbor 04662, tel. 207/276–3344. 27 rooms with bath, 23 suites, 6 cottages. Facilities: clay tennis court, heated pool. MC, V. Inn closed mid-Sept.–mid-June; cottages, lodge closed Jan.–Mar. Rates are MAP in summer. Very Expensive (lodge, Moderate–Expensive).*

Southwest Harbor
Dining

Claremont Hotel. The large, airy dining room of the inn, open to the public for dinner only, is awash in light streaming through the picture windows. The atmosphere is on the formal side, with crystal, silver, and china service. Rack of lamb, baked stuffed shrimp, coquilles St. Jacques, and tournedos au poivre are specialties. *Tel. 207/244–5036. Reservations required. Jacket required. No credit cards. Closed mid-Sept.–mid-June. Closed for lunch Sept.–June. Moderate.*

Lodging

Claremont Hotel. Built in 1884 and operated continuously as an inn, the Claremont calls up memories of long, leisurely vacations of days gone by. The yellow-clapboard structure commands a view of Somes Sound, croquet is played on the lawn, and cocktails are served at the boathouse from mid-July to the end of August. Guest rooms are bright, white, and quite plain; cottages and two guest houses on the grounds are homier and woodsier. Modified American Plan is in effect from mid-June to mid-September. *Box 137, 04679, tel. 207/244–5036. 22 rooms, 20 with bath; 3 suites, 12 cottages, 2 guest houses. Facilities: clay tennis court, croquet, bicycles, private dock and moorings. No credit cards. Hotel closed mid-Sept.–mid-June. Cottages closed Nov.–mid-May. Rates are MAP. Expensive–Very Expensive.*

The Arts

Music

Arcady Music Festival (tel. 207/288–3151) schedules concerts around Mount Desert Island from mid-July through August.

Bar Harbor Festival (59 Cottage St., Bar Harbor, tel. 207/288–5744; 120 W. 45th St., 7th floor, New York, NY 10036, tel. 212/222–1026) programs recitals, jazz, chamber music, and pops concerts by up-and-coming young professionals from mid-July to mid-August.

Domaine School (Hancock, tel. 207/422–6251) presents public concerts by faculty and students at Monteux Memorial Hall.

Theater **Acadia Repertory Company** (Masonic Hall, Rte. 102, Somesville, tel. 207/244–7260) mounts plays in July and August.

Nightlife

Acadia has little nighttime activity. The lounge at the **Moorings Restaurant** (Manset, tel. 207/244–7070), accessible by boat and car, is open until midnight from May through October, and the company is a lively boating crowd.

Western Lakes and Mountains

Less than 20 miles northwest of Portland and the coast, the lakes and mountains of western Maine begin their stretch north along the New Hampshire border to Québec. In winter this is ski country; in summer the woods and waters draw vacationers to recreation or seclusion in areas less densely populated than much of Maine's coast.

The Sebago–Long Lake region has antiques stores and lake cruises on a 42-mile waterway. Kezar Lake, tucked away in a fold of the White Mountains, has long been a hideaway of the wealthy. Bethel, in the Androscoggin River valley, is a classic New England town, its town common lined with historic homes. The far more rural Rangeley Lake area brings long stretches of pine, beech, spruce, and sky—and stylish inns and bed-and-breakfasts with easy access to golf, boating, fishing, and hiking.

Important Addresses and Numbers

Visitor Information **Bethel Area Chamber of Commerce** (Box 121, Bethel, 04217, tel. 207/824–2282).

Bridgton–Lakes Region Chamber of Commerce (Box 236, Bridgton, 04009, tel. 207/647–3472).

Rangeley Lakes Region Chamber of Commerce (Box 317, Rangeley, 04970, tel. 207/864–5571).

Emergencies **Bethel Area Health Center** (tel. 207/824–2193).

Getting Around the Western Lakes and Mountains

By Plane **Mountain Air Service** (Rangeley, tel. 207/864–5307) provides air access to remote areas.

By Car A car is essential to a tour of the western lakes and mountains. Of the variety of routes available, the itinerary that follows takes Route 302, Route 26, Route 2, Route 17, Route 4/16, and Route 142.

Guided Tours

Naples Flying Service (Naples Causeway, tel. 207/693–6591) offers sightseeing flights over the lakes in summer.

Exploring the Western Lakes and Mountains

Numbers in the margin correspond to points of interest on the Western Maine map.

❶ A tour of the lakes begins at **Sebago Lake,** west of Route 302, less than 20 miles northwest of Portland. At the north end of the lake, the **Songo Lock** (tel. 207/693–6231), which permits the passage of watercraft from Sebago Lake to Long Lake, is the one surviving lock of the Cumberland and Oxford Canal. Built of wood and masonry, the original lock dates from 1830 and was expanded in 1911; today it sees heavy traffic during the summer months.

The 1,300-acre **Sebago Lake State Park** on the north shore of Sebago Lake offers opportunities for swimming, picnicking, camping, boating, and fishing (salmon and togue). *Tel. 207/ 693–6613, June 20–Labor Day; 207/693–6231, other times.*

Route 302 continues north to Naples, where the Naples Causeway has rental craft for fishing or cruising on Long Lake, and rather drab Bridgton, near Highland Lake, which has antiques shops in and around the town.

The most scenic route to Bethel, 30 miles to the north, follows Route 302 west from Bridgton, across Moose Pond to Knight's Hill Road, turning north to Lovell and Route 5, which will take you on to Bethel. It's a drive that lets you admire the jagged crests of the White Mountains outlined against the sky to the west and the lush, rolling hills that alternate with brooding for-

❷ ests at roadside. At **Center Lovell** you can barely glimpse the secluded Kezar Lake to the west, the retreat of wealthy and very private people; Sabattus Mountain, which rises behind Center Lovell, has a public hiking trail and stupendous views of the Presidential range from the summit.

❸ **Bethel** is pure New England, a town with white-clapboard houses and white-steeple churches and a mountain vista at the end of every street. In the winter this is ski country, and Bethel serves the Sunday River area (*see* Chapter 2). A stroll of Bethel should begin at the **Moses Mason House and Museum,** a Federal-period home of 1813. On the town common, across from the sprawling Bethel Inn and Country Club, the Mason Museum has nine period rooms and a front hall and stairway wall decorated with murals by Rufus Porter. You can also pick up materials for a walking tour. *Broad St., tel. 207/824–2908. Admission: $2 adults, $1 children under 12. Open July–Labor Day, Tues.–Sun. 1–4; day after Labor Day–June, by appointment.*

The **Major Gideon Hastings House** nearby on Broad Street has a columned front portico typical of the Greek Revival style. Around the common, on Church Street, stands the severe white **West Parish Congregational Church** (1847), with its unadorned triangular pediment and steeple supported on open columns. Beyond the church is the campus of **Gould Academy,** a preparatory school chartered in 1835; the dominant style of the school buildings is Georgian, and the tall brick main campus

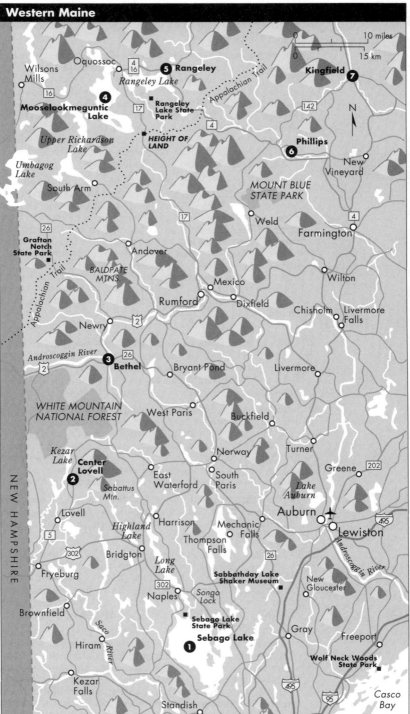

Western Maine

10 miles
15 km

Wilsons Mills

Oquossoc

⑤ Rangeley

Kingfield ⑦

Rangeley Lake

④ Mooselookmeguntic Lake

Rangeley Lake State Park

142

Upper Richardson Lake

HEIGHT OF LAND

Phillips ⑥

New Vineyard

Umbagog Lake

South Arm

MOUNT BLUE STATE PARK

Grafton Notch State Park

17

Weld

Farmington

BALDPATE MTNS.

Andover

Mexico

Wilton

Androscoggin River

Rumford

Dixfield

Chisholm

Livermore Falls

Newry

2

③ Bethel

Bryant Pond

Livermore

WHITE MOUNTAIN NATIONAL FOREST

West Paris

Buckfield

Kezar Lake

Center Lovell ②

East Waterford

Norway

South Paris

Turner

Greene

202

Sabattus Mtn.

Lake Auburn

N E W   H A M P S H I R E

Lovell

Highland Lake

Harrison

Mechanic Falls

Auburn

Lewiston

5

Bridgton

Thompson Falls

26

495

Fryeburg

302

Naples

Long Lake

Songo Lock

Sabbathday Lake Shaker Museum

New Gloucester

Saco River

Sebago Lake State Park

Brownfield

Sebago Lake ①

Gray

Freeport

Hiram

Wolf Neck Woods State Park

Kezar Falls

95

Standish

Casco Bay

Androscoggin River

building is surmounted by a white cupola. Main Street will take you from the common past the Town Hall-Cole Block, built in 1891, to the shops.

The routes north from Bethel to the Rangeley district are all scenic, particularly in the autumn when the maples are aflame. On Route 26 it's about 12 miles to **Grafton Notch State Park,** where you can hike to stunning gorges and waterfalls and into the Baldpate Mountains. En route to the park, in the town of Newry, you will cross "**Artist's Bridge,**" the most painted and photographed of Maine's eight covered bridges. Route 26 continues on to Errol, New Hampshire, where Route 16 will return you east around the north shore of Mooselookmeguntic Lake, through Oquossoc, and into Rangeley.

A more direct—if marginally less scenic—tour follows Route 2 north and east from Bethel to the twin towns of Rumford and Mexico, where Route 17 continues north to Oquossoc, about an hour's drive. When you've gone about 20 minutes beyond Rumford, the signs of civilization all but vanish and you pass through what seems like virgin territory; in fact, the lumber companies have long since tackled the virgin forests, and sporting camps and cottages are tucked away here and there. The high point of this route is **Height of Land,** about 30 miles north of Rumford, with its unforgettable views of range after range of mountains and the huge, island-studded blue mass of Mooselookmeguntic Lake directly below. Turnouts on both sides of the highway allow you to pull over for a long look.

❹ Route 4 ends at Haines Landing on **Mooselookmeguntic Lake,** 7 miles west of Rangeley. Here you can stand at 1,400 feet above sea level and face the same magnificent scenery you admired at 2,400 feet from Height of Land on Route 17. Boat and canoe rentals are available at Mooselookmeguntic House.

❺ **Rangeley,** north of Rangeley Lake on Route 4/16, has lured fisherfolk, hunters, and winter-sports enthusiasts for a century to its more than 40 lakes and ponds within a 20-mile radius and 450 square miles of woodlands. Rangeley makes only a mediocre first impression, for the town has a rough, wilderness feel to it, and its best parts—including the choice lodgings—are tucked away in the woods, around the lake, and along the golf course.

On the south shore of Rangeley Lake, **Rangeley Lake State Park** (tel. 207/289–3824) offers superb lakeside scenery, swimming, picnic tables, a boat ramp, showers, and camping sites set well apart in a spruce and fir grove.

❻ In **Phillips,** 14 miles southeast of Rangeley on Route 4, the Sandy River & Rangeley Lakes Railroad, a restored narrow-gauge railroad, has a mile of track through the woods, where you can board a century-old train drawn by a replica of the Sandy River No. 4 locomotive. *Tel. 207/639–3352. Admission: $3 adults, $1.50 children 6–12. Open May–Nov., 1st and 3rd Sun. each month, rides at 11, 1, and 3.*

❼ Just west of Phillips on Route 4, Route 142 takes you northeast to **Kingfield,** prime ski country in the heart of the western mountains. In the shadows of Mt. Abraham and Sugarloaf Mountain, Kingfield is a picture-postcard Maine town, complete with a general store, historic inns, and a white-clapboard church. The **Stanley Museum** houses a collection of original Stanley Steamer cars built by the Stanley twins, Kingfield's most famous natives. *School St., tel. 207/265–2729. Suggested donation: $2 adults, $1 children. Open July 4–Oct., Tues.–Sun. 1–4; Nov.–July 3, call for hours.*

Western Lakes and Mountains for Free

Bridgton Historical Society Museum, housed in a former fire station built in 1902, displays artifacts of the area's history and materials on the local narrow-gauge railroad. *Gibbs Ave., tel. 207/647–2765. Admission free. Open June–Aug., Mon.–Sat. 1–4.*

Naples Historical Society Museum includes a jailhouse, a bandstand, and slides of the Cumberland and Oxford Canal and the Sebago–Long Lake steamboats. *Village Green, Rte. 302, no phone. Admission free. Open July–Aug., Tues.–Fri. 10–4, Sat. 10–1.*

What to See and Do with Children

Songo River Queen II, a 92-foot stern-wheeler, takes passengers on hour-long cruises on Long Lake and longer voyages down the Songo River and through Songo Lock. *Rte. 302, Naples Causeway, tel. 207/693–6861. Admission: Songo River ride, $8 adults, $5 children; Long Lake cruise, $5 adults, $4 children. July–Labor Day, 5 trips daily; June and Sept., weekends.*

Off the Beaten Track

Sabbathday Lake Shaker Museum on Route 26, 20 miles north of Portland, is part of one of the oldest Shaker communities in the United States (established in the late 18th century) and the last one in Maine. Members continue to farm crops and herbs, and visitors are shown the meetinghouse of 1794—a paradigm of Shaker design—and the ministry shop with 14 rooms of Shaker furniture, folk art, tools, farm implements, and crafts of the 18th to early 20th centuries. On Sunday, the Shaker day of prayer, the community is closed to visitors. *Rte. 26, New Gloucester, tel. 207/926–4597. Admission: introductory tour, $4 adults, $2 children 6–12; extended tour, $5.50 adults, $2.75 children. Open Memorial Day–Columbus Day, Mon.–Sat. 10–4:30.*

Shopping

Antiques
Bridgton
Wales & Hamblen Antique Center (134 Main St., tel. 207/647–8344), the region's best-known antiques store, displays the goods of 30 dealers: quilts, jewelry, country furniture, wicker, and Depression glass.

Hanover
The Lyons' Den (Rte. 2, near Bethel, tel. 207/364–8634), a great barn of a place, carries glass, china, tools, prints, rugs, and some furniture.

Crafts
South Casco
Cry of the Loon Shop and Art Gallery (Rte. 302, tel. 207/655–5060) has crafts, gifts, gourmet foods, and a gallery upstairs.

Pottery
Bethel
Bonnema Potters (Lower Main St., Bethel, tel. 207/824–2821) features modern designs in plates, lamps, tiles, and vases.

Sports and Outdoor Activities

Biking **Sunday River Ski Resort** in Newry operates a mountain bike park (Sunday River Access Rd., tel. 207/824–3000) with lift-accessed trails.

Canoeing The Saco River (near Fryeburg) is a favorite route, with a gentle stretch from Swan's Falls to East Brownfield (19 miles) and an even gentler, scenic stretch from East Brownfield to Hiram (14 miles). Rangeley and Mooselookmeguntic lakes are good for scenic canoeing.

For canoe rentals, try **Canal Bridge Canoes** (Rte. 302, Fryeburg Village, tel. 207/935–2605), **Mooselookmeguntic House** (Haines Landing, Oquossoc, tel. 207/864–2470), **Rangeley Region Sport Shop** (Main St., Rangeley, tel. 207/864–5615), or **Saco River Canoe and Kayak** (Rte. 5, Fryeburg, tel. 207/935–2369).

Camping *See* National and State Parks and Forests, *below*. Maine Campground Owners Association (655 Main St., Lewiston 04240, tel. 207/782–5874) has a statewide listing of private campgrounds.

Hunting and Fishing Freshwater fishing for brook trout and salmon is at its best in May, June, and September, and the Rangeley area is especially popular with fly-fishermen. Nonresident freshwater anglers over the age of 12 must have a fishing license, which is available at many sporting-goods and hardware stores and at local town offices. The deep woods of the Rangeley area are popular with hunters. Game includes woodcock and partridge, deer and bear. The season for deer is usually the first three weeks of November; for game birds, usually October through November. State regulations are strictly enforced; licenses, available at town offices and many sporting-goods and hardware stores, are required of all hunters 10 years old or older. The **Department of Inland Fisheries and Wildlife** (284 State St., Augusta 04333, tel. 207/289–2043) can provide further information.

Guides Recommended guides in the Rangeley area include: **Clayton (Cy) Eastlack** (Mountain View Cottages, Oquossoc, tel. 207/864–3416), **Grey Ghost Guide Service** (Box 24, Oquossoc, tel. 207/864–5314), and **Rangeley Region Guide Service** (Box 19HF, Rangeley, tel. 207/864–5761).

Snowmobiling The snowmobile is a popular mode of transportation in the Rangeley area during the winter months, with trails linking lakes and towns to wilderness camps. **Maine Snowmobile Association** (Box 77, Augusta 04330) has information on Maine's nearly 8,000-mile Interconnecting Trail System.

Water Sports Sebago, Long, Rangeley, and Mooselookmeguntic lakes are the most popular areas for sailing and motorboating. For rentals, try **Grant's Kennebago Camps** (Kennebago Lake, tel. 207/864–3608), **Long Lake Marina** (Rte. 302, Naples, tel. 207/693–3159), **Mountain View Cottages** (Rte. 17, Oquossoc, tel. 207/864–3416), **Naples Marina** (Naples Causeway, Naples, tel. 207/693–6254), or **Sunny Breeze Sports** (Rte. 302, Naples, tel. 207/693–3867).

National and State Parks and Forests

Grafton Notch State Park (tel. 207/824–2912), on Route 26, 14 miles north of Bethel on the New Hampshire border, offers unsurpassed mountain scenery, picnic areas, caves to explore, swimming holes, and camping. You can take an easy nature walk to Mother Walker Falls or Moose Cave and see the spectacular Screw Auger Falls; or you can hike to the summit of Old Speck Mountain, the state's third-highest peak. If you have the stamina and the equipment, you can pick up the Appalachian Trail here, hike over Saddleback Mountain, and continue on to Katahdin. The **Maine Appalachian Club** (Box 283, Augusta 04330) publishes a map and trail guide.

Rangeley Lake State Park (tel. 207/289–3824) has 50 campsites on the south shore of the lake (*see* Exploring the Western Lakes and Mountains, *above*).

Sebago Lake State Park (tel. 207/693–6613, June 20–Labor Day; 207/693–6231, other times) has 250 campsites on the lake's north shore (*see* Exploring the Western Lakes and Mountains, *above*).

White Mountain National Forest straddles New Hampshire and Maine. Although the highest peaks are on the New Hampshire side, the Maine section includes lots of magnificent rugged terrain, camping and picnic areas, and hiking opportunities from hour-long nature loops to a 5½-hour scramble up Speckled Mountain—with open vistas at the summit. *Evans Notch Ranger District, FRD 2, Box 2270, Bethel 04217, tel. 207/824–2134. Open weekdays 8–4:30.*

Dining and Lodging

Bethel has the largest concentration of inns and bed-and-breakfasts, and its Chamber of Commerce (tel. 207/824–3585) has a central lodging reservations service.

Bethel Dining ★ **Four Seasons Inn.** The three small dining rooms of the region's front-running gourmet restaurant reveal tables draped with linens that brush the hardwood floors, and prim bouquets on the tables. The dinner menu is classic French: escargot, caviar, sautéed mushrooms, or onion soup to start; tournedos, beef Wellington, chateaubriand, veal Oscar, and bouillabaisse for entrées. *63 Upper Main St., tel. 207/824–2755. Reservations advised. Dress: neat but casual. AE, MC, V. Closed Mon. Dinner and Sun. brunch only. Expensive.*

Mother's Restaurant. This gingerbread house furnished with wood stoves and bookshelves is a cozy place to enjoy the likes of veal with ginger and lime; broiled trout; and a variety of pasta offerings. In summer one can dine on the porch. *Upper Main St., tel. 207/824–2589. Reservations accepted. Dress: casual. MC, V. Closed Wed. Moderate.*

Lodging **Bethel Inn and Country Club.** Bethel's grandest accommodation, once a rambling country inn on the town common, is now a full-service resort offering golf, a health club, and conference facilities. Guest rooms in the main inn, sparsely furnished with Colonial reproductions and George Washington bedspreads, are the most desirable, if not very large; the choice rooms have fireplaces and face the mountains over the golf course. The 40 two-bedroom condos on the fairway are clean and a bit sterile, but all units face the mountains. The health club facility has Nautilus, two saunas, a games room with billiards, a heated outdoor pool, and a Jacuzzi. The formal dining room, done in lemon yellow with pewter accents, serves elaborate dinners of roast duck, prime rib, lobster, scampi, and swordfish. *Village Common, Box 49, 04217, tel. 207/824–2175 or 800/654–0125, fax 207/824–2233. 57 rooms with bath, 40 condo units. Facilities: restaurant, tavern, all-weather tennis court, 18-hole golf course, health club, conference center. AE, D, DC, MC, V. Rates are MAP or EP. Moderate–Very Expensive.*

The Hammons House. A sunny two-story conservatory with wicker furniture and exotic plants is the focal point of this charming, friendly bed-and-breakfast situated in an historic home on the town common. The rooms are furnished with antique spool beds and pine chests. A large sitting room downstairs has a crackling fire in the winter and a bookshelf containing, among other things, a well-worn collection of Nancy Drew and Hardy Boy mysteries. *Broad St., tel. 207/824–3170. 2 rooms without bath, 1 suite. No smoking or pets. MC, V. Moderate.*

Sudbury Inn. The classic white-clapboard inn on Main Street offers good value, basic comfort, and a convenient location. Guest rooms sport country antiques, white bedspreads, and window shades. On weekends, second-floor rooms get the drumbeats of the bands performing in the basement pub; third-floor rooms are quieter and more spacious. The parlor's fireplace, brick-red furniture, and pressed-tin ceiling are warm and welcoming. The dining room (upholstered booths and square wood tables) has a country charm; the dinner menu runs to prime rib, sirloin au poivre, broiled haddock, and lasagna. The pub, with a large-screen TV, is a popular hangout. *Box 369, 04217, tel. 207/824–2174 or 800/395–7837. 15 rooms with bath, 5 suites, 2 apartments. Facilities: restaurant, pub. MC, V. Inexpensive–Moderate.*

Bridgton
Dining

Black Horse Tavern. The 200-year-old gray cape contains a country-style restaurant with a shiny bar, horse blankets and stirrups for decor, and an extensive menu of Mexican and Cajun specialties. A predominantly young crowd dines here on pan-blackened swordfish or sirloin; scallop pie; and ribs. Starters include nachos, buffalo wings, and chicken and smoked sausage gumbo. *8 Portland St., tel. 207/647–5300. No reservations. Dress: casual. MC, V. Moderate.*

Lodging

Noble House. Set amid white pines on a hill on a quiet residential street overlooking Highland Lake and the White Mountains, the stately bed-and-breakfast with the wide porch dates from the turn of the century. The parlor is dominated by a grand piano and fireplace; in the dining room beyond, hearty breakfasts (fruit, eggs, blueberry pancakes, waffles, muffins) are served family-style on china and linen. Guest rooms are small and a bit spartan in their furnishings. The honeymoon suite, a single large room, has a lake view, a whirlpool bath, and white wicker furniture. *Box 180, 04009, tel. 207/647–3733. 9 rooms, 6 with bath; 2 suites. Facilities: croquet, canoe, pedal boat, dock, swimming float. AE, MC, V. Closed mid-Oct.–mid-June. Moderate–Very Expensive.*

Center Lovell
Lodging

Westways. Built in the 1920s as a corporate retreat for the president and executives of the Diamond Match Company, Westways on Kezar Lake was opened to the public as a sumptuous, secluded hotel in 1975. A stay here today is like a visit with relatives everyone hopes for—rich, discreet, and very generous. Kezar Lake, the secret of a small set of exclusive summer people, brims at the back door of the gray-shingled main lodge

(10 privately owned cottages, rented by the week through the inn, are tucked away on the densely wooded grounds). The rustic splendor continues inside in a palatial living room with massive stone fireplace, wood floors, and overstuffed easy chairs. The inn is suffused with a dim, silvery light reflected off the lake and filtered through the surrounding pines. It is restful in the height of summer, though it can be a touch somber for those who prefer bright sunshine. The Horses Room, a large, masculine room decorated with fox-hunt prints and maple furniture, has the best lake view. The Maple Room, in the southwest corner, is another choice room, with Italian Renaissance prints, floral bedspreads, and water views from all windows. The East Wing rooms, once the servants' quarters, are smaller (but by no means cramped), more spartan in their furniture, and less expensive. The dining room (open to the public for dinner by reservation) is a glassed-in porch facing the lake, where hearty meals are served on china and linen. *Center Lovell 04016, tel. 207/928–2663. 7 rooms, 3 with bath; 10 cottages with 3, 4, or 7 bedrooms. Facilities: clay tennis court; lake swimming and boating; 2 canoes; recreation hall with bowling, ping-pong, billiards; softball field; fives court. Rates include Continental breakfast. No pets. AE, MC, V. Closed Nov. and Mar.–Apr. Expensive–Very Expensive.*

Kingfield
Lodging

The Inn on Winter's Hill. Designed in 1895 by the Stanley brothers (of Stanley Steam Engine fame), this Georgian Revival mansion was the first home in Maine to have central heating. Today it's an inn with a restaurant renowned for rich Sunday brunches and seven-course traditional New England dinners, including stuffed pork tenderloin, beef Wellington, and poached pears. The mansion's four rooms are eclectically furnished, with pressed tin ceilings and picture windows overlooking an apple orchard and the mountains beyond; the renovated barn's 16 rooms are simply and brightly furnished. *RR 1, Box 1272, tel. 207/265–5421 or 800/233–9687. 20 rooms with bath. Facilities: tennis court, pool, outdoor hot tub, cross-country skiing, ice skating. AE, D, DC, MC, V. Expensive–Very Expensive.*

Naples
Dining

Epicurean Inn. The rambling pink Victorian building on the edge of town, originally a stagecoach stop, serves classic French and new American cuisine in its small dining rooms done in muted colors, with wood floors and paisley drapes. Entrées can include cranberry-ginger duck, shrimp curry, tournedos with shrimp, and coho salmon. *Rte. 302, tel. 207/693–3839. Reservations advised. Dress: neat but casual. AE, D, DC, MC, V. No lunch. Closed Mon.; closed Tues. Sept.–June. Expensive.*

Lodging

Augustus Bove House. Built as the Hotel Naples in 1850, the brick bed-and-breakfast at the crossroads of Routes 302 and 114 looks as though it was last renovated about a century ago. Nothing matches; the color schemes run riot on rugs, bedspreads, and wallpaper; yet you get good value—king-size beds in some rooms, lake views from the front rooms, full breakfast, and a location convenient to water activities. *RR 1, Box 501, 04055, tel. 207/693–6365. 7 rooms, 3 with bath. Facilities: rental boat. D, MC, V. Inexpensive–Moderate.*

Oquossoc
Dining

Oquossoc House. Stuffed bears and bobcats keep you company as you dine on lobster, prime rib, filet mignon, or pork chops. The lunch menu promises chili, fish chowder, and lobster roll.

Junction Rtes. 17 and 4, tel. 207/864-3881. Reservations required on summer weekends. Dress: casual. Closed Nov.-mid-May. Inexpensive-Moderate.

Rangeley
Lodging

Country Club Inn. This retreat, built in the 1920s on the Mingo Springs Golf Course, enjoys a secluded hilltop location and sweeping lake and mountain views. The inn's baronial living room has a cathedral ceiling, a fieldstone fireplace at each end, and game trophies. Guest rooms downstairs in the main building and in the motel-style wing added in the 1950s are cheerfully if minimally decorated with wood paneling or bright wallpaper. The dining room—open to nonguests by reservation only—is a glassed-in porch where the linen-draped tables are set well apart and the menu features roast duck with cherry sauce and filet mignon. *Box 680, Mingo Loop Rd., 04970, tel. 207/864-3831. 19 rooms with bath. Facilities: restaurant, outdoor pool, lounge, public golf course next door. Charge for pets. AE, MC, V. Closed Apr.-mid-May, mid-Oct.-Dec. 25. Rates are MAP. Expensive.*

Hunter Cove on Rangeley Lake. These lakeside cabins, which sleep two to six people, offer all the comforts of home in a rustic setting. The interiors are unfinished knotty pine and include fully furnished kitchens, screened porches, full baths, and comfortable, if plain, living rooms. Cabin No. 1 has a fieldstone fireplace and all others have wood-burning stoves for backup winter heat. Cabins No. 5 and No. 8 have hot tubs. Summer guests can take advantage of a sand swimming beach, boat rentals, and a nearby golf course. *Mingo Loop Rd., tel. 207/864-3383. 8 cabins with bath. Facilities: some cabins have hot tubs. Charge for pets. AE. Moderate-Very Expensive.*

Waterford
Lodging

The Waterford Inne. This gold-painted, curry-trimmed house on a hilltop provides a good home base for trips to local lakes, ski trails, and antiques shops. The bedrooms, each furnished on a different theme, have lots of nooks and crannies. Nicest are the Nantucket Room, with whale wallpaper and a harpoon, and the Chesapeake Room, with private porch and fireplace. A converted wood shed has five additional rooms, and though they have slightly less character than the inn rooms, four of them have the compensation of sunny decks. *Box 149, 04088, tel. 207/583-4037. 9 rooms, 6 with bath; 1 suite. Facilities: TV in common room, apple picking in orchard, antiques shop in barn, cross-country ski trails, ice-skating pond, badminton. Charge for pets. AE. Moderate-Expensive.*

The Arts

Rangeley Friends of the Arts (Box 333, Rangeley, tel. 207/864-5364) sponsors musical theater, fiddlers' contests, rock and jazz, pipers, and other summer fare, mostly at Lakeside Park.

Sebago-Long Lake Region Chamber Music Festival (Bridgton Academy Chapel, North Bridgton, tel. 207/627-4939) schedules concerts from mid-July to mid-August.

The North Woods

Maine's north woods, a vast area of the north central section of the state, is best experienced by canoe or raft, hiking trail, or on a fishing or hunting trip. The driving tour below takes in the three great theaters for these activities—Moosehead Lake, Baxter State Park, and the Allagash Wilderness Waterway—as well as the summer resort town of Greenville, dramatically situated Rockwood, and the no-frills outposts that connect them.

Important Addresses and Numbers

Visitor Information
Baxter State Park Authority (64 Balsam Dr., Millinocket 04462, tel. 207/723–5140).

Millinocket Chamber of Commerce (Box 5, Millinocket 04462, tel. 207/723–4443).

Moosehead Lake Region Chamber of Commerce (Box 581MI, Greenville 04441, tel. 207/695–2702).

North Maine Woods (Box 421, Ashland 04732, tel. 207/435–6213), a private organization, publishes maps, canoeing guides, and lists of outfitters, camps, and campsites.

Emergencies
Police (Greenville, tel. 207/695–3835, 207/564–3304, or 800/432–7372; Millinocket, tel. 207/723–9731).

Getting Around the North Woods

By Plane
Charter flights, usually by seaplane, from the Bangor area to smaller towns and remote lake and forest areas can be arranged with flying services, which will transport you and your gear and help you find a guide: **Currier's Flying Service** (Greenville Jct., tel. 207/695–2778), **Folsom's Air Service** (Greenville, tel. 207/695–2821), **Jack's Air Service** (Greenville, tel. 207/695–3020), and **Scotty's Flying Service** (Patten, tel. 207/528–2528).

By Car
A car is essential to negotiating this vast region but may not be useful to someone spending a vacation entirely at a wilderness camp. While public roads are scarce in the north country, lumber companies maintain private roads that are often open to the public (sometimes by permit only). When driving on a logging road, always give lumber company trucks the right of way. Be aware that loggers often take the middle of the road and will neither move over nor slow down for you.

Exploring the North Woods

Moosehead Lake, Maine's largest, offers more in the way of rustic camps, restaurants, guides, and outfitters than any other northern locale. Its 420 miles of shorefront, three quarters of which is owned by paper manufacturers, is virtually uninhabited.

Rockwood, on the lake's western shore, is a good starting point for a wilderness trip or a family vacation on the lake. While not offering much in the way of amenities, Rockwood has the most striking location of any town on Moosehead: The dark mass of **Mt. Kineo,** a sheer cliff that rises 1,860 feet out of the lake, looms just across the narrows (you get an excellent view just north of town on Route 6/15). Once a thriving summer resort, the original Mount Kineo Hotel (built in 1830 and torn down in the 1940s) was accessed primarily by steamship. An effort to renovate the remaining buildings in the early 1990s failed. Kineo makes a pleasant day trip from Rockwood: Rent a boat or take the shuttle operated by **Rockwood Cottages** (tel. 207/534–7725) and hike one of the trails to the summit for a picnic lunch and panoramic views of the region.

From Rockwood, follow Route 6/15 south, with Moosehead Lake on your left. After about 10 miles you'll come to a bridge with a dam to the left; this is the **East Outlet of the Kennebec River,** a popular class II and III whitewater run for canoeists and whitewater rafters that ends at the Harris Station Dam at Indian Pond, headwaters of the Kennebec.

Farther south on Route 6/15, **Greenville,** the largest town on the lake, has a smattering of shops, restaurants, and hotels. Turn left at the "T" intersection in town, following signs for Lily Bay State Park and Millinocket (the road is called both Lily Bay Road and Greenville Road). On your left is the **Moosehead Marine Museum** (tel. 207/695–2716), with exhibits on the local logging industry and the steamship era on Moosehead Lake, plus photographs of the Mount Kineo Hotel. The museum also runs cruises on the restored, 110-foot SS *Katahdin* (fondly called the *Kate*), a steamer (now diesel) built in 1914 that carried passengers to Kineo until 1942. It's a good idea to get a full tank of gas before leaving town, as it's almost 90 nearly deserted miles to Millinocket, some of it on dirt roads (they're well maintained, though).

Eight miles northeast of Greenville is **Lily Bay State Park** (tel. 207/695–2700), with a 93-site campground, swimming beach, and two boat-launching ramps.

Lily Bay Road continues northeast to the outpost of **Kokadjo** on First Roach Pond, population "not many," where one can have a snack or a meal at the **Kokadjo Store** (tel. 207/695–2904). Kokadjo is easily recognizable by the sign, "Keep Maine Green. This is God's country. Why set it on fire and make it look like hell?"

As you leave town, bear left at the fork in the road and follow signs to Baxter State Park. Fifteen miles along this road (now a dirt road) brings you to the Bowater/Great Northern Paper Company checkpoint, where June–November you'll need to sign in and pay a user fee ($8 per car for nonresidents; $4 per car for Maine residents to travel the next 10 miles of this road. Now you enter the working forest; you're likely to encounter logging trucks (yield right of way), logging equipment, and work in progress. At the bottom of the hill after the checkpoint, look to your right—there's a good chance you'll spot a moose in this boggy area.

At the end of the logging road on your left sits **Chesuncook Lake,** with **Chesuncook Village** at its far end, accessible only by boat or seaplane in summer. This tiny wilderness settlement has a church (open in summer), an inn, a few houses, a small store, and a spectacularly remote setting (it's home to two sporting camps).

Next to Chesuncook is Ripogenus Lake. Bear left at the sign for Pray's Cottages to reach **Ripogenus Dam** and the granite-walled gorge, the jumping-off point for the famous 12-mile West Branch of the Penobscot whitewater rafting trip and the most popular jumping-off point for Allagash trips. The **Allagash Wilderness Waterway** is a 92-mile corridor of lakes and rivers that cuts across 170,000 acres of wilderness, beginning at the northwest corner of Baxter and running north to the town of Allagash, 10 miles from the Canadian border. The river drops more than 70 feet per mile through these sections, giving rafters a hold-on-for-your-life ride.

The best spot to watch the rafters is from Pray's Big Eddy Wilderness Campsite, overlooking the rock-choked **Crib Works rapid**; be careful not to get too close to the edge. To get here, return to the main road, continue northeast, and head left on Telos Road; the campsite is about 10 yards after the bridge.

Take the main road (here called the Golden Road for the amount of money it took the Great Northern Paper Company to build it) southeast toward Millinocket. The road soon becomes paved. After you pass over the one-lane Abol Bridge and pass through the Bowater/Great Northern Paper Company checkpoint, bear left to reach Togue Pond Gatehouse, the southern entrance to **Baxter State Park** (tel. 207/723–5140). A gift from Governor Percival Baxter, the park is the jewel in the crown of northern Maine, a 201,018-acre wilderness area that surrounds **Katahdin**, Maine's highest mountain (5,267 feet at Baxter Peak) and the terminus of the Appalachian Trail. A 50-mile road makes a semicircle around the western side of the park; maximum speed is 20 miles per hour.

From the Togue Pond Gatehouse it's 24 miles to **Millinocket**, home to the **Bowater/Great Northern Paper Company mill**, which produces more than 800,000 tons of paper annually, and the **Ambejejus Boom House**, listed on the National Register of Historic Places, displays log drive memorabilia and artifacts. *Accessible by watercraft. Ambajejus Lake, Millinocket, no tel.*

Off the Beaten Track

For a worthwhile day trip from Millinocket, take Route 11 west to a trailhead just north of Brownville Junction. Follow the trail to **Katahdin Iron Works,** the site of a once-flourishing mining town, which employed nearly 200 workers in the mid-1800s; a deteriorated kiln and stone furnace is all that remains. The trail continues into **Gulf Hagas,** the Grand Canyon of the east, with natural chasms, cliffs, a 2.5-mile gorge, waterfalls, pools, and natural rock formations.

Lumberman's Museum. This museum comprises 10 buildings filled with exhibits depicting the history of logging, including models, dioramas, and equipment. *Shin Pond Rd., Patten, tel. 207/528–2650. Open Memorial Day–mid-Sept., Tues.–Sat. 9–4, Sun. 11–4. Admission: $2.50 adults, $1 children 6–12, under 6 free.*

Shopping

Crafts **The Corner Shop** (Rte. 6/15, tel. 207/695–2142) has a selection
Greenville of books, gifts, and crafts.
Currier's on Moosehead Gift Shop (Next to Currier's Flying Service, Greenville Jct., tel 207/695–2921) has wood carvings and other hand-crafted items.

Pottery *Greenville*	**Sunblower Pottery** (Rte. 6/15, tel. 207/695–2870) offers pottery and local art.
Sporting Goods *Greenville*	**Indian Hills Trading Post** (Rte. G/15, tel. 207/695–2104) stocks just about anything you might possibly need for a north woods vacation, including sporting and camping equipment, canoes, casual clothing, shoes, hunting and fishing licenses; there's even an adjacent grocery store.

Sports and Outdoor Activities

Boating	**Mt. Kineo Cabins** (Rte. 6/15 Rockwood, tel. 207/534–7744) rents boats and canoes on Moosehead Lake for the trip to Kineo.
Moosehead Lake *Cruises*	The **Moosehead Marine Museum** (tel. 207/695–2716) offers two 1/2-hour, six-hour, and full-day trips on Moosehead Lake aboard the *Katahdin*, a 1914 steamship (now diesel).
	Jolly Roger's Moosehead Cruises (tel. 207/534–8827 or 534–8817) has scheduled scenic cruises aboard the 48-foot *Socatean* from Rockwood. Charters are also available.
Camping	Reservations for state park campsites can be made from January until August 15 through the **Bureau of Parks and Recreation** (tel. 207/287–3824 or 800/332–1501 in ME). Make reservations as far in advance as possible (at least 14 days in advance), because sites go quickly. The camping season in Baxter State Park is mid-May to mid-October, and it's important that you reserve in advance by mail when you plan to camp inside the park; write to Baxter State Park Authority, 64 Balsam Dr., Millinocket 04462. Camping is permitted only in authorized locations, and when campgrounds are full, you will be turned away. The state maintains primitive backcountry sites that are available without charge on a first-come, first-served basis.
Camping and Fire *Permits*	Camping and fire permits may be required for areas outside of state parks. The **Bureau of Parks and Recreation** (State House Sta. 22, Augusta 04333, tel. 207/289–3821) will tell you if you need a camping permit and where to obtain one; the **Bureau of Forestry, Department of Conservation** (State House Sta. 22, Augusta 04333, tel. 207/287–2791) will direct you to the nearest ranger station, where you can get a fire permit.
	North Maine Woods (Box 421, Ashland 04732, tel. 207/435–6213) maintains many wilderness campsites on commercial forest land; early reservations are recommended.
	Maine Publicity Bureau (Box 2300, Hallowell 04347, tel. 207/582–9300) publishes a listing of private campsites and cottage rentals.
Canoeing	The Allagash rapids are ranked classes I and II (very easy and easy), but that doesn't mean the river is a piece of cake; river conditions vary greatly with the depth and volume of water, and even a class I rapid can hang your canoe up on a rock, capsize you, or spin you around in the wink of an eye. On the lakes, strong winds can halt your progress for days. The Allagash should not be undertaken lightly or without advance planning; the complete course requires from seven to 10 days. The best bet for a novice is to go with a guide; a good outfitter will help you plan your route and provide your craft and transportation. The Mount Everest of Maine canoe trips is the 110-mile route

on the St. John River from Baker Lake to Allagash Village, with a swift current all the way and two stretches of class III rapids. Bureau of Parks and Recreation, Department of Conservation (State House Station 22, Augusta 04333, tel. 207/ 289–3821) provides information on canoeing and camping in the Allagash area.

Those with their own canoe who want to go it alone can take the Telos Road north from Ripogenus Dam, putting in at Chamberlain Bridge at the southern tip of Chamberlain Lake, or at Allagash Lake, Churchill Dam, or Umsaskis Bridge.

One popular and easy route follows the Upper West Branch of the Penobscot River from Lobster Lake (just east of Moosehead Lake) to Chesuncook Lake. From Chesuncook Village you can paddle to Ripogenus Dam in a day.

The Aroostook River from Little Munsungan Lake to Fort Fairfield (100 miles) is best run in late spring. More challenging routes include the Passadumkeag River from Grand Falls to Passadumkeag (25 miles with class I–III rapids); the East Branch of the Penobscot River from Matagamon Wilderness Campground to Grindstone (38 miles with class I–III rapids); and the West Branch of the Pleasant River from Katahdin Iron Works to Brownville Junction (10 miles with class II–III rapids).

Outfitters   Most canoe rental operations will arrange transportation, help you plan your route, and provide a guide when you need one. Transport to wilderness lakes can be arranged through the flying services listed above (*see* Getting Around the North Woods by Plane, *above*).

Allagash Canoe Trips (Greenville, tel. 207/695–3668) offers guided trips on the Allagash, Penobscot, and St. John rivers.

Allagash Sporting Camp (Allagash, tel. 207/398–3555) rents canoes and camping equipment and provides guides.

Allagash Wilderness Outfitters/Frost Pond Camps (Greenville, tel. 207/695–2821 or 207/723–6622 in winter) provides equipment and guides for trips on the Allagash.

North Country Outfitters (Rockwood, tel. 207/534–2242) rents equipment and sponsors guided trips on the Allagash and Penobscot rivers.

Willard Jalbert Camps (115 W. Main St., Fort Kent 04743, tel. 207/834–3448) has been sponsoring guided Allagash trips since the late 1800s.

Fishing   Salmon, trout, and togue lure thousands of fisherfolk to the region from ice-out in early May through September, and the hardiest return in winter for the ice-fishing.

Licenses   Licenses, required of all freshwater fishermen over the age of 12, may be purchased at many sporting-goods and hardware stores and outfitters.

Guides   Guides are available through most wilderness camps, sporting goods stores, and canoe outfitters. For assistance in finding a guide, contact **Maine Professional Guides Association** (Box 159, Orono, tel. 207/866–0305) or **North Maine Woods** (*see* Camping, *above*).

A few well-established guides are **Gilpatrick's Guide Service** (Box 461, Skowhegan 04976, tel. 207/453–6959), **Maine Guide Fly Shop and Guide Service** (Box 1202, Main St., Greenville 04441, tel. 207/695–2266), **Professional Guide Service** (Box 346, Sheridan 04775, tel. 207/435–8044), and **Taiga Outfitters** (RFD 1, Box 147–8, Ashland 04732, tel. 207/435–6851).

Hiking **Katahdin,** in Baxter State Park, draws thousands of hikers every year for the daylong climb to the summit and the stunning views of woods, mountains, and lakes from the hair-raising Knife Edge Trail along its ridge. Roaring Brook Campground, which you can drive to in the park, gives direct access to the quickest way up Katahdin. Katahdin Stream and Nesowdnehunk. Field campgrounds, both reached by the park's Perimeter Road, put you on the west side of Katahdin.

Because the crowds at Katahdin can be formidable on clear summer days, those who seek a greater solitude might choose to tackle instead one of the 45 other mountains in the park, all accessible from a 150-mile trail network. South Turner can be climbed in a morning (if you're fit), and it affords a great view of Katahdin across the valley. On the way you'll pass Sandy Stream Pond, where moose are to be seen at dusk. The Owl, the Brothers, and Doubletop Mountain are good day hikes.

Hunting Hunters penetrate the woods, marshes, hillsides, and rivers of the north woods in November and early December in pursuit of deer, bear, pheasant, partridge, and moose (limited by lottery). The season for each animal is different, so you must be certain of the regulations—which are strictly enforced. **Maine's Department of Inland Fisheries and Wildlife** (284 State St., Augusta 04333, tel. 800/322–1333) can provide information about hunting and fishing regulations.

Licenses Licenses, available at town offices and sporting-goods and hardware stores, are required of all hunters over the age of nine. Applicants for an adult firearms hunting license must show proof of having previously held an adult license to hunt with firearms or having successfully completed an approved hunter safety course.

Guides *See* Guides in Fishing, *above.*

Rafting The Kennebec, Dead, and West Branch of the Penobscot River offer thrilling white-water rafting (guides are strongly recommended for these trips). These rivers are dam-controlled also, so trips run rain or shine daily from May through October (day trips and multi-day trips are offered). Most guided raft trips on the Kennebec and Dead rivers leave from The Forks, southwest of Moosehead Lake, on Route 201; Penobscot River trips leave from either Greenville or Millinocket. Many rafting outfitters offer resort facilities in their base town.

Outfitters The following outfitters lead trips down the West Branch of the Penobscot, Kennebec, and Dead rivers: **Crab Apple Whitewater** (Crab Apple Acres Inn, The Forks 04985, tel. 207/663–2218), **Eastern River Expeditions** (Box 1173, Greenville 04441, tel. 207/695–2411 or 800/634–7238), **Maine Whitewater** (Suite 454, Bingham 04920, tel. 207/622–2260, Oct.–Apr.; 207/672–4814, May–Sept.), **Northern Outdoors** (Box 100, The Forks 04985, tel. 207/663–4466), **Voyagers Whitewater** (Rte. 201, The Forks 04985, tel. 207/663–4423), and **Unicorn Expeditions** (Box T, Brunswick 04011, tel. 800/UNICORN).

Dining and Lodging

Greenville and Rockwood offer the largest selection of restaurants and accommodations in the region. Casual dress is the rule at dinner.

Greenville   **Greenville Inn.** Two dining rooms overlook Moosehead Lake. A
Dining   third, with ornate cherry and mahogany paneling and ladderback chairs, has a subdued, gentlemanly air. The Continental menu, revised daily, reflects the owners' Austrian background: shrimp with mustard dill sauce; fresh salmon marinated in olive oil and basil; veal cutlet with mushroom cream sauce. Popovers accompany the meal. *Norris St., tel. 207/695–2206. Reservations advised. D, MC, V. Closed Apr. Dinner only. Moderate–Expensive.*

Kelly's Landing. This casual, family-oriented restaurant in a large log cabin perched on a hill above Moosehead Lake has both indoor and outdoor seating, and excellent views. The fare includes sandwiches, burgers, spaghetti, and lasagna. *Rte. 6/15, Greenville Jct., tel. 207/695–4438. Reservations accepted. MC, V. Inexpensive.*

Lodging   **Greenville Inn.** A rambling gray-and-white structure, built a century ago as the retreat of a wealthy lumbering family, the inn stands on a rise over Moosehead Lake, a block from town. Indoors the cherry and mahogany paneling, Oriental rugs, and leaded glass create an aura of masculine ease. Two of the sparsely furnished, sunny bedrooms have fireplaces; two have lake views; and two clapboard cottages were built in the 1960s. *Norris St., 04441, tel. 207/695–2206. 6 rooms, 4 with bath; 1 suite; 2 cottages. D, MC, V. Moderate.*

Wilson's on Moosehead Lake. Wilson's claims to be the oldest continuously operated sporting camp on Moosehead Lake. The log cabins, situated at the headwaters of the Kennebec River, halfway between Greenville and Rockwood, cater to anglers, hunters, and families in summer. Cabins have screened porches and two to five bedrooms, and kitchens are fully equipped. There's a one-week minimum stay, mid-June to Labor Day; guide service is available; leashed pets are accepted. *Greenville Jct. 04442, tel. 207/695–2549. 15 cottages with bath. Facilities: private beach, dock, barbecue. MC, V. Inexpensive–Moderate.*

Chalet Moosehead. Just 50 yards off Route 6/15, the efficiencies, motel room, and cottages are right on Moosehead Lake. The attractive grounds lead to a private beach, pets are welcome, and no minimum stay is required. *Box 327, Greenville Jct. 04442, tel. 207/695–2950. 9 rooms with bath, 1 cabin with bath. Facilities: beach, canoes, volleyball. MC, V. Inexpensive.*

Jackman   **Attean Lake Lodge.** About an hour west of Rockwood, Attean
Lodging   Lake Lodge has been owned and operated by the Holden family since 1900; the 18 log cabins (sleeping two to six) offer a secluded, island environment. Each cabin has hot and cold running water and a full bath; a central lodge has a library, games, and a public telephone. *Birch Island, Box 457, tel. 207/668–3792. 18 cabins with bath. Facilities: beach; boats; canoes; fishing licenses, supplies, and guides available. 3 meals included in the rate. AE, MC, V. Very Expensive.*

Millinocket   **Scootic Inn and Penobscot Room.** This informal restaurant and
Dining   lounge offers a varied menu of steak, seafood, pizza, and sand-

wiches, and a large-screen TV usually tuned to sports. *70 Penobscot Ave., tel. 207/723–4566. Reservations advised for 5 or more. AE, D, MC, V. Inexpensive–Moderate.*

Lodging **Atrium Motor Inn.** Located off Route 157 in a shopping center, this motel offers facilities that make up for its unappealing location and standard motel furnishings: a large central atrium with an indoor pool, plus a Jacuzzi and health club. *970 Central Ave., tel. 207/723–4555. 82 rooms. Facilities: breakfast room, lounge, Jacuzzi, indoor pool, wading pool and sand box, health club. Rates include Continental breakfast. AE, D, MC, V. Moderate.*

Rockwood **The Birches Resort.** The family-oriented resort offers the full
Dining and Lodging north-country experience: Moosehead Lake, birch woods, log cabins, and boats for rent. The turn-of-the-century main lodge has four guest rooms, a living room dominated by a fieldstone fireplace, and a dining room overlooking the lake. The dining room is open to the public for breakfast and dinner; the fare is pasta, seafood, and steak. Most guests occupy one of the 17 cottages that have wood-burning stoves or fireplaces and sleep from two to 15 people. An additional charge is made for pets; Full American Plan is available. *Box 81, 04478, tel. 207/534–7305 or 800/825–9453. 4 lodge rooms, 1 with bath; 17 cottages with bath. Facilities: dining room; boats, kayaks, canoes, sailfish for rent; private marina; horseback riding available; outdoor hot tub and sauna. AE, D, MC, V. Dining room closed late Nov.–Dec., Apr. Moderate.*

Lodging **Rockwood Cottages.** Eight white cottages with blue trim, on Moosehead Lake, off Route 15, and convenient to the center of Rockwood, are ideal for families; they have screened porches and fully equipped kitchens, cribs are provided, and pets are welcome. Cottages sleep two to seven, and there is a one-week minimum stay in July and August. *Box 176, 04478, tel. 207/534–7725. 8 cottages. Facilities: dock, rental craft, cable TV. MC, V. Inexpensive.*

4 Vermont

by Mary H. Frakes, with an introduction by William G. Scheller

A restaurant columnist for the Boston Phoenix, *Mary Frakes also writes on travel, business, and contemporary art and crafts.*

Updated by Tara Hamilton

Everywhere you look around Vermont, the evidence is clear: This is not the state it was 25 years ago.

That may be true for the rest of New England as well, but the contrasts between present and recent past seem all the more sharply drawn in the Green Mountain State, if only because an aura of timelessness has always been at the heart of the Vermont image. Vermont was where all the quirks and virtues outsiders associate with upcountry New England were supposed to reside. It was where the Yankees were Yankee-est and where there were more cows than people.

Not that you should be alarmed, if you haven't been here in a while; Vermont hasn't become southern California, or even, for that matter, southern New Hampshire. This is still the most rural state in the Union (meaning that it has the smallest percentage of citizens living in statistically defined metropolitan areas), even if there are, finally, more people than cows. It's still a place where cars occasionally have to stop while a dairyman walks his cows across a secondary road; and up in Essex County, in what George Aiken dubbed the Northeast Kingdom, there are townships with zero population. And the kind of scrupulous, straightforward, plainspoken politics practiced by Governor (later Senator) Aiken for 50 years has not become outmoded in a state that still turns out on town-meeting day.

How has Vermont changed? In strictly physical terms, the most obvious transformations have taken place in and around the two major cities, Burlington and Rutland, and near the larger ski resorts, such as Stowe, Killington, Stratton, and Mt. Snow. Burlington's Church Street, once a paradigm of all the sleepy redbrick shopping thoroughfares in northern New England, is now a pedestrian mall complete with chic bistros; outside the city, suburban development has supplanted dairy farms in towns where someone's trip to Burlington might once have been an item in a weekly newspaper. As for the ski areas, it's no longer enough simply to boast the latest in chairlift technology. Stratton has an entire "Austrian Village" of restaurants and shops, while a hillside adjacent to Bromley's slopes has sprouted instant replica Victorians for the second-home market. The town of Manchester, convenient to both resorts, is awash in designer-fashion discount outlets.

But the real metamorphosis in the Green Mountains has to do more with style, with the personality of the place, than with the mere substance of development. The past couple of decades have seen a tremendous influx of outsiders—not just skiers and "leaf peekers," but people who've come to stay year-round—and many of them are determined either to freshen the local scene with their own idiosyncrasies or to make Vermont even more like Vermont than they found it. On the one hand, this translates into the fact that one of the biggest draws to the tiny town of Glover each fall is an outdoor pageant that promotes leftist political and social causes; on the other, it means that sheep farming has been reintroduced into the state, largely to provide a high-quality product for the hand-weaving industry.

This ties in with another local phenomenon, one best described as Made in Vermont. Once upon a time, maple syrup and sharp cheddar cheese were the products that carried Vermont's name to the world. The market niche that they created has since been widened by Vermonters—a great many of them refugees from

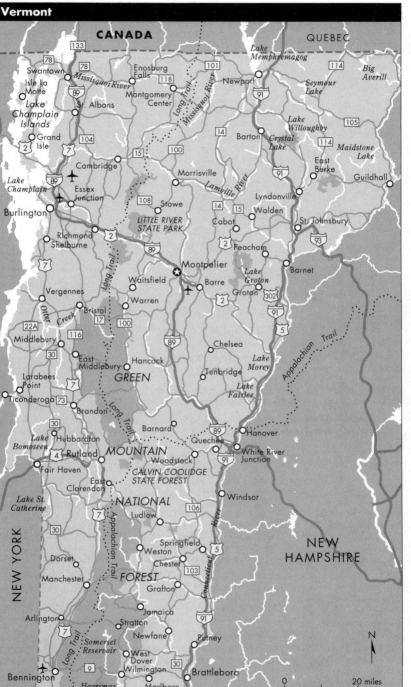

Vermont

CANADA   QUEBEC

133

Swantown

78

Lake Memphremagog

101

Missisquoi River

Enosburg Falls

118

Newport

91

Big Averill

114

Isle La Motte

78

Montgomery Center

Seymour Lake

89

St. Albans

105

Lake Champlain Islands

Grand Isle

2

7

104

15

100

14

Barton

Crystal Lake

Lake Willoughby

East Burke

114

Maidstone Lake

Guildhall

Cambridge

Morrisville

Lamville River

91

Lake Champlain

89

Essex Junction

108

Stowe

LITTLE RIVER STATE PARK

14

15

Walden

Lyndonville

St. Johnsbury

Burlington

2

Richmond

Shelburne

Cabot

2

Peacham

93

7

Montpelier

Waitsfield

Barre

Lake Groton

Barnet

Vergennes

89

Warren

Groton

302

91

5

Otter Creek

22A

Bristol

17

100

116

Middlebury

30

East Middlebury

Hancock

Chelsea

Tunbridge

Lake Morey

Appalachian Trail

GREEN

Larabees Point

7

Lake Fairlee

Ticonderoga

73

Brandon

Long Trail

Barnard

89

Hanover

30

Quechee

White River Junction

Lake Bomoseen

Hubbardton

MOUNTAIN

Woodstock

91

4

Rutland

Fair Haven

CALVIN COOLIDGE STATE FOREST

East Clarendon

NATIONAL

Windsor

Lake St. Catherine

7

106

30

Ludlow

Dorset

Springfield

5

Weston

Chester

NEW HAMPSHIRE

Manchester

FOREST

103

Grafton

NEW YORK

Jamaica

91

Arlington

Stratton

Newfane

Putney

7

Long Trail

Somerset Reservoir

West Dover

Wilmington

30

Brattleboro

N

Bennington

9

Marlboro

Harriman Reservoir

0   20 miles

0   30 km

more hectic arenas of commerce in places like Massachusetts and New York—offering a dizzying variety of goods with the ineffable cachet of Vermont manufacture. There are Vermont wood toys, Vermont apple wines, Vermont chocolates, even Vermont gin. All of it is marketed with the tacit suggestion that it was made by Yankee elves in a shed out back on a bright autumn morning.

The most successful Made in Vermont product is the renowned Ben & Jerry's ice cream. Neither Ben nor Jerry comes from old Green Mountain stock, but their product has benefited immensely from the magical reputation of the place where it is made. Along the way, the company (which started in Burlington under the most modest circumstances a little more than a decade ago) has become the largest single purchaser of Vermont's still considerable dairy output. Proof that the modern and the traditional—wearing a red-plaid cap and a Johnson Woolen Mills hunting jacket—can still get along very nicely in Vermont.

Essential Information

Visitor Information

Vermont Department of Travel and Tourism (134 State St., Montpelier 05602, tel. 802/828–3236).

Vermont Chamber of Commerce (Box 37, Montpelier 05601, tel. 802/223–3443).

Tour Groups

General-Interest Tours **New England Vacation Tours** (Box 560, Rte. 100, West Dover 05356, tel. 802/464–2076 or 800/742–7669).

Special-Interest Tours
Biking Vermont is great bicycle touring country and a number of companies offer weekend tours and week-long trips that range throughout the state. The state travel division has prepared an information sheet on biking, and many bookstores have *25 Bicycle Tours in Vermont* by John Freidin, the founder of **Vermont Bicycle Touring** (Box 711, Bristol 05443, tel. 802/453–4811), the first bike tour operator in the United States and one of the most respected. It operates numerous tours throughout the state.

Canoeing **Umiak Outdoor Outfitters** (Gale Farm Center, 1880 Mountain Rd., Stowe 05672, tel. 802/253–2317) has shuttles to nearby rivers for day excursions as well as customized overnight trips.

Vermont Canoe Trippers/Battenkill Canoe, Ltd. (Box 65, Arlington 05250, tel. 802/362–2800) organizes canoe tours.

Hiking **North Wind Touring** (Box 46, Waitsfield 05673, tel. 802/496–5771) offers guided inn-to-inn walking tours.

Vermont Hiking Holidays (Box 750, Bristol 05443, tel. 802/453–4816) leads guided hikes and walks from May through October, with lodging in country inns.

Package Deals for Independent Travelers

Country Inns Along the Trail (Churchill House Inn, RD 3, Box VTG, Brandon 05733, tel. 802/247–3300) organizes inn-to-inn vacations for independent travelers.

Festivals and Seasonal Events

Mid-Jan.: Stowe Winter Carnival, among the country's oldest such celebrations, features winter sports competitions. *Tel. 802/253–7321.*

Late Jan.: Brookfield Ice Harvest Festival is one of New England's last ice-harvest festivals. *Tel. 802/276–3415.*

Mid-Feb.: Mad River Valley Winter Carnival hosts a week of winter festivities including dogsled races and a masquerade ball. *Tel. 802/496–3409.*

Late Feb.: Benson Fishing Derby hosts ice-fishing competitions. *Tel. 802/773–2747.*

Late Feb.: Vermont Mozart Festival in Burlington features the Winter Chamber Music Series. *Tel. 802/862–7352.*

Late Mar.: Craftsbury Common Annual Spring Fling is held at the Nordic Ski Center. *Tel. 802/586–7767.*

Early–mid-Apr.: Vermont Maple Festival, St. Albans, celebrates the end of the spring sugaring. *Tel. 802/524–4966.*

Late Apr.: St. Johnsbury Maple Sugar Festival comes at the close of the sugaring season. *Tel. 802/748–3678.*

Mid-May: The Festival of Traditional Crafts at the Fairbanks Museum in St. Johnsbury demonstrates such old Vermont skills as blacksmithing. *Tel. 802/748–3678.*

Late May–early June: Vermont Dairy Festival at Enosburg Falls celebrates the products of all those Holsteins you see in the fields alongside the roads. *Tel. 802/933–2513.*

Late June: The Quechee Balloon Festival sponsors a regional hot-air balloon competition. *Tel. 802/295–7900.*

Late June: Vermont Canoe and Kayak Festival takes place at Waterbury State Park. *Tel. 802/253–2317.*

July 4: Burlington's month-long **Lake Champlain Discovery Festival** ends with a large-scale version of the July 4 celebrations held throughout the state. *Tel. 802/863–3489.*

July: One of the state's largest **antiques festivals** takes place in Dorset in odd-numbered years, in Manchester in even-numbered years. *Tel. 802/362–2100.*

Mid-July: Vermont Quilt Festival in Northfield draws visitors and exhibitors alike from throughout New England. *Tel. 802/485–7092.*

July–Aug.: Marlboro College hosts the celebrated Marlboro Music Festival of classical music. *Tel. 802/254–8163.*

Early Aug.: Art on the Mountain, a week-long show at Haystack Mountain, presents the work of Vermont artists and craftspeople. *Tel. 802/464–5321.*

Early Aug.: The Southern Vermont Crafts Fair in Manchester has juried exhibits of contemporary crafts. *Tel. 802/362–2100.*

Mid-Aug.: Bennington Battle Days commemorates the state's most important conflict of the Revolutionary era. *Tel. 802/447–3311.*

Late Aug.: The Domestic Resurrection Day Circus of the Bread and Puppet Theater, an outdoor pageant on social and political themes, draws thousands to Glover. *Tel. 802/525–3031.*

Early Sept.: The Vermont State Fair, held in Rutland over the

Labor Day weekend, has agricultural exhibits, a midway, and entertainment. *Tel. 802/775–5200.*

Early Sept.: Burlington's **Champlain Valley Exposition** has all the attributes of a large county fair. *Tel. 802/878–5545.*

Early Sept.: **Tunbridge World's Fair,** a large agricultural fair, has rides and farm-horse competitions. *Tel. 802/889–3458.*

Mid-Sept.: Stratton Arts Festival, Stratton Mountain, brings together artists and well-known performers in various media. *Tel. 802/297–2200.*

Late Sept.: The **National Traditional Old-Time Fiddler's Contest** in Barre celebrates folk music. *Tel. 802/229–5711.*

Late Sept.–early Oct.: The **Northeast Kingdom Fall Foliage Festival** is a week-long affair hosted by the six small towns of Walden, Cabot, Plainfield, Peacham, Barnet, and Groton. *Tel. 802/ 563–2472.*

Late Oct.: Montpelier's **Festival of Vermont Crafts** focuses on traditional and contemporary crafts. *Tel. 802/229–5711.*

Mid-Nov.: Vermont Hand Crafters Crafts Fair, Burlington. *Tel. 802/453–4240.*

Late Nov.: Thanksgiving Weekend Crafts Show takes place in Killington. *Tel. 802/422–3783.*

Late Nov.: The **Bradford Wild Game Supper** draws thousands to sample a variety of large and small game animals and birds. *Tel. 802/222–4670.*

Mid-Dec.: St. Lucia Pageant, in Arlington, is a "Festival of Lights" that celebrates the winter solstice. *Tel. 802/375–2800.*

Late Dec.: Hildene in Manchester holds candlelight tours of this historic home. *Tel. 802/362–1788.*

Dec. 31: The **First Night celebration** sees downtown Burlington transformed by musical and theatrical performances, street happenings, a parade, and fireworks. *Tel. 802/863–6005.*

Hints for Disabled Travelers

A recent Vermont law requires that new construction include facilities for the disabled, so the newer hotels and those that have added new sections are the most likely to have disabled access and disabled-equipped rooms. A list of facilities is available from the Vermont Travel Division.

The official state map indicates public recreation areas at state parks that are disabled-accessible.

Hints for Older Travelers

Many country inns are happy to accommodate a request for a room on the ground floor, but it should be made when booking the reservation. Older visitors may want to make sure they reserve a room with a shower—or at least a room without a Victorian clawfoot tub that requires climbing in and out.

Arriving and Departing

By Plane **Burlington International Airport** (tel. 802/863–2874) has scheduled daily flights by six major U.S. airlines. West of Bennington and convenient to southern Vermont, **Albany–Schenectady County Airport** in New York State is served by 10 major U.S. carriers.

By Car I-91, which stretches from Connecticut and Massachusetts in the south to Québec (highway 55) in the north, reaches most points along Vermont's eastern border. I–89, from New Hampshire to the east and Québec (highway 133) to the north, crosses central Vermont from White River Junction to Burlington. Southwestern Vermont can be reached by Route 7 from Massachusetts and Route 4 from New York.

By Train Amtrak's (tel. 800/872–7245) *Montrealer*, an overnight train linking Washington D.C., New York City, and Montréal, stops at Brattleboro, Bellows Falls, Claremont, White River Junction, Montpelier, Waterbury, Essex Junction, and St. Albans. Service to Albany and Glens Falls, New York, is convenient to western Vermont.

By Bus A subsidiary of Greyhound Lines, **Vermont Transit** (135 St. Paul St., Burlington 05401, tel. 802/864–6811 or 800/451–3292) connects Bennington, Brattleboro, Burlington, Rutland, and other cities with Boston, Springfield, Albany, New York, Montréal, and cities in New Hampshire.

Getting Around Vermont

By Plane Aircraft charters are available at Burlington International Airport from **Montair** (tel. 802/862–2246), **Mansfield Heliflight** (tel. 802/864–3954), **Northern Airways** (tel. 802/658–2204), and **Valley Air Services** (tel. 802/863–3626).

Southern Vermont Helicopter (Box 15G, West Brattleboro 05301, tel. 802/257–4354) provides helicopter transportation throughout New England.

By Car The official state map, available free from the Vermont Travel Division, is very helpful for driving in the state; a table shows the mileage between principal towns, and there are enlarged maps of major downtown areas. *The Vermont Atlas and Gazetteer,* sold in many bookstores, has more detail on the smaller roads. Information centers are located on the Massachusetts border at I–91, the New Hampshire border at I–89, the New York border at Route 4A, and the Canadian border at I–89.

By Bus **Vermont Transit** (tel. 802/864–6811 or 800/451–3292) links Bennington, Brattleboro, Bellows Falls, Rutland, White River Junction, Middlebury, Montpelier, Burlington, St. Johnsbury, and Newport, with intermediate stops at smaller towns.

Dining

Vermont restaurants have not escaped recent efforts to adapt traditional New England fare in order to offset its reputation for blandness. The New England Culinary Institute, based in Montpelier, has trained a number of Vermont chefs who have now turned their attention to such native New England foods as fiddlehead ferns (available only for a short time in the spring); maple syrup (Vermont is the largest producer in the United States); dairy products, especially cheese; native fruits and berries that are often transformed into sauces, jams, jellies, and preserves; "new Vermont" products such as salsa and salad dressings; and venison, quail, pheasant, and other game.

Your chances of finding a table for dinner will vary dramatically with the season: Many restaurants have lengthy waits during peak seasons (when it's always a good idea to call about reservations) and then shut down during the slow months of April and November. Some of the best dining will be found in country inns. Casual dress is the general rule in Vermont restaurants; the formal dining rooms of a few upscale country inns are the dressiest places, but even there you'll rarely need a tie—though you'll often find wearing a jacket useful on nippy Vermont evenings.

Highly recommended restaurants in each price category are indicated by a star ★.

Category	Cost*
Very Expensive	over $35
Expensive	$25–$35
Moderate	$15–$25
Inexpensive	under $15

average cost of a three-course dinner, per person, excluding drinks, service, and 8% sales tax

Lodging

Vermont's largest hotels are in Burlington and in the vicinity of the major ski resorts. Elsewhere throughout the state travelers will find a variety of inns, bed-and-breakfasts, and small motels. Rates are generally highest during foliage season, from late September to mid-October, and lowest in late spring and November, when many properties close. It makes sense to inquire about package rates if you plan a stay of several days, especially at the larger hotels. Some inns whose furnishings are largely antiques may not welcome children as guests; if you are traveling with youngsters, you will want to discuss this question in advance.

Organizations that provide referral services for bed-and-breakfasts throughout Vermont include **American Country Collection of Bed and Breakfast** (984 Gloucester Place, Schenectady, NY 12309; tel. 518/370–4948) and **American–Vermont Bed and Breakfast Reservation Service** (Box 1, E. Fairfield 05448, tel. 802/827–3827). In addition, many ski resort areas operate lodging referral services.

The Vermont Chamber of Commerce publishes the *Vermont Travelers' Guidebook,* which is an extensive list of lodgings, and additional guides to country inns and vacation rentals. The Vermont Travel Division (*see* Visitor Information, *above*) has a brochure that lists lodgings at working farms.

Highly recommended lodgings in each price category are indicated by a star ★.

Category	Cost*
Very Expensive	over $150
Expensive	$100–$150
Moderate	$60–$100
Inexpensive	under $60

All prices are for a standard double room during peak season, with no meals unless noted, and excluding service charge.

Southern Vermont

The Vermont tradition of independence and rebellion began in southern Vermont. Many towns founded in the early 18th century as frontier outposts or fortifications were later important as trading centers. In the western region the Green Mountain Boys fought off both the British and the claims of land-hungry New Yorkers—and some say their descendants are still fighting. In the 19th century, as many towns turned to manufacturing, the eastern part of the state preserved much of its rich farming and orchard areas. Many of the people who have moved to Vermont in the last 20 years have settled in the southern part of the state.

Important Addresses and Numbers

Weather (tel. 802/464–2111).

Visitor Information **Bennington Area Chamber of Commerce** (Veterans Memorial Dr., Bennington 05201, tel. 802/447–3311).

Brattleboro Chamber of Commerce (180 Main St., Brattleboro 05301, tel. 802/254–4565).

Chamber of Commerce, Manchester and the Mountains (Adams Park Green, Box 928, Manchester 05255, tel. 802/362–2100).

Great Falls Regional Chamber of Commerce (Box 554, Bellows Falls 05101, tel. 802/463–3537).

Mt. Snow/Haystack Region Chamber of Commerce (E. Main St., Box 3, Wilmington 05363, tel. 802/464–8092).

Windsor Area Chamber of Commerce (Box 5, Windsor 05089, tel. 802/672–5910).

Emergencies Vermont's **Medical Health Care Information Center** has a 24-hour line (tel. 802/864–0454).

Brattleboro Memorial Hospital (9 Belmont Ave., tel. 802/257–0341) is the largest in the region.

Telecommunications Device for the Deaf (TDD) has a 24-hour emergency hot line (tel. 802/253–0191).

Getting Around Southern Vermont

By Car In the south the principal east–west highway is Route 9, the Molly Stark Trail, from Brattleboro to Bennington. The most important north–south roads are Route 7, the more scenic Route 7A to the west, and I–91 and Route 5 to the east. Route 100, which runs north–south through the state's center, and Rte. 30 from Brattleboro to Manchester are scenic drives. All routes may be heavily traveled during peak tourist seasons.

By Bus **Vermont Transit** (tel. 802/864–6811 or 800/451–3292) links Bennington, Manchester, Brattleboro, and Bellows Falls.

Guided Tours

Back Road Country Tours (tel. 802/442–3876) offers jeep tours on the back roads of Bennington County during September and October—a great way to experience the fall foliage.

Exploring Southern Vermont

Numbers in the margin correspond to points of interest on the Southern Vermont map.

Travelers in southern Vermont will see verdant farmland, built-up ski resorts, newly rejuvenated towns, tourist-clogged highways, and quiet back roads. Our tour begins in the east, south of the junction of I–91 and Route 9.

❶ Brattleboro, a town of about 13,000, originated as a frontier scouting post and became a thriving industrial center and resort town in the 1800s. More recently, such organizations as the Experiment in International Living (which trains Peace Corps volunteers) have helped build the area's reputation as a haven for left-leaning political activists and aging hippies.

The **Brattleboro Museum and Art Center** selects an annual theme and gears each exhibit to it. The converted railroad station hosts art and historical exhibits as well as an Estey organ from the days when the city was home to one of the world's largest organ companies. *Canal and Bridge Sts., tel. 802/257–0124. Admission: $2 adults, $1 senior citizens and college students. Open May–Oct., Tues.–Sun. noon–6.*

Larkin G. Mead Jr., a Brattleboro resident, stirred 19th-century America's imagination with an 8-foot snow angel he built at the intersection of Routes 30 and 5. **Brooks Memorial Library** has a replica of the angel as well as art exhibits that change frequently. *224 Main St., tel. 802/254–5290. Open Mon.–Thurs. 9–9, Fri. 9–6, Sat. 9–5.*

Time Out | **Hamelmann's Bakery** on Elliot Street in Brattleboro has crusty country breads in hand-shaped loaves, thick napoleons, and delicate fruit and almond tarts.

From Brattleboro one can head north along the eastern edge of the state to Putney, where **Harlow's Sugar House** (Rte. 5, 2 mi north of Putney, tel. 802/387–5852) offers maple sugaring in spring, berry picking in summer, and sleigh rides in winter.

❷ Nearly 10 miles west of Brattleboro on Route 9 (the Molly Stark Trail) is **Marlboro,** a tiny town that draws musicians and audiences from around the world each summer to the Marlboro Music Festival, founded by Rudolf Serkin and led for many years by Pablo Casals. Marlboro is also home to the New England Bach Festival in the fall.

Perched high on a hill just off Route 9, **Marlboro College** is the center of the musical activity. The demure white frame buildings have an outstanding view of the valley below, and the campus is studded with apple trees.

The **Luman Nelson New England Wildlife Museum** (tel. 802/464–5494), housed in a gift shop on Route 9 opposite the Skyline Restaurant, is taxidermy heaven. The display of large animals includes majestic deer heads, a bobcat eyeing a couple of concerned-looking squirrels, and a wild boar who seems surprised to be there. The large room downstairs is filled with stuffed bird species in cages with hand-lettered signs.

❸ Wilmington, the shopping and dining center for the Mount Snow ski area to the north, lies 8 miles west of Marlboro on Route 9. Here you can take one of Vermont's most scenic

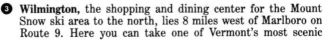

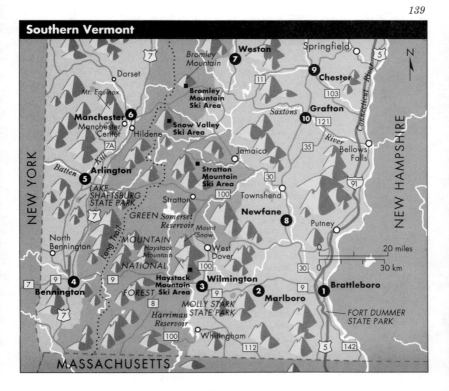

Southern Vermont

(though well-trodden) drives, a 35-mile circular tour that affords panoramic views of the region's mountains, farmland, and abundant cow population: Drive west on Route 9 to the intersection with Route 8, turn south and continue to the junction with Route 100, follow Route 100 through Whitingham (the birthplace of the Mormon prophet Brigham Young), and stay with the road as it turns north again and takes you back to Route 9. On this last leg you will pass the **North River Winery,** which occupies a converted farmhouse and barn on Route 112. The winery produces such fruit wines as Green Mountain Apple and offers tours and tastings. *Rte. 112, 6 mi south of Wilmington, tel. 802/368–7557. Admission free. Open late May–Dec., daily 10–5; Jan.–late May, Fri.–Sun. 11–5.*

❹ Bennington, now the state's third-largest city and the commercial focus of Vermont's southwest corner has retained much of the industrial character it developed in the 19th century, when paper mills, grist mills, and potteries formed the city's economic base. It was in Bennington, at the Catamount Tavern, that Ethan Allen organized the Green Mountain Boys, who helped capture Fort Ticonderoga in 1775. Here also, in 1777 the American general John Stark urged his militia to attack the Hessians across the New York border: "There are the Redcoats; they will be ours or tonight Molly Stark sleeps a widow!"

A Chamber of Commerce brochure describes two self-guided walking tours; the more interesting is the tour of **Old Bennington,** a National Register Historic District just west of downtown, where impressive white-column Greek Revival and sturdy brick Federal homes stand around the village green. In the graveyard of the **Old First Church,** at the corner of Church Street and Monument Avenue, the tombstone of the poet Robert Frost proclaims, "I had a lover's quarrel with the world."

The **Bennington Battle Monument,** a 306-foot stone obelisk with an elevator to the top, commemorates General Stark's victory over the British, who attempted to capture Bennington's stockpile of supplies. The battle, which took place near Walloomsac Heights in New York State, helped bring about the surrender two months later of the British commander, "Gentleman Johnny" Burgoyne. *15 Monument Ave., tel. 802/447-0550. Admission: $1 adults, 50¢ children 6–11. Open Apr.–Oct., daily 9–5.*

The **Bennington Museum**'s rich collections of early Americana include artifacts of rural life piled high in large cases. The decorative arts are well represented; one room is devoted to early Bennington pottery, then known as Norton pottery, the product of one of the first ceramic makers in the country. Another room covers the history of American glass and contains fine Tiffany specimens. Devotees of folk art will want to see the largest public collection of the work of Grandma Moses, who lived and painted in the area. Among the 30 paintings and assorted memorabilia is her only self-portrait and the famous painted caboose window. *W. Main St. (Rte. 9), tel. 802/447-1571. Admission: $5 adults, $4 senior citizens and children 12–18, $12 family. Open daily 9–5.*

The **Park-McCullough House,** a 35-room restored mansion in North Bennington, shows what the forty-niners did with the money they made in the California gold rush. The elaborately carved Second Empire mahogany furnishings, massive oak staircase, and etched glass doors are original. Guided tours begin on the hour. *Rte. 67A, North Bennington, tel. 802/442-5441. Admission: $4 adults, $2.50 children 12–17. Open May–Oct., weekdays 9–4.*

Bennington College's placid campus features green meadows punctuated with contemporary stone sculpture, white frame neo-Colonial dorms, and acres of cornfields. The small coeducational liberal arts college, one of the most exclusive in the country, is noted for its progressive program in the arts. To reach the campus, take Route 67A off Route 7 and look for the stone entrance gate.

⑤ Don't be surprised to see familiar-looking faces among the roughly 2,200 people of **Arlington,** about 15 miles north of Bennington on Route 7A. The illustrator Norman Rockwell lived here for 14 years, and many of the models for his portraits of small-town life were his neighbors. Settled first in 1763, Arlington was called Tory Hollow for its Loyalist sympathies—even though a number of the Green Mountain Boys lived here as well. Smaller than Bennington and less sophisticated than Manchester to the north, Arlington displays a certain Rockwellian folksiness. It's also known as the home of Dorothy Canfield Fisher, a novelist popular in the 1930s and 1940s.

Don't expect to find original paintings at the **Norman Rockwell Exhibition;** it has none. Instead, the exhibition rooms are crammed with reproductions, arranged in every way conceivable: chronologically, by subject matter, and juxtaposed with photos of the models, some of whom work at the exhibition. A gift shop in the white church (ca. 1875) that houses the exhibition sells yet more reproductions. *Rte. 7A, Arlington, tel. 802/ 375–6423. Admission: $1, children under 6 free. Open May– Oct., daily 9–5; Nov.–Apr., daily 10–4.*

❻ **Manchester,** where Ira Allen proposed financing Vermont's participation in the American Revolution by confiscating Tory estates, has been a popular summer retreat since the mid-19th century, when Mary Todd Lincoln visited. Manchester Village's tree-shaded marble sidewalks and stately old homes reflect the luxurious resort lifestyle of a century ago, while Manchester Center's upscale factory outlet stores appeal to the 20th-century's affluent ski crowd drawn by nearby Bromley and Stratton mountains.

Time Out At the **Gourmet Deli** in Factory Point Square, Route 7A, Manchester, you'll find homemade soups, sandwiches, baked goods, and outdoor tables with umbrellas in summer.

Hildene, the summer home of Abraham Lincoln's son Robert, on Route 7A, 2 miles south of the intersection with Route 11/30, is situated on a 412-acre estate that the former chairman of the board of the Pullman Company built for his family and their descendants, who lived here as recently as 1975. With its Georgian Revival symmetry, gracious central hallway, and grand curved staircase, the 24-room mansion is unusual in that its rooms are not roped off. When "The Ride of the Valkyries" is played on the 1,000-pipe Aeolian organ, the music comes out of the mansion's very bones. Tours include a short film on the owner's life and a walk through the elaborate formal gardens. *Rte. 7A, Manchester, tel. 802/362–1788. Admission: $7 adults, $4 children 6–15. Open mid-May–Oct., daily 9:30–4.*

For fly-fishing devotees, the **American Museum of Fly Fishing** displays more than 1,500 rods, 800 reels, 30,000 flies, and the tackle of such celebrities as Bing Crosby, Daniel Webster, and Winslow Homer. Its 2,500 books on angling comprise the largest public library devoted to fishing. Only the fish are missing here. *Rte. 7A, Manchester, tel. 802/362–3300. Admission: $2 adults, children under 12 free. Open May–Oct., daily 10–4; Nov.–Apr., weekdays 10–4.*

The **Southern Vermont Art Center's** 10 rooms are set on 375 acres dotted with contemporary sculpture. Here are a permanent collection, changing exhibits, and a serene botany trail; the graceful Georgian mansion is also the site of concerts, dramatic performances, and films. *West Rd., Box 617, Manchester, tel. 802/362–1405. Admission: $3 adults, 50¢ students. Open Memorial Day–Oct. 15, Tues.–Sat. 10–5, Sun. noon–5, and for occasional winter concerts.*

Time Out **Mother Myrick's** on Route 7A offers sugar in all its forms: icecream sundaes, cakes, cookies, handmade chocolates, and fudge. The waiting lines even in winter attest to its popularity.

You may be tempted to keep your eye on the temperature gauge of your car as you drive the 5.2 miles to the top of 3,825-foot **Mount Equinox.** Remember to look out the window periodically for views of the Batten Kill trout stream and the surrounding Vermont countryside. Picnic tables line the drive, and there's an outstanding view down both sides of the mountain from a peak known as "the Saddle." *Rte. 7A, Manchester, tel. 802/*

362–1114. Admission: $4.50 car. Open May–Oct., daily 8 AM–10 PM.

Head east on Route 11 and then north on Route 100 to reach **Weston,** perhaps best known for the Vermont Country Store (Rte. 100, tel. 802/362–4667), which may be more a way of life than a shop. For years the retail store and its mail-order catalogue have carried such nearly forgotten items as Lilac Vegetal aftershave, Monkey Brand black tooth powder, Flexible Flyer sleds, pickles in a barrel, and tiny wax bottles of colored syrup. Nostalgia-laden implements dangle from the store's walls and ceiling.

Weston Priory, a Benedictine monastery just north of the junction of Routes 100 and 155, is a tranquil spot in an already fairly serene state. Guests are welcome to join in services (evening vespers is the most impressive), walk by the pond, picnic under the trees, and visit the gift shop, which has records of the well-known monastery choir. *⅒ mi north of junction of Rtes. 100 and 155.*

From Weston you might head south on Route 100 and then down Route 30 through Jamaica, Townshend, and Newfane, pretty hamlets typical of small-town Vermont. **Newfane** is especially attractive for its crisp white buildings surrounding the village green. Just south of Townshend, near the Townshend Dam on Route 30, is the state's longest single-span bridge, which is now closed to traffic.

Another option is to travel east to Route 11, which will take you to **Chester.** There, on North Street, look for Stone Village, two rows of buildings constructed from quarried stone, all built by two brothers and said to have been used during the Civil War as stations on the Underground Railroad.

To examine the oldest one-room schoolhouse in the state, take Route 11 east almost to I–91. Completed in 1790, the **Eureka Schoolhouse** has a collection of 19th-century primers and other education materials. *Rte. 11, off I–91, tel. 802/828–3226. Admission free. Open Memorial Day–mid-Oct., daily 9–4.*

It's 8 miles south on Route 35 from Chester to **Grafton,** the picturesque village that got a second lease on life when the Windham Foundation provided funds for the restoration of most of the town, now one of the best-kept in the state. The Grafton Historical Society documents the change and shows other exhibits. *Townshend Rd., tel. 802/843–2388. Admission free. Open Memorial Day–Columbus Day, Sat. 2:30–4:40; July–Aug., Sun. 2:30–4:40.*

Southern Vermont for Free

Grafton Historical Society, Grafton
North River Winery, Wilmington
Stone Village, Chester
Weston Priory, Weston

What to See and Do with Children

Battle Monument and Museum, Bennington
Harlow's Sugar House, Putney
Luman Nelson New England Wildlife Museum, Marlboro
Mt. Equinox, Arlington

American Express offers Travelers Cheques built for two.

American Express® Cheques *for Two*. The first Travelers Cheques that allow either of you to use them because both of you have signed them. And only one of you needs to be present to purchase them.

Cheques *for Two* are accepted anywhere regular American Express Travelers Cheques are, which is just about everywhere. So stop by your bank, AAA* or any American Express Travel Service Office and ask for Cheques *for Two*.

Travelers Cheques

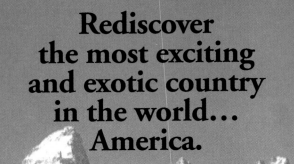

Off the Beaten Track

In Bellows Falls, on the Connecticut River at the eastern edge of the state, about 12 miles east of Grafton, you can board the *Green Mountain Flyer* for a 26-mile round-trip to Chester and Ludlow in cars that date from the golden age of railroading. The journey takes you through scenic countryside that includes the Brockway Mills gorge. *Island St. off Bridge St. (Rte. 12), tel. 802/463–3069. Round-trip fare: $9–$21 adults, $5–$14 children 3–12, depending on destination. Open mid-June–mid-Oct., daily 11–2.*

Native American petroglyphs can be found on the banks of the Connecticut River in Bellows Falls, but you'll have to scramble down the side of the riverbank to examine the carvings. The Bellows Falls Chamber of Commerce (tel. 802/463–4280) has a map showing the site; follow the small sign off Bridge Street near the river.

Shopping

Shopping Districts **Candle Mill Village** (tel. 802/375–6068), on Old Mill Road, off Route 7A in East Arlington, offers shops that specialize in community cookbooks from around the country, bears in all forms, and music boxes. A waterfall makes a pleasant backdrop for a picnic.

Manchester Commons (tel. 802/362–3736), at the intersection of Routes 7 and 11/30, the largest and spiffiest of three large factory-direct shopping minimalls, has such big-city names as Joan and David, Coach, Boston Trader, Ralph Lauren, Hickey-Freeman, and Cole-Haan. Not far off are Factory Point Square on Route 7 and Battenkill Place on Route. 11.

Flea Market **Wilmington Flea Market** (Junction Rtes. 9 and 100 South, tel. 802/464–3345), a cornucopia of leftovers and never-solds, operates weekends and holidays from Memorial Day to mid-October.

Food and Drink **Allen Bros.** (Rte. 5 south of Bellows Falls, tel. 802/722–3395) offers its own apple pies, cider doughnuts, other baked goods, and a selection of Vermont food products and produce.

Equinox Nursery (Rte. 7A, between Arlington and Manchester, tel. 802/362–2610) carries a wide selection of Vermont-made food and produce, including locally manufactured ice cream.

H & M Orchard (Dummerston Center, tel. 802/254–8100) lets you watch sugaring in spring and pick your own fruit in other seasons.

Vermont Country Store (Rte. 100, Weston, tel. 802/824–3184) sets aside one room of its old-fashioned emporium for Vermont Common Crackers and bins of fudge and other candy.

Specialty Stores **Carriage Trade** (tel. 802/362–1125) and **1812 House** (tel. 802/362–1189) are two antiques centers just north of Manchester Center on Route 7. They hold room after room of Early American antiques gathered by many dealers; Carriage Trade has especially fine collections of clocks and ceramics.

Antiques

Danby Antiques Center (⅛ mi off Rte. 7, 13 mi north of Manchester, tel. 802/293–9984) has 11 rooms and a barn filled with furniture and accessories, folk art, textiles, and stoneware.

Four Corners East (307 North St., Bennington, tel. 802/442–2612) has a selection of Early American antiques.

Newfane Antiques Center (Rte. 30, south of Newfane, tel. 802/365–4482) displays antiques from 20 dealers on three floors.

Books **The Book Cellar** (120 Main St., Brattleboro, tel. 802/254–6026), with three floors of books, is strong on Vermont and New England volumes.
Johnny Appleseed (tel. 802/362–2458), next to the Equinox Hotel in Manchester Village, specializes in Vermont lore and the hard-to-find.
Northshire Bookstore (Main St., Manchester, tel. 802/362–2200) has excellent selections of travel and children's books in a large inventory.

Crafts **Basketville** (Rte. 5, Putney, tel. 802/387–5509), as its name suggests, is an immense space filled with baskets from around the world.
Bennington Potters Yard (324 County St., tel. 802/447–7531) has seconds from the famed Bennington Potters. Prepare to get dusty digging through the bad stuff to find an almost-perfect piece at a modest discount. The complex of buildings also houses a glass factory outlet and John McLeod woodenware.
Green Mountain Spinnery offers yarns, knit items, and tours of its yarn factory at 1:30 on the first and third Tuesday of each month. *Exit 4, I–91, Putney, tel. 802/387–4528. Tour: $1 adults, 50¢ children.*
Handworks on the Green (Rte. 7, Manchester, tel. 802/362–5033) deals in contemporary crafts—ceramics, jewelry, glass, with an emphasis on sophisticated, brightly colored decorative work.
Newfane Country Store (Rte. 30, Newfane, tel. 802/365–7916) has an immense selection of quilts—they can be custom ordered as well—and homemade fudge.
Vermont Artisan Design (115 Main St., Brattleboro, tel. 802/257–7044) displays contemporary ceramics, glass, wood, and clothing from Vermont.
Weston Bowl Mill (Rte. 100, Weston, tel. 802/824–6219) has finely crafted wood products at mill prices.

Men's Clothing **Orvis Retail Store** (Rte. 7A, Manchester, tel. 802/362–3750) carries the outdoorsman's clothing and home furnishings featured in its popular mail order catalog (don't overlook the bargain basement). The company also offers three-day fly fishing courses.

Women's Clothing **Anne Klein, Liz Claiborne, Donna Karan, Esprit, London Fog,** and **Coach** are among the shops on Routes 11/30 and 7 South in Manchester—a center for women's designer factory stores.
The Silver Forest (Westminster West Rd., Putney, tel. 802/387–4149) carries natural-fiber clothing and jewelry reminiscent of the 1960s.

Sports and Outdoor Activities

Biking A Dorset–Manchester trail of about 20 miles runs from Manchester Village north on West Street to Route 30, turns west at the Dorset village green to West Road, and heads back south to Manchester. **Battenkill Sports** (Rte. 7, at Rtes. 11/30, tel. 802/362–2634) and **Pedal Pushers** (Rtes. 11/30, ½ mi east of Rte. 7A, tel. 802/362–5200) in Manchester have bike rentals and information.

Chester is the start of a 26-mile loop that follows the Williams River along Route 103 to Pleasant Valley Road north of Bellows Falls. Pleasant Valley Road meets Route 121 at Saxtons River; turn west on Route 121 as it runs beside Saxtons River, to connect with Route 35. When the two routes separate, follow Route 35 north back to Chester. **Neal's Wheels** (Rte. 11, tel. 802/875–3627) has rentals.

Mountain Bike Peddlers (954 E. Main St., tel. 802/447–7968) and **Up and Downhill** (160 Benmont Ave., tel. 802/442–8664) in Bennington both offer rentals, repairs, and route information.

Canoeing The stretch of the Connecticut River between Bellows Falls and the Massachusetts border, interrupted by one dam at Vernon, is relatively easy. A good resource is *The Complete Boating Guide to the Connecticut River*, available from **CRWC Headquarters** (125 Combs Rd., Easthampton, MA 01027, tel. 413/584–0057). **Connecticut River Safari** (Rte. 5, Brattleboro, tel. 802/257–5008) has guided and self-guided tours as well as canoe rentals. **Battenkill Canoe** (River Rd., Box 65, Arlington, tel. 802/375–9559) offers day trips and rentals on the Batten Kill and can arrange custom inn-to-inn tours.

Fishing **The Orvis Co.** (Manchester Center, tel. 802/362–3900) hosts a nationally known fly-fishing school on the Batten Kill, the state's most famous trout stream, with three-day courses given weekly, April–October. The Connecticut River contains smallmouth bass, walleye, and perch; shad are beginning to return via the fish ladders at Vernon and Bellows Falls. Harriman and Somerset reservoirs in the central part of the state offer both warm- and cold-water species; Harriman has a greater variety.

Strictly Trout (RFD 3, Box 800, Westminster West 05346, tel. 802/869–3116) will arrange a fly-fishing trip on any Vermont stream or river.

Hiking One of the most popular segments of the Long Trail starts at Route 11/30 west of Peru Notch and goes to the top of Bromley Mountain (four hours). About 4 miles east of Bennington, the Long Trail crosses Route 9 and runs south to the summit of Harmon Hill (two–three hours). On Route 30 about 1 mile south of Townshend is Townshend State Park; from here the hiking trail runs to the top of Bald Mountain, passing an alder swamp, a brook, and a hemlock forest (two hours). The **Mountain Goat** (Rte. 7A just south of Rtes. 11/30, Manchester, tel. 802/362–5159) specializes in hiking, backpacking, and climbing equipment; it also offers climbing clinics.

Water Sports **Lake Front Restaurant** (Harriman Reservoir, tel. 802/464–5838) rents sailboats, canoes, and rowboats by the hour or day.

West River Canoe (Rte. 100, off Rte. 30, Townshend, tel. 802/896–6209) has sailboard rentals and lessons.

National and State Parks

The 275,000 acres of Green Mountain National Forest extend down the center of the state, providing scenic drives, picnic areas, 95 campsites, lakes, and hiking and cross-country ski trails. Information is available from the **Forest Supervisor, Green Mountain National Forest** (151 West St., Box 519, Rutland 05701, tel. 802/773–0300). The **Green Mountain Club** (Rte. 100, Box 650, Waterbury Center 05677, tel. 802/244–7037) publishes a number of helpful maps and guides and can offer advice and suggestions for hiking in Vermont.

The waterfalls at the **Lye Brook Wilderness Area** are a popular attraction. Maps and information are available at the U.S. Forest Service Office. *Rte. 11/30, east of Manchester, tel. 802/362–2307. Open weekdays 8–4:30.*

Emerald Lake State Park has a marked nature trail and an on-site naturalist. *Rte. 7, 9 mi north of Manchester, tel. 802/362–1655. 430 acres. Facilities: 105 campsites (no hookups), toilets, showers, picnic tables, fireplaces, phone, boat and canoe rentals, snack bar.*

Fort Dummer State Park's hiking trails afford views of the Connecticut River Valley. *S. Main St., 2 mi south of Brattleboro, tel. 802/254–2610. 217 acres. Facilities: 61 campsites (no hookups), toilets, showers, picnic tables, fireplaces, phone.*

Lake Shaftsbury State Park is one of the few in Vermont with a group camping area. *Rte. 7A, 10½ mi north of Bennington, tel. 802/375–9978. 101 acres. Facilities: group camping area (with hookups), picnic tables and shelter, swimming beach, bathhouse, self-guided nature trails, boat and canoe rentals, phone.*

Molly Stark State Park has a hiking trail to a vista from a fire tower on Mt. Olga. *Rte. 9, east of Wilmington, tel. 802/464–5460. 158 acres. Facilities: 34 campsites (no hookups), toilets, showers, picnic tables and shelter, fireplaces, phone.*

Townshend State Park, the largest in southern Vermont, is popular for the swimming at Townshend Dam and the stiff hiking trail to the top of Bald Mountain. *3 mi north of Rte. 30, between Newfane and Townshend, tel. 802/365–7500. 856 acres. Facilities: 34 campsites (no hookups), toilets, showers, picnic tables and shelter, fireplaces.*

Woodford State Park is popular for its activities center on Adams Reservoir; there are also marked nature trails. *Rte. 9, east of Bennington, tel. 802/447–4169. 400 acres. Facilities: 102 campsites (no hookups), toilets, showers, picnic tables, fireplaces, phone, playground, boat and canoe rentals.*

Dining and Lodging

The ski lodges around Stratton, Bromley, Mount Snow, and Haystack boast Vermont's largest hotels. The Manchester area has a lodging referral service (tel. 802/824–6915). In the region's restaurants, dress is casual and reservations are unnecessary except where noted.

Arlington
Dining
★

Arlington Inn. The recent arrival of chef Ken Panquin will certainly help the restaurant retain its reputation as one of the most respected in the state. Using local products from Vermont farms whenever possible, his seasonal mix of contemporary and classic Continental cuisines might include venison Carpacio in apple chutney and maple mustard vinaigrette, and house-cured Gravlax with sauce rangote and field greens. Polished hardwood floors, green napkins and walls, candlelight, and soft piano music complement the food; so could a bottle of wine from the restaurant's extensive collection, recipient of the prestigious Award of Excellence from *The Wine Spectator. Rte. 7A,* *tel. 802/375–6532. Reservations advised. AE, MC, V. Closed Dec. 25, Jan. 1. Expensive.*

West Mountain Inn. A low-beamed, paneled, candlelit room is the setting for prix-fixe dinners featuring such specialties as veal chops topped with sun-dried tomatoes and Asiago cheese. Aunt Min's Swedish rye and other toothsome breads, as well as desserts, are all made on the premises. Tables by the windows allow a glorious view of the mountains. *Rte. 313, tel. 802/375–6516. Reservations advised. AE, MC, V. Moderate.*

Lodging ★ **West Mountain Inn.** A llama ranch on the property, African violets and chocolate llamas in the rooms, quilted bedspreads, and a front lawn with a spectacular view of the countryside were elements in Michael J. Fox's decision to be married here. This former farmhouse of the 1840s, restored over the last 13 years, sits on 150 acres and seems to be a world apart. Rooms 2, 3, and 4 in the front of the house overlook the front-lawn; the three small nooks of room 11 resemble railroad sleeper berths and are perfect for kids. Plush carpeting, complimentary hors d'oeuvres (chicken fingers, fruit), and copies of the books of Dorothy Canfield Fisher adorn the rooms. *Rte. 313, 05250, tel. 802/375–6516. 13 rooms with bath, 3 suites. Facilities: bar, walking and ski trails, disabled-access room. AE, MC, V. Rates are MAP. Expensive.*

Arlington Inn. The Greek Revival columns at the entrance to this railroad magnate's home of 1848 give it an imposing presence, yet the inn is more welcoming than forbidding. The cozy charm is created by clawfoot tubs in some bathrooms, linens that coordinate with the Victorian-style wallpaper, and the house's original moldings and wainscoting. The carriage house, built at the turn of the century and renovated in 1985, has country French and Queen Anne furnishings. *Rte. 7A, 05250, tel. 802/375–6532. 13 rooms with bath, 5 suites. Facilities: cable TV and VCR in public area, bar, tennis court. AE, MC, V. Rates include Continental breakfast. Moderate.*

Hill Farm Inn. This homey inn still has the feel of the country farmhouse it used to be: The mix of sturdy antiques and hand-me-downs, the spinning wheel in a corner of the hallway, the paintings by a family member, the buffalo that roam the 50 acres, the jars of homemade jam that visitors may take away— all convey the relaxed, friendly personalities of the owners, George and Joanne Hardy. Room 7, the newest, has a beamed cathedral ceiling and a porch with a view of Mount Equinox; the rooms in the guest house of 1790 are very private. *Rte. 7, Box 2015, 05250, tel. 802/375–2269 or 800/882–2545. 11 rooms, 6 with bath; 2 suites; 4 cabins in summer. Facilities: restaurant, cable TV in public area. AE, D, MC, V. Rates include full breakfast. Moderate.*

Bennington Dining **Four Chimneys.** Those who seek classic French cuisine in Bennington are inevitably drawn here. Heavy silverware, crisply starched linens, candlelight, and the delicately rose-colored walls complement a menu that recently included steak flambéed in cognac with green peppercorns. *21 West Rd., tel. 802/447–3500. Reservations advised. Jacket and tie advised. AE, DC, MC, V. Closed Mon. and Jan. 2–Feb. 14. Expensive.*

Main Street Café. Since it opened in 1989, this small storefront with the polished hardwood floors, candlelit tables, and fresh flowers has drawn raves, its Northern Italian cuisine judged well worth the few minutes' drive from downtown Bennington. Favorites include the rigatoni tossed with Romano, Parmesan, broccoli, and sausage in a cream sauce; and the chicken stuffed with ham, provolone, and fresh spinach and served in a Marsala-onion sauce. The look is casual chic, like that of a New York loft transplanted to a small town. *Rte. 67A, North Bennington, tel. 802/442-3210. Reservations advised. AE, DC, MC, V. Dinner only. Closed Mon. and Tues.; Thanksgiving, Dec. 25. Expensive.*

Alldays and Onions. It may look like a deli—it *is* a deli during the day—yet its dinner menus (changed weekly) have featured such creative dishes as sautéed scallops and fettuccine in a jalapeño-ginger sauce; and rack of lamb with a honey-thyme sauce. Desserts are baked on the premises. *519 E. Main St., tel. 802/447-0043. MC, V. Closed Sun. Moderate.*

The Brasserie. The Brasserie's fare is some of the city's most creative. A mozzarella loaf swirls cheese through bread topped with anchovy-herb butter, and the soups are filling enough for a meal. The decor is as clean-lined and contemporary as the Bennington pottery that is for sale in the same complex of buildings. *324 County St., tel. 802/447-7922. MC, V. Closed Tues. Moderate.*

★ **Blue Benn Diner.** Breakfast is served all day in this authentic diner, and the eats are as down-home as turkey hash and as off-the-wall as tabbouleh or breakfast burritos that wrap scrambled eggs, sausage, and chiles in a tortilla. There can be a long wait. *Rte. 7 N, tel. 802/442-8977. No credit cards. No dinner Sun.-Tues. Inexpensive.*

Lodging **South Shire Inn.** Canopy beds in lushly carpeted rooms, ornate plaster moldings, and a dark mahogany fireplace in the library create turn-of-the-century grandeur. The inn is in a quiet residential neighborhood within walking distance of the bus depot and downtown stores. Furnishings are antique except for the reproduction beds that provide contemporary comfort. Breakfast is served in the peach-and-white wedding cake of a dining room. *124 Elm St., 05201, tel. 802/447-3839. 9 rooms with bath. Facilities: fireplaces in 7 rooms, whirlpool baths in 4 rooms. No smoking. AE, MC, V. Rates include full breakfast. Moderate-Expensive.*

★ **Molly Stark Inn.** Tidy blue plaid wallpaper, gleaming hardwood floors, antique furnishings, and a wood-burning stove in a brick alcove of the sitting room give a country charm to this recently renovated inn of 1860 on the main road to Brattleboro. The Rockwell Room on the first floor is spacious but opens onto the sitting room; Molly's Room at the back of the building gets less noise from Route 9. *1067 E. Main St., 05201, tel. 802/442-9631. 6 rooms, 2 with bath. Facilities: cable TV in public area. No smoking. MC, V. Rates include full breakfast. Inexpensive-Moderate.*

Brattleboro **Walker's Restaurant.** Green café curtains hanging from brass
Dining railings, oak Windsor chairs, and a long bar give this family-style restaurant a turn-of-the-century feel. Food is adequately prepared, and the menu generally sticks to such basics as broiled fish, steak, baked stuffed shrimp, plus daily specials. *132 Main St., tel. 801/254-6046. AE, MC, V. Moderate.*

Common Ground. The political posters and concert fliers that line the staircase make you conscious of Vermont's strong progressive element. Owned cooperatively by the staff, this vegetarian restaurant serves the likes of cashew burgers and the "humble bowl of brown rice." A chocolate cake with peanut butter frosting and other desserts will lure confirmed meat-eaters. *25 Elliot St., tel. 802/257-0855. No credit cards. Closed Tues. Inexpensive-Moderate.*

Lodging **Latchis Hotel.** Restoration of the downtown landmark's Art Deco grandeur was completed in 1989, and everything old is new again: black-and-white-check bathroom tiles, painted geometric borders along the ceiling, multicolored patterns of terrazzo on the lobby floor. All deluxe rooms have refrigerator, complimentary Continental breakfast, movie passes, and shopping discounts at Brattleboro stores. Odd-numbered rooms offer a view of the Connecticut River and Main Street. *50 Main St., 05301, tel. 802/254-6300. 35 rooms with bath. Facilities: cable TV, telephones, air-conditioning. AE, MC, V. Inexpensive-Moderate.*

Chester **Inn at Long Last.** An army of toy soldiers fills a glass case beside the enormous fieldstone fireplace in the pine-floored lobby
Lodging of this Victorian inn, where guests like to gather for after-dinner drinks, lounging on one of the large couches in front of the fire. Bookshelves in the large wood-paneled library hold volumes in literature, science, biography, music, history, and labor economics; one entire shelf is devoted to George Orwell. Individual rooms are named after people, places, and things important to innkeeper Jock Coleman, former president of Haverford College in Pennsylvania, and are decorated simply with personal memorabilia; a pamphlet in each room explains the significance of the room names. The Dickens Room, with a high carved headboard, is the most spacious, and the Audubon and Tiffany rooms offer access to the second-story porch. Some of the bathrooms are fairly small. The quietest section of the house is at the back. *Main St., Box 589, 05143, tel. 802/875-2444. 30 rooms, 1 with bath in hall. Facilities: restaurant, TV in public area; 2 tennis courts. No pets. MC, V. Rates include full breakfast. Expensive.*

Grafton **The Old Tavern at Grafton.** Two dining rooms, one with formal
Dining Georgian furniture and oil portraits, the other with rustic paneling and low beams, serve such hearty traditional New England dishes as venison stew or grilled quail; some offerings feature cheeses made just down the road. *Rte. 35, tel. 802/843-2231. AE, MC, V. Closed Apr., Dec. 24-25. Expensive.*

Lodging **The Old Tavern at Grafton.** The white-column porches on both stories of the main building wrap around a carefully restored structure that dates to 1788 and has hosted Daniel Webster and Nathaniel Hawthorne. The inn has 14 rooms in the main building and 21 rooms in two structures across the street. Individually decorated, all rooms have private bath; rooms in the older part of the inn are furnished in antiques, and some have crocheted canopies or four-poster beds. Homes in town can also be rented through the inn. *Rte. 35, 05146, tel. 802/843-2231. 35 rooms with bath. Facilities: restaurant, lounge, swimming pond, 2 tennis courts, platform tennis in winter, games room. AE, MC, V. Closed Apr., Dec. 24-25. Moderate-Expensive.*

★ **Eaglebrook of Grafton.** A mix of well-preserved antiques and abstract art give this small country inn an air of city sophistication. The cathedral-ceilinged sun room, built overlooking the Saxtons River, the seven fireplaces with soapstone mantels, and the watercolor stencils in the hallways warrant this elegant retreat being featured in a glossy interior-design magazine. Blue-checked fabric gives one of the three rooms a French provincial air; another leans toward American country; the third has a Victorian flavor. Outside, the landscaped stone terrace is a perfect place to sit with a bottle of wine on a summer evening. Although the inn is small, the lush furnishings and care extended by the innkeepers toward their guests assures an indulgent stay. *Main St., 05146, tel. 802/843-2564. 1 room with bath, 2 rooms share 1 bath. Facilities: TV in public area. No pets. No credit cards. Rates include Continental breakfast. Moderate.*

Manchester
Dining

Chantecleer. Five miles north of Manchester, intimate dining rooms have been created in a converted dairy barn with a large fieldstone fireplace. The menu reflects the chef's Swiss background: The appetizers include *Bündnerfleisch* (air-dried Swiss beef); recent entrées were Wiener schnitzel and frogs' legs in garlic butter. *Rte. 7, East Dorset, tel. 802/362-1616. Reservations required. DC, MC, V. Dinner only. Closed Mon.-Tues. Expensive-Very Expensive.*

Wildflowers. As the dining room of the Reluctant Panther inn, Wildflowers has long been known for elegant cuisine, and the new owner, Robert Bachofen, former director of food and beverage at New York's Plaza Hotel, is upholding that tradition. A huge fieldstone fireplace dominates the larger of the two dining rooms; the other is a small greenhouse with five tables. Glasses and silver sparkle in the candlelight, the service is impeccable, and the menu, which changes daily, might include boneless stuffed chicken with spinach, Gruyère, and Chardonnay-thyme sauce; or fricassee of lobster with Nantucket Bay scallops and Gulf shrimp. *West Rd. at Rte. 7A, tel. 802/362-2568. Reservations required. AE, MC, V. Closed Tues. and Wed. Expensive.*

Garden Cafe. This sunny room with hanging plants has a terrific view of the spacious Southern Vermont Art Center grounds and an outdoor terrace; the menu includes such fare as sautéed trout with almonds; ragout of mushrooms in puff pastry; and home-baked fruit tart. *West Rd., tel. 802/362-4220. No credit cards. Closed mid-Oct.-Memorial Day. Moderate.*

Garlic John's. Italian specialties such as veal (piccata, Marsala, saltimbocca, parmigiana) and calamari fra diavolo; red sauce and lots of it; and a dangling thicket of straw-covered Chianti bottles give this large and popular family-oriented restaurant the feel of a busy trattoria. *Rte. 11/30, tel. 802/362-9843. MC, V. Dinner only. Moderate.*

Quality Restaurant. Gentrification has reached the down-home neighborhood place that was the model for Norman Rockwell's *War News* painting. The Quality now has Provençal wallpaper and polished wood booths, and the sturdy New England standbys of grilled meat loaf and hot roast beef or turkey sandwiches have been joined by tortellini Alfredo with shrimp and smoked salmon. *Main St., tel. 802/362-9839. AE, MC, V. Inexpensive-Moderate.*

Lodging

The Equinox. This white-column resort was a fixture on the tourism scene even before the family of Abraham Lincoln began spending summers here. A complete overhaul in 1992 restored all the rooms and public spaces, as well as the Marsh Tavern restaurant and the golf course, which is now a member of the Gleneagles group. The rooms and public areas are furnished in the casually elegant Vermont country-grand style. Unusual for a Vermont inn are the spa programs in the hotel's fitness spa, which have medical supervision and are tailored to the needs of the individual. The resort is often the site of large conferences. *Rte. 7A, Manchester Village 05254, tel. 802/362-*

4700 or 800/362–4747. 119 rooms with bath, 18 suites, 9 3-bedroom town houses. Facilities: restaurant, tavern, cable TV, 3 tennis courts, 18-hole golf course, and health club with sauna, steam room, indoor and outdoor pools, fitness classes, exercise equipment. AE, D, DC, MC, V. Very Expensive.

Reluctant Panther. The spacious rooms each have goose-down duvets and a complimentary half-bottle of wine. The decor features soft, elegant grays and peaches, while the furnishings are an eclectic mix of antique, country, and contemporary. Ten rooms have fireplaces—the Mary Porter suite has two—and all suites have whirlpools. The best views are from rooms B and D. *West Rd., Box 678, 05254, tel. 802/362–2568 or 800/822–2331. 16 rooms with bath, 4 suites. Facilities: restaurant, lounge, conference room. AE, MC, V. Rates are MAP. Expensive–Very Expensive.*

★ **1811 House.** The atmosphere of an elegant English country home can be enjoyed without crossing the Atlantic. A pub-style bar that serves 26 kinds of single-malt scotches and is decorated with horse brasses, the Waterford crystal in the dining room, equestrian paintings, and the English floral landscaping of three acres of lawn all contribute to an inn worthy of Princess Di. The rooms contain period antiques; six have fireplaces, and many have four-poster beds. Bathrooms are old-fashioned but serviceable, particularly the Robinson Room's marble-enclosed tub. *Rte. 7A, 05254, tel. 802/362–1811 or 800/432–1811. 14 rooms with bath. Facilities: lounge, air conditioning. No smoking. AE, MC, V. Rates include full breakfast. Expensive.*

Wilburton Inn. The stone-wall Tudor estate sits atop 20 acres of manicured grounds enhanced with sculpture, and the dining room and outdoor terrace overlook the Battenkill Valley. Rooms are spacious, especially those on the second floor, but the chenille-covered beds date to the home's conversion to an inn in 1946 (the country chintz decor in the six outlying cottages is newer). The public areas—with an ornately carved mantel on the first floor, mahogany paneling and stained-glass door in one of the small dining rooms, and a sweeping stone staircase to the lawn—are as elaborate as a railroad magnate's fortune could make them. *River Rd., 05254, tel. 802/362–2500 or 800/648–4944. 34 rooms with bath. Facilities: restaurant, lounge, outdoor pool, 3 tennis courts. AE, MC, V. Rates include full breakfast and afternoon tea. Expensive.*

Barnstead Innstead. A barn of the 1830s was transformed in 1968 into a handful of rooms that combine the rustic charm of exposed beams and barnboard walls with modern plumbing and cheerful wallpaper. *Rte. 30, 05255, tel. 802/362–1619. 12 rooms with bath, 1 suite. Facilities: cable TV, outdoor pool. MC, V. Moderate.*

Aspen Motel. Set well back from busy Route 7A, this family-owned motel has clean rooms with standardized motel furnishings. *Box 548, 05255, tel. 802/362–2450. 24 rooms with bath, 2-bedroom house with kitchen and bath. Facilities: cable TV, outdoor pool, shuffleboard courts, social room with fireplace. AE, D, MC, V. Inexpensive–Moderate.*

Marlboro
Dining

Tamarack House. Soft classical music accompanies a variety of ethnic dishes that make the most of traditional Vermont ingredients; the menu changes weekly and may include cuisine from regions—like France and the Caribbean, Italy and Cambodia—as distinct as they are miles apart. Game is a specialty in the fall and winter. Diners have a view of the inn's rolling lawn, and an antique leaded-glass cabinet with spice tins, salt dishes, and painted fans adds elegance. *Rte. 9, tel. 802/257–1093. Reservations advised. MC, V. Closed Mon.–Tues. and early Apr. Moderate.*

Lodging **Tamarack House.** Originally a farmhouse built in 1769, the inn has hand-stenciled willows in the halls, gleaming pine floors, and is updated with contemporary furnishings. The carriage house has four efficiency apartments that sleep three to six people. The newer rooms have larger windows and carpeting; one has a Jacuzzi. *Rte. 9, Box 275, 05344, tel. 802/257–1093. 15 rooms, 13 with bath. Facilities: restaurant, trout pond. MC, V. Rates include full breakfast. Moderate–Expensive.*

Whetstone Inn. A favorite of visitors to the Marlboro Music Festival, the 200-year-old inn mixes authentic Colonial architecture and furnishings with pottery lamps, stenciled curtains, Scandinavian-style wall hangings, and a library filled with the works of Thoreau, Tolstoy, Zola, Hugo, and Proust. Three rooms have kitchenettes, and two can be joined to form a suite. During the music festival, mid-July through mid-August, a one-week minimum stay is required. *South Rd., 05344, tel. 802/254–2500. 12 rooms, 8 with bath. Facilities: restaurant, skating pond. No credit cards. Inexpensive–Moderate.*

Newfane **The Four Columns.** Chef Greg Parks has introduced such nou-
Dining velle American dishes as mixed grilled game sausages, jumbo
★ shrimp with poblano butter and tapenade toast, and grilled marinated quail with pesto couscous. The elegant, Colonial-style dining room is decorated with antique tools and copper pots, and the tables sport such coverings as Towle place settings and Limoges china. *West St. on the village green, tel. 802/365–7713. Reservations advised. Jacket and tie advised. AE, MC, V. Closed Tues.; weekdays Apr.; early Dec. Expensive–Very Expensive.*

Lodging **The Four Columns.** Erected 150 years ago for a homesick Southern bride, the majestic white columns of the Greek Revival mansion are more intimidating than the Colonial-style rooms inside. Room 1 in the older section has an enclosed porch overlooking the town common; three rooms and a suite were added in an annex eight years ago. All rooms have antiques, brass beds, and quilts; some have fireplaces. The third-floor room in the old section is the most private. *West St., Box 278, 05345, tel. 802/365–7713. 17 rooms with bath. Facilities: restaurant, cable TV in public area, hiking trails. AE, MC, V. Rates are MAP in foliage season. Very Expensive.*

Weston **The Inn at Weston.** The food served in the large candlelit
Dining room—such entrées as lamb sautéed with mushrooms and Dijon mustard sauce; grilled chicken breast marinated in olive oil and lemon and served with raspberry sauce—has been praised by gourmet magazines. Breads and desserts are made on the premises. *Main St., tel. 802/824–5804. Reservations advised. No credit cards. Dinner only. Closed Wed. in winter, Mon. in summer. Moderate–Expensive.*

Lodging **Darling Family Inn.** The rooms in this renovated farmhouse of 1830 have baskets of apples and hand-stenciling by Joan Darling, and some rooms have folk art or an antique silver pitcher. Two cottages in back are less meticulously furnished, with twin beds, refrigerator, and shower stall. *Rte. 100, 05161, tel. 802/824–3223. 5 rooms with bath, 2 cottages. Facilities: outdoor* *pool, TV in public area. Pets in cottages only. No credit cards. Rates include full breakfast. Moderate.*

The Arts

Music **Marlboro Music Festival** (Marlboro Music Center, tel. 802/257–4333) presents a broad range of classical and contemporary music in weekend concerts during July and August.

New England Bach Festival (Brattleboro Music Center, tel. 802/257–4523), with a chorus under the direction of Blanche Moyse, is held in the fall.

Vermont Symphony Orchestra (tel. 802/864–5741) performs in Bennington and Arlington in winter, in Manchester and Brattleboro in summer.

Opera **Brattleboro Opera Theatre** (tel. 802/254–6649) stages a complete opera once a year and holds an opera workshop.

Theater **Dorset Playhouse** (north of Manchester, tel. 802/867–5777) hosts performances by a community group in winter and a resident professional troupe in the summer months.

Oldcastle Theatre Co. (Southern Vermont College, Bennington, (tel. 802/447–0564) performs from April to October.

Whetstone Theatre (River Valley Playhouse, Putney, tel. 802/387–5678) stages six productions from April to December.

Nightlife

Southern Vermont nightlife centers on Wilmington and other ski areas. In ski season you can expect to find live entertainment most nights; during the slower summer months it will be limited to weekends—or nonexistent. Most of the larger ski resorts have live entertainment. Performers may be listed in local newspapers.

Bars and Lounges **Avalanche** features a little of everything—country, blues, soft rock. *Rte. 11/30, Manchester, tel. 802/362–2622.*

Marsh Tavern, the lounge in the Equinox Hotel, hosts individual performers Tuesday to Saturday in summer. *Rte. 7A, Manchester, tel. 802/362–4700.*

Mole's Eye Cafe. This basement room offers Mexican food, burgers, and live bands: perhaps acoustic or folk on Wednesday, danceable R&B, blues, or reggae on the weekend. *High St., Brattleboro, tel. 802/257–0771. Cover charge, Fri.–Sat.*

Poncho's Wreck. Acoustic jazz or mellow rock is the rule here. *S. Main St., south of Rte. 9, Wilmington, tel. 802/464–9320.*

Nightclubs **Colors** has a DJ Thursday–Saturday; Thursday is ladies' night, Friday belongs to the guys. *20 Elliot St., Brattleboro, tel. 802/254–8646. Cover charge.*

Flat Street Night Club has a DJ on the weekend, an oldies band Thursday, and a huge video screen. *17 Flat St., Brattleboro, tel. 802/254–8257. Cover charge.*

Central Vermont

Manufacturing has dwindled in central Vermont even as strip development and the creation of service jobs in tourism and recreation have increased. Some manufacturing is still to be found, particularly in the west around Rutland, the state's second-largest city. Yet the southern tip of Lake Champlain and a major ski resort, Killington, make the area an economically diverse section of the state. Freshwater lakes are here, as are the state's famed marble industry and large dairy herds. But the heart of the area is the Green Mountains, running up the state's spine, and the surrounding wilderness of the Green Mountain National Forest, which offers countless opportunities for outdoor recreation and soulful pondering of the region's intense natural beauty—even for those inclined not to venture beyond the confines of their vehicle.

Important Addresses and Numbers

Weather (tel. 802/773–8056).

Visitor Information
Addison County Chamber of Commerce (2 Court St., Middlebury 05753, tel. 802/388–7951).

Bristol Area Chamber of Commerce (Box 291, Bristol 05443, tel. 802/453–4062).

Quechee Chamber of Commerce (Box 106, Quechee 05059, tel. 802/295–7900).

Rutland Region Chamber of Commerce (7 Court Sq., Box 67, Rutland 05701, tel. 802/773–2747).

Sugarbush Chamber of Commerce (Rte. 100, Box 173, Waitsfield 05673, tel. 802/496–3409).

Windsor Area Chamber of Commerce (Main St., Box 5, Windsor 05089, tel. 802/674–5910).

Woodstock Area Chamber of Commerce (4 Central St., Woodstock 05091, tel. 802/457–3555 or 802/457–1042 in summer).

Emergencies
Vermont's **Medical Health Care Information Center** has a 24-hour line (tel. 802/864–0454).

Telecommunications Device for the Deaf (TDD) has a 24-hour emergency hot line (tel. 802/253–0191).

Getting Around Central Vermont

By Car
The major east–west road is Route 4, from White River Junction in the east to Fair Haven in the west. Route 125 connects Middlebury on Route 7 with Hancock on Route 100; Route 100 splits the region in half along the eastern edge of the Green Mountains. Route 17 travels east–west from Waitsfield over the Appalachian Gap through Bristol and down to the shores of Lake Champlain. I–91 and the parallel Route 5 follow the eastern border; Routes 7 and 30 are the north–south highways in the west. I–89 links White River Junction with Montpelier to the north.

By Bus
Vermont Transit (tel. 802/864–6811 or 800/451–3292) links Rutland, White River Junction, Burlington, and many smaller towns.

Guided Tours

Land o' Goshen Farm raises llamas for sale and offers guided day or overnight trips in which llamas carry the luggage. *Rte. 73, Brandon, tel. 802/247–6015. Fares: day trip $75 per person (2-person minimum), overnight $210–$250 (6-person minimum). Treks mid-May–mid-Oct.*

Exploring Central Vermont

Numbers in the margin correspond to points of interest on the Central Vermont map.

Mountains, freshwater lakes, dairy herds, and unlimited recreational possibilities await visitors to central Vermont. Our tour begins in Windsor, on Route 5 near I–91, at the eastern edge of the state.

❶ **Windsor** was the delivery room for the birth of Vermont. The **Old Constitution House,** where in 1777 grantholders declared Vermont an independent republic, was originally a tavern that was moved to the present site. It now holds 18th- and 19th-century furnishings, American paintings and prints, and Vermont-made tools, toys, and kitchenware. *Rte. 5, tel. 802/674–6628. Admission: $1. Open late May–mid-Oct., Wed.–Sun. 10–4.*

The firm of Robbins & Lawrence became famous for applying the "American system"—the use of interchangeable parts—to the manufacture of rifles. Although the company no longer exists, one of its defunct factories houses the **American Precision Museum,** whose displays extol the Yankee ingenuity that created a major machine-tool industry here in the 19th century. *Rte. 5, tel. 802/674–5781. Admission: $2 adults, 75¢ children 6–12. Open mid-May–mid-Nov., weekdays 9–5, weekends and holidays 10–4.*

The **covered bridge** just off Route 5 that spans the Connecticut River between Windsor and Cornish, New Hampshire, is the longest in the state.

❷ **White River Junction,** on the Connecticut River 14 miles north of Windsor, is the home of the **Catamount Brewery,** one of the state's several microbreweries. Still relatively new, Catamount's popularity is growing with its golden ale, a British-style amber, a dark porter, and occasional seasonal specialties like their hearty Christmas ale. Samples are available at the conclusion of the brewery tour, and there's a company store. *58 S. Main St., tel. 802/296–2248. Open Mon.–Sat. 9–5, Sun. 1–5. Brewery tour July–Oct., Mon.–Sat. 11, 1, and 3; Sun., 1 and 3; Nov.–June, Sat. 11, 1, and 3. Additional tours given in summer and foliage season.*

❸ The village of **Quechee,** 6 miles west of White River Junction, is perched astride the Ottauquechee River. Nearby, the 165-foot-deep **Quechee Gorge** is fairly impressive and worth a look if you are in the area, though you should be wary of the large tourist crowds drawn to the gorge during summer and fall. The mile-long gorge, carved with the help of a glacier, is visible from Route 4, but many visitors spend time picnicking nearby or scrambling down one of the several descents to get a closer look. More than a decade ago **Simon Pearce** set up a glassblowing factory by the bank of a waterfall here, using the

Central Vermont

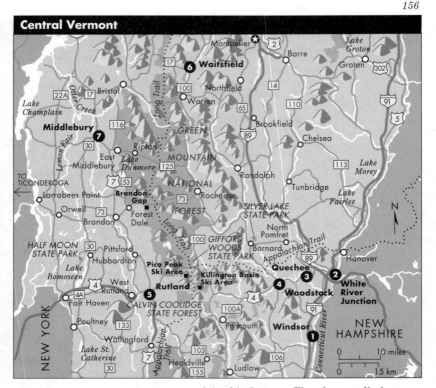

water power to drive his furnace. The glass studio is now a small complex that also houses a pottery workshop, a retail shop, and a restaurant; visitors can watch both potters and glassblowers at work. *Main St., tel. 802/295-2711. Workshops open weekdays 10–5, store open daily 9–9.*

❹ Four miles east of Quechee on Route 4, **Woodstock** fulfills virtually every expectation most people have of a quiet New England town (except for the crowds). The tree-lined village green is surrounded by exquisitely preserved Federal houses, streams flow around the center of town, and there's a covered bridge at the center. The interest of Rockefeller family members in historic preservation and land conservation is in part responsible for the town's pristine appearance.

The **Billings Farm and Museum** is one example of Rockefeller money at work (Billings's granddaughter married Laurance Rockefeller). The exhibits in the reconstructed farmhouse, school, general store, and workshop demonstrate the daily activities and skills of early Vermont settlers. Splitting logs doesn't seem nearly so quaint when you've watched the effort that goes into it! Visitors can contrast the older methods with those of a contemporary working dairy farm on the site. *Rte. 12, ½-mi north of Woodstock, tel. 802/457-2355. Admission: $6 adults, $3.50 children. Open early May–late Oct., daily 10–5.*

The Woodstock Historical Society has filled the rooms of the white clapboard **Dana House,** built in 1807, with its collection of period furnishings from the 18th and 19th centuries. Exhibits on the first floor include the town charter, furniture, maps, and locally minted silver. The elaborate sleigh owned by Frederick Billings, displayed in the barn, conjures up visions of romantic sleigh rides at the turn of the century. *26 Elm St., tel. 802/457–1822. Admission: $3.50 adults, $2.50 senior citizens, $1 children 12–18. Open May–late Oct., Mon.–Sat. 10–5, Sun. 2–5.*

Near Woodstock, the **Raptor Center** of the **Vermont Institute of Natural Science** houses 26 species of birds of prey, among them a bald eagle, a peregrine falcon, and the three-ounce saw-whet owl. All the caged birds have been found injured and unable to survive in the wild. The institute is a nonprofit, environmental research and educational resource center situated on a 77-acre nature preserve with self-guided walking trails. *Church Hill Rd., tel. 802/457–2779. Admission: $5 adults, $1 children 5–15. Open May–Oct., daily 10–4; Nov.–Apr., Mon.–Sat. 10–4.*

Time Out   Relax at one of the outdoor tables at the **Dunham Hill Bakery** on Central Street and enjoy a light lunch or pastry and cappuccino.

Plymouth Notch, where Calvin Coolidge was born, inaugurated president of the United States, and buried, has the character of the man himself: low-key and quiet. South of Route 4 on Route 100A, the small cluster of buildings, now owned by the state, looks more like a large farm than a town; in addition to the homestead itself there's the general store once run by Coolidge's father, a visitor center, an operating cheese factory, a one-room schoolhouse, the summer White House, and a film about Coolidge's life. Coolidge is buried in the cemetery on the other side of Route 100A. *Rte. 100A, 6 mi south of Rte. 4, east of Rte. 100, tel. 802/672–3773. Admission: $3.50 adults, children under 12 free. Open Memorial Day–mid-Oct., daily 9:30–5:30.*

The intersection of Routes 4 and 100 is at the heart of central Vermont's ski country, with the Killington, Pico, and Okemo resorts nearby. For a side trip into the area's principal city, **Rutland,** continue west 10 miles on Route 4.

⑤ Founded in the late 1700s, **Rutland** is at the heart of marble country—except the homes of blue-collar workers vastly outnumber the mansions of the marble magnates, as do strips of shopping centers and a seemingly endless row of traffic lights. Rutland's traditional economic ties to railroading and marble are rapidly being displaced by the growth of the Pico and Killington ski areas to the east.

The **Chaffee Art Gallery** is housed in a former Victorian mansion complete with parquet floors and grand staircases. The 250 Vermont artists work in a variety of media, and the gallery contains both abstract and representational pieces. Most of the work is for sale. The gallery's rotating exhibits may deal with such subjects as trains, folk art, and airplanes. *16 S. Main St., tel. 802/775–0356. Contribution. Open June–Oct., daily 10–5; Nov.–May, Wed.–Mon. 11–4.*

At the **Vermont Marble Exhibit,** 4 miles north of Rutland, visitors can see the transformation of the rough stone into slabs, blocks, and works of art by the full-time sculptor-in-residence. There is also a walkway above the production floor that lets visitors watch the industrial applications. A gift shop carries factory seconds and both foreign and domestic marble items. Expect crowds here; this is one of the state's most popular tourist attractions. *Take Route 3 north from Route 4, turn left after 4.4 miles, and follow the signs. Tel. 802/459-3311. Admission: $3.50 adults, $1.50 children 6–12. Open Memorial Day–Oct. 31, daily 9–5:30; Nov.–Memorial Day, Mon.–Sat. 9–4.*

Just what goes into producing all those jugs of maple syrup? The **New England Maple Museum** in Pittsford gives the historical perspective (the process originated with Native Americans, who cooked the sap over an open fire) and shows antique sugaring implements, folk murals, and a film. When your sweet tooth is aching, you'll find that the gift shop has all syrup grades for sale. *Rte. 7, Pittsford, tel. 802/483-9414. Admission: $1.50 adults, 50¢ children 6–12. Open late May–late Oct., daily 8:30–5:30; late Oct.–Dec. and Apr.–May, daily 10–4.*

Wilson Castle, a tribute to 19th-century America's infatuation with European culture, is a 32-room Romanesque mansion complete with turrets, stone portico, fresco ceilings, and a potpourri of Oriental and European furniture and objets d'art. Quite an anomoly in rural Vermont, it represents the Gilded Age at its most indulgent. *W. Proctor Rd., Proctor, tel. 802/ 773-3284. Admission: $6 adults, $5.50 senior citizens, children 6–12. Open late May–Oct., daily 9–6.*

Head north on Route 100 for a scenic drive into the heart of the Green Mountains. The intersection of Routes 100 and 125 in Hancock offers options for two of Vermont's most inspiring mountain drives. The shorter, Route 125 West, meanders past a waterfall and the Texas Falls Recreation Area, then traverses a moderately steep mountain pass before reaching the town of Middlebury. This is Robert Frost country; Vermont's late poet laureate spent 23 summers at a farm just east of Ripton. The farm isn't open to the public, but 2 miles east of Ripton and 12 miles east of Middlebury, the **Robert Frost Wayside Trail** is an easy ¾-mile gravel path that winds through quiet woodland. Plaques along the way bear quotations from Frost's poems. A picnic area is ¼ mile to the east.

The longer option continues on Route 100 and after snaking through the Granville Gulf Nature Reserve enters the **Mad River Valley,** home to the Sugarbush and Mad River Glen ski areas. Although in close proximity to these popular resorts, the valley **⑥** towns of **Warren** and **Waitsfield** have maintained a decidedly low-key atmosphere.

Time Out The gourmet deli and bakery in the **Warren Store** on Main Street has innovative sandwich, salad, and pastry offerings that can be enjoyed on an outdoor deck overlooking a cascading brook.

Route 17 West winds up and over the Appalachian Gap, one of Vermont's most panoramic mountain passes: The views from the top and on the way down the other side toward the town of Bristol are a just reward for the challenging drive.

⑦ In the late 1800s **Middlebury** was the largest community in the state west of the Green Mountains, an industrial center with wool, grain, and marble mills powered by the river that runs through the town. **Middlebury College,** founded in 1800, was conceived as an alternative to the more worldly University of Vermont, and its grey limestone buildings give a unified look to the campus, located near the center of town. The college's

Johnson Memorial Art Gallery, located in the Fine Arts Building, has a permanent collection of paintings and sculpture that includes work by Rodin and Hiram Powers. *Fine Arts Bldg., tel. 802/388–3711, ext. 5235. Admission free. Open weekdays, Sun. noon–5; Sat. 9–noon, 1–5.*

The **Vermont Folk Life Center** is housed in the basement of the restored 1801 home of Gamaliel Painter, the founder of Middlebury College. The rotating exhibits explore all facets of Vermont life, which could mean contemporary photography, antiques, paintings by folk artists, or manuscripts. *2 Court St., tel. 802/388–4964. Donations accepted. Open weekdays 9–5.*

At the **Sheldon Museum,** an 1829 marble merchant's house, a guide walks groups through period rooms that range from Colonial to turn-of-the-century and hold not only furniture but also toys, clothes, kitchen tools, and paintings. The museum archives contain 30,000 letters, account books, ledgers, manuscripts, and photos. *1 Park St., tel. 802/388–2117. Admission: $3.50 adults, $3 senior citizens and students, 50¢ children under 12. Open June–Oct., Mon.–Sat. 10–5; Nov.–May, Wed., Fri. 1–4.*

Time Out   An old-fashioned marble-counter soda fountain, and an extensive menu of ice-cream dishes, are the attractions at **Calvi's** on Merchants Row in Middlebury.

More than a crafts store, the **Vermont State Craft Center** at Frog Hollow is a juried display of the work of more than 250 Vermont artisans. The center sponsors classes with some of those artists. *Mill St., tel. 802/388–3177. Open year-round Mon.–Sat. 9:30–5; also June–Dec., Sun. noon–5.*

The Morgan horse—the official state animal—is known for its even temper and stamina even though its legs are a bit truncated in proportion to its body. The University of Vermont's **Morgan Horse Farm,** about 2½ miles from Middlebury, is a breeding and training farm where visitors may tour the stables and paddocks. *Rte. 23, tel. 802/388–2011. Admission: $3.50 adults, $1 children 13–19. Open May–Oct., daily 9–4.*

Central Vermont for Free

Catamount Brewery, White River Junction
Johnson Art Gallery, Middlebury
Robert Frost Trail, Ripton
Simon Pearce Glass Studio, Quechee
Vermont State Craft Center, Middlebury

What to See and Do with Children

Billings Farm and Museum, Woodstock
Morgan Horse Farm, Middlebury
New England Maple Museum, Rutland
Raptor Center, Woodstock

Off the Beaten Track

At the **Crowley Cheese Factory**'s converted barn, visitors can watch the process that turns milk into cheese. What's different here is that the curds are manipulated by hand rather than by a machine. Turn south from Route 103 about 5 miles west of Ludlow (at the sign for Healdville) and continue 1 mile to the factory. *Tel. 802/259–2340. Open Mon.–Sat. 8–4, Sun. 11–5.*

Crossing the **floating bridge at Brookfield** feels like driving on water. The bridge, supported by almost 400 barrels, sits at water level and is the scene of the annual ice harvest festival in January (the bridge is closed in winter). Take Route 65 off I–89 to Brookfield and follow the signs.

Shopping

Shopping Districts **Historic Marble Works** (Middlebury, tel. 802/388–3701), a renovated marble manufacturing facility, is a collection of unique shops set amid quarrying equipment and factory buildings.

The Marketplace at Bridgewater Mills (Rte. 4, west of Woodstock, tel. 802/672–3332) is a converted mill that houses three stories of boutiques with Vermont crafts, including Vermont Clock Craft and Vermont Marble, as well as The Mountain Brewers, producers of Long Trail Ale, where tours and tastings are available.

Timber Rail Village (Rte. 4, Quechee, tel. 802/295–1550) bills itself as an antiques mall and stocks inventory from 225 dealers in its immense reconstructed barn. If you enjoy antiques, allow plenty of time; many people stay an entire afternoon. A small-scale working railroad will take the kids for a ride while Mom and Dad browse.

Food and Drink **The Village Butcher** (Elm St., Woodstock, tel. 802/457–2756) is an emporium for Vermont comestibles.

Bristol Market (28 North St., Bristol, tel. 802/453–2448), open since the early 1900s, features a comprehensive selection of health-oriented foods and Vermont-made products.

Specialty Stores
Art and Antiques **Antiques Center at Hartland** (Rte. 5, Hartland, tel. 802/436–2441), one of the best known in Vermont, displays, in two 18th-century houses, inventory from 50 dealers around the state.

Foundation Antiques (148 N. Main St., Fair Haven, tel. 802/265–4544) has a strong selection of Quimper china, graniteware, art pottery, lighting, and ephemera.

Luminosity (Rte. 100, Waitsfield, tel. 802/496–2231) is situated in a converted church and, fittingly, specializes in stained glass. And windows are just the beginning.

Minerva (61 Central St., Woodstock, tel. 802/457–1940) is a cooperative of eight artisans whose work includes stoneware, porcelain, and jewelry, as well as handwoven clothing, rugs, and blankets.

North Wind Artisans' Gallery (81 Central St., Woodstock, tel. 802/457–4587) has contemporary artwork with sleek, jazzy designs.

Park Antiques (75 Woodstock Ave., Rutland, tel. 802/775–4184) has furniture, folk art, glass, china, jewelry, paintings, and quilts.

Windsor Antiques Market (53 N. Main St., Windsor, tel. 802/674–9336) occupies a Gothic Revival church and features Oriental, Native American, and military items in addition to American furniture, folk art, and accessories.

Books **Charles E. Tuttle** (28 S. Main St., Rutland, tel. 802/773–8930) is a major publisher of books on Oriental subjects, particularly art. In addition to its own publications, Tuttle has rare and out-of-print books, genealogies, and local histories.

Crafts **All Things Bright and Beautiful** (Bridge St., Waitsfield, tel. 802/496–3997) is a 12-room Victorian house jammed to the rafters with stuffed animals of all shapes, sizes, and colors.

East Meets West (Rte. 7 at Sangamon Rd., north of Rutland, tel. 802/443–2242) shows carvings, masks, statues, textiles, pottery, and baskets from the Third World, the American Southwest, the Pacific Northwest, and the Arctic.

Folkheart (18 Main St., Bristol, tel. 802/453–4101 and 71 Main St., Middlebury, tel. 802/388–0367) carries an unusual selection of jewelry, toys, and crafts from around the world.

Log Cabin Quilts (9 Central St., Woodstock, tel. 802/457–2725) has an outstanding collection of quilts in traditional designs and quilting supplies for the do-it-yourself enthusiast.

Warren Village Pottery (Main St. Warren, tel. 802/496–4162) sells unique, hand-crafted wares from their home-based retail shop.

Three Bags Full (at the Black Sheep Farm, Rte. 100, Waitsfield, tel. 802/496–4298) features everything wool, including handmade sweaters, blankets, sheep pelts, and yarn.

Women's Clothing **Scotland by the Yard** (Rte. 4, Quechee, tel. 802/295–5351) has authentic Scottish kilts, kilt pins in imaginative designs, and jewelry bearing traditional Scottish emblems and symbols.

Who Is Sylvia? (26 Central St., Woodstock, tel. 802/457–1110) is stocked with vintage clothing and antique linens and jewelry.

Sports and Outdoor Activities

Biking The popular 14-mile Waitsfield–Warren loop begins by crossing the covered bridge in Waitsfield and keeping right on East Warren Road to the four-way intersection in East Warren; continue straight, then bear right, riding down Brook Road to the village of Warren; return by turning right (north) on Route 100 back toward Waitsfield. **Mad River Bike Shop** (Rte. 100, Waitsfield, tel. 802/496–9500) offers rentals, mountain bike tours, route suggestions, and maps of the area.

A more challenging, 32-mile ride starts in Bristol: Take North Street from the traffic light in town and continue north to Monkton Ridge and on to Hinesburg; to return follow Route 116 south through Starksboro and back to Bristol. The **Bike and Ski Touring Center** (74 Main St., Middlebury, tel. 802/388–6666) rents both road and mountain bikes and provides information and advice for bicycling in the Champlain Valley.

A bike trail runs alongside Route 106 south of Woodstock. **Four Seasons Sports** (Clubhouse Rd., Woodstock, tel. 802/295–7527) rents equipment and schedules daily bike trips.

Canoeing **Otter Falls Outfitters** (Marble Works, Middlebury, tel. 802/388–4406) has an excellent selection of maps, guides, and canoeing equipment.

North Star Canoes (Balloch's Crossing, tel. 603/542–5802) in Cornish, New Hampshire, rents canoes for half-day, full-day, and overnight trips on the Connecticut River.

Fishing Central Vermont is the heart of the state's warm-water lake and pond fishing. **Lake Dunmore** produced the state record rainbow trout; **Lakes Bomoseen** and **St. Catherine** are good for rainbows and largemouth bass. In the east, **Lakes Fairlee** and **Morey** feature bass, perch, and chain pickerel, while the lower part of the **Connecticut River** has bass, pickerel, walleye, and perch.

Yankee Charters (20 S. Pleasant St., Middlebury 05753, tel. 802/388–7365) arranges sport-fishing trips on Lake Champlain and provides equipment.

Golf Spectacular views and challenging play can be found at the 18-hole championship course designed by Robert Trent Jones at **Sugarbush Resort** (Golf Course Rd., Warren, tel. 802/583–2722). He also designed the 18-hole championship course of the **Woodstock Country Club** (South St., Woodstock, tel. 802/457–2112), which is operated by the Woodstock Inn and Resort and is open to the public.

Hiking Several day hikes in the vicinity of Middlebury take in the scenery of the Green Mountains. About 8 miles east of Brandon on Route 73, one trail starts at Brandon Gap and climbs steeply up **Mount Horrid** (one hour). On Route 116, about 5½ miles north of East Middlebury, a U.S. Forest Service sign marks a dirt road that forks to the right and leads to the start of the hike to **Abbey Pond,** which has a view of Robert Frost Mountain (two–three hours).

About 5½ miles north of Forest Dale on Route 53, a large turnout marks a trail to the **Falls of Lana** (two hours). Three other trails—two short ones of less than a mile each and one of 2½ miles—lead to the old abandoned fortifications at **Mount Independence;** to reach them, take Route 22A west of Orwell for 3½ miles and continue on the right fork almost 2 miles to a parking area.

Polo **Quechee Polo Club** draws several hundred spectators every Saturday afternoon in summer to its matches with visiting teams on a field near the Quechee Gorge. *Deweys' Mills Rd., ½ mi off Rte. 4, Quechee, tel. 802/295–7152. Admission: $2 adults, $1 children, or $5 car.*

Water Sports Boat rentals are available at **Chipman Point Marina** (Rte. 73A, Middlebury, tel. 802/948–2288), where there is dock space for 60 boats. This is also headquarters for **Vermont Houseboat Vacations** (90 Forbes St., Riverside, RI 02915, tel. 401/437–1277), which operates from May through August and rents houseboats that sleep six to eight persons.

State Parks

Ascutney State Park has a scenic mountain toll road and snowmobile trails. *Rte. 5, 2 mi north of Exit 8 from I–91, tel. 802/674–2060. 1,984 acres. Facilities: 49 campsites (no hookups), toilets, showers, picnic tables, fireplaces.*

Coolidge State Park, part of Calvin Coolidge National Forest, includes the village where Calvin Coolidge was born. *Rte. 100A, 2 mi north of junction with Rte. 100, tel. 802/672–3612. 500 acres. Facilities: 60 campsites (no hookups), toilets, showers, picnic tables, fireplaces, phone, snowmobile trails.*

Gifford Woods State Park, between Woodstock and Rutland, includes Kent Pond, a popular spot for fishing. *Rte. 100, ½ mi north of junction with Rte. 4, tel. 802/775–5354. 114 acres. Facilities: 47 campsites (no hookups), toilets, showers, picnic tables and shelter, fireplaces, phone.*

Half Moon State Park's principal attraction is Half Moon Pond, which has approach trails, nature trails, and a naturalist on duty. *Town Rd., 3½ mi off Rte. 30 from Hubbardton, tel. 802/ 273–2848. Facilities: 69 campsites (no hookups), toilets, showers, picnic tables, fireplaces, phone, boat and canoe rentals.*

Dining and Lodging

The large hotels are in Rutland and near the Killington ski area just to the east; elsewhere, travelers stay at inns, bed-and-breakfasts, or small motels. The **Woodstock Area Chamber of Commerce** provides a lodging referral service (tel. 802/457–2389). In the restaurants, dress is casual and reservations are unnecessary except where noted.

Bristol
Dining
★

Mary's. Walking off the sleepy streets of Bristol and into this little storefront restaurant is like finding a precious antique in a dusty attic. Mary's has earned a reputation as one of the most inspired dining experiences in the state. Seasonal offerings include Vermont rack of lamb with a rosemary mustard sauce, Norwegian salmon szechuan style, and venison au poivre. For dessert try the Bailey's white chocolate chip cheesecake. *11 Main St., tel. 802/453–2432. Reservations advised. AE, MC, V. Moderate–Expensive.*

Middlebury
Dining

Middlebury Inn. At lunchtime the big bay window of the blue and white Colonial dining room lets in lots of light, and in the evening the candles above the fireplace give the pristine white columns, curtains, and lace tablecloths a romantic glow. Entrées include such dishes as veal Madeira; bourbon shrimp; and chicken teriyaki; the specialty of the house is hot popovers. *Court House Sq., tel. 802/388–4961. Reservations advised. AE, MC, V. Expensive.*

★ **Woody's.** The peach walls with diner-Deco fixtures, the abstract paintings, and the cool jazz create a setting where assistant professors celebrate special occasions. Of the three levels, the lowest has the best view of Otter Creek. The nightly specials might include a homemade soup of roast pheasant broth with barley; a dinner entrée could be charbroiled strip steak with smoked cheddar nachos and salsa butter; and there's usually a Vermont lamb offering. *5 Bakery La., tel. 802/388–4182. Reservations advised. DC, MC, V. Moderate–Expensive.*

Lodging **Middlebury Inn.** Queen Anne furniture, white fluted columns, a baby grand piano, and a black marble fireplace in the lobby reflect the heritage of Middlebury's foremost lodging place since 1827. The Otis elevator dates from 1926. Rooms in the main building mix the formal with country antiques: Reproduction mahogany cabinets house television sets. Bathrooms are early 20th-century, though they are stocked with contemporary features such as hairdryers, scales, and a phone. The 20 motel rooms have newer plumbing, sofa beds for a third person, quilt hangings, and floor-to-ceiling windows. *Court House Sq., 05753, tel. 802/388–4961 or 800/842–4666. 75 rooms with bath. Facilities: restaurant, lounge. AE, MC, V. Rates include afternoon tea. Moderate–Expensive.*

★ **Swift House Inn.** The white paneled wainscoting, elaborately carved mahogany and marble fireplaces, and cherry paneling in the dining room give this Georgian home of a 19th-century governor and his philanthropist daughter a formal elegance. Rooms, each with Oriental rugs and nine of them with fireplaces, are decorated with antique reproductions that might include canopy beds, swag curtains, or a clawfoot Victorian tub. Bathrooms have double whirlpool tubs, bath pillows, and guest robes. *25 Stewart La., 05753, tel. 802/388-9925. 21 rooms with bath. Facilities: restaurant, lounge, cable TV in public area and in some rooms, sauna and steam room, disabled-access room. AE, D, MC, V. Rates include full breakfast. Moderate–Expensive.*

Waybury Inn. The Waybury Inn may look familiar; it appeared as the "Stratford Inn" on television's *Newhart.* Guest rooms, some of which have the awkward configuration that can result from the conversion of a building of the early 1800s, have quilted pillows, antique furnishings, and middle-aged plumbing. Comfortable sofas around the fireplace create a homey living room, and the pub—which serves more than 100 different kinds of beer—is a favorite local gathering spot. *Rte. 125, 05740, tel. 802/388-4015 or 800/348-1810. 14 rooms with bath. Facilities: restaurant, lounge, cable TV in public area. AE, MC, V. Moderate–Expensive.*

Quechee **Isabelle's.** Located in the Parker House Inn, this formal dining
Dining room was completely redecorated in 1990, resulting in a lighter, more contemporary feel. Lace window panels, high-backed chairs, and traditional period stencilling on peach walls give Isabelle's an elegant atmosphere. The menu features such entrées as roasted local rabbit with homemade plum chutney as well as lighter bistro fare. When the weather's warm, check out the terrace with its spectacular river view. *Main St., tel. 802/295-6077. AE, MC, V. Dinner only. Closed Mon.–Tues. except summer, mid-April, early Nov. Expensive.*

Simon Pearce. Candlelight and fresh flowers, sparkling glassware from the studio downstairs, contemporary dinnerware, and large windows that overlook the banks of the Ottauquechee River all contribute to a romantic setting. Beef and Guinness stew (which reflects the owner's Irish background), and roast duck with mango chutney sauce are specialties of the house. *Main St., tel. 802/295-1470. Reservations advised. AE, MC, V. Moderate–Expensive.*

Rosalita's. *Ay yi yi yi*—who would expect Mexican cuisine in the heart of Yankeedom? This casual place has the right decorative touches—cacti, stucco, clay tiles—and the standard burritos, nachos, and enchiladas, plus such entrées as steak and chicken fajitas and broiled chicken breast topped with tomatoes and Monterey Jack cheese. *Waterman Pl., Rte. 4, tel. 802/295-1600. AE, MC, V. Inexpensive–Moderate.*

Lodging **Quechee Inn at Marshland Farm.** The home of Vermont's first lieutenant governor, this 1793 building has Queen Anne furniture and wide-plank pine floors. The sitting room flaunts an enormous fireplace; a piano stands in one corner, and a 5-foot teddy bear looks comfy sitting at a table in another. *Clubhouse Rd., 05059, tel. 802/295-3133. 24 rooms with bath. Facilities: restaurant, lounge, cable TV, air-conditioning, conference rooms, ski center, fly-fishing school, bike and canoe rentals. AE, DC, MC, V. Rates are MAP. Expensive–Very Expensive.*

Parker House. The spacious peach and blue rooms of this renovated Victorian mansion of 1857 are named for former residents. Emily boasts a marble fireplace and an iron-and-brass bed. The armoire and dressing table in Rebecca have delicate faux inlays. Walter is the smallest room. Joseph has a spectacular view of the Ottauquechee River. The new rooms on the third floor are air-conditioned. *Main St., Box 0780, 05059, tel. 802/295-6077. 7 rooms with bath. Facilities: restaurant. AE, MC, V. Closed mid-Apr., early Nov. Expensive.*

★ **Quechee Bed and Breakfast.** Dried herbs hang from the beams in the living room, where a wood settee sits before a floor-to-ceiling fireplace that dates to the original structure of 1795. In the guest rooms, handwoven throws cover the beds and soft pastels coordinate linens and decor. Jessica's Room is the smallest; the Bird Room with its exposed beams is one of four that overlook the Ottauquechee River. Rooms at the back are farther from busy Route 4. Luminarias or cornstalks decorate the wide front porch seasonally, and the inn is within walking distance of Quechee Gorge. *Rte. 4, 05059, tel. 802/295-1776. 8 rooms with bath. Facilities: air-conditioning. MC, V. Rates include full breakfast. Moderate–Expensive.*

Rutland **Vermont Marble Inn.** The dining room, with 16 tables, is inti-
Dining mate enough to allow diners to make new friends. Anything
★ less than the classical music, crystal chandelier, and candle-light would scarcely do justice to a meal that might include veal loin sautéed in saffron oil with sweet peppers and olives in a chive pesto; or braised duckling in port and raspberry sauce with wild rice. A vegetarian plate may offer lentil-and-vegetable stuffed zucchini and grilled polenta, and there's a selection of home-baked desserts. All food is prepared to order, and special diets can be accommodated. *Fair Haven, tel. 802/265-8383. AE, MC, V. Moderate–Expensive.*

Ernie's Hearthside. Known also as Royal's Hearthside, Royal's Grill and Bar, and Ernie's Grill and Bar, the Rutland institution features an open hearth with hand-painted tiles, behind which the staff prepares mesquite-grilled chicken with basil, tomato, and mushrooms; roast prime rib; and lamb chops grilled with ginger and rosemary. *37 N. Main St., tel. 802/775-0856. Reservations advised. AE, DC, MC, V. Moderate.*

121 West. The menu features Wiener schnitzel and other Continental entrées as well as New England standbys—broiled fish; and lobster and shrimp casserole. The decor is as middle-of-the-road as the menu: red tablecloths, white stucco walls. Portions are ample, and the restaurant is popular locally. *121 W. Central St., tel. 802/773-7148. Reservations advised. AE, MC, V. Closed Sun. Moderate.*

★ **Back Home Cafe.** Wood booths, black and white linoleum tile, and exposed brick give this second-story café the air of a hole-in-the-wall in New York City—where the owners come from. Dinner might be baked stuffed fillet of sole with spinach, mushrooms, feta cheese, and tarragon sauce; or any of a number of Italian specialties. Daily lunch specials offer soup, entrée, and dessert for less than $5. *21 Center St., tel. 802/775-2104. MC, V. Inexpensive–Moderate.*

Lodging **Vermont Marble Inn.** The innkeepers are the sort of people who
★ beg you to put on your coat so you don't catch cold and later present an elaborate afternoon tea on a sterling silver service. Two ornate Carrara marble living room fireplaces look and feel as though they were carved from solid cream. Guest rooms are named for authors (Byron, Elizabeth Barrett Browning) whose works are placed beside the bed. The antique furnishings may include a canopy bed, a working fireplace, an antique trunk; the bathrooms are large enough to have accommodated the full, flowing dresses of 1867, when the inn was built as a private home. Eight baths have shower stall only. *Fair Haven, 05743,*

tel. 802/265–8383. 13 rooms with bath. Facilities: restaurant, lounge. AE, MC, V. Rates include 5-course breakfast, afternoon tea, dinner. Very Expensive.

The Inn at Rutland. Mary and Michael Clark gave Rutland an alternative to motel and hotel chain accommodations when they renovated a Victorian mansion in 1988. The ornate oak staircase lined with heavy embossed metallic paper wainscoting leads to rooms that blend modern bathrooms with turn-of-the-century touches: botanical prints, elaborate ceiling moldings, frosted glass, pictures of ladies in long white dresses. Rooms on the second floor are larger than those on the third (once the servants' quarters). *70 N. Main St., 05701, tel. 802/773–0575. 12 rooms with bath. Facilities: phones, cable TV. AE, D, MC, V. Rates include Continental breakfast. Moderate.*

Comfort Inn. This hotel just in back of the Trolley Barn shops may look as though it's intended for business travelers, but it also has a large tourist clientele. Guest room decor is a cut above the hotel chain standard, though the bathrooms are a bit small. Rooms with even numbers face away from the parking lot. *170 S. Main St., 05701, tel. 802/775–2200 or 800/432–6788. 103 rooms with bath. Facilities: restaurant, lounge, indoor pool, racquetball and tennis courts, sauna, whirlpool, exercise equipment, cable TV, phones. Rates include Continental breakfast. AE, D, DC, MC, V. Inexpensive–Moderate.*

Waitsfield
Dining

Chez Henri. Though located adjacent to the Sugarbush ski area, this bistro has garnered a year-round following with traditional French dishes such as grilled swordfish with a coulis, rabbit in red wine sauce, and filet of beef peppercorn. After dinner, there is dancing in the "Back Room." *Sugarbush Village, tel. 802/583–2600. AE, MC, V. Moderate–Expensive.*

Richard's Special Vermont Pizza (RSVP). Walk through the door, and you're immediately transported through time (to the 1950s) and space (to anywhere but Vermont). The pizza—legendary around these parts with its paper-thin crust and toppings like cilantro pesto, cob-smoked bacon, pineapple, and sautéed spinach—has become known for transport as well: Richard will Federal Express a frozen pie almost anywhere in the world overnight. And there are plenty of takers. Salads and sandwiches are also available. *Bridge St., tel. 802/496–RSVP. MC, V. Inexpensive.*

Lodging

The Inn at the Round Barn Farm. Art exhibits have replaced cows in the big round barn here, but the Shaker-style building still dominates the farm's 85 countryside acres. One of the 12 remaining round barns in the state, it's used for summer concerts, weddings, and parties and is on the National Register of Historic Places. The inn's 10 rooms are in the 1806 farmhouse where books line the walls of the cream-colored library and breakfast is served in a cheerful solarium that overlooks a small landscaped pond and rolling acreage. The rooms are elegance country-style, with eyelet-trimmed sheets, new quilts on four-poster beds, and brass wall lamps for easy bedtime reading. The inn makes a terrific retreat, in fact, you could relax here until the cows come home. *E. Warren Rd., RR 1, Box 247, 05673, tel. 802/496–2276. 10 rooms with bath. Facilities: TV in public area, whirlpools; swimming pool, full breakfast. AE, MC, V. Moderate–Expensive.*

Windsor
Dining

Windsor Station. Yet another converted main-line railroad station serves such main-line entrées as chicken Kiev or filet mignon (prime rib on Saturday night). The booths with their curtained brass railings were created from the high-back railroad benches in the depot. *Depot Ave., tel. 802/674–2052. AE, MC, V. Closed early Nov. Moderate.*

Lodging **Juniper Hill Inn.** An expanse of green lawn with Adirondack chairs and a garden of perennials sweeps up to the portico of this Greek Revival mansion, built at the turn of the century and now on the National Historic Register. The central living room with its hardwood floors, oak paneling, Oriental carpets, and thickly upholstered wing chairs and sofas has a stately feel. The spacious rooms are furnished with some antiques, and some have fireplaces. The four-course dinners served in the candlelit dining room may include roast pork glazed with mustard and brandy sauce. *Juniper Hill Rd., Box 79, 05089, tel. 802/674–5273. 16 rooms with bath. Facilities: restaurant, pool, walking trails. MC, V. Rates include full breakfast. Moderate.*

Woodstock **Woodstock Inn.** The dinner fare is nouvelle New England in this
Dining large dining room with several dozen tables. The menu changes seasonally and may include such entrées as salmon steak with avocado beurre blanc; Maine lobster and scallops with fresh vegetable melange; and such standbys as beef Wellington and prime rib. The wall of windows affords diners a view over the inn's putting green. *Rte. 4, tel. 802/457–1100. Reservations advised. Jacket requested after 6 PM. AE, MC, V. Expensive–Very Expensive.*

Kedron Valley Inn. The chef trained at La Varenne cooking school in Paris, and that means such classical French dishes as fillet of Norwegian salmon stuffed with herb seafood mousse in puff pastry; and shrimp, scallops, and lobster with wild mushrooms sautéed in shallots and white wine and served with a Fra Angelico cream sauce. The decor, too, is striking; antique linens are displayed in frames like works of art, and a terrace looking onto the grounds is open in summer. *Rte. 106, tel. 802/457–1473. D, MC, V. Closed Apr. Expensive.*

★ **The Prince and the Pauper.** Here is a romantically candlelit Colonial setting, a prix fixe menu, and nouvelle French fare with a Vermont accent. The roast duckling might be served with a black cherry or Cointreau glaze; escalopes de veau could have a madeira demiglace or creamed onions with tarragon vinegar. Homemade lamb and pork sausage in puff pastry with a honey-mustard sauce is another possibility. *24 Elm St., tel. 802/457–1818. Reservations advised. D, MC, V. Dinner only. Closed Sun.–Mon. some seasons. Expensive.*

Bentleys. In addition to the standards—burgers, chili, homemade soups, omelets, croissants with various fillings—entrées at this informal and often busy restaurant include duck in raspberry purée, almonds, and Chambord; and tournedos with red zinfandel sauce. Remy rum raisin ice cream is one of the tempting desserts. You'll find jazz or blues here on weekends. *3 Elm St., tel. 802/457–3232. AE, MC, V. Moderate.*

Lodging **Kedron Valley Inn.** The inn is imbued with the personalities of
★ its owners, Max and Merrily Comins; in 1985 they began the renovation of what in the 1840s had been the National Hotel, one of the state's oldest. A collection of family quilts is displayed throughout the inn (with a handwritten history of each one), and framed antique linens deck the walls. Many rooms have either a fireplace or a Franklin stove, and each is decorated with a quilt. Two rooms have private decks, another has a

private veranda, and a fourth has a private terrace overlooking the stream that runs through the inn's 15 acres. The exposed log walls in the motel units in back are more rustic than the rooms in the main inn, but they're decorated in similar fashion. *Rte. 106, 05071, tel. 802/457–1473. 28 rooms with bath. Facilities: restaurant, lounge, 1½-acre pond with sand beach, riding center. D, MC, V. Closed Apr. Rates include full breakfast. Expensive–Very Expensive.*

Woodstock Inn and Resort. The hotel's floor-to-ceiling field-stone fireplace in the lobby with its massive wood-beam mantel embody the spirit of New England, and it comes as no surprise to learn that the resort is owned by the Rockefeller family, which has been instrumental in preserving the town's charm. The rooms' modern ash furnishings are high-quality institutional, enlivened by patchwork quilts on the beds; the inoffensive decor is designed to please the large clientele of corporate conference attendees. Some of the newer rooms, constructed in 1990, have fireplaces. *Rte. 4, 05091, tel. 802/457–1100 or 800/448–7900. 146 rooms, with bath. Facilities: conference rooms, indoor and outdoor pools, indoor and outdoor tennis courts, sports center with fitness equipment, squash and racquetball courts, whirlpool, saunas, ski center, putting green, 18-hole Robert Trent Jones golf course, croquet court, restaurant, gift shop, lounge, cable TV. AE, MC, V. Expensive–Very Expensive.*

Village Inn at Woodstock. This renovated Victorian mansion features oak wainscoting, ornate pressed-tin ceilings, and a front porch perfect for studying the passersby on the sidewalks of Main Street; it's also convenient to downtown. Rooms are decorated simply with country antiques, quilts or chenille bedspreads, and dried flowers. *Rte. 4, 05091, tel. 802/457–1255. 8 rooms, 6 with bath. Facilities: restaurant, lounge, cable TV in public area, air-conditioning. Rates include full breakfast. MC, V. Closed early Nov., Thanksgiving. Moderate.*

★ **Pond Ridge Motel.** The strip of rooms was renovated in 1989, so the furnishings are simple but fresh and tidy. Unlike many motels, it's set far enough back from Route 4 to mute the noise of the traffic. The big surprise here is the spacious back lawn that runs down to the Ottauquechee River. Many visitors choose one of the two-bedroom apartments with refrigerator, table, and stove. *Rte. 4, 05091, tel. 802/457–1667. 21 rooms with bath. Facilities: air-conditioning. AE, MC, V. Inexpensive–Moderate.*

The Arts

Middlebury College (tel. 802/388–3711) sponsors music, theater, and dance performances throughout the year at Wright Memorial Theatre.

The **Pentangle Council on the Arts** in Woodstock organizes performances of music, theater, and dance at the Town Hall Theater (tel. 802/457–3981).

In Rutland, the **Crossroads Arts Council** (tel. 802/775–5413) presents music, opera, dance, jazz, and theater events.

Music **Point-Counterpoint Chamber Players** (tel. 802/247–8467) gives a summer series of concerts.

Vermont Symphony Orchestra (tel. 802/864–5741) performs in Rutland and, during the summer, in Woodstock.

Opera **Opera North** (Norwich, tel. 802/649–1060) does three opera productions annually at locations throughout the state.

Theater **Vermont Ensemble Theater** (tel. 802/388–2676 or 802/388–3001) has a three-week summer season in a tent on the Middlebury College campus.

Nightlife

Most of the nighttime activity of central Vermont takes place around the ski resorts of Killington, Pico, and Sugarbush.

Bars and Lounges **The Doghouse Pub** (Powderhound Inn, Rte. 100, Warren, tel. 802/496–7394) is a comfortable place to play pool or darts while sampling an eclectic beer selection.

Jazz **Bentleys** (3 Elm St., Woodstock, tel. 802/457–3232), a popular restaurant, also offers live jazz and blues on weekends.

Rock **Gallaghers** (Rtes. 100 and 17, Waitsfield, tel. 802/496–8800) is a popular spot with danceable local bands.

The Pickle Barrel (Killington Rd., Killington, tel. 802/422–3035), a favorite with the après-ski crowd, presents up-and-coming acts.

Northern Vermont

Northern Vermont, where much of the state's logging and dairying takes place, is a land of contrasts: It has the state's largest city, some of New England's most rural areas, and many rare species of wildlife. With Montréal only an hour from the border, the Canadian influence can be felt and Canadian accents and currency encountered. On the west, Lake Champlain and the islands are the closest Vermont comes to having a seacoast.

Important Addresses and Numbers

Weather (tel. 802/862–2375).

Visitor **Central Vermont Chamber of Commerce** (Box 336, Barre 05641,
Information tel. 802/229–5711).

Greater Newport Area Chamber of Commerce (The Causeway, Newport 05855, tel. 802/334–7782).

Lake Champlain Regional Chamber of Commerce (209 Battery St., Box 453, Burlington 05402, tel. 802/863–3489).

St. Johnsbury Chamber of Commerce (30 Western Ave., St. Johnsbury 05819, tel. 802/748–3678).

Smugglers' Notch Area Chamber of Commerce (Box 3264, Jeffersonville 05464, tel. 802/644–2239).

Stowe Area Association (Main St., Box 1320, Stowe 05672, tel. 802/253–7321).

Emergencies Vermont's **Medical Health Care Information Center** has a 24-hour line (tel. 802/864–0454).

Telecommunications Device for the Deaf (TDD) has a 24-hour emergency hot line (tel. 802/253–0191).

Getting Around Northern Vermont

By Car In north central Vermont, I–89 heads west from Montpelier to Burlington and continues north to Canada. I–91 is the principal north–south route in the east, and Route 100 runs north–south through the middle of Vermont. North of I–89, Routes 15 and 104 provide a major east–west transverse.

By Bus **Vermont Transit** (tel. 802/864–6811 or 800/451–3292) links Burlington, Stowe, Montpelier, Barre, St. Johnsbury, and Newport.

Guided Tours

The **Lamoille Valley Railroad,** a working line, augments its income by carrying passengers on two-hour, 40-mile excursions along the Lamoille River, where the green and gold cars crisscross the water and pass through one of the rare covered railroad bridges in the country. *Stafford Ave., Morrisville 05661, tel. 802/888–4255. Reservations advised. Fare: $15 adults, $7 children; children under 5, when held, free. MC, V. July–Aug., Tues.–Fri. at 10, 1; mid-Sept.–mid-Oct., weekends at 10, 1.*

Exploring Northern Vermont

Numbers in the margin correspond to points of interest on the Northern Vermont map.

Visitors to northern Vermont find points of interest in the busy ski area at Stowe; in Burlington, the state's cultural center; and in rural and even remote areas in the Lake Champlain islands and the Northeast Kingdom. We begin at Montpelier, Vermont's capital.

1 The Vermont legislature anointed **Montpelier** as the state capital in 1805. Today, with less than 10,000 residents, the city holds the distinction of being the country's least populous seat of government. Built in 1859, following its predecessor's destruction by fire, the current **Vermont State House**—with its gold dome and granite columns 6 feet in diameter—has an impressive scale. Inside, the relatively intimate House chamber conjures up visions of *Mr. Smith Goes to Montpelier,* and the even smaller Senate chamber looks like a rather grand committee room. The center hall is decorated with quotations reflecting on the nature of Vermont. *State St., tel. 802/828–2228. Admission free. Open weekdays 8–4.*

Are you wondering what the last panther shot in Vermont looked like? why New England bridges are covered? what a niddy-noddy is? or what Christmas was like for a Bethel boy in 1879? ("I skated on my new skates. In the morning Papa and I set up a stove for Gramper.") The **Vermont Museum,** on the ground floor of the Vermont Historical Society offices in Montpelier, has the answers. *109 State St., tel. 802/828–3391. Suggested contribution: $2. Open Tues.–Fri., 9–4:30; Sat. 9–4; Sun. noon–4.*

The **T. W. Wood Art Gallery** is named for a Montpelier artist, a prominent painter of the Academy school of realism, who endowed this facility with his collection of his own work and that of his peers. Changing exhibits feature contemporary work.

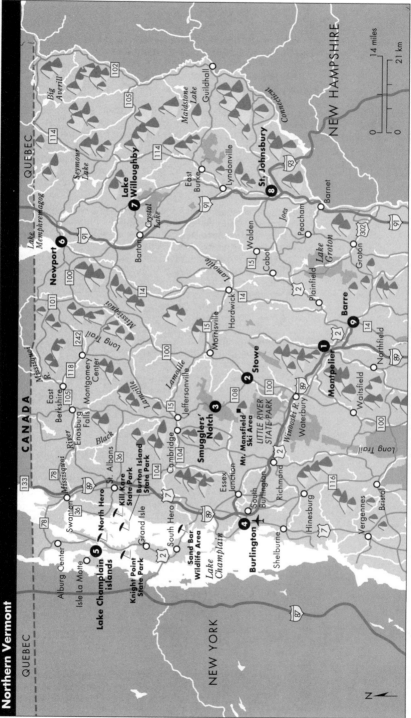

Northern Vermont

QUEBEC

CANADA

QUEBEC

NEW HAMPSHIRE

NEW YORK

14 miles
21 km

Big Averill

Seymour Lake

Lake Memphremagog

Maidstone Lake

Guildhall

Connecticut

St. Johnsbury 🔞

East Burke

Lyndonville

Lake Willoughby 🔧

Crystal Lake

Barton

Barnet

Peacham

Lake Groton

Groton

Walden

Joes

Newport 🔧

Lamoille

Hardwick

Cabot

Plainfield

Barre 🔧

Northfield

Montpelier

Waitsfield

Missisquoi

East Berkshire

Montgomery Center

Long Trail

Enosburg Falls

Black

Jeffersonville

Lamoille

Morrisville

Stowe 🔧

Smugglers' Notch 🔧

Mt. Mansfield Ski Area

LITTLE RIVER STATE PARK

Winooski R.

Waterbury

Long Trail

Swanton

Mississquoi

St. Albans

Kill Kare State Park

Burton Island State Park

Cambridge

Essex Junction

South Burlington

Richmond

Hinesburg

Alburg Center

Isle La Motte

North Hero

Grand Isle

South Hero

Sand Bar Wildlife Area

Knight Point State Park

Burlington 🔧

Shelburne

Vergennes

Bristol

Lake Champlain Islands 🔧

Lake Champlain

N

Vermont College Arts Center, E. State St., tel. 802/828–8743. Admission: $2. Open Tues.–Sun. noon–4.

Northwest of Montpelier, one of Vermont's best-loved attractions is **Ben and Jerry's Ice Cream Factory**, a mecca, nirvana, and Valhalla for ice-cream lovers. Ben and Jerry, who began selling ice cream from a renovated gas station in the 1970s, have created a business that has grown to become one of the most influential voices in community-based activism in the country. Their action-oriented social and environmental consciousness—which initiated such projects as the "1 Percent for Peace" program—have made the company a model of corporate responsibility. Fifty percent of tour proceeds go to Vermont community groups. And don't forget about their gooey, chewy, out-of-this-world ice cream. *Rte. 100, 1 mi north of I–89, tel. 802/244–5641. Admission: $1, children under 12 free. Open Mon.–Sat. 9–5. Tour every ½ hour.*

2 For more than a century the history of **Stowe**—northwest of Montpelier on Route 100, 10 miles north of I–89—has been determined by the town's proximity to Mt. Mansfield, the highest elevation in the state. As early as 1858 visitors were trooping to the area to view the mountain whose shape suggests the profile of the face of a man lying on his back. In summer, visitors can take the 4½-mile **toll road** to the top for a short scenic walk and a magnificent view. *Mountain Rd., 7 mi from Rte. 100, tel. 802/253–3000. Admission: $9 car, $6 motorcycle. Open late May–early Oct., daily 10–5.*

Time Out The **Blue Moon Café** serves hearty bistro fare in a renovated landmark building on Stowe's School Street.

An alternative means of reaching the Mt. Mansfield summit is the eight-seat **gondola** that shuttles continuously up 4,393 feet to the area of "the Chin," which has a small restaurant (dinner reservations required). *Mountain Rd., 7 mi from Rte. 100. Admission: $9.50 adults, $5 children, under 5 free. Open June–early Oct., daily 10–5; Oct.–late June, weekends 10–5.*

The Mount Mansfield Co. also operates a 2,300-foot **Alpine slide** on Spruce Peak. *Spruce Peak Lodge, Mountain Lodge. Admission: single ride $6 adults, $4 children; unlimited rides $18 adults, $14 children. Open June–early Sept., daily 10–5; early Sept.–early Oct., weekends 10–5.*

3 Northwest of Stowe lies a scenic but not very direct route to Burlington: **Smugglers' Notch,** the narrow pass over Mt. Mansfield that is said to have given shelter to 18th-century outlaws in its rugged, bouldered terrain. There are picnic tables and places to park at roadside and, as you begin the descent on the western side of the mountain, a spectacular waterfall to your left, though you may have to look over your shoulder to see it. Note that the notch road is closed in winter. Follow Route 108 to Route 15, which turns west and south at Jeffersonville.

Time Out **Windridge Bakery and Cafe** on Route 15 in Jeffersonville prepares positively incredible breads, pies, and other pastries.

4 Vermont's largest population center, **Burlington** was founded in 1763 and had a long history as a trade center following the growth of the shipping industry on Lake Champlain during the 18th century. More recently, energized by the roughly 10,000 students at the University of Vermont and an abundance of culture-hungry, transplanted urban dwellers, Burlington was for years the only city in America to have a socialist mayor. The **Church Street Marketplace**—a pedestrian mall boasting down-to-earth shops, chic boutiques, and an appealing menagerie of sidewalk cafés, food and craft vendors, and street performers—is an animated downtown focal point. Burlington's festival-like town center, where most people in central and northern Vermont are drawn at least occasionally to do errands or see a show, is reminiscent of bustling New England village greens of 200 years ago.

During the warm-weather months, Burlington's recently revitalized **waterfront** teems with outdoor enthusiasts along its recreation path, and in boats on the waters of Lake Champlain. A replica of an old Champlain paddlewheeler, *The Spirit of Ethan Allen,* hosts narrated cruises on Lake Champlain and, in the evening, dinner and moonlight dance sailings that drift by the Adirondacks and the Green Mountains. *Perkins Pier, tel. 802/ 862–9685. $7.90 adults, $3.50 children 5–11. Cruises June–mid-Oct., daily at 10, noon, 2, 4.*

Time Out	The food and ambience of **Leunig's Cafe**, at Church and College streets in Burlington, recall a European bistro. In summer there is an outdoor café that looks onto the Church Street Marketplace parade.

After emerging from the built-up strip heading south out of Burlington, Route 7 opens up, affording chin-dropping views of the rugged Adironacks across Lake Champlain. Five miles from the city, one could trace all New England history simply by wandering the 45 acres of the **Shelburne Museum,** whose 37 buildings seem a collection of individual museums. The large collection of Americana contains 18th- and 19th-century period homes and furniture, fine and folk art, farm tools, more than 200 carriages and sleighs, Audubon prints, even a private railroad car from the days of steam. And an old-fashioned jail. And an assortment of duck decoys. And an old stone cottage. And a display of early toys. And the *Ticonderoga*, an old sidewheel steamship. *Rte. 7, 5 mi south of Burlington, tel. 802/985–3346. Admission (good for 2 consecutive days): $14 adults, $6 children 6–14. Open mid-May–mid-Oct., daily 9–5.*

Shelburne Farms, 6 miles south of Burlington, has a history of improving the farmer's lot by developing new agricultural methods. Founded in the 1880s as the private estate of a gentleman farmer, the 1,000-acre property is now an educational and cultural resource center. Visitors can see a working dairy farm, listen to nature lectures, or simply stroll the immaculate grounds on a scenic stretch of Lake Champlain waterfront. The original landscaping, designed by Frederick Law Olmsted, the creator of Central Park and Boston's Emerald Necklace, gently channels the eye to expansive vistas and aesthetically satisfying views of such buildings as the five-story, 2-acre Farm Barn. *East of Rte. 7, 6 mi south of Burlington, tel. 802/985–8686. Admission: $5.50 adults, $5 senior citizens, $2.50 children 6–15. Guided tour $2.50. Visitor center and shop open daily 9:30–5, last tour at 3:30; tours given Memorial Day–mid-Oct.*

At the 6-acre **Vermont Wildflower Farm,** the display along the flowering pathways changes constantly: violets in the spring, daisies and black-eyed Susans for summer, and fall colors that rival the foliage. The farm is the largest wildflower seed center in the eastern part of the country. The gift shop has seeds, crafts, and books. *Rte. 7, 5 mi south of the Shelburne Museum, tel. 802/425–3500. Admission: $3 adults, $1.50 senior citizens. Open mid-May–Oct., daily 10–5.*

Retrace Route 7 back through Burlington and head toward northern Vermont where more of the state's history is revealed. Ethan Allen, Vermont's famous early settler, is a figure of some mystery. The visitor center at his **homestead** by the Winooski River both answers and raises questions about his flamboyant life. The house, about 70% original, has such frontier hallmarks as nails pointing through the roof on the top floor, rough saw-cut boards, and an open hearth for cooking. The Ethan Allen commemorative tower, within walking distance of the homestead, has been restored by a private organization. *North Ave., off Rte. 127, north of Burlington, tel. 802/865–4556. Admission: $3.50 adults, $3 senior citizens, $2 children over 6, $10 family. Open May, Tues.–Sun. 1–5; June–Aug., Mon.–Sat. 10–5, Sun. 1–5; Sept.–Oct., daily 1–5.*

The **Discovery Museum,** northeast of Burlington in Essex Junction, is a cornucopia of hands-on natural science, art, and history, with changing exhibits and an outdoor area where injured animals are cared for and children can pet healthy ones. *51 Park St., Essex Junction, tel. 802/878–8687. Admission: $3 adults, $2 children. Open July–Aug., Tues.–Sat. 10–5, Sun. 1–5; Sept.–June, Tues.–Fri., Sun. 1–5, Sat. 10–5.*

❺ The **Lake Champlain islands** lie between the Adirondacks to the west and the Green Mountains to the east. Their great moment in history was their discovery by Samuel de Champlain, represented on Isle La Motte by a granite statue that looks south to the shrine to St. Anne on the site of the first French settlement. Today the islands are a center of water recreation in summer, ice fishing in winter. North of Burlington, the scenic drive through the islands on Route 2 begins at I–89 and travels north through South Hero, Grand Isle, and Isle La Motte to Alburg Center, 5 miles from the Canadian border. Here Route 78 will take you east to the mainland.

To cross northern Vermont, take Route 78 east to Route 105, continue to Route 118 in East Berkshire, and follow that to Route 242 and the Jay Peak area. From the top of the mountain pass there are vast views of Canada to the north, and to the east of Vermont's rugged **Northeast Kingdom.**

❻ The descent from Jay Peak on Route 101 leads to Route 100, which takes you east to the city of **Newport** on Lake Memphremagog (accent on *gog*). The waterfront is the dominant view of the city, which is built on a peninsula. The grand hotels of the last century are gone, yet the buildings still drape themselves along the lake's edge and climb the hills behind.

❼ The drive south from Newport on I–91 encounters some of the most unspoiled areas in all Vermont. This is the Northeast Kingdom, named for the remoteness and stalwart independence that has helped to preserve its rural nature; some of the towns here still have no people living in them. From the northern shore of **Lake Willoughby,** 7 miles northwest of Barton off I–91, the cliffs of surrounding Mounts Pisgah and Hor dropping to water's edge give this glacially carved, 500-feet-deep lake a striking resemblance to a Norwegian fjord. The lake is popular for both summer and winter recreation, and the trails to the top of Mt. Pisgah reward hikers with glorious views. Contact the St. Johnsbury Chamber of Commerce (30 Western Ave., tel. 802/748–3678) for more information on hiking and water activities.

The southern gateway to this section of the state is the city of **8** **St. Johnsbury,** directly off I–91. Though chartered in 1786, St. Johnsbury's identity was not firmly established until 1830 when Thaddeus Fairbanks invented the platform scale, a device that revolutionized weighing methods that were in use since the beginning of recorded history. The impact of his company on the city is still pervasive: a distinctly 19th-century industrial feel that is superimposed by a strong cultural and architectural imprint, the result of the Fairbanks family's philanthropic bent. The **Fairbanks Museum and Planetarium** attests to the family inquisitiveness about all things scientific. The redbrick building in the squat Romanesque architectural style of H. H. Richardson houses collections of Vermont plants and animals, Vermont items, and an intimate 50-seat planetarium. *Main and Prospect Sts., tel. 802/748–2372. Admission: $3 adults, $2.50 children, $7.50 family; planetarium $1.50. Open Sept.–June, Mon.–Sat. 10–4, Sun. 1–5; July–Aug., Mon.–Sat. 10–6, Sun. 1–5.*

The **St. Johnsbury Athenaeum,** with its dark rich paneling, polished Victorian woodwork, and ornate circular staircases that rise to the gallery around the perimeter, is a tiny gem. The gallery at the back of the building has the overwhelming *Domes of Yosemite* by Albert Bierstadt and a lot of sentimental 19th-century material. *30 Main St., tel. 802/748–8291. Admission free. Open Tues., Thurs., Fri. 10–5:30; Mon., Wed. 9–8; Sat. 9:30–4.*

Heading east from St. Johnsbury along Route 2, an 8-mile detour to the south leads to the village of **Peacham.** This tiny hamlet's almost-too-picturesque scenery and 18th-century charm have made it a favorite for urban refugees and artists seeking solitude and inspiration, as well as movie directors looking for the quintessential New England village: The critically acclaimed *Ethan Frome* was filmed here.

Time Out   Stop into the **Peacham Store,** in St. Johnsbury, for a quirky combination of Yankee Vermont sensibility and Hungarian eccentricity. Transylvanian goulash, stuffed peppers, and lamb-and-barley soup are among the takeout specialties.

9 **Barre** has been famous as the source of Vermont granite ever since two men began working the quarries in the early 1800s, and the large number of immigrant laborers attracted to the industry made the city prominent in the early years of the American labor movement.

The attractions of the **Rock of Ages granite quarry** (take Exit 6 from I–89 and follow Route 63) range from the awe-inspiring— the quarry resembles a man-made miniature of the Grand Canyon—to the absurd: The company invites you to consult a directory of tombstone dealers throughout the United States. At the craftsman center, which you pass on the drive to the visitor center, the view seems to take in a scene out of Dante's *Inferno:* A dusty, smoky haze hangs above the acres of men at work, with machines screaming as they bite into the rock. The process that transfers designs to the smooth stone and etches them into it is fascinating. *Rte. 63, tel. 802/476–3115. Quarry and visitor center open May–mid-Oct., daily 8:30–5. Quarry shuttlebus tour weekdays 9:30–3:30; admission: $2 adults, $1 children 5–12. Craftsman center open weekdays 8–3:30.*

Northern Vermont for Free

Robert Hull Fleming Museum, Burlington
St. Johnsbury Athenaeum, St. Johnsbury
Recreational Path, Stowe
Vermont State House, Montpelier

What to See and Do with Children

Ben and Jerry's Ice Cream Factory, Waterbury
The Discovery Museum, Essex Junction
Lamoille Valley Railroad, Morrisville
Shelburne Museum, Shelburne
The Spirit of Ethan Allen, Burlington

Off the Beaten Track

The **Lake Champlain Maritime Museum** commemorates the days when steamships sailed along the coast of northern Vermont carrying logs, livestock, and merchandise bound for New York City. The exhibits housed here in a one-room stone schoolhouse 25 miles south of Burlington include historic maps, nautical prints, and a collection of small craft. *Basin Harbor Rd., 5 mi west of Vergennes, tel. 802/475–2317. Admission: $3 adults. Open Memorial Day–mid-Oct., Wed.–Sun. 10–5.*

South of I–91 (Exit 25) in the town of Glover is the **Bread and Puppet Museum,** an unassuming, ramshackle barn that houses a surrealistic collection of props used in past performances by the world-renowned Bread and Puppet Theater. The troupe, whose members live communally on the surrounding farm, have been performing social and political commentary with the towering (they're supported by people on stilts), eerily expressive puppets for almost 30 years. *Rte. 122, Glover, 1 mi east of Rte. 16, tel. 802/525–3031. Admission free, donations accepted. Call for current hours.*

North of Rte. 2, midway between Barre and St. Johnsbury, the biggest cheese producer in the state, the **Cabot Creamery,** has a visitor center with an audiovisual presentation about the state's dairy and cheese industry, tours of the plant, and—best of all—samples. *Cabot, 3 mi north of Rte. 2, tel. 802/563–2231. Admission: $1. Open Mon.–Sat. 8–4:30.*

Shopping

Shopping Districts **Church Street Marketplace** (tel. 802/863–1648), a pedestrian thoroughfare that runs from Main Street to Pearl Street in downtown Burlington, is lined with boutiques, cafés, and street vendors. Burlington Square Mall, entered from Church Street, has Porteous (the city's major department store) and some 50 shops.
The Champlain Mill (tel. 802/655–9477), a former woolen mill

on the banks of the Winooski River on Route 2/7 northeast of Burlington, has three floors of stores.

The **Mountain Road** in Stowe is crowded with shops lining the way from town up toward the ski area.

Food and Drink **The Cheese Outlet Shop** (400 Pine St., Burlington, tel. 802/863–3698) has Vermont and imported cheeses, its own cheesecake, imported crackers and cookies, and wines.

Cold Hollow Cider Mill (Rte. 100, Stowe, tel. 802/244–8771) offers cider, baked goods, Vermont produce, and free samples at the pressing machine.

Harrington's (Rte. 7 opposite Shelburne Museum, south of Burlington, tel. 802/985–2000) cob-smoked hams, bacon, turkey, and summer sausage will generate thoughts of lunch at any hour. The store also stocks cheese, syrup, and other New England specialties.

Morse Farm (County Rd., 2 mi north of Montpelier, tel. 802/223–2740) has been producing maple syrup for three generations. The sugar house is open for viewing in spring when the syrup is being made; the gift shop is open year-round.

Specialty Stores **English Country at Stowe** (1 Pond St., Stowe, tel. 802/253–4420)
Antiques offers English country antiques.

Ethan Allen Antique Shop (1 mi east of Exit 14E from I–89, Burlington, tel. 802/863–3764) has a large stock of early American and period country furniture and accessories.

Great American Salvage (3 Main St., Montpelier, tel. 802/223–7711) supplies architectural detailing: moldings, brackets, stained-glass and leaded windows, doors, and trim retrieved from old homes.

Sign of the Dial Clock Shop (63 Eastern Ave., St. Johnsbury, tel. 802/748–5044) specializes in antique clock sales, repairs, and restorations.

Tailor's Antiques (68 Pearl St., Burlington, tel. 802/862–8156) carries small primitive paintings as well as glass and china for collectors.

Books **Chassman & Bem Booksellers** (1 Church St., Burlington, tel. 802/862–4332), voted best bookstore in Vermont, has more than 20,000 titles, with a discriminating selection of children's books and a large magazine rack.

Clothing **Moriarty Hat and Sweater Shop** (Mountain Rd., Stowe, tel. 802/253–4052) is the home of the original ski hat with the funny peak on top; the assortment is mind-boggling, and you can order a custom knit.

Crafts **Bennington Potters North** (127 College St., Burlington, tel. 802/863–2221) has glassware, baskets, small household items, and a seconds outlet downstairs.

Ducktrap Bat Trading Co. (84 Church St., Burlington, tel. 802/865–0036) is one of the only wildlife and marine art galleries in New England.

Vermont State Craft Center (85 Church St., Burlington, tel. 802/863–6458) is an elegant gallery displaying contemporary and traditional crafts by more than 200 Vermont artisans.

Women's Clothing **Handblock** (97 Church St., Burlington, tel. 802/962–8211) carries a fun collection of casual yet indulgent women's clothing; it also specializes in rich, hand-dyed linens and colorful stoneware.

Vermont Trading Company (2 State St., Montpelier, tel. 802/

223–2142, and 151 N. Main St., Barre, tel. 802/476–6865) has natural-fiber clothing and funky accessories.

Sports and Outdoor Activities

Biking In Burlington a recreational path runs 9 miles along the waterfront. South of Burlington, a moderately easy 18½-mile trail begins at the blinker on Route 7, Shelburne, and follows Mt. Philo Road, Hinesburg Road, Route 116, and Irish Hill Road. **Earl's** (135 Main St., tel. 802/862–4203) and **North Star Cyclery** (100 Main St., tel. 802/863–3832) rent equipment and provide maps and information.

Stowe's recreational trail begins behind the Community Church on Main Street and meanders for 5.3 miles behind the shops that line Mountain Road. The intersection of Routes 100 and 108 is the start of a 21-mile tour with scenic views of Mt. Mansfield; the route takes you along Route 100 to Stagecoach Road, to Morristown, over to Morrisville, and south on Randolph Road. **Mountain Bike** (Mountain Rd., tel. 802/253–7919) supplies equipment and information.

Canoeing **Sailworks** (176 Battery St., Burlington, tel. 802/864–0111) rents canoes and gives lessons at Sand Bar State Park during the summer.

Umiak Outdoor Outfitters (Gale Farm Center, 1880 Mountain Rd., Stowe, tel. 802/253–2317) specializes in canoes and rents them for day trips; they also lead guided overnight excursions.

The **Village Sport Shop** (Lyndonville, tel. 802/626–8448) rents canoes for use on the Connecticut River.

Fishing Rainbow trout can be found on the Missisquoi, Lamoille, Winooski, and Willoughby rivers, and there's warm-water fishing at many smaller lakes and ponds in the region. Lakes Seymour, Willoughby, and Memphremagog and Big Averill in the Northeast Kingdom are good for salmon and lake trout. The **Fly Rod Shop** (Rte. 100, 3 mi south of Stowe, tel. 802/253–7346) rents and sells equipment and provides information.

Lake Champlain, stocked annually with salmon and lake trout, has become the state's ice-fishing capital; walleye, bass, pike, pickerel, muskellunge, yellow perch, steelhead, and channel catfish are also taken. Ice fishing is also popular on Lake Memphremagog. Marina services are available north and south of Burlington. **Malletts Bay Marina** (228 Lakeshore Dr., Colchester, tel. 802/862–4077) and **Point Bay Marina** (Thompson's Point, Charlotte, tel. 802/425–2431) both provide full service and repairs.

Groton Pond (Rte. 302, off I–91, 20 mi south of St. Johnsbury, tel. 802/584–3829) is popular for trout fishing; boat rentals are available at the site.

Health and Fitness Club The **Fitness Advantage** (137 Iroquois Ave., Essex Junction, tel. 802/878–6568) offers spa and fitness equipment, a licensed daycare center, and massage therapy.

Hiking **Mount Mansfield State Forest** and **Little River State Park** (Rte. 2, 1½ mi west of Waterbury) provide an extensive trail system, including one that reaches the site of the Civilian Conservation Corps unit that was here in the 1930s.

For the climb to Stowe Pinnacle, go 1½ miles south of Stowe on Route 100 and turn east on Gold Brook Road opposite the Nichols Farm Lodge; bear left at the first fork, continue through an intersection at a covered bridge, turn right after 1.8 miles, and travel 2.3 miles to a parking lot on the left. The trail crosses an abandoned pasture and takes a short, steep climb to views of the Green Mountains and Stowe Valley (two hours).

Tennis The **Stowe Area Association** (tel. 802/253–7321) hosts a grand prix tennis tournament in early August.

Water Sports **Burlington Community Boathouse** (foot of College St., Burlington Harbor, tel. 802/865–3377) has sailboard and boat rentals (some captained) and lessons.

Chiott Marine (67 Main St. Burlington, tel. 802/862–8383) caters to all realms of water sports with two floors of hardware, apparel, and accessories.

International Yacht Sales (Colchester, tel. 802/864–6800) makes the yacht *Intrepid,* an America's Cup winner, available for charter.

Beaches

Some of the most scenic Lake Champlain beaches are on the Champlain islands. **North Hero State Park** (tel. 802/372–8727) has a children's play area nearby; **Knight Point State Park** (tel. 802/372–8389) is the reputed home of "Champ," Lake Champlain's answer to the Loch Ness monster; and **Sand Bar State Park** (tel. 802/372–8240) is near a waterfowl preserve. Summer crowds make it wise to arrive early. *Admission: $1 adults, 50¢ children. Open mid-May–Oct.*

The **North Beaches** are on the northern edge of Burlington: North Beach Park (North Ave., tel. 802/864–0123), Bayside Beach (Rte. 127 near Malletts Bay), and Leddy Beach, which is popular for sailboarding.

State Parks

Burton Island State Park is accessible only by passenger ferry or boat; at the nature center a naturalist discusses the island habitat. *Rte. 105, 2 mi east of Island Pond, then south on marked local road, tel. 802/524–6353. 253 acres. Facilities: 42 campsites (no hookups), 100-slip marina with power hookups and 20 moorings, toilets, showers, picnic tables, fireplaces, phone, playground, snack bar.*

Grand Isle State Park has a fitness trail and a naturalist. *Rte. 2, 1 mi south of Grand Isle, tel. 802/372–4300. 226 acres. Facilities: 155 campsites (no hookups), toilets, showers, picnic tables, fireplaces, recreation building, phone.*

Kamp Kill Kare State Park is popular for sailboarding, and it provides ferry access to Burton Island. *Rte. 36, 4½ mi west of St. Albans Bay, then south on town road 3½ mi, tel. 802/524–6021. 17.7 acres. Facilities: 60 campsites (no hookups), toilets, showers, picnic shelter, fireplaces, phone, boat rentals and ramp.*

Little River State Park features marked nature trails for hiking on Mount Mansfield and Camel's Hump. *Little River Rd., 3½ mi north of junction with Rte. 2, 2 mi east of Rte. 100, tel. 802/*

*244–7103. 12,000 acres. Facilities: 101 campsites (no hook-
ups), toilets, showers, picnic tables, fireplaces, boat rentals
and ramp, phone.*

Smugglers' Notch State Park is good for picnicking and hiking
on wild terrain among large boulders. *Rte. 108, 10 mi north of
Mt. Mansfield, tel. 802/253–4014. 25 acres. Facilities: 38 campsites (no hookups), toilets, showers, picnic tables, fireplaces,
phone.*

Dining and Lodging

Burlington and Stowe have the large resort hotels; the rest of
the region offers inns, bed-and-breakfasts, and small motels.
The Stowe area has a **lodging referral service** (tel. 800/247–
8693). In the restaurants, dress is casual and reservations may
be helpful in the peak season.

Barton **Fox Hall Inn.** Moose are a passionate subject of debate in Ver-
Lodging mont these days, and the innkeepers here have responded by
creating a sort of sanctum to the re-emergence in the state of
this previously scarce animal: Throughout this 1890 Cottage
Revival, listed on the Register of Historic Places, furnishings
and rooms are embellished by many a moose miscellany. The
generous wraparound veranda that overlooks Lake Willoughby is well-appointed with swinging seats and comfortable
chairs, perfect for a summer evening spent listening to the
loons. While the two corner turret rooms are the most distinctive and spacious, and have the most expansive views of the
lake, the other rooms are also extremely light and delicately
furnished with white wicker and antique quilts. *Rte. 16, 05822,
tel. 802/525–6930. 9 rooms, 4 with bath. Facilities: 2 fireplaces
in public areas; hiking and cross-country ski trails, canoes; afternoon snacks. No smoking. No pets. 2-night minimum during fall foliage. MC, V. Rates include full breakfast; dinner is
available upon request. Inexpensive–Moderate.*

Burlington **Butler's.** At Butler's—one of two restaurants at the Inn at
Dining Essex—the food is prepared by an outpost of the New England
★ Culinary Institute, and the style is updated New England: pan-
seared salmon fillet with pistachio pesto; lobster in yellow corn
sauce with spinach pasta. *70 Essex Way, Essex Junction, tel.
802/878–1100. Reservations advised. AE, D, DC, MC, V. Expensive.*

The Ice House. For a great view of Lake Champlain, the outdoor terrace is the place to be in summer; in winter the picture
windows are almost as good. The menu is mainstream: grilled
swordfish, boiled lobster, steak, a seafood combination plate
that changes daily. *171 Battery St., tel. 802/864–1800. Reservations advised. AE, DC, MC, V. Moderate–Expensive.*

The Daily Planet. Contemporary plaid oilcloth, an old jukebox
playing Aretha Franklin, a solarium, and a turn-of-the-century
bar add up to one of Burlington's hippest restaurants. This is
Marco Polo cuisine—basically Mediterranean with Oriental in-
fluences: lobster risotto with peas; braised lamb loin with polenta and chutney; various stirfries. *15 Center St., tel. 802/862–
9647. Reservations advised. AE, DC, MC, V. Moderate.*

★ **Déjà Vu.** High Gothic booths made from ornately carved church
pews, fringed silk lampshades, and brass accents that gleam in
the candlelight create a lushly romantic yet informal dining
room. Dinner entrées might be smoked duck breast and confit

leg with a Concord grape demi-glacé; or Vermont pheasant stuffed with apples, cranberries, and pecans. Sandwiches and crepes are available, too. *185 Pearl St., tel. 802/864–7917. AE, DC, MC, V. Moderate.*

Sakura. The serene Japanese setting has *samisen* music in the background and tatami seating for up to 15. On the menu are a popular combination platter, à la carte items, tempura, and other Japanese specialties. *2 Church St., tel. 802/863–1988. AE, DC, MC, V. No lunch Sun. Moderate.*

★ **Five Spice Cafe.** This tiny spot has only a dozen tables set against whitewashed barnboard walls enlivened with framed sheet music or perhaps a drawing of Laurel and Hardy. The chef experiments with Asian cuisines to create such specialties as the searing Thai Fire Shrimp and a more traditional Kung Pao chicken. The menu has an extensive selection of vegetarian dishes, and there's a dim sum brunch on Saturday and Sunday. *175 Church St., tel. 802/864–4045. AE, DC, MC, V. Inexpensive–Moderate.*

Lodging **The Inn at Essex.** This new Georgian-style facility about 10 miles from downtown is a hotel and conference center in country-inn clothing. Flowered wallpaper and matching dust ruffles, working fireplaces in some rooms, and library books on the reproduction desks give innlike touches to spacious rooms. Room service and the restaurants are run by the New England Culinary Institute. *70 Essex Way, off Rte. 15, Essex Junction 05452, tel. 802/878–1100 or 800/288–7613. 97 rooms with bath. Facilities: 2 restaurants, pool, health club with Jacuzzi. AE, D, DC, MC, V. Moderate–Very Expensive.*

Radisson Hotel–Burlington. This sleek corporate giant is the hotel closest to downtown shopping, and it faces the lakefront. Odd-numbered rooms have the view; rooms whose number end in 1 look onto both lake and city. *60 Battery St., 05401, tel. 802/ 658–6500 or 800/333–3333. 256 rooms with bath. Facilities: restaurant, lounge, indoor pool, whirlpool, indoor garage, complimentary airport shuttle. AE, D, DC, MC, V. Moderate–Expensive.*

Sheraton-Burlington. Now the biggest hotel in the city (90% of the rooms and the health club were added in 1989) and the closest to the airport, the Sheraton accommodates large groups as well as individuals. Upholstered wing chairs and dust ruffles give a New England touch to the upscale mauve and burgundy decor of the rooms. On the concierge level are a cocktail bar, complimentary hors d'oeuvres, and Continental breakfast. *870 Williston Rd., 05403, tel. 802/862–6576 or 800/325–3535. 309 rooms with bath, 30 disabled-equipped rooms. Facilities: restaurant, conference center, health club, pool with retractable roof, complimentary airport shuttle, in-room modems, corporate business center with clerical services. AE, D, DC, MC, V. Moderate–Expensive.*

Queen City Inn. This Victorian home of 1881 was restored in 1989 and its 12 rooms individually decorated; rich architectural details include a magnificent mahogany staircase and (in room 24, for example) polished oak arches that frame a bay window alcove. Although it's on a busy main road, the back rooms get little traffic noise. Motel accommodations, while simple, include Continental breakfast in a sunny sitting room with white wicker and a red marble fireplace. *428 Shelburne Rd., South Burlington 05403, tel. 802/864–4220. 25 rooms with bath. Facilities: cable TV, phones. AE, MC, V. Inexpensive–Expensive.*

Montpelier **Tubb's.** Waiters and waitresses are students at the New En-
Dining gland Culinary Institute, and this is their training ground. Yet
the quality and inventiveness are anything but beginner's luck;
while the menu changes daily, it runs along the lines of swordfish with spinach and cherry tomatoes. The atmosphere is more
formal than that of the Elm Street Cafe, the sister operation
down the block. *24 Elm St., tel. 802/229-9202. Reservations
advised. MC, V. Closed Sun. Moderate–Expensive.*

Horn of the Moon. Bowls of honey, mismatched wooden chairs
and tables, and the bulletin board of political notices at the entrance hint at Vermont's prominent progressive contingent.
This vegetarian restaurant has attracted a following for an in-
ventive cuisine that includes a little Mexican, a little Thai, a lot
of flavor, and not too much tofu. *8 Langdon St., tel. 802/223-
2895. No credit cards. No dinner Sun., Mon. Inexpensive–
Moderate.*

Lodging **The Inn at Montpelier.** This spacious home built in the early
★ 1800s was renovated in 1988 with the business traveler in mind,
yet the architectural detailing, antique four-poster beds,
Windsor chairs, stately upholstered wing chairs, and the classical guitar on the stereo attract casual visitors as well.
Maureen's Room has a private sundeck, and the wide wraparound Colonial Revival porch is conducive to relaxing. The
rooms in the annex across the street are equally elegant. *147
Main St., 05602, tel. 802/223-2727. 19 rooms with bath, 2
suites. Facilities: conference rooms, phones, cable TV, fax.
AE, MC, V. Rates include Continental breakfast. Moderate–
Expensive.*

Newport **East Side Restaurant and Lounge.** The green napkins match the
Dining green padded booths, which match the green lampshades,
which match the plants. This is the sort of family restaurant
that will comply with customers' pleas to keep the fried chicken
livers on the menu along with burgers, sandwiches, soups, and
bar food. *E. Main St., tel. 802/334-2340. MC, V. Closed Mon.
Inexpensive–Moderate.*

Lodging **Top of the Hills Motel.** The motel rooms are attached to a small
inn whose Victorian architectural detailing is meticulous and
well cared for. One of the five rooms in the inn has a kitchenette, another a private bath. *Rtes. 5 and 105, 05855, tel. 802/
334-6748 or 800/258-6748. 15 rooms with bath. Facilities: picnic area, gas grill, cable TV, phones, snowmobile trail. AE, D,
MC, V. Rates include full breakfast. Inexpensive.*

St. Johnsbury **Rabbit Hill Inn.** There is a feeling of intimacy here in this low-
Dining ceilinged, traditional dining room. And the care extended by
chef Russell Stannard in the preparation of his eclectic, regional cuisine only adds to the restaurant's already substantial
appeal. Entrées might include grilled sausage of Vermont
pheasant with pistachios or smoked chicken and red lentil
dumplings nestled in red pepper linguine. Many of the meats
and fish served at the restaurant are smoked on the premises,
and the herbs and vegetables served in season are grown in gardens out back. *Rte. 18, Lower Waterford, tel. 802/748-5168.
Reservations advised. MC, V. Closed Apr. and first 3 weeks in
Nov. Moderate–Expensive.*

Tucci's Bistro. Veal topped with crisp fried eggplant, mozzarella, and ham; and beef scallopini sautéed with capers and ancho-
vies go beyond the standard red-sauce recipes. The
whitewashed barnboard trim and kelly green tablecloths com-

plete the simple but tasteful decor. *41 Eastern Ave., tel. 802/ 748-4778. AE, MC, V. Moderate.*

Lodging **Rabbit Hill Inn.** When the door swings open and you are wel-
★ comed—often by name—into a warmth that will melt away
even the most stressful of journeys, you'll know you've found
the place. There is an obvious fondness for the gentility of days
past that lives on in the formal, Federal-period parlor, where
mulled cider from the fireplace crane is served on chilly afternoons. The low, wooden beams and cozy warmth of the Irish-
style pub right next door create a comfortable contrast that is
carried throughout the rest of the inn. The individually decorated rooms are as stylistically different as they are consistently indulgent: The Loft, with its 8-foot Palladian window, king
canopy bed, double Jacuzzi, and corner fireplace, is one of the
most requested, while the abundant windows, Victrola, and
working pump organ with period sheet music make the Music
Chamber another favorite. Rooms toward the front of the inn
get views of the Connecticut River and the White Mountains in
New Hampshire beyond. *Rte. 18, Lower Waterford 05848, tel.
802/748-5168 or 800/76-BUNNY. 6 double rooms with baths,
7 suites. Facilities: restaurant, pub, TV in public area,
whirlpools in some rooms, fireplaces in many rooms, walking/
cross-country ski trails on property, canoes. No smoking. No
pets. 3-night minimum stay Christmastime and holiday weekends. MC, V. Rates are MAP. Closed Apr. and first 3 weeks in
Nov. Moderate–Expensive.*

Fairbanks Motor Inn. A location convenient to I–91, a putting
green, a view that makes visitors want to sit for hours on the
balcony, and a honeymoon suite with whirlpool and wet bar
make this more than the average Holiday Inn clone. *Rte. 2 E,
05819, tel. 802/748-5666. 44 rooms with bath. Facilities: cable
TV, phones, pool, nonsmoking rooms. AE, MC, V. Moderate.*

Stowe **Foxfire Inn.** A restored Colonial building might seem an unusu-
Dining al place in which to find such superb Italian delicacies as veal
rollantine, steak saltimbocca, and *tartufo* (vanilla and chocolate gelato in a chocolate cup with a raspberry center). However, this old farmhouse a couple of miles north of Stowe proper
blends the two well, and its popularity with locals proves it's
worth the short drive. *Rte. 100, Stowe, tel. 802/253-4887. MC,
V. Moderate–Expensive.*

Number One Main Street. The low-ceiling Colonial dining room
livens cuisine basics with a hint of creativity: broiled swordfish
with garlic butter and Pernod in a cream sauce; roast pork with
red currant and crème de cassis sauce. *1 Main St., tel. 802/253-
7301. Reservations advised. AE, MC, V. Moderate–Expensive.*

Stubb's. Jim Dinan is one of those New England chefs who are
rethinking such traditional dishes as calves' liver—he prepares
it with a balsamic vinegar shallot sauce—and Vermont ham,
which he combines with veal ribs, sage, and apples. The mar-
bleized walls and pink-on-burgundy linens add a sophisticated
note to the rustic beams and fireplaces at either end of the two
rooms. *Mountain Rd., tel. 802/253-7110. Reservations advised. AE, DC, MC, V. Moderate–Expensive.*

★ **Villa Tragara.** A converted farmhouse has been carved into intimate dining nooks where romance reigns over such specialties as ravioli filled with four cheeses and served with half-
tomato, half-cream sauce. The tasting menu is a five-course
dinner for $35 (plus $15 for coordinating wines). *Rte. 100, south*

of Stowe, tel. 802/244–5288. Reservations advised. AE, MC, V. Moderate–Expensive.

Lodging **10 Acres Lodge.** The 10 rooms in the main inn are cozier and more inn-like than those in the new building high on the hill, which have a definite condominium feel to them. Contemporary pottery or low-key abstract art complement the antique horse brasses over the fireplace in the living room. This is truly in the country; the cows are just across the road. *Luce Hill Rd., Box 3220, 05672, tel. 802/253–7638 or 800/327–7357. 18 rooms, 16 with bath; 2 cottages. Facilities: restaurant, lounge, phones, cable TV in some rooms, outdoor pool, tennis court. AE, MC, V. Rates include full breakfast. Moderate–Very Expensive.*

★ **The Inn at the Brass Lantern.** Home-baked cookies in the afternoon, a basket of logs by your fireplace, and stenciled hearts along the wainscoting reflect the care taken in turning this 18th-century farmhouse into a place of welcome. All rooms have quilts and country antiques; most are oversize. The honeymoon room has a brass and iron bed with a heart-shape headboard; the breakfast room (like some guest rooms) has a terrific view of Mt. Mansfield. *Rte. 100, ½ mi north of Stowe, 05672, tel. 802/253–2229 or 800/729–2980. 9 rooms with bath. No smoking. Facilities: some fireplaces, TV in public area, air-conditioning. AE, MC, V. Rates include full breakfast. Moderate.*

The Arts

Barre Opera House (City Hall, Main St., Barre, tel. 802/476–8188) hosts music, opera, theater, and dance performances.

Catamount Arts (60 Eastern Ave., St. Johnsbury, tel. 802/748–2600) brings avant-garde theater and dance performances to the Northeast Kingdom, as well as classical music.

Flynn Theatre for the Performing Arts, a grandiose old structure, is the cultural heart of Burlington; it schedules the Vermont Symphony Orchestra, theater, dance, and lectures. The box office also has tickets for other performances and festivals in the area. *153 Main St., Burlington, tel. 802/864–8778 for theater information, 802/863–5966 for ticket information.*

Music **Stowe Performing Arts** (tel. 802/253–7321) sponsors a series of classical and jazz concerts during July and August in a meadow high above the village, next to the Trapp Family Lodge.

Vermont Symphony Orchestra (tel. 802/864–5741) performs at the Flynn Theatre in Burlington in winter and outdoors at Shelburne Farms in summer.

Theater **Champlain Shakespeare Festival** performs each summer at the Royall Tyler Theater (tel. 802/656–0090) at the University of Vermont.

Stowe Stage Co. does musical comedy, July to early October. *Stowe Playhouse, Mountain Rd., Stowe, tel. 802/253–7944.*

Vermont Repertory Theater (tel. 802/655–9620) mounts five productions in a season from September through May.

Nightlife

Nighttime activities are centered in Burlington, with its business travelers and college students, and in the ski areas. Many resort hotels have après-ski entertainment.

Bars and Lounges **Vermont Pub and Brewery** (College and St. Paul Sts., Burlington, tel. 802/865–0500) is the only pub in Vermont that makes its own beer and fruit seltzers. It also serves a full lunch and dinner menu and late-night snacks.

The Butter Tub at Topnotch (Mountain Rd., Stowe, tel. 802/253–8585) has live entertainment most nights in ski season.

Comedy **Comedy Zone** (Radisson Hotel, 60 Battery St., Burlington, tel. 802/658–6500) provides the laughs in town Friday and Saturday nights.

Dance **Sha-na-na's** plays music from the 1950s and 1960s. *101 Main St., Burlington, tel. 802/865–2596.*

Folk **Last Elm Cafe** (N. Wiooski Ave., no phone), a good old-fashioned coffeehouse, is a good bet for folk music.

Jazz and Blues **Papa's Blues Cellar** (1 Lawson Ln., Burlington, tel. 802/860–7272), a comfortable spot with dark, cozy corners, is the place to go for jazz and blues; it also serves dinner.

Rock **Club Metronome** (188 Main St., Burlington, tel. 802/865–4563) stages an eclectic musical mix that ranges from the newest in cutting edge to funk, blues, reggae, and the occasional big name.

K.D. Churchill's (167 Church St., Burlington, tel. 802/860–1226) offers local musicians in addition to danceable bar bands.

5 New Hampshire

by Betty Lowry, with an introduction by William G. Scheller

A freelance travel correspondent, Betty Lowry has written extensively on New England, the Caribbean, and Europe for magazines and newspapers throughout the United States.

Updated by Ed and Roon Frost

When General John Stark coined the expression Live Free or Die, he knew what he was talking about. Stark had been through the Revolutionary War battles of Bunker Hill and Bennington—where he was victorious—and was clearly entitled to state the choice as he saw it. It was, after all, a choice he was willing to make. But Stark could never have imagined that hundreds of thousands of his fellow New Hampshire men and women would one day display the same fierce sentiment as they traveled the streets and roads of the state: Live Free or Die is the legend of the New Hampshire license plate, the only state license plate in the Union to adopt a sociopolitical ultimatum instead of a tribute to scenic beauty or native produce.

The citizens of New Hampshire are a diverse lot who cannot be tucked neatly into any pigeonhole. To be sure, a white-collar worker in one of the high-tech industries that have sprung up around Nashua or Manchester is no mountaineer defending his homestead with a muzzle-loader, no matter what it says on his license plate.

Yet there is a strong civic tradition in New Hampshire that has variously been described as individualistic, mistrustful of government, even libertarian. This tradition manifests itself most prominently in the state's long-standing aversion to any form of broad-based tax: There is no New Hampshire earned-income tax, nor is there a retail sales tax. Instead, the government relies for its revenue on property taxes, sales of liquor and lottery tickets, and levies on restaurant meals and lodgings—the same measures that other states use to varying degrees. Nor are candidates for state office likely to be successful unless they declare themselves opposed to sales and income taxes.

Another aspect of New Hampshire's suspiciousness of government is its limitation of the gubernatorial term of service to two years: With the running of the reelection gauntlet ever imminent, no incumbent is likely to take the risk of being identified as a proponent of an income or a sales tax—or any other similarly unpopular measure.

And then there's the New Hampshire House of Representatives. With no fewer than 400 members, it is the most populous state assembly in the nation and one of the largest deliberative bodies in the world. Each town with sufficient population sends at least one representative to the House, and he or she had better be able to give straight answers on being greeted—on a first-name basis—at the town hardware store on Saturday.

Yankee individualism, a regional cliché, may or may not be the appropriate description here, but New Hampshire does carry on with a quirky, flinty interpretation of the Jeffersonian credo that that government governs best that governs least. Meanwhile, visitors to New Hampshire see all those license plates and wonder whether they're being told that they've betrayed General Stark's maxim by paying an income tax or a deposit on soda bottles—still another indignity the folks in the Granite State have spared themselves.

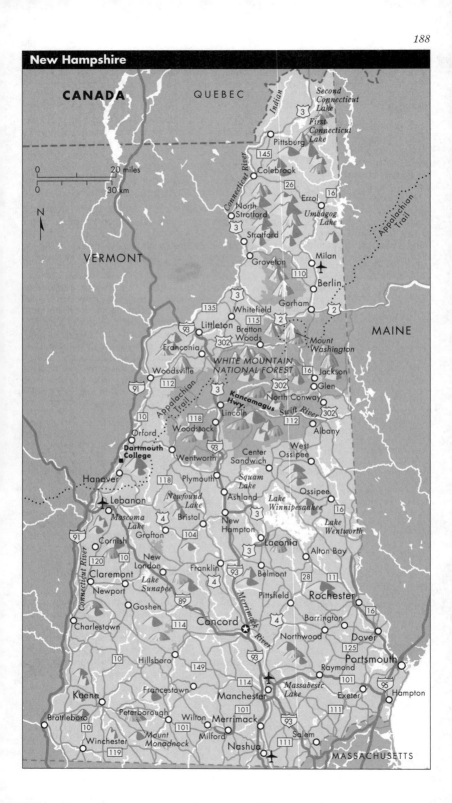

188

Essential Information

Visitor Information

New Hampshire Office of Travel and Tourism Development (Box 856, Concord 03302, tel. 603/271–2343 or 800/944–1117).

Events, foliage, and ski conditions (tel. 800/258–3608 or 800/262–6660).

New Hampshire Council on the Arts (40 N. Main St., Concord 03301, tel. 603/271–2789).

Tour Groups

Special-Interest Tours   **Bike & Hike New Hampshire's Lakes** (43 Highland St., Ashland 03217, tel. 603/968–3775), **Bike the Whites** (tel. 800/933–3902), **Granite State Wheelmen** (various locations, tel. 603/898–9926), **Great Outdoors Hiking & Biking Tours** (tel. 603/356–3271 or 800/525–9100), **Monadnock Bicycle Touring** (Box 19, Harrisville 03450, tel. 603/827–3925), **New England Hiking Holidays,** (tel. 603/356–9696 or 800/869–0949), and **Sunapee Inns Hike & Bike Tours** (tel. 800/662–6005) all organize bike tours.

Festivals and Seasonal Events

Mar.–Apr.: **Sugaring Off** goes public as many sugarhouses demonstrate procedures from maple-tree tapping to sap boiling. Many offer tastings of various grades of syrup, sugar-on-snow, traditional unsweetened doughnuts, and pickles. For a statewide listing of sugar house tours call 603/271–3788.
Mid-May: **New Hampshire Sheep and Wool Festival,** New Boston, demonstrates shearing, carding, and spinning. *Tel. 603/763–5859.*
Late May: **Lilac festivals** involve variety shows, parades, and flea markets in Bristol. *Tel. 603/744–8714.*
Late June: **Market Square Day Weekend** features a street fair with some 300 exhibitors, a road race, a concert, historic house tours, and fireworks in Portsmouth. *Tel. 603/431–5388.*
Early July: **Independence Day weekend** sees parades, flea markets, music, and fireworks in many towns across the state.
Late July: **Wolfeboro Antiques Fair** has been a perennial for nearly 40 years. *Tel. 603/539–5126.*
Early Aug.: **Fair of the League of New Hampshire Craftsmen Foundation,** the nation's oldest crafts fair, schedules special events daily along with exhibits, sales, and demonstrations at Mt. Sunapee State Park, Newbury. *Tel. 603/224–1471.*
Early Aug.: Sullivan's **Zucchini Festival** has spoofed the prolific vegetable for more than a decade with zany competitions, music, and food. *Tel. 603/357–3906.*
Mid-Aug.: **Trail by Candlelight** is a romantic summer evening tour of six historic Portsmouth homes. *Tel. 603/436–1118.*
Mid-Sept.: **Highland Games** brings pipe bands, athletics, music, and dance to Lincoln. *Tel. 603/964–9634 or 603/745–8111.*
Late Sept.: **Deerfield Fair** is New England's oldest county fair, with agricultural exhibits, competitions, and entertainment. *Tel. 603/463–7421.*

Arriving and Departing

By Plane **Manchester Airport** (tel. 603/624–6556), south of the city, has scheduled flights by American, Business Express (Delta Connection), Continental Express, Northwest, United, and USAir. **Keene Airport** (tel. 603/357–9835) has flights via Skymaster to Boston and Newark. **Laconia Airport** (tel. 603/524–5003) is served by Skymaster to Boston and Newark. **Lebanon Municipal Airport** (tel. 603/298–8878), near Dartmouth College, is served by Northwest and Business Express (Delta Connection). **Pease Airport** (tel. 603/427–0350) is served by Business Express (Delta Connection).

By Car I–95 is a toll road as it passes through the coastal area of southern New Hampshire. I–93, the principal north–south route through Manchester, Concord, and central New Hampshire, joins eastern Massachusetts in the south with Vermont in the north. I–89 links Concord with central Vermont.

By Train **Amtrak's** (tel. 800/872–7245) *Montrealer* stops at Claremont on its Washington, DC–Montréal runs. This is New Hampshire's only rail service.

By Bus **Greyhound Lines** (tel. 800/231–2222) and its subsidiary **Vermont Transit** (tel. 603/228–3300) link the cities of New Hampshire with major cities in the eastern United States.

Getting Around New Hampshire

By Plane Small local airports that handle charters and private planes are **Berlin Airport** (tel. 603/449–7383) in Milan, **Concord Airport** (tel. 603/224–4033), **Jaffrey Municipal Airport** (tel. 603/532–7763), **Keene Airport** (tel. 603/357–9835), **Laconia Airport** (tel. 603/524–5003), **Nashua Municipal Airport** (tel. 603/882–0661), **Sky Haven Airport** (tel. 603/332–0005) in Rochester, and **Pease Airport** (tel. 603/427–0350) in Newington (Portsmouth).

By Car The official state map, available free from the Office of Travel and Tourism Development, has directories for each of the tourist areas and is useful for driving the state's larger roads. It gives the locations of the 17 safety rest areas throughout the state that provide rest rooms, picnic facilities, public phones, and vacation information; those at Hooksett (I–93 northbound and southbound) and Seabrook (I–95 northbound) are open 24 hours.

By Bus **Coast** (Durham, tel. 603/862–2328), **C&J** (tel. 603/742–5111), **Vermont Transit** (tel. 603/228–3300 or 800/451–3292), **Concord Trailways** (tel. 800/639–3317), and **Peter Pan Bus Lines** (tel. 603/889–2121) provide bus service between the cities and towns of the state.

Dining

New Hampshire cuisine ranges in character from down-home Yankee to classic French, with ethnic and vegetarian menus well represented. Seafood is plentiful and prepared in a variety of ways. Country inns are known for the quality of their dining rooms and the diversity of their menus. In rural New England, even the roadside diner is an institution, a place where young professionals lunch on spinach pie and herbal tea while truckers and families dine on pot roast, mashed potatoes, and apple or blueberry pie. Ice-cream parlors, too, flourish here, especially in college towns. Restaurants and/or specialty food shops are often associated with nearby small farms that operate orchards or maple-sugar groves.

Highly recommended restaurants in each price category are indicated by a star ★.

Category	Cost*
Very Expensive	over $35
Expensive	$25–$35
Moderate	$15–$25
Inexpensive	under $15

average cost of a three-course dinner, per person, excluding drinks, service, and 8% meals tax.

Lodging

While the hotel chains are well represented in and around the major cities, the lodging of choice in New Hampshire remains the country inn. Usually a family-owned facility with 10 to 30 rooms, most with private bath, the inn's eclectic furnishings (and often a good restaurant) contribute to the charm of vintage houses.

Highly recommended lodgings in each price category are indicated by a star ★.

Category	Cost*
Very Expensive	over $150
Expensive	$100–$150
Moderate	$60–$100
Inexpensive	under $60

All prices are for a standard double room during peak season, with no meals unless noted, and excluding service charge and 8% occupancy tax.

The Coast

In 1603 the first English explorer sailed into the mouth of the Piscataqua River, and in 1623 the first colonists settled at Odiorne Point. Yet the New Hampshire coast today is more than 18 miles of Early Americana. Six state parks and beaches provide picnicking space, walking trails, swimming, boating, fishing, and water sports. Hampton Beach has a boardwalk right out of the 1940s—and the coastal area includes a scramble of patchy retail and housing development. Portsmouth's restaurants, galleries, special events, historic houses, and an outdoor museum at Strawbery Banke attract a trendsetting Boston crowd. Inland, Exeter is an important Colonial capital with 18th- and early 19th-century homes clustered around Phillips Exeter Academy. The crowds are heaviest on summer weekends; weekdays in summer and weekends in June or September are more likely to provide quiet times along the dunes and salt marshes.

Important Addresses and Numbers

Visitor Information **Exeter Area Chamber of Commerce** (120 Water St., Exeter 03833, tel. 603/772–2411).

Greater Dover Chamber of Commerce (299 Central Ave., Dover 03820, tel. 603/742–2218).

Greater Portsmouth Chamber of Commerce (500 Market St., Portsmouth 03801, tel. 603/436–1118).

Hampton Beach Area Chamber of Commerce (836 Lafayette Rd., Hampton 03842, tel. 603/926–8717).

Seacoast Council on Tourism (235 West Rd., Suite 10, Portsmouth 03801, tel. 603/436–7678 or 800/221–5623 outside NH).

Emergencies **New Hampshire State Police** (tel. 800/852–3411).

Poison Center (tel. 800/562–8236).

Portsmouth Regional Hospital (333 Borthwick Ave., tel. 603/436–5110).

Exeter Hospital (10 Buzzell Ave., tel. 603/778–7311).

Late-Night Pharmacy **Kingston Rexall** (Kingston Plaza, Main St., Kingston, tel. 603/642–3323).

Getting Around the New Hampshire Coast

By Car Route 1 and, along the coast, Route 1A are the principal highways through an area where most points are within 30 minutes of Portsmouth, although summer beach traffic in the Hamptons may lengthen driving times considerably along Route 1A.

Guided Tours

Audubon Society of New Hampshire (Box 528B, Concord 03302, tel. 603/224–9909) conducts field trips in various parts of the state.

Insight Tours (tel. 603/436–4223) offers tours from June to Labor Day.

New Hampshire Seacoast Cruises (tel. 603/964–5545) operates June to Labor Day from Rye Harbor Marina.

Portsmouth Livery Company (tel. 603/427–0044) provides horse-and-carriage tours of the Portsmouth area.

Exploring the New Hampshire Coast

Numbers in the margin correspond to points of interest on the New Hampshire Coast map.

❶ Our tour of the coast begins at **Seabrook,** on Route 1 almost 2 miles north of the Massachusetts state line. Seabrook is an old town where whaling boats were once built and residents were known for their Yorkshire accents. Today Seabrook is virtually a one-industry town, and the nuclear power plant, finally granted an operating license early in 1990, is visible from the road.

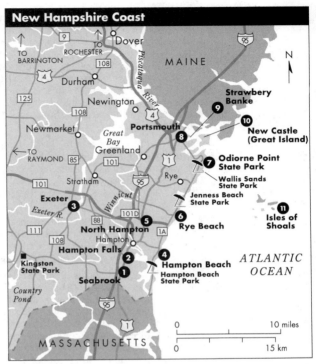

New Hampshire Coast

Two miles farther north, where Route 1 meets Route 88, **2** **Hampton Falls** offers a jogging trail, cross-country skiing in winter, and the **Applecrest Farm Orchards,** a pick-your-own apple grove and berry patch, with a picnic ground, shop, and bakery where you can put together a bread-and-cheese lunch or add fresh fruit and farm apple cider to the contents of your own picnic basket. *Rte. 88, Hampton Falls, tel. 603/926–3721. Open daily 10–dusk.*

Route 88 at Hampton Falls affords the opportunity to visit **3** **Exeter,** the state's Revolutionary capital, 8 miles to the northwest. Today the town is known best for **Phillips Exeter Academy,** one of the nation's oldest prep schools and an assembly of Georgian architecture on a verdant campus. Settled in 1638, Exeter was a radical and revolutionary counterpoint to Tory Portsmouth in 1776. Among the handsome Colonial homes is the **Gilman Garrison House** (Water St., Exeter, tel. 603/227–3956), where settlers once fortified themselves against Native Americans and the Governor's Council met during the American Revolution.

Time Out The **Loaf and Ladle,** at 9 Water Street in Exeter, is a bistro where the chowders, soups, and stews are homemade and even the sandwiches come on homebaked bread. Overlooking the river, the Loaf and Ladle is handy to shops, galleries, and historic houses.

Returned to (or continuing on) Route 1 at Hampton Falls, it's 2 miles north to the junction with Route 101, where the coastal

4 Route 1A veers east and passes near **Hampton Beach.** Sometimes bawdy, never boring, its two-beach and 3-mile-boardwalk complex has the look of a location for a movie taking place in the 1940s and 1950s. This is an area of pizza and cotton candy, palm readers and performers, fireworks and fast-talking pitchmen. Young people swarm across Ocean Boulevard, oblivious to honking cars and blaring radios. Bands play swing in the amphitheater on the beach, and big names perform in the club of the 7-acre, multiple-arcade Hampton Beach Casino (tel. 603/926–4541).

Route 1A continues north to North Hampton and Rye Beach.
5 In **North Hampton,** Millionaires' Row sits just beyond the blare of Hampton Beach. At Fuller Gardens there are 2 acres of estate flower gardens, circa 1939, where 1,500 rose bushes bloom all summer. *10 Willow Ave., North Hampton, tel. 603/964–5414. Open mid-May–Oct., daily 10–6.*

6 At **Rye Beach** is Rye harbor, where one can embark on naturalist-led whale watches and narrated trips to the Isles of Shoals with New Hampshire Seacoast Cruises (tel. 603/382–6743), though Portsmouth offers a larger selection of such cruises.

Jenness Beach and Wallis Sands State Park, north of Rye
7 Beach, have attractive white beaches. **Odiorne Point State Park** and the Seacoast Science Center, site of the first New Hampshire settlement (Pannaway Plantation), require a leisurely afternoon to make the most of the 230 acres of tidal pools, nature trails, and bird walks. The museum and Science Center have programs on ecology and the environment, and you can find further information in the Audubon bookstore. *Rte. 1A, Rye, tel. 603/436–8043. Open year-round.*

8 Routes 1, 1A, and 1B all converge on **Portsmouth,** the state's principal coastal city, the conclusion of the 18-mile New Hampshire coast, and the launch of I–95 and Route 1 on their long journeys up the coast of Maine.

Unlike the museum villages of New England—where historical buildings sometimes are moved into a tourist-oriented mock town—maritime Portsmouth is the real thing, preserved and restored. Shops, galleries, and restaurants are tucked between and into historic houses, some of which date from the late 17th century, when this side of the Piscataqua River was home to a Pilgrim settlement named Strawbery Banke.

After picking up a map from the tourist booth on Market Square or from any of the marked historic houses, you can easily tour the old Colonial town on foot without concern for sequence. As you go, remember that Paul Revere rode to Portsmouth before Lexington and Concord, warning patriots to hide the town's precious supply of gunpowder before the British arrived.

On entering the city from the south, turn right on Little Harbor Road to visit the yellow Georgian **Wentworth-Coolidge Mansion** (tel. 603/436–6607), once the official residence of the Royal Governor. No furnishings are original to the house, but all are of the period. What is said to be the oldest lilac bush in New Hampshire still blooms in the garden.

Time Out **Ceres Street Bakery,** at 51 Penhallow, is a bright, simple place to go for an apricot brioche and coffee mid-morning; homemade soup and quiche at lunch; tea and an almond torte mid-afternoon.

The **Portsmouth Historical Society** is located in the **John Paul Jones House** (Middle and State Sts., tel. 603/436–1118), which has been restored and furnished as it might have been when it was the boardinghouse residence of the naval hero. It is now one of six historic houses on the Portsmouth Trail, a historic walking tour. Tickets good for one or all may be purchased at each house.

Along the waterfront, Prescott Park is an ever-blooming retreat between Strawbery Banke and the river, with a fishing pier and two historic warehouses that date from the early 17th century. One of them contains the **Sheafe Warehouse Museum** (tel. 603/431–8748), with its carved mastheads, ship models, and waterfowl carvings. *Prescott Park, tel. 603/431–8748. Admission free. Open Memorial Day–Labor Day, Wed.–Sun. 8–4.*

The **Port of Portsmouth Maritime Museum,** in Albacore Park, has the USS *Albacore,* built here in 1953 as a prototype and testing submarine for the U.S. Navy. A film, followed by a tour, shows visitors how the 55-man crew lived and worked aboard the vessel. A section of Albacore Park has been dedicated as a memorial to submariners. *500 Market St., tel. 603/ 436–3680. Admission: $4 adults, $3 senior citizens, $2 children 7–12, $10 family. Open May–Columbus Day, daily 9:30–5:30; call for winter hours.*

Time Out Children of all ages will appreciate the confections at **Annabelle's** on Ceres Street. This restaurant offers rich and creamy homemade ice cream, or lunch to take out or eat in the converted warehouse space. For the health conscious, **Izzy's Frozen Yogurt** at the corner of Bow and Ceres streets has frozen delights and specialty coffees.

The **Children's Museum** has hands-on exhibits and activities for children of all ages, from toddlers to young teens. Lobstering, art, geography, computers, and space are among the subjects treated. Special programs may require advance reservations. *South Meeting House, 280 Marcy St., tel. 603/436–3853. Admission: $3.50 adults and children over 1, $3 senior citizens. Open Tues.–Sat. 10–5, Sun. 1–5. Open Mon. in summer and during school vacations.*

9 Portsmouth's ever-changing major attraction is **Strawbery Banke,** a 10-acre outdoor museum with period gardens, monthly activities, and more than 40 original buildings that date from the years 1695 to 1820. The Candlelight Tours in early December are downright romantic. The boyhood home of Thomas Bailey Aldrich (author of *The Story of a Bad Boy)* is the **Nutter House,** where you can climb into his garret, stand in his bedroom (kept just as he described it right down to the patchwork quilt and the bird wallpaper), and look through the window that was his exit into further mischief. The **Wheelwright House** affords a daily demonstration of 18th-century cooking. Snacks, lunch, and dinner (featuring creamy chowders and seafood stews, home-baked scones, and mouth-watering desserts) are served daily in the museum restaurant, the Washington Street Eatery. *Marcy St., tel. 603/433–1100 or 603/433–1106 for 24-*

hour recorded information. Admission: $9 adults, $8 senior citizens, $5 children under 17, $25 family. Tickets good for 2 consecutive days. Open May–Oct., daily 10–5; first 2 weekends in Dec., 3:30–8:30.

⑩ New Castle, once known as Great Island, just east of Portsmouth and overlooking the Piscataqua River, is reached by Route 1B (New Castle Avenue). Its attractions are New Castle Path and **Fort Constitution.** The fort, then a British bastion, was raided by rebel patriots in 1774 and the stolen munitions were used against the British at the Battle of Bunker Hill four months later. Take the paved walking trail from the fort through the 18th-century town for a close-up look at the former Colonial residences that are now private homes. *Fort Constitution, Great Island. Open mid-June–Labor Day, daily 9–5; Labor Day–mid-June, weekends 9–5.*

Island Excursions **Isles of Shoals** is an archipelago of nine Atlantic Ocean islands
⑪ (eight at high tide), one hour by boat from Portsmouth, that was one of the region's major attractions for settlers. The islands were named for the shoals (schools) of fish that supposedly jumped into the nets of fishermen. A dispute between Maine and New Hampshire over the ownership of the islands caused them to be divided between the two states, but the invisible boundary is only of academic interest. In the 19th century the islands were an offshore retreat for the literary and art circle of the poet Celia Thaxter, whose Appledore Island is now used by the Marine Laboratory of Cornell University; Star Island houses a conference center for Unitarian, Universalist, and Congregational church organizations. In summer scheduled cruises take visitors to Star in the morning, leave them long enough for a nonalcoholic picnic and a narrated walking tour, and return them to the mainland in mid-afternoon (only conference attendees may stay overnight in the rambling hotel and cottages). The Isles of Shoals Steamship Company also runs whale-watch expeditions, and its M/V *Thomas Leighton*, a Victorian-era steamship replica, schedules minivoyages on which ghost and pirate stories—the islands have them in abundance—are told; other excursions include some meals. Breakfast, lunch, and light snacks are available on board, or you can bring your own. *Isles of Shoals Steamship Company, Barker Wharf, 315 Market St., Portsmouth, tel. 603/431–5500 or 800/441–4620. Reservations advised. Cruises mid-June–Labor Day; foliage cruises Oct. Christmas cruises. Whale-watching expeditions May–Oct.*

New Hampshire Coast for Free

Boardwalk, Hampton Beach
Fort Constitution, New Castle, Portsmouth
Sheafe Warehouse Museum, Portsmouth
Summer musicals at Prescott Park, Portsmouth

What to See and Do with Children

Children's Museum, Portsmouth
Hampton Playhouse, Hampton (*see* Theater, *below*)
Port of Portsmouth Maritime Museum and Albacore Park, Portsmouth

Off the Beaten Track

Great Bay. The magnificent Great Bay estuary, 4 miles west of Portsmouth, is the haunt of seabirds, migrating land birds, herons, and harbor seals. Upland and wetland game-management areas are kept much as they were when the first visitors arrived, and today's visitors are cautioned to respect the natural environment. Every species of regional aquatic fowl may be seen here and, in Great Bay Access on the southeastern shore, every species of indigenous animal except moose and bear. The early morning hours are the best time to appreciate the area; its isolation from populated centers nearby brings out the Thoreau in all of us. Great Bay Acess is reached by taking Route 101 to Greenland and turning north on the unmarked road near Winnicut River; leave your car at the railway track and walk in. The University of New Hampshire maintains the Jackson Estuan Laboratory on the western shore, an area that can be toured on Durham Point Road, which loops east from Route 108 at points south of Durham and north of Newmarket.

Shopping

Portsmouth's harborside district has unusual and high-quality gift and clothing specialty shops, though you will find art and craft galleries of particular note in the towns of Dover and Exeter as well. The shopping malls are divided between designer and name-brand outlets and an amalgam of department and big stores where slight discounts are commonplace. Shopping hours in general are Monday through Saturday from 10 to 9 and Sunday from 10 to 6.

Antiques stores tend to be scattered; in Portsmouth, look on Chapel and Market streets. Along Route 4 in Northwood is a row of barns and shops overflowing with antiques. From May through October, street fairs, yard sales, and flea markets may be found all along the seacoast. Look for posted notices and in the classified section of the newspapers. There is a regular Sunday **flea market** in the Star Center (25 Fox Run Rd., Newington, tel. 603/431–9403).

Country and farm products such as homemade jams and pickles are available at Applecrest Farm and Raspberry Farm, Hampton Falls; Emery Farm, Durham; Tuttle's Farm, Dover; and Calef's Country Store, Barrington.

Factory Outlets **North Hampton Factory Outlet Center** promises 20% to 70% savings on brand names like Van Heusen, Old Mill, and Aileen. Bass and Timberland have their own factory outlet stores. Visit American Tourister for luggage and Toy Liquidators for zillions of nationally advertised toys. *Rte. 1 (Lafayette Rd.), North Hampton, tel. 603/964–9050.*

Galleries and Crafts Shops **Alie Jewelers** (1 Market St., Portsmouth, tel. 603/436–0531) has gifts as well as gold, silver, and gems.
N.W. Barrett (53 Market St., Portsmouth, tel. 603/431–4262) is a good source for art and local crafts, especially in wood, leather, and pottery. Silver and gold jewelry are also sold here.
Country Curtains (2299 Woodbury Ave., Newington, tel. 603/431–2315), located on the Old Beane Farm, has ready-made curtains, bedding, furniture, gifts, and folk art.
Exeter League of New Hampshire Craftsmen (61 Water St., Exeter, tel. 603/778–8282) is the seacoast shop for originals by

select, juried members of L.N.H.C. Exhibits feature a different local craftsperson each month.

The Museum Shop at the Dunaway Store (Marcy St., Portsmouth, tel. 603/433–1114) stocks reproduction and contemporary furniture, quilts, crafts, and books. Profits support Strawbery Banke.

Partridge Replications (63 Penhallow St., tel. 603/431–8733), in a former customs house, stocks fine Early American–style furniture made by contemporary craftsmen.

A Pictures Worth a Thousand Words (65 Water St., Exeter, tel. 603/778–1991) has a large showroom of antique and contemporary prints, old maps, and rare books.

Salmon Falls Stoneware (The Engine House on Oak St., Dover, tel. 603/749–1467 or 800/621–2030) is handmade, American salt-glaze stoneware decorated with traditional, country, and whimsical designs. Potters are on hand if you want to place a special order.

Tulips (19 Market St., Portsmouth, tel. 603/431–9445) was Portsmouth's first crafts gallery and is still the city's leading venue for both local and national craftspeople. Wood crafts and quilts are specialties.

Malls **Fox Run Mall** (Fox Run Rd., Newington, tel. 603/431–5911) is the largest hereabouts, with Filene's, Jordan Marsh, JC Penney, Sears, and 100 other stores.

Newington Mall (45 Gosling Rd., Newington, tel. 603/431–4104) has Bradlees, Montgomery Ward, and 70 more stores as well as restaurants and a supermarket.

Sports and Outdoor Activities

Biking The Durham-to-Exeter route is a flat, pleasant round-trip of about 30 miles. Start off on Route 108/85 and return by crossing Route 101 and taking back roads along and across the Piscassic and Lamprey rivers. Avoid Route 1. A bike trail runs along part of Route 1A, and you can take a break at Odiorne Point. For **group rides** in various locations from April through October, tel. 603/898–9926.

Boating There are rentals aplenty, along with deep-sea fishing charters, at Hampton, Portsmouth, Rye, and Seabrook piers, available from **Eastman Fishing & Marine** (Seabrook 03874, tel. 603/474–3461), **Atlantic Fishing Fleet** (Rye Harbor 03870, tel. 603/964–5220), **Al Gauron Deep Sea Fishing** (Hampton Beach 03842, tel. 603/926–2469), and **Smith & Gilmore** (Hampton Beach 03842, tel. 603/926–3503).

Camping **Pine Acres Family Campground** (55 Prescott Rd., Raymond 03077, tel. 603/895–2519) has a giant water slide.

Tidewater Campground (160 Lafayette Rd., Hampton 03842, tel. 603/926–5474).

Tuxbury Pond Camping Area (W. Whitehall Rd., South Hampton 03842, tel. 603/394–7660) is convenient to the Hampton Casino action.

Hiking There are good short hikes at **Blue Job Mountain** (Crown Point Rd. off Rte. 202A, 1 mi from Rochester) and walking trails at the Urban Forestry Center, Portsmouth, and at Odiorne Point State Park, Rye. Serious hikers should move on to the White Mountains.

Beaches

Swimming beaches on the New Hampshire shore and one inland freshwater pond are maintained and supervised by the Division of Parks and Recreation. You will usually find Jenness, Rye, and Wallis Sands less congested than Hampton, but you can view them and take your choice as you cruise Route 1A. For freshwater swimming, try Kingston State Park at Kingston on Great Pond (not to be confused with Great Bay). Beaches outside the state park system include Foss Beach, Rye, and New Castle Common, New Castle.

Dining and Lodging

Portsmouth has many high quality restaurants. In warm weather, the eateries along Bow and Ceres streets open their decks for dining with a sea breeze, and diners can watch the tugboats and harbor traffic.

All the lodgings described here are convenient to both town and shore, and all require advance reservations, at least during the period from mid-June to mid-October.

Durham **New England Center Hotel.** This is a quiet spot set in a pine
Lodging grove on the campus of the University of New Hampshire. The rooms are larger in the new wing, and none are noisy. *15 Strafford Ave., Durham 03824, tel. 603/862–2800. 115 rooms with bath. Facilities: 2 restaurants, lounge, cable TV. No pets. AE, MC, V. Moderate.*

Exeter **Exeter Inn Dining Room.** The restaurant on the Phillips Exeter
Dining Academy campus serves chateaubriand on a plank that goes miles beyond any student's dream night out with Mom and Dad. On Friday and Saturday night, look for cherries flambé or some equally spectacular flaming dessert. Sunday brunch, with at least 60 savory items (including a variety of omelets), provides a bright start to the day: the dining room is enclosed within a circle of windows and has a fig tree growing in the center. *90 Front St., Exeter, tel. 603/772–5901. Reservations advised; not accepted for Sunday brunch. Dress: neat but casual. AE, D, DC, MC, V. Moderate–Expensive.*

Lodging **Exeter Inn.** A three-story, Georgian-style inn with handsomely appointed guest rooms is properly set on the campus of the Phillips Exeter Academy, in the heart of Exeter's historic district. This is understated elegance, New England–preppie style. *90 Front St., Exeter 03833, tel. 603/772–5901 or 800/782–8444, fax 603/778–8757. 50 rooms with bath. Facilities: restaurant, cable TV, fitness room. No pets. AE, D, DC, MC, V. Moderate.*

Hampton **Ron's Beach House.** Cioppino, pasta with white clam sauce, and
Dining a fish chowder with Cajun-style mushroom caps lead a menu of imaginative specialties that has made an overnight success of this family-run restaurant. In the Plaice Cove section of Hampton, Ron's occupies a restored house on the waterfront, 3 miles north of the boardwalk. *965 Ocean Blvd., Hampton, tel. 603/926–1870. Reservations advised. Dress: casual. AE, D, MC, V. Moderate–Expensive.*

Lodging **The Victoria Inn.** In 1875 it was carriage house to a mansion; today it is a romantic bed-and-breakfast done in the style and colors Victorians loved best. Franklin Pierce, 14th president of the United States, had a summer home next door, and there is a Pierce Room named in his honor. Whether you breakfast in the dining room or in the morning room, which overlooks the garden and gazebo, the meals prepared by innkeepers Linda and Leon Lamson are always hearty and sumptuous. After Saturday's Logger's Breakfast or Sunday's Eggs Leon (Leon's version of eggs Benedict), you certainly will need that ½-mile walk to the beach. *430 High St., Hampton 03842, tel. 603/929–1437. 6 rooms, 3 with bath. Facilities: cable TV, air-conditioning, off-street parking. No smoking. No pets. Rates include full breakfast. MC, V. Moderate.*

Hampton Beach **Ashworth by the Sea.** Since this centrally located hotel opened
Lodging in 1912, it has been renovated, rebuilt, and renovated again; most rooms now have decks, and the furnishings are either period or contemporary, depending on the room. Be sure to specify whether you want sea view or quiet, because you can't have it both ways. *295 Ocean Blvd., Hampton Beach 03842, tel. 603/ 926–6762 or 800/345–6736. 105 rooms with bath. Facilities: 3 restaurants, pool, room service. AE, D, DC, MC, V. Moderate–Expensive.*

Newmarket **Moody Parsonage Bed and Breakfast.** This historic red clap-
Lodging board Colonial built in 1730 for John Moody, the first minister
★ of Newmarket, is 2 miles south of Newmarket center. Today's world and worries seem far away in a house where a spinning wheel sits on the landing, and where you can still see the original paneling, staircases, and wide pine floors. Five fireplaces— one is always going in the dining room on chilly mornings—are cozy reminders of days when even the seacoast was on the edge of the wilderness. One bedroom and bath are on the first floor. The other three rooms are upstairs and share a bath, making a good arrangement for a family. Great Bay, the magnificent estuary and wildlife sanctuary for migrating waterfowl, is within walking distance, and so is a golf course. *15 Ash Swamp Rd., Newmarket 03857, tel. 603/659–6675. 4 rooms, 1 with bath. Facilities: air-conditioning, fireplaces in bedrooms. No pets. No credit cards. Rates include Continental breakfast. Inexpensive.*

Portsmouth **The Blue Strawbery Restaurant.** The label "American Cuisine"
Dining understates the inventiveness of this six-course menu that
★ changes every night according to what is freshest in the local market that morning. The prix-fixe, reservations-only policy of this small waterfront restaurant never deters diners; in fact, some drive hours to get here. *29 Ceres St., Portsmouth, tel. 603/431–6420. Reservations required. Dress: neat but casual. No credit cards. Dinner only. Closed Oct. 15–July 3, Mon.– Wed. Very Expensive.*

★ **Guido's Trattoria.** This second-story dining room overlooking the harbor serves traditional Tuscan cuisine. Guido offers a fine selection of Italian vintages, but even the house Chiantis are choice. Because the cooking is light and healthful, it's possible to polish off four generous courses and not feel stuffed. Appetizers include grilled bread that diners rub with fresh garlic; calamari simmered in white wine with red peppers, porcini, and garlic; and *tortelli alla Bolognese* (cheese-stuffed pasta topped with ground veal, tomatoes, herbs, and wine). Entrée selections include the wild boar, grilled breast of duck, rack of lamb, or moist halibut garnished with capers and leeks. Save room for poached pears or tiramisù for dessert. *67 Bow St., 2nd* *floor, Portsmouth, tel. 603/431–2989. Reservations advised. Dress: casual. AE, MC, V. No lunch. Closed Sun.–Mon. Moderate–Expensive.*

The Library at the Rockingham House. A Portsmouth landmark, this restaurant has its walls lined with bookcases filled with old books, and it presents its bill in the pages of a vintage bestseller. *Moo sate* (skewered strips of marinated pork with peanut curry sauce), oysters Rockingham, New Zealand rack of lamb with an apricot mint sauce, and fresh swordfish are highlights. *401 State St., Portsmouth, tel. 603/431–5202. Reservations advised on weekends. Dress: casual. AE, DC, MC, V. Moderate–Expensive.*

The Oar House and Deck. For cocktails and dining in the summer on the deck next to the Heritage Cruise dock, or year-round in the stone warehouse, the Oar House is consistently first-rate. Try the bouillabaisse; veal Barbara with avocado, crab, cheese, and mushroom topping; or Oar House delight (fresh fish, scallops, and shrimp lightly sautéed and then baked with a sour cream–crumb topping). *55 Ceres St., Portsmouth, tel. 603/436–4025. Valet parking. Reservations advised. Dress: neat but casual. AE, MC, V. Moderate–Expensive.*

The Brewery. Local brews (you can watch the process), intriguing collages, and a long, long bar enhance such dishes as Caesar salad garnished with seared swordfish steak, spicy shrimp, stir-fried combinations, burritos, fresh tuna steak au poivre, and fish and chips. There's live entertainment Wednesday through Saturday. *56 Market St., Portsmouth, tel. 603/431–1115. Dress: casual. AE, D, MC, V. Inexpensive–Moderate.*

Karen's. A favorite with locals, Karen's has long been known for good food at reasonable prices. Design your own breakfast omelet, enjoy chicken fajitas or quiche and salad for lunch, or dine on grilled, uncultured mussels in pistachio garlic butter and salmon en papillote. Dinner guests are invited to bring their own wine. *105 Daniel St., Portsmouth, tel. 603/431–1948. No dinner Sun.–Wed. No reservations. No smoking. Dress: casual. AE, D. Inexpensive–Moderate.*

Lodging **Sheraton Portsmouth Hotel.** This five-story redbrick Sheraton blends nicely with the 19th-century architecture of the historic district. Despite its harbor views and central location, it's more of a conference center than a cozy inn. *250 Market St., Portsmouth 03801, tel. 603/431–2300 or 800/325–3535. 148 rooms, 29 suites with bath. Facilities: restaurant, lounge, nightclub, room service, cable TV, health spa, indoor pool. No pets. AE, D, DC, MC, V. Expensive.*

★ **Sise Inn.** With silks and polished chintz, rubbed woods and armoires, this inn re-creates the lifestyle of the affluent of the 1880s. The Queen Anne town house is in Portsmouth's historic district and is ideally located for waterfront strolling and dining. No two rooms are alike. *40 Court St., Portsmouth 03801, tel. 603/433–1200 or 800/267–0525. 34 rooms with bath. Facilities: cable TV, VCR, some whirlpool tubs. No pets. AE, DC, MC, V. Rates include breakfast. Expensive.*

★ **Governor's House B&B.** Although it's located within a short walk of Portsmouth's historic downtown, this comfortable Georgian Colonial mansion retains a real sense of the rural, surrounded as it is by nearly an acre of lawn and wood. The house, originally built in 1917, was once owned by Governor Charles Dale of New Hampshire. In 1992 it was opened as a bed and breakfast, and its new owners have fully restored the four cozy, antiques-decorated rooms (and refurbished the private tennis court). An ample breakfast of traditional New England treats—including savory homemade popovers—is served in the small but elegant dining room. *32 Miller Ave., Portsmouth 03801, tel. 603/431–6546, fax 603/427–0803. 4 rooms with bath. Facilities: tennis, cable TV, ceiling fans, off-street parking. No smoking. No pets. MC, V. Rates include full breakfast. Moderate.*

Martin Hill Inn. Actually two buildings, this downtown inn is within walking distance of Portsmouth's historic district and waterfront; quiet rooms are comfortably furnished with antiques. *404 Islington St., Portsmouth, tel. 603/436–2287. 4 rooms with bath; 3 suites. Facilities: off-street parking, air-conditioning. No smoking. No pets. MC, V. Moderate.*

Inn at Christian Shore. The inn is owned—and decorated—by former antiques dealers who came to bed-and-breakfast innkeeping after restoring and furnishing houses elsewhere. It is a 10-minute walk from the historic district, the harbor, and shops; and you'll need the walk after breakfasting on fruit, eggs, a meat dish, vegetables, and homemade muffins. *335 Maplewood Ave., Portsmouth 03801, tel. 603/431–6770. 5 rooms with bath. Facilities: cable TV. No credit cards. Rates include full breakfast. Inexpensive–Moderate.*

Rochester
Dining

The Governor's Inn. Candlelight dinners are served in the period dining room of this 1920 brick mansion, once owned by former New Hampshire governor Huntley Spaulding. The fixed menu, served to the public by reservation only, may include openers of black-sturgeon caviar or curried butternut soup with apple. The main course may be medallions of beach tenderloin with salsa and guacamole or sautéed tuna Maltaise followed perhaps by coconut cake with Grand Marnier oranges. The Governor's Inn is located in the center of Rochester and doubles as a commendable bed-and-breakfast inn with five plush rooms, each with bath. *78 Wakefield St., Rochester, tel. 603/332–0107. Dress: casual. AE, MC, V. Moderate.*

Rye
Lodging

Rock Ledge Manor. This bed-and-breakfast was once part of a late-19th-century resort colony, and its sun room and white wicker are signs of its past. The owners speak French, and you may well find crepes served one morning in the sunny dining room overlooking the Atlantic. All the bedrooms have sea views. *1413 Ocean Blvd. (Rte. 1A), Rye 03870, tel. 603/431–1413. 4 rooms, 2 with bath. No pets. No smoking. No credit cards. Rates include full breakfast. Moderate.*

The Arts

Music

Music in Market Square (tel. 603/436–9109) is a free Friday-afternoon show of vocal and instrumental artists in the heart of Portsmouth.

Prescott Park Arts Festival (Marcy St., Portsmouth, tel. 603/436–2848), on the waterfront, provides art, music, theater, and dance for the family, July 4 to mid-August.

Strawbery Banke Chamber Music Festival (Box 1529, Portsmouth, tel. 603/436–3110) schedules performances from October through June.

Theater

Hampton Playhouse (357 Winnacunnet Rd., Rte. 101E, Hampton, tel. 603/926–3073) has children's theater and Equity summer theater with familiar TV, Broadway, and Hollywood faces from July through September. Tickets are available at the box office or at the Chamber of Commerce Sea Shell office on Ocean Boulevard.

The Seacoast Repertory Company (125 Bow St., Portsmouth, tel. 603/433–4472) is the only year-round professional theater in the Portsmouth area. The Portsmouth Academy of Performing Arts and the Bow Street Theater combine to bring classical, traditional, musical, and children's presentations to the waterfront.

Nightlife

Hampton Beach Casino Ballroom. As many as 2,500 people can crowd the floor on a summer night, and because people have been coming here for 30 years all generations are well represented. As for the nightly show, Tina Turner, The Monkees, Jay Leno, and Loretta Lynn have played here. *Ocean Beach Blvd., Hampton Beach, tel. 603/926–4541. Open Apr.–Oct.*

The Press Room. Media folk come from Boston, Portland, and towns in New Hampshire to hang out in the old three-story brick building. The shows are good, but the preliminaries are better. From 5 PM to 9 PM, it's usually piano or guitar music. Tuesday night the open mike starts at 9; Friday look for sea shanties, pre-1850 Celtic ballads, or maybe just open jams. *77 Daniel St., Portsmouth, tel. 603/431–5186. No reservations. Dress: casual. Name entertainment upstairs, Fri.–Sat. 9–closing, Sun. 7–11. Open gig Tues.–Sat. 5–9. Cover upstairs only.*

Lakes Region

Lake Winnipesaukee ("Smiling Water") is the largest of the dozens of lakes scattered across the eastern half of central New Hampshire; Squam Lake took on a new identity when *On Golden Pond* was filmed here; and Lake Wentworth is named for the first Royal Governor of the state, who in building his country manor here established North America's first summer resort. The lake islands number more than 200, and there are preserved Colonial and 19th-century villages minutes away. Swimming, boating, fishing, and other water recreation abound. Hiking, biking, and 11 golf courses help fill time not spent on, in, or about the water. Every summer weekend hosts some major event. Yet there's still plenty of people who come specifically to poke about in musty antiques and craft shops, or to do absolutely nothing except ponder intense lakeland views.

Important Addresses and Numbers

Visitor Information
Lakes Region Association (Center Harbor 03226, tel. 603/253–8555).

Lakes Region Chamber of Commerce (11 Veterans Square, Laconia 03246, tel. 603/524–5531 or 800/531–2347).

Emergencies
State Police (tel. 800/852–3411).

Poison Center (tel. 800/562–8236).

Lakes Region General Hospital (Highland St., Laconia, tel. 603/524–3211 or 800/852–3311).

Getting Around the Lakes Region

By Car Interstate 93, on the western side of the region, is the principal
artery, with exits to the lakes. From the coast, Route 11
reaches southwestern Lake Winnipesaukee, and Route 16
stretches to the White Mountains, with roads leading to the
lakeside towns.

By Bus **Concord Trailways** (tel. 800/639–3317).

Guided Tours

Cruising Golden Pond visits filming sites of the 1981 movie *On
Golden Pond* (a.k.a. Squam Lake) aboard the *Lady of the Manor*, a 28-foot pontoon craft. *Manor Resort, Holderness, tel. 603/
968–3348 or 800/545–2141. Fare: $10 adults, $5 children.*

Squam Lake Tours can be chartered for guided fishing trips and
wedding or anniversary parties, as well as for lake excursions.
*Box 185, Holderness 03245, tel. 603/968–7577. Closed Nov.–
late May.*

M/S *Mount Washington's* (Box 5367, Weirs Beach 03247, tel.
603/366–2628) three-hour cruises of Winnipesaukee allow time
for breakfast or lunch aboard while touring the lake. From May
through October departures are daily from Weirs Beach and
Wolfeboro, three times a week from Center Harbor, and four
times a week from Alton Bay.

Winnipesaukee Railroad departures are timed to connect with
the boat, but rides can be taken independently. Historic equipment carries passengers along the lakeshore for just under two
hours; boarding is at Weirs Beach or Meredith. *Box 9, Lincoln
03251, tel. 603/279–3196. Fare: $7 adults, $4.50 children. Season: Memorial Day–late June, late Sept.–mid-Oct., weekends.*

Exploring the Lakes Region

*Numbers in the margin correspond to points of interest on the
New Hampshire Lakes map.*

❶ Each of the more than two dozen major lakes in this region has
its advocates. Our tour will concentrate on **Winnipesaukee**, the
state's largest lake, with a 283-mile shoreline and more than
200 islands. We'll begin at Alton Bay, at the southernmost tip,
and move clockwise around the lake, starting off on Route 11.
Visitors to the lakes region often plan a shopping excursion to
the outlet strip at the southern end of North Conway (*see* The
White Mountains, *below*).

Two mountain ridges hold 7 miles of Winnipesaukee in a bay. Of
the twin towns at the southern extremity of the lake, Alton is
❷ the quiet village while **Alton Bay** is where the lake's cruise
boats dock and where you will find a dance pavilion, minigolf, a
public beach, and a Victorian-style bandstand used for summer
concerts.

❸ One of the larger public beaches is at **Gilford,** an affluent community that traces its origins to Colonial days. The **Gunstock
Recreation Area** (tel. 603/293–4341), with an Olympic pool, a

New Hampshire Lakes

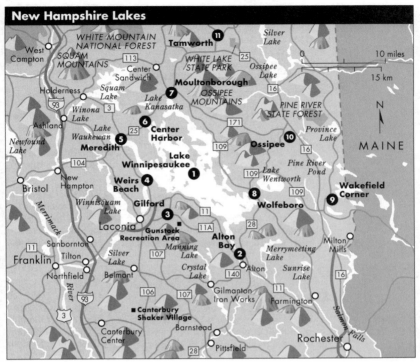

children's playground, hiking trails, and a campground, is east of Gilford on Route 11A.

4 North of Gilford on Route 11A, **Weirs Beach** provides the boardwalk atmosphere of the lakes. Fireworks are common here on summer evenings; cruise ships (M/S *Mount Washington*, M/V *Sophie C.*, and M/V *Doris E.*, tel. 603/366–2628) depart from its dock; and the **Winnipesaukee Railroad** (tel. 603/279–3196) picks up passengers here for an hour-long tour of the shore. You can do crazy water things at Surf Coaster, descend four giant water slides at Water Slide, or work your way through the games, minigolf, and 20 lanes of bowling at Funspot.

Time Out **Kellerhaus,** just north of Weirs Beach and overlooking the lake, is a candy shop beloved by lake visitors since 1906. At the half-timbered, Alpine-style building you'll find an ice-cream smorgasbord with a variety of toppings to dress as much ice cream as you can pile in your dish. The price is based on dish size.

5 At **Meredith,** on Route 3 at the western extremity of Winnipesaukee, **Annalee's Doll Museum** (tel. 603/279–4144), an adjunct to a gift shop, has hundreds of felt dolls, and there are shops and galleries. An information center is located across from the Town Docks.

6 The town of **Center Harbor,** set on the middle of three bays at the northern end of Winnipesaukee, borders on Lakes Squam, Waukewan, and Winona.

❼ Farther north on Route 25, **Moultonborough** has 6½ miles of shoreline on Lake Kanasatka as well as a piece of Squam. Moultonborough, oriented to leisure, has restaurants of good quality. **Castle in the Clouds** (tel. 603/476–2352 or 800/729–2468), a mansion on 6,000 acres offering horseback rides and hayrides, is open mid-May–mid-October.

❽ **Wolfeboro** has been a resort since John Wentworth built his summer home on the shores of Lake Wentworth in 1763. The original Wentworth house burned down in 1820, but by then summering at the lake was a well-established routine. The sedate village is headquarters of the **Hampshire Pewter Company** (tel. 603/569–4944), where 17th-century techniques are still used to make hollowware and accessories, and there are antiques shows and crafts events all summer.

Between Winnipesaukee and the border of Maine to the east lie several villages with historical districts and considerable charm that differ markedly from the heavily visited lakeside towns. With their own lakes close at hand, and their proximity to Route 16, they are good stopping-off places for those headed to Mt. Washington Valley.

❾ **Wakefield Corner** is a registered historic district, with church, houses, and inn looking just as they did in the 18th century. The
❿ larger Wakefield encompasses 10 lakes. **Ossipee** consists of three villages around Lake Ossipee and satellite ponds. Good antiques (and other) shops are here for those who don't want to spend all their time fishing, swimming, boating, and hiking.
⓫ **Tamworth** has a clutch of villages within its borders. The view through the birches of Chocorua Lake has been so often photographed that you may get a sense of having been here before.

Lakes Region for Free

Hampshire Pewter Company (tours), Wolfeboro
Old Print Barn, Meredith
Old Village Barn, Chocorua

What to See and Do with Children

Annalee's Doll Museum, Meredith
Center Harbor Children's Museum is a hands-on learning facility with a gift shop. *Senter's Market, Center Harbor, tel. 603/253–8697. Admission: $4. Open Tues.–Sat. 9:30–5, Sun. 11–5.*
Funspot, Surf Coaster, and **Water Slide,** Weirs Beach
Museum of Childhood's displays include a one-room schoolhouse, model trains, 30 dollhouses, and 3,000 dolls. *Wakefield Corner, tel. 603/522–8073. Admission: $3 adults, $1.25 children. Open June–Oct., Wed.–Mon. 11–4, Sun. 1–4.*
New Hampshire Farm Museum, Milton (tel. 603/652–7840)
Winnipesaukee Railroad, Meredith and Weirs beaches

Off the Beaten Track

Canterbury Shaker Village. Established in 1792, the Canterbury community flourished in the 1800s. Shakers were known for fine workmanship and for the simplicity and integrity of their design, especially in household furniture. They were also prolific inventors (of the clothespin, for example). The village is now an outdoor museum with guided tours, crafts demonstrations, and a large shop offering books and reproductions. At the heart of the village, the Creamery Restaurant practices the plain cookery of people who made the most of the freshest ingredients; even the butter is home-churned. Authentic Shaker recipes create the raised-squash biscuits, the rosewater apple pie, and everything else on the menu. Consider this a four-hour stop. From I–93 Exit 18, follow signs; the village is 7 miles from the exit. *288 Shaker Rd., Canterbury, tel. 603/783–9511. Admission: $7 adults, $3.50 children. Open May–Oct., Mon.–Sat. 10–5, Sun. noon–5; Apr., Nov.–Dec., Fri.–Sat. 10–5, Sun. noon–5.*

Shopping

Crafts shops, galleries, and sportswear boutiques dominate the shopping scene around the lakes. Antiques shops (mostly open by chance or by appointment) are thickest along the eastern side of Winnipesaukee near Wolfeboro and around Ossipee.

Art   **The Old Print Barn** (Meredith, tel. 603/279–6479). Hundreds of rare prints from the Middle Ages to modern times are available in this extraordinary barn. It's the largest print gallery in northern New England. From Route 104 in Meredith follow Winona Road and look for "Lane" on the mailbox. *Closed Columbus Day–Memorial Day.*

Crafts   **Keepsake Quilting & Country Pleasures** (Senter's Marketplace on Rte. 25, Center Harbor, tel. 603/253–4026). New England's largest quilt shop has fabrics, supplies, books, and country-style accessories.

Meredith League of New Hampshire Craftsmen (Rte. 3, ½ mi north of intersection of Rtes. 3 and 104, Meredith, tel. 603/279–7920). Work of juried craftspeople is on display and for sale in all price ranges.

The Old Country Store (tel. 603/476–5750) in Moultonboro Corner has been selling handmade soaps, regional crafts, maple products, aged cheeses, penny candy, and pickles in the crock since 1781. There's a free museum in the back.

Sandwich Home Industries. (Rte. 109, Center Sandwich, tel. 603/284–6831). This 65-year-old grandparent of the League of New Hampshire Craftsmen was formed to foster cottage crafts. There are crafts demonstrations in July and August and sales of home furnishings and accessories mid-May–October.

Crystal   **Pepi Hermann Crystal** (Gilford, tel. 603/528–1020). You can buy all your wedding gifts plus stemware and even handcut crystal chandeliers in this famous hand-factory shop. Take a tour of the workshop while you're there.

Dolls   **Annalee's Gift Shop and Museum** (Reservoir Rd., off Rte. 3, Meredith, tel. 603/279–6542). Annalee's whimsical felt dolls are known all over the world. Here you will see hundreds of dolls no longer manufactured that are treasured by collectors. You can also buy the latest.

Mall   **Mills Falls Marketplace** (tel. 603/279–7006), in Meredith, contains 22 shops and galleries.

Sports and Outdoor Activities

Biking   Traffic can be heavy on main arteries in midsummer (particularly between Gilford and Meredith), and even the region's small backroads are sometimes overwhelmed by four-wheeled tourists. The best bet for solitude is Squam Lake on Routes 113 and 109.

Boating   **The Lakes Region Association** (Box 1545, Center Harbor 03226, tel. 603/253–8555) can answer questions about boating opportunities. Boats can be rented in Meredith from **Meredith Marina and Boating Center** (tel. 603/279–7921) and in Weirs Beach from **Thurston's Marina** (tel. 603/366–4811).

Camping   **Gunstock** (Rte. 11A, Gilford, Box 1307, Laconia 03247, tel. 603/293–4344) offers multiple sports facilities including a pool and children's playground.

Meredith Woods (New Hampton 03256, tel. 603/279–5449 or 800/848–0328) offers year-round camping and RV facilities, as well as an indoor heated pool.

Yogi Bear's Jellystone Park (Ashland 03217, tel. 603/968–3654) is especially good for families.

Clearwater Campground (New Hampton 03256, tel. 603/279–7761).

Len Kay (Barrington 03825, tel. 603/664–9333).

Squam Lakeside Camp Resort and Marina (Rte. 3, Holderness 03245, tel. 603/968–7227) is open all year with full hookups; cable TV.

White Lake State Park (Tamworth 03886, tel. 603/323–7350), between Tamworth and Ossipee, has two camping areas.

Fishing   Lake trout and salmon in Winnipesaukee, trout and bass in the smaller lakes, and trout streams all around make this a fisherman's paradise. Alton Bay has an "Ice Out" salmon derby in spring. During winter, on all the lakes including Winnipesaukee, intrepid ice fishers fish from huts known as "ice bobs." For up-to-date fishing information, call the regional New Hampshire Fish and Game office (tel. 603/744–5470).

Hiking   There are many trails, but just to get you started: Mt. Major, Alton; Squam Range, Holderness; Red Hill, off Route 25 on Bean Road northeast of Centre Harbor; Pine River State Forest, east of Route 16.

Water Sports   The lake is crowded with boats in summer, and waterskiing regulations are posted at every marina. Scuba divers can explore a sunken paddle wheeler off Wolfeboro. Instruction, rentals, repairs, and sales are available at **North Country Scuba & Sports, Inc.** (tel. 603/524–8606 or 603/569–2120) in both Laconia and Wolfeboro.

State Parks

White Lake State Park, between Tamworth and West Ossipee, is the only state park in the lakes region. Picnicking, swimming, camping, and fishing are available.

Beaches

There are many private beaches around the lake. **Ellacoya State Beach,** in Gilford, is 600 feet long and is the major public beach. **Wentworth State Beach,** at Wolfeboro, has good swimming and a bath house.

Dining and Lodging

Because restaurants around the lakes serve throngs of visitors during the summer, grilling is the usual means of preparing meats, and you should be able to find a steak or prime rib in almost any dining room.

Bridgewater
Dining and Lodging

Pasquaney Inn on Newfound Lake. Just across the road from Newfound Lake, only the sunset can distract diners from the French-Belgian cuisine. Start with smoked salmon with endive and mustard-truffle dressing, and then try veal sweetbreads with mushrooms and Madeira wine or monkfish with tomato *coulis.* The mousse, made with real Belgian chocolate, is a good choice for dessert. The restaurant's vegetables, herbs, and flowers are grown in the inn's gardens. Owner-chef Bud Edrick also gives lessons in French cookery at the inn during the off-season. The 26 antiques-filled bedrooms in this 1840s house tempt you to stay the night after you've worked your way through the ever-changing menu. *Rte. 3A, Bridgewater, tel. 603/744-9111. Reservations advised. Dress: neat but casual. AE, D, DC, MC, V. Closed June–Oct., Mon.; Nov.–May, Mon.–Wed. Moderate–Expensive.*

Center Harbor
Lodging

Red Hill Inn. This once-upon-a-time summer mansion overlooks "Golden Pond" from a respectful distance. Furnished with Victorian period pieces, many of the rooms have fireplaces, and some have whirlpool baths. Hiking and ski trails on the inn's 50 acres provide opportunities for activity. *RD 1, Box 99M (Rte. 25B), Center Harbor 03226, tel. 603/279-7001. 21 rooms with bath. Facilities: restaurant. AE, D, DC, MC, V. Rates include full breakfast. Moderate–Expensive.*

Center Sandwich
Dining and Lodging

The Corner House Inn. This quaint Victorian inn serves home-cooked meals in cozy dining rooms decorated with local arts and crafts. Lobster and mushroom bisque, a New England version of Chesapeake Bay crab cakes, as well as the traditional veal Oscar are favorites here. Storytelling by the pot-bellied stove makes for interesting dining one night a week, and there are four comfortable, old-fashioned rooms upstairs (one with private bath) if you get too sleepy to drive home. *Rte. 113, Center Sandwich, tel. 603/284-6219 or 800/832-7829. Dress: casual. AE, MC, V. Closed Thanksgiving, Christmas, and Mon. and Tues. Nov.–May. Inexpensive–Moderate.*

East Hebron
Lodging
★

Six Chimneys. Six Chimneys (count them) sits on a knoll at the northeast corner of Newfound Lake, midway between Bristol and Plymouth, as convenient now for visitors to the lakes and White Mountains as when the building was a tavern 200 years ago and the room rate was 10¢ a night. There are three cozy common rooms on the first floor warmed in winter by wood-burning stoves or a fireplace. One is a quiet back parlor, and two have their own cable TV and VCRs, with more than 200 tapes stored in an English monk's bench. The old wide-board floors tilt a bit, and there are gun-stock corner posts and pine wainscoting in several of the bedrooms. An upstairs sitting room furnished with Oriental rugs and old pine and cherry furniture has been created under the sloping roof. In space once reserved for drovers, a family can have a suite by combining the twin and single bedrooms (which share a bath) with the sitting ell. Bountiful country breakfasts (fruit compote, French toast, sausage, and raspberry muffins, for example) are cooked on a 125-year-old "Dairy Household" wood-burning range, then served in a dining room where the exposed original beams and pegs complement the rush-seat chairs. *Star Rte. 114, East Hebron 03232, tel. 603/744–2029. 6 rooms, 2 with bath. Facilities: cable TV and VCRs in 2 common rooms; lake beach. MC, V. Closed late Mar.–early Apr. Inexpensive.*

Holderness
Lodging

The Inn on Golden Pond. This relaxed country home, built in 1879 and set on 50 wooded acres, is just across the road from Squam Lake. Visitors enjoy the variety of the lake, then take refuge on the screened porch or walk one of the property's nature trails. The rooms have braided rugs and easy chairs. The rear of the third floor is where it's the most quiet. *Rte. 3, Box 680, Holderness 03245, tel. 603/968–7269. 9 rooms with bath. Facilities: cable TV in common room. No pets. No smoking. MC, V. Rates include full breakfast. Moderate.*

Laconia
Dining
★

Hickory Stick Farm. The specialty is roast duckling with country herb stuffing and orange-sherry sauce, and you order by portion—the quarter, half, or whole duck. The entrée price includes salad, orange rolls, vegetable, and potato. Also on the menu are seafood, beef tenderloin, rack of lamb, and a vegetarian casserole. Two large, old-fashioned upstairs rooms with bath are available as bed-and-breakfast year-round. The inn is 4 miles from Laconia. Follow signs off Union Road into the woods, all on paved roads. *75 Bean Hill Rd., Laconia 03246, tel. 603/524–3333. Reservations required. Dress: casual. AE, D, MC, V. Dinner only. Closed Mon.–Wed., except holidays Oct.–May. Inexpensive–Moderate.*

Meredith
Lodging

The Nutmeg Inn. The Cape-style house was built in 1763 by a sea captain who dismantled his ship to get the timber for the beams and paneled what is now a dining room with illegal "king's boards," those extrawide cuts reserved for royal needs. An 18th-century ox yoke, said to have been used during the original construction, is bolted to the wall over a walk-in-size fireplace, and the wide-board floors are also original. All the rooms are named after spices and decorated accordingly. The walls of Sage, for example, are just *that* shade of green. The white inn with black shutters is located on a rural side street off Route 104, the main road that runs between I-93 and Lake Winnipesaukee. *Pease Rd., RFD 2, Meredith 03253, tel. 603/279–8811. 7 rooms with bath; 1 suite. Facilities: air-conditioning, some rooms with working fireplaces; swimming pool, 3 rooms for private parties and meetings. D, MC, V. Rates include full breakfast. Moderate.*

Moultonborough
Dining

Sweetwater Inn. Pasta made daily is the basis of such dishes as lobster ravioli (with a white-wine-and-tomato sauce) and fettuccine jambalaya (sautéed chicken, scallops, and andouille sausage with garlic, sherry, peppers, and Cajun spices). Spanish offerings include paellas and *pollo con gambas* (chicken breast and shrimp sautéed with brandy). Even the butter is home-churned, with blackberry honey and fresh orange. Only herbs and spices are used as seasonings; no salt is used. *Rte. 25, Moultonborough, tel. 603/476–5079. Reservations advised. Dress: casual. AE, DC, MC, V. Moderate.*

The Woodshed. Beef and seafood are the basics here, all cooked to order. Try a New England menu of clam chowder, scrod, and Indian pudding; an alternative is escargots Rockefeller, prime rib, and cheesecake. *Lee's Mill Rd., Moultonborough, tel. 603/476–2311. Reservations advised. Dress: casual. AE, MC, V. Moderate.*

Tamworth **Tamworth Inn.** Across the street from Barnstormers, the vin-
Dining tage summer theater of the lakes region, the inn offers a pre-
★ theater dinner. The new American cuisine includes blackened
swordfish and veal Picasso (mustard, white wine, onions, and
capers over rice or fettuccini). Among the desserts are
homebaked pie, carrot cake, and profiterole Tamworth (with
the chef's own chocolate sauce). In summer you can dine on the
porch, which looks over the back meadow and the river. Lighter
fare is available in the pub. Sunday brunch is popular with day
trippers. *Main St., Tamworth, tel. 603/323–7721 or 800/642–
7352). Reservations advised. Dress: neat but casual. MC, V.
Closed Mon. (summer), Mon.–Tues. (winter). Moderate–Expensive.*

Lodging **Tamworth Inn.** The touch of show-biz sophistication may be the
★ result of sharing the stage with the Barnstormers across the
street. Whatever the reason, this friendly country inn has
much of the romantic charm of an old movie. Every room is different, and all are comfortably furnished and decorated with
19th-century American pieces. Fresh flowers in your room are
the rule in summer, fresh fruit in winter. The field behind the
inn slopes to a trout-filled brook. The gazebo is used sometimes
for weddings. *Main St., Box 189, Tamworth 03886, tel. 603/
323–7721 or 800/642–7352. 15 rooms with bath. Facilities: restaurant, pub, pool, video film library with VCR. No smoking.
MC, V. Rates include breakfast. Moderate–Expensive.*

Tilton **Le Chalet Rouge.** Located on the west side of Tilton, the modest
Dining yellow house with a small, simply decorated dining room is not
★ unlike the country bistros of France. The menu features a re-
markable house pâté; steak au poivre; duck with raspberry
sauce; and tarte au citron. *321 W. Main St., Tilton, tel. 603/
286–4035. Reservations advised. Dress: casual. AE, D. Closed
Nov. Moderate–Expensive.*

Wakefield **Wakefield Inn.** The restoration of the house and coaching inn of
Lodging 1815, located in a historic district, has been done with care.
★ Among the inn's many features is a freestanding spiral staircase that rises three stories. Rooms are named for famous
guests, including John Greenleaf Whittier. The weekend Quilting Package could send you home with a finished quilt. *RFD 1,
Box 2185, Wakefield 03872, tel. 603/522–8272 or 800/245–0841.
7 rooms with bath. Facilities guest-only: restaurant. No pets.
No smoking in rooms. AE, MC, V. Rates include full breakfast. Moderate.*

Wolfeboro **The Wolfeboro Inn.** This landmark resort has 19th- and 20th-
Lodging century additions, which extend from the original white clapboard house on Main Street to the waterfront of Wolfeboro
Bay. Polished cherry and pine furnishings, flowered chintzes,
and armoires (to hide the TVs) help create an elegant ambience. The old Wolfe's Tavern has a bake-oven fireplace and
more than 45 brands of beer. *44 N. Main St., Wolfeboro 03894,
tel. 603/569–3016 or 800/451–2389, fax 603/569–5375. 38
rooms, 5 suites with bath. Facilities: 2 restaurants, tavern, cable TV, air-conditioning, VCR, elevator, private lake beach,
excursion boat, canoes, bicycles, golf and tennis nearby. No
pets. AE, D, MC, V. Rates include Continental breakfast. Off-
season packages. Moderate–Very Expensive.*

The Arts

The Belknap Mill Society (Mill Plaza, Laconia, tel. 603/524–8813) is a year-round cultural center housed in a 19th-century textile mill.

Music   **Arts Council of Tamworth** (tel. 603/323–7793) produces concerts—soloists, string quartets, revues, children's programs—from September through June.

Theater   **Barnstormers** (Main St., Tamworth, tel. 603/323–8500), an Equity summer theater and New Hampshire's oldest professional theater, performs in July and August.

Nightlife

The Red Rib (Rte. 3, Meredith, tel. 603/279–7777), with dining and dancing in a railway station of 1849, provides the nightly entertainment for the under-thirties summering on the lakes. In the newest part of the building, windows overlook Winnipesaukee. The fare is smokehouse style.

Funspot (Weirs Beach, tel. 603/366–4377) remains open 24 hours, July to Labor Day. You can bowl, snack, and play the 500 advertised games all night long.

M/S *Mount Washington* (tel. 603/366–2628) has dinner/dance Moonlight Cruises Tuesday–Saturday evenings with a different menu each night and two bands. Departure points vary; ticket prices range from $26 to $33.

The White Mountains

Northern New Hampshire has the highest mountains in New England, the 750,000 acres of White Mountain National Forest, and wilderness that stretches north into Canada. Hikers, climbers, and motorists who seek dramatic vistas are at home here, where gorges slash the mountain range and rivers are born and flow south. Southeast of the national forest, on the eastern side of the state, North Conway's miles of factory outlets and off-price designer boutiques draw heavy shopping traffic throughout the year. Yet the heaviest traffic is seasonal: The two-week autumn explosion of color sees carloads and busloads of people, bumper-to-bumper on the Kancamagus Highway.

Important Addresses and Numbers

Visitor   **Mt. Washington Valley Visitors Bureau** (Box 2300, North
Information   Conway 03860, tel. 603/356–3171 or 800/367–3364).

White Mountain Attractions Association (Box 10, North Woodstock 03262, tel. 603/745–8720).

Emergencies   **State Police** (tel. 800/852–3411).

Poison Center (tel. 800/562–8236).

Memorial Hospital (Intervale Rd., North Conway, tel. 603/356–5461).

Getting Around the White Mountains

By Plane **Berlin Airport** (Milan, tel. 603/449–7383) has facilities for charters and private planes.

By Car You will need a car to see this region if you aren't taking a bus tour during foliage season. I–93 and Route 3 bisect the White Mountain National Forest on their south–north extent between Massachusetts and Québec. On the eastern side of the area, Route 16 is the main artery from the coast, past the Mt. Washington valley and on toward Maine. The Kancamagus Highway (Route 112) is the east–west thoroughfare through the White Mountain National Forest.

By Bus **Concord Trailways** (tel. 800/639–3317 in NH).

Exploring the White Mountains

Numbers in the margin correspond to points of interest on the White Mountains map.

Our tour begins at the southeastern gateway to the Mt. Washington valley, where the towns are downright sweet and the discount shopping opportunities cause frequent gridlock. We take Route 16/302 through the Conways to Glen and continue west to Bethlehem, then south to Franconia Notch, Lincoln, and the Kancamagus Highway.

❶ The winter sports area and shopper's world of **North Conway** has a high concentration of lodging and dining facilities. Here the **Conway Scenic Railroad** (Main St., tel. 603/356–5251 or 800/232–5251) operates from May through October out of a railroad station built circa 1874. A steam (or sometimes diesel) engine pulls the antique coaches 11 miles in one hour, and it's necessary to make reservations early during foliage season.

Overlooking the valley are **White Horse** and **Cathedral ledges.** Trails from **Echo Lake State Park** lead up to the 1,000-foot cliffs. Look for rockclimbers going up and skydivers coming down. To reach them, turn left two stoplights north of the railway station and follow the signs to the park and ledges.

❷ From North Conway you can follow Route 16 north through Jackson to **Mt. Washington,** the highest mountain (6,288 feet) in the northeastern United States. It has measured at its summit the greatest velocity of winds ever recorded—231 miles per hour—and its Antarctic-like temperatures are the ultimate lows broadcast to New Englanders every winter.

The **Mount Washington Auto Road,** a toll road open when weather conditions permit, begins at Glen House, 16 miles north of Glen; allow two hours for the round-trip. You use low gear all the way, and there are frequent rests, yet this is a route for the experienced mountain driver only. At the top the Sherman Adams Summit Building has a museum and glassed-in viewing area. A slide show and exhibits illuminate the rich natural and human history of the "Home of the World's Worst Weather." One-and-a-half-hour guided tours in Auto Road vans are available at Glen House; you can also hike the mountain or take the cog railway at Bretton Woods. *Tel. 603/466–3988. Toll: $12 car and driver, $5 each adult passenger, $3 children 5–12. Guided-tour fees: $17 adults, $10 children 5–12. Open mid-May–mid-Oct.*

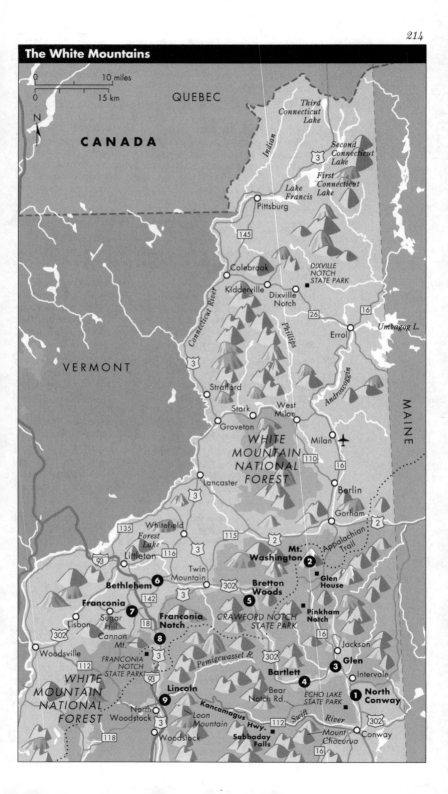

The White Mountains

0 ___ 10 miles
0 ___ 15 km

N

QUEBEC

CANADA

Third Connecticut Lake

Second Connecticut Lake

③ 3

First Connecticut Lake

Lake Francis

Pittsburg

[145]

Colebrook

DIXVILLE NOTCH STATE PARK

Kidderville

Dixville Notch

[26]

Errol

Umbagog L.

[16]

Connecticut River

Phillips

Stratford

Stark

West Milan

Groveton

Androscoggin

WHITE MOUNTAIN NATIONAL FOREST

Milan ✈

[110]

Lancaster

[16]

Berlin

Whitefield

Forest Lake

Gorham

[135]

[115]

② 2

[93]

Littleton

[116]

[3]

Twin Mountain

[2]

Mt. Washington

Appalachian Trail

Glen House

❻ 6

Bethlehem

[142]

[302]

Bretton Woods

❺ 5

❼ 7

Franconia

Sugar Hill

[18]

Franconia Notch

CRAWFORD NOTCH STATE PARK

Pinkham Notch

Cannon Mt.

❽ 8

Lisbon

[93]

[16]

Jackson

Woodsville

[302]

FRANCONIA NOTCH STATE PARK

[3]

Pemigewasset R.

[302]

❸ 3 **Glen**

Intervale

[112]

WHITE MOUNTAIN NATIONAL FOREST

Lincoln

❾ 9

❹ 4 **Bartlett**

ECHO LAKE STATE PARK

❶ 1 **North Conway**

North Woodstock

Kancamagus Hwy.

Bear Notch Rd.

[302]

[3]

Loon Mountain

[112]

Swift River

Conway

Woodstock

[118]

Sabbaday Falls

Mount Chocorua

[16]

VERMONT

MAINE

③ Few traveling families can resist one or the other of **Glen's** entertainments. **Storyland** theme park has life-size storybook and nursery-rhyme characters, an African safari, Cinderella's castle, a Victorian-theme river-raft ride, a voyage to the moon, and visits to other lands. You can figure on a full day for this one. *Rte. 16, Glen, tel. 603/383–4293. Admission: $13 (free under 4) includes rides and entertainment. Open Father's Day–Labor Day, daily 9–6; Labor Day–Columbus Day, weekends 10–5.*

Heritage New Hampshire, next door to Storyland, offers a simulated journey into the past that begins with a village street in 1634 England. Sights, sounds, and animation usher you aboard the *Reliance* and carry you over tossing seas. You stop at the cabin of a snowbound settler, walk Portsmouth's streets in the late 1700s, applaud George Washington's presidency, and plunge into the dark side of the Industrial Revolution. The trip ends cheerily aboard a train heading through Crawford's Notch during foliage season. Other exhibits include a glass silo and New England's largest historic mural. *Rte. 16, Glen, tel. 603/383–9776. Admission: $7 adults, $4.50 children 4–12. Open mid-May–mid-Oct., daily 9–5.*

The Bear Notch road south from Route 302 in Bartlett provides the only midpoint access to the Kancamagus Highway, and it is **④** closed in winter. **Bartlett** is primarily a recreation area and a place to pick up picnic ingredients for the drive ahead. The **Attitash Ski Area** (Rte. 302, tel. 603/374–2368) in Bartlett has a "dry" Alpine slide, a water slide, and a scenic chair-lift ride.

At the mountain pass, **Crawford Notch State Park** (tel. 603/374–2272) is a good place for a picnic and a leg-stretching hike along the well-trodden trails to Arethusa Falls or Silver and Flume cascades. A shop sells soft drinks and items made by blind New Hampshire craftspeople.

Twenty miles north of Bartlett on Route 302 lies the secluded **⑤** **Bretton Woods.** In the early decades of this century, as many as 50 trains a day brought the private railway cars of the rich and famous from New York and Philadelphia to Mt. Washington Hotel. In July 1944 the World Monetary Fund Conference convened here and established the American dollar as the basic medium of international exchange. The hotel contains a small museum.

The **Mt. Washington Cog Railway** is a steam-powered mountain-climbing railway, operating since 1869, that provides an alternative to driving the corkscrew road up the mountain or climbing it on foot (first accomplished by Darby Field in 1642). Allow three hours for the round-trip. To reach the railway from Bretton Woods, take the marked road 6 miles northeast from Route 302; if the weather is poor, forget it. *Rte. 302, Bretton Woods, tel. 603/846–5404 or 800/922–8825, ext. 7 outside NH. Round-trip: $32 (ask about discounts). Reservations advised. Operates May, weekends 8:30–4:30; June–Oct., daily 8:30–4:30, weather conditions permitting.*

⑥ The pure air of **Bethlehem,** where Route 142 meets Route 302 north and west of the national forest, drew hay-fever sufferers to the mountains, where Hasidic Jews established a kosher resort in the Arlington and Alpine hotels.

❼ Take Route 142 south to Route 18 to reach **Franconia,** where Route 116 will take you south (follow the signs) to the poet Robert Frost's 1915 home, known as **The Frost Place.** Two rooms contain memorabilia and signed editions of his books, and on summer evenings visiting poets give readings. Behind the house a ½-mile nature trail is posted with lines from Frost's poems. *Ridge Rd., tel. 603/823–5510. Admission: $3 adults, $2 senior citizens, $1.25 children 6–15. Open Memorial Day–June, weekends 1–5; July–Columbus Day, Wed.–Mon. 1–5.*

Franconia is just north of Cannon Mountain, where the **New England Ski Museum** (tel. 603/823–7177) lies at the foot of the aerial tramway. Slide and film presentations, art, photographs, and ski clothing and equipment are shown.

The **Cannon Mountain Aerial Tramway** will lift nonskiers 2,022 feet in five minutes during the summer. Foot trails lead from the summit observation platform to other vistas. *Cannon Mt. Ski Area, tel. 603/823–5563. Admission: $7. Open Memorial Day–3rd weekend in Oct., daily 9–4.*

❽ A series of scenic spectacles along a 13-mile stretch of Route 3 in **Franconia Notch** has been stopping travelers for centuries. The granite profile of the **Old Man of the Mountains** is the most famous feature, but the point of greatest viewing advantage remains in dispute. Is it from the shore of Profile Lake or from the highway parking area? At what time of day? P. T. Barnum wanted to buy it; Nathaniel Hawthorne told the world about it in his tale "The Great Stone Face." Travelers who saw it in 1805 thought it looked like Thomas Jefferson.

The Flume (tel. 603/823–5563), open from May through October, is an 800-foot-long natural chasm through which you make your way on a series of boardwalks and stairways. **The Basin** is a glacial pothole, 20 feet across, at the base of a waterfall. **Echo Lake** will tempt you to try its acoustics.

❾ North Woodstock and Lincoln, two towns on opposite sides of the Pemigewasset River, anchor the western end of Route 112, the Kancamagus Highway. **Lincoln** is the center for the resort communities; it has shops, restaurants, and an amusement park, the **Whale's Tale** (Rte. 3, tel. 603/745–8810), with flume water slides, a wave pool, and a kiddie pool.

The **Kancamagus Highway,** the state's most popular single route for viewing the foliage in fall, is a 33-mile stretch interrupted by only one cutoff, Bear Notch Road (closed in winter) to Bartlett. Connecting Lincoln in the west with bustling North Conway in the east, this road offers six well-equipped campgrounds, four picnic areas, and four scenic overlooks. Numerous hiking trails and fishing spots attract those who are willing to venture farther afield. At the **Passaconaway Information Center** near the Bear Notch road is the beginning of the Rain 'n River Forest Trail, an easy, half-mile loop ideal for families wanting to learn more about the mountains. There is wheelchair and stroller access to the trail from the parking lot.

Park at the Sabbaday Falls parking lot and follow the trail to **Sabbaday Falls,** a multilevel cascade that plunges through two potholes and a flume. You can also leave the road to climb the Champney Falls and Piper trails to the top of Mount Chocorua. Spectacular views can be had at many points, but it is easy to get lost when you leave the main trail, so keep an eye on the signs.

The eastern terminus of the Kancamagus Highway is Route 16.

The White Mountains for Free

Abenaki Indian Shop, Intervale
Bretzfelder Park, Bethlehem

What to See and Do with Children

Attitash Alpine Slide, Bartlett
Conway Scenic Railroad, North Conway
Mt. Washington Cog Railway, Bretton Woods
Storyland, Glen

Off the Beaten Track

Pittsburg (Indian Stream Republic). Beyond the White Mountains lies the far north of New Hampshire, with many miles of forest and lakes but few roads. Here bubble the springs that become the Connecticut River, and here in 1829 a small band of settlers, disgusted with the slow processes of politics, proclaimed themselves citizens of a separate territory. By 1832 the United States and Canada still had not fixed an international border, and the "Streamers" declared their independence and wrote a constitution providing for an assembly, council, courts, and militia. They called their country Indian Stream Republic, after the river that came down from Québec and melded into the newborn Connecticut. The republic encompassed 250 square miles between Halls Stream and the brook at the Third Connecticut Lake. The capital was Pittsburg. In 1835 the feisty, 40-man Indian Stream militia invaded Canada, causing the New Hampshire Militia to invade Indian Stream—which convinced residents they were de facto citizens of the United States after all. The Indian Stream war ended more by common consent than surrender, and in 1842 the Webster-Ashburton Treaty fixed the international boundary. Indian Stream was incorporated as Pittsburg, making that hamlet the largest township in the state. The town of Pittsburg still has the feeling of an outpost, for it serves primarily as a supplier to campers, hunters, anglers, lumbermen, gold miners, and the like. A marker on Highway 3 attests to its former status. Information on the town is available at the Colebrook-Pittsburg Chamber of Commerce (Colebrook 03576, tel. 603/237–8939).

Dixville Notch. Midway between Errol and Colebrook, Dixville Notch is the home of The Balsams Grand Resort Hotel but is better known nationally as the election district first in the nation to vote and report its returns in the presidential elections. The polling place where the 34 ballots (more or less) are cast is a small meeting room next to the hotel bar, a location chosen for the convenience of the media. Dixville Notch won its distinction over such smaller towns as Hart's Location (population 9 or 10) because the resort has its own phone company—a convenience journalists appreciate.

Shopping

Custom-made hiking boots are the pride of the valley, but the area is known for good family sportswear, especially ski clothes. Popular stores for sportswear are the **Jack Frost Shop** (tel. 603/383–4391) in Jackson, and **Joe Jones** (tel. 603/356–9411) and **Carroll Reed** (tel. 603/356–3122) in North Conway. As for crafts, the local **League of New Hampshire Craftsmen** (tel. 603/356–2441) and neighboring **Windsor Fair** (tel. 603/356–3982), both on Main Street in North Conway, are among the best.

Antiques **Antiques & Collectibles Barn** (Rte. 302, North Conway, tel. 603/356–7118), 1½ miles north of the village, is a 35-dealer group with everything from furniture and quilts to coins and jewelry.

Richard M. Plusch (Main St., North Conway, tel. 603/356–3333) deals in period furniture, glass, sterling silver, Oriental porcelains, rugs, and paintings.

Custom-Made Made-to-order **Limmerboots** (Intervale, tel. 603/356–5378)
Hiking Boots take about a year from measurements to wear and cost $220 plus shipping.

Factory Outlets **Lincoln Square Outlet Stores** (Rte. 112, Lincoln) stock predominantly factory seconds. North Face, Van Heusen, Bass, and London Fog are some of the names you'll see; interspersed are restaurants if you need a break. Take Exit 32 off I–93 and go 1½ miles east.

The Mount Washington Valley Visitors Bureau (Box 2300, North Conway 03860, tel. 603/356–3171) can answer your questions about the 150-plus outlets in Mt. Washington Valley. On Route 16 in North Conway, look for names like Anne Klein, Dansk, L. L. Bean, Corning, Barbizon, Calvin Klein, Reebok, and Ralph Lauren.

Malls **Millfront Marketplace, Mill at Loon Mountain** (tel. 603/745–2245) is a clutch of specialty stores and restaurants at the junction of I–93 and the Kancamagus Highway. Nonshoppers are entertained by free concerts and carriage rides in summer, and horse-drawn sleighs and an ice-skating rink in winter.

Sports and Outdoor Activities

Biking There are 86 major mountains in the area, so you may be biking in short stretches, but at least there's a bike path in Franconia Notch State Park, at Lafayette Campground.

Camping **New Hampshire Campground Owners Association** (Box 320, Twin Mountain 03595, tel. 603/846–5511 or 800/822–6764) will send a list of all private, state, and national-forest campgrounds.

White Mountain National Forest (Box 638, Laconia 03247, tel. 603/528–8721 or 800/283–2267) has 20 roadside campgrounds on a no-reserve and 14-day-limit basis.

Appalachian Mountain Club headquarters at Pinkham Notch was built in 1920 and now offers lectures, workshops, slide shows, and movies June–October. The 100-bunk main lodge and six rustic cabins aside, you may also want to look into other programs like AMC–The Friendly Huts and the AMC Backcountry Host Program. *Box 298, Gorham 03581, tel. 603/*

466–2721. Trail information, tel. 603/466–2725; reservations, tel. 603/466–2727.

Lafayette Campground (Franconia Notch State Park, 03580) has good hiking and biking, easy access to the Appalachian Trail, and 97 tent sites and showers. Other state parks have camping facilities, too. Reservations are not accepted.

Canoeing Canoe-kayak whitewater runs on the Swift River are fast and intricate. If you go with river outfitters **Saco Bound–Northern Waters** (Box 119, Center Conway 03813, tel. 603/447–2177), day's end is the full-facility (Jacuzzi, sauna, pool, racquetball, and more) Mt. Cranmore Racquet Club. Saco Bound handles rentals as well as organized trips April–November. **Saco Bound/Downeast River Trips** (Box 119, Center Conway 03812, tel. 603/447–3801) offers canoe and kayak trips, whitewater rafting on seven rivers, lessons, and equipment.

Fishing For serious trout and salmon fishing, try the Connecticut Lakes (*see* Off the Beaten Track, *above*) though any clear stream in the White Mountains will do. Many are stocked, and there are 650 miles of them in the national forest alone. Some 45 lakes and ponds contain trout and bass. For up-to-date fishing information, call the regional New Hampshire Fish and Game office (tel. 603/788–3164).

Hiking The web of trails through the White Mountains can keep a hiker busy for years. Overnight hiking is a regional specialty, and the Appalachian Trail runs across the state. Short hikes include Artist's Bluff, Lonesome Lake, and Basin-Cascades Trails, Franconia Notch State Park; Boulder Loop and Greely Ponds off the Kancamagus Highway; and Sanguinari Ridge Trail, Dixville Notch.

Appalachian Mountain Club (Box 298, Pinkham Notch, Gorham 03581, tel. 603/466–2725).

AMC Hut System (Box 298, Gorham 03581, tel. 603/466–2721) provides reasonably priced meals and dorm-style lodging on a network of trails throughout the mountains.

White Mountain National Forest (U.S. Forest Service, Box 638, Laconia 03246, tel. 603/528–8721 or 800/283–2267).

New England Hiking Holidays–White Mountains (Box 1648, North Conway 03860, tel. 603/356–9696) offers inn-to-inn, guided hiking tours that include two, three, or five nights in country inns.

White Mountain Trekkers (tel. 603/837–2285 in the evening) arranges one- to seven-day wilderness experiences of various levels of difficulty.

Gourmet Hikes **Snowvillage Inn** (Snowville 03849, tel. 603/447–2818 or 800/447–4345) conducts guided mountain hikes complete with an elegant picnic (teriyaki beef on skewers, phyllo stuffed with spinach and feta cheese, wine, and more) on a checkered tablecloth.

White Mountain Llamas at the Stag Hollow Inn (Jefferson 03583, tel. 603/586–4598) will introduce you to llama trekking, with one- to four-day treks on beautiful, secluded trails. Gourmet picnics, with such delicacies as melon balls in Cointreau and chicken-pear salad, are toted by friendly, sure-footed llamas as you hike.

Recreation Areas

Bretzfelder Park (Bethlehem), a 77-acre nature and wildlife park, has a picnic shelter.

Lost River Reservation (North Woodstock 03293, tel. 603/745–8031). From May through October tour the gorge on boardwalks, as the river appears and vanishes.

Loon Mountain Recreation Area, on the western terminus of the Kancamagus Highway, has aerial rides, hiking, picnics, tennis, and a pool, hotel, and restaurant. *Lincoln 03251, tel. 603/745–8111. Open May–Oct.*

Waterville Valley Recreation Area (Waterville Valley 03215, tel. 603/236–8311 or 800/258–8988) is a full-facility complex with hotels, restaurants, pool, tennis, and skiing.

State Parks

Crawford Notch State Park (Harts Location). The 6 miles of scenic mountain pass include waterfalls, picnic sites, fishing, and hiking.

Dixville Notch State Park (Dixville). This most-northern notch has a waterfall, hiking, and picnic areas.

Echo Lake State Park (Conway). The mountain lake beneath White Horse Ledge has swimming, picnic sites, and a road to Cathedral Ledge.

Franconia Notch State Park (Franconia and Lincoln) has swimming, camping, picnicking, biking, and hiking on a 27-mile network of Appalachian-system trails. The top attraction is the Old Man of the Mountains ("Great Stone Face"), a 40-foot granite profile that is the official symbol of New Hampshire. Also in the park are the Flume, Echo Lake, Liberty Gorge, the Cascades, and the Basin.

White Mountain National Forest is managed by the U.S. Forest Service (tel. 603/528–8721 or 800/283–2267) and covers nearly 763,000 acres. It includes most of New England's highest peaks.

Dining and Lodging

Some of the best food in the area can be found in the many cozy inns whose dining rooms are open to the public. Be sure to call for dining reservations any time of year. In peak season an inn may be booked solid, while in late fall or spring innkeepers often close for renovation or travel.

Resorts, motels, country inns, and bed-and-breakfasts are thick as snowflakes, and only during foliage season should you hesitate to travel without reservations. (Getting into a special place requires advance calling in any season.) The **Mt. Washington Valley Visitors Bureau** (tel. 603/356–3171 or 800/367–3364) and **Country Inns in the White Mountains** (tel. 603/356–9460 or 800/562–1300) will find you a room when you need one.

Bethlehem **The Bells.** A pagoda-shape bed-and-breakfast across the street
Lodging from a Jewish synagogue in a town called Bethlehem is an anomaly. It's also a charmer, filled with family heirlooms and choice bits from the owners' antiques shop. The white room in

the cupola, a honeymoon favorite, has a four-way view. *Straw-berry Hill St., Bethlehem 03574, tel. 603/869–2647. 1 room, 3 suites, all with bath. No pets. AE, MC, V. Rates include full breakfast. Moderate.*

Bretton Woods
Lodging

Mount Washington Hotel. The grand dowager, with its stately public rooms and its large, traditionally furnished bedrooms and suites, has a formal atmosphere; jacket and tie are expected in the dining room at dinner and in the lobby after 6 PM. The 2,600-acre property has a recreation center with pool, tennis courts, and spa, and a 27-hole golf course. *Rte. 302, Bretton Woods 03575, tel. 603/278–1000 or 800/258–0330. 200 rooms with bath. Facilities: restaurant, golf, indoor and outdoor pools, sauna, tennis, extensive family activities. AE, MC, V. Rates are MAP. Closed mid-Oct.–mid-May. Very Expensive.*

Conway
Dining

Darby Field Inn. If you call after 4 PM, you will be told the four daily specials, which depend on what was freshest and best in the market. Or choose from menu regulars like chicken marquis (a sautéed breast of chicken with mushrooms, tomatoes, and white wine); or duckling glazed with Chambord or Grand Marnier. The recipe for Darby cream pie may be coaxed from the chef. *Bald Hill, Conway, tel. 603/447–2181. Reservations advised. Dress: casual. AE, MC, V. Expensive.*

Lodging

Darby Field Inn. Every room is different at this inn, but what most have in common—besides all being on the second and third floors—is the spectacular mountain view. A fieldstone fireplace is the centerpiece of the living room; the dining room is paneled in pine; the bar has a wood stove and a piano. *Bald Hill, Conway 03818, tel. 603/447–2181 or 800/426–4147. 16 rooms, 14 with bath. Facilities: restaurant, cross-country trails, pool. No pets. No smoking in rooms. AE, MC, V. Closed Apr., Nov. Rates are MAP. Expensive.*

Tanglewood Motel & Cottages. Swim or fish in a mountain stream just outside the door of this neat, family-operated, single-story motel-inn. Some rooms in the motel sleep up to six, and the two-person cottages have screened porches and fully equipped kitchens, though you provide your own maid service. *Rte. 16, Conway 03818, tel. 603/447–5932. 13 rooms with bath. Facilities: cribs. AE, MC, V. Inexpensive.*

Dixville Notch
Dining
★

The Balsams Grand Resort Hotel. The chef and his staff are culinary award-winners, and they prepare a different menu each evening. On a warm night you might begin with chilled strawberry soup Grand Marnier; go on to poached salmon fillet with golden caviar sauce; and end with chocolate hazelnut cake. Because the dining room is essentially for guests of the resort, reservations are necessary if you are staying elsewhere. *Dixville Notch, tel. 603/255–3400 or 800/255–0600. Reservations required. Jacket required. AE, MC, V. Closed Apr. 1–May 15 and Oct. 15–Dec. 15. Expensive.*

Lodging
★

The Balsams Grand Resort Hotel. Getting away from it all luxuriously is only part of the appeal of this famous full-service resort. Families can divide according to interest and regroup at meals; couples can find any number of cozy nooks for private conversation. The Tower Suite, with its 20-foot conical ceiling, is located in a Victorian turret; its view is 360 degrees. More-standard accommodations have views, too, as well as all the deluxe amenities. Incidentally, guests wear jackets and ties to dinner. *Dixville Notch 03576, tel. 603/255–3400 or 800/255–*

0600. 232 rooms with bath. Facilities: restaurant, biking, boating, children's program, dancing, golf, pool, tennis, downhill and cross-country skiing. AE, D, MC, V. Closed Apr. 1–May 15 and Oct. 15–Dec. 15. Rates are AP in summer, MAP in winter, and include sports and entertainment. Very Expensive.

East Madison
Lodging

Purity Spring Resort. Before the first guests came, in the late 1800s, Purity Spring consisted of a farm, sawmill, and private lake. It is now a four-season, American-plan resort that has been operated by the same family for nearly a century. It's a place to swim, fish, hike, and play tennis or lawn games. There is a supervised program for children, and King Pine Ski Area is on the property. Whether you choose rooms in the main inn, adjacent lodges, or cottages, the decor is sturdy, old-fashioned New England. *Rte. 153, East Madison 03849, tel. 603/367–8896 or 800/367–8897. 45 rooms, 35 with bath. Facilities: restaurant, private lake, tennis, volleyball. No pets. MC, V. Rates are MAP (or include 3 meals). Inexpensive–Moderate.*

Franconia
Dining

Franconia Inn. While you dine on medallions of veal with apple-mustard sauce, or filet mignon with sun-dried tomatoes, your child can have "The Young Epicurean Cheeseburger" or a "Petite Breast of Chicken." The two brothers who own and operate Franconia Inn understand how families work. *Easton Rd., Franconia, tel. 603/823–5542. Reservations advised. Dress: casual. AE, MC, V. Closed Apr.–mid-May. Moderate–Expensive.*

Lodging

Franconia Inn. A year-round resort like this one will supply you with anything from a bike to a babysitter. Movies are shown each evening in the lounge, and there is croquet in summer and skiing in winter. Greens fees are waived for inn guests at Sunset Hill's nine-hole course. You can play tennis, ride horseback, swim in the pool or swimming hole, order your lunch-to-go for a day of hiking—even try soaring from the inn's own airstrip. The rooms have designer chintzes and canopied beds; some have whirlpools, some have fireplaces. *Easton Rd., Franconia 03580, tel. 603/823–5542. 34 rooms with bath. Facilities: restaurant, pool, bicycles, croquet, golf privileges, hot tub, movies, soaring center, stable, tennis. No pets. Limited smoking. AE, MC, V. Rates include full breakfast or are MAP. Closed Apr.–mid-May. Moderate–Expensive.*

Glen
Dining

The Bernerhof. The cuisine is primarily classic French but perhaps is better described as high Continental. This may be because of the ambience of the Alpine dining room, with its rubbed wood and flowers—too charming to be merely classic. The wine list is heavily French and Austrian, and veal is a specialty. *Rte. 302, Glen, tel. 603/383–4411. Reservations advised. Dress: neat but casual. AE, MC, V. Closed Apr.–mid-May, mid-Nov.–mid-Dec. Moderate–Expensive.*

★ **Margaritaville.** The taste of the authentic Mexican food is enhanced by outdoor dining on the patio in summer. The appropriately named restaurant is family run, with five daughters waiting tables. *Rte. 302, Glen, tel. 603/383–6556. Reservations accepted. Dress: casual. No credit cards. Inexpensive.*

Lodging

The Bernerhof. This small, Old World hotel, built a century ago, is at home in its Alpine setting. There's a Finnish sauna on the third floor, a coal stove in the living room, and lace curtains in the bedrooms. The inn was completely refurbished in 1988, and four deluxe rooms now have oversize spa tubs. Stay three days in any room, and you are served a champagne breakfast in bed. *Rte. 302, Glen 03838, tel. 603/383–4414 or 800/548–8007. 12 rooms with bath. Facilities: restaurant, playground, sauna. No pets. No smoking in rooms. AE, MC, V. Rates include full breakfast. Moderate–Expensive.*

Jackson **Christmas Farm Inn.** The food is Mixed Menu, and you might
Dining start with ravioli of smoked chicken with tomato-basil dressing; poached scallops with diced tomato and fines herbes; or sautéed venison with spinach, wild mushrooms, and dark game sauce. The menu alerts diners to "heart-healthy" dinners approved by the American Heart Association. *Jackson Village, tel. 603/383–4313. Reservations advised. Dress: casual. AE, MC, V. Expensive.*

Inn at Thorn Hill. Candlelight, wine, and contemporary New England cuisine bring diners here from all over the valley. The chef smokes his own meats, including a notable chicken sausage. Lobster pie Thorn Hill, a specialty of the house, is lobster in a brandy Newburg sauce. For dessert there's cranberry-walnut tart, saffron poached pears with raspberry coulis, and pumpkin crème brûlée, among others. *Thorn Hill Rd., Jackson, tel. 603/383–4242. AE, MC, V. Closed Apr. Moderate–Expensive.*

Lodging **Inn at Thorn Hill.** The inn was designed by Stanford White in
★ 1895, and its rooms are decorated as if White were the expected guest, with polished dark woods and rose-motif papers and fabrics. *Thorn Hill Rd., Jackson 03846, tel. 603/383–4242 or 800/289–8990, fax 603/383–8082. 20 rooms with bath. Facilities: restaurant, pub, pool. No smoking. No pets. AE, MC, V. Closed Apr. Rates are MAP. Expensive.*

★ **Christmas Farm Inn.** Despite its name, this 200-year-old village inn is an all-season retreat. Rooms in the main inn and the salt box are decorated with Laura Ashley prints; the cottages, log cabin, and dairy barn suites have beam ceilings and fireplaces and are better suited to active families. *Box CC, Rte. 16B, Jackson 03846, tel. 603/383–4313 or 800/443–5837, fax 603/ 383–6495. 38 rooms with bath. Facilities: restaurant, children's play area, games rooms, pool, putting green, sauna, volleyball. No pets. AE, MC, V. Rates are MAP. Moderate–Expensive.*

North Conway **The Scottish Lion.** The dining room overlooks meadows and
Dining mountains, and Sunday brunch is a full meal that attracts local
★ residents as well as visitors. Until the inn became a bed-and-breakfast a decade ago, it was solely a restaurant. Now the tartan-papered pub has more than 50 varieties of Scotch, and the American-Scottish cuisine includes hot oatcakes in the evening bread basket. *Rte. 16, North Conway, tel. 603/356–6381. Reservations advised. Dress: casual. AE, MC, V. Moderate.*

Lodging **Hale's White Mountain Hotel and Resort.** Mount Washington Valley's newest full-service hostelry, this resort nestled beneath Cathedral and Whitehorse ledges offers spectacular mountain views from every room. *Golf* magazine calls Hale's 18-hole course "one of the most unique and singularly beautiful golf developments in the country." With 30 kilometers of groomed cross-country trails on the grounds, and proximity to the White Mountain National Forest and Echo Lake State Park, the hotel makes guests feel light-years away from the crowded outlet malls across the valley. *Box 1828, West Side Rd., North Conway, 03860 tel. 603/356–7100 or 800/533–6301.*

80 rooms with bath; 11 suites. Facilities: restaurant, tavern, golf, tennis, health club, hiking and cross-country trails, movies, video games, heated outdoor pool and Jacuzzi, room service. AE, D, MC, V. Moderate–Very Expensive.

Red Jacket Mountain View Inn. How often do you find a motor inn/resort that feels like a country inn? The bedrooms are large and traditionally furnished with all the amenities of a fine hotel. Deep chairs and plants fill the cozy public rooms. The grounds are expansive and attractively landscaped. The manager has been here for nearly three decades and runs a friendly albeit tight ship. *Rte. 16, Box 2000, North Conway 03860, tel. 603/356–5411 or 800/752–2538. 159 rooms with bath. Facilities: restaurant, cable TV, indoor and outdoor pools, saunas, whirlpool, tennis, supervised children's activities in summer, playground. No pets. AE, MC, V. Expensive.*

Cranmore Inn. This easygoing lodge at the foot of Mt. Cranmore has the atmosphere of an upcountry guest house. High school students serve the meals, and the print of the wallpaper harmonizes with the spreads and curtains in the rooms. The furnishings date from the mid-1800s to the 1930s, in keeping with the history and atmosphere of the inn. *Kearsage St., North Conway 03860, tel. 603/356–5502 or 800/822–5502. 19 rooms, 9 with bath. Facilities: restaurant, pool. No smoking in rooms. AE, MC, V. Rates include full breakfast. Moderate.*

Pittsburg
Lodging

The Glen. A rustic lodge on the First Connecticut Lake, this sportsman's resort has log cabins, boats to rent, and uncomplicated cookery. A stone fireplace in the dining room and wood paneling throughout set the tone. The dining room is open to the public by reservation only. *Box 77, Pittsburg 03592, tel. 603/538–6500. 8 rooms with bath, 10 cabins with bath. Facilities: restaurant, dock. No credit cards. Rates include 3 meals. Closed mid-Oct.–mid-May. Moderate.*

Snowville
Dining

Snowvillage Inn. There's a touch of Austria in the cuisine here. Walnut-beer bread? Bourbon in the salad dressing? Reservations are essential, and you will be told the day's main course and several alternatives when you call. *Snowville, tel. 603/447–2818. Reservations required. Dress: casual. AE, MC, V. Closed Apr. Moderate–Expensive.*

Lodging
★

Snowvillage Inn. Cheerful barn-red exteriors and guest rooms filled with such Americana as four-poster beds and working fireplaces are only part of the scene. The owners/innkeepers are ardent conservationists who can take you on gourmet hikes up the mountains. They are also builders who have added a Tyrolean chalet to their turn-of-the-century farmhouse, converted a 150-year-old barn to guest quarters, and built libraries in each of the inn's three buildings. *Box A–50, Snowville 03849, tel. 603/447–4414 or 800/447–4345. 18 rooms with bath. Facilities: restaurant, cross-country trails, sauna, tennis. AE, MC, V. Closed Apr. Rates include full breakfast or are MAP. Moderate–Expensive.*

Sugar Hill
Lodging

Sugar Hill Inn. There's an old carriage on the lawn and wicker chairs on the wraparound porch of this converted 1789 farmhouse. Many rooms are hand-stenciled, and much of the antique furniture came from neighboring farms. Not a single room is square, level, or without at least some rippled window-glass. Climb out of your four-poster, canopy, or brass bed, and set foot on braided rugs strategically placed to show off the pumpkin-pine and northern-maple floors. There are 10 rooms in the inn and six in three country cottages. *Rte. 117, Sugar Hill 03585, tel. 603/823–5621 or 800/548–4748. 16 rooms with bath. Facilities: restaurant. No pets. No smoking. MC, V. Rates include full breakfast (spring–summer) or are MAP (fall–winter). Closed Apr., Christmas week. Cottages closed Nov.– May. Moderate–Expensive.*

The Arts

Theater **Mt. Washington Valley Theater Company** (Eastern Slope Playhouse, North Conway, tel. 603/356–5776) has musicals and Equity summer theater from July through September.

North Country Center for the Arts (Mill at Loon Mountain, Lincoln, tel. 603/745–2141) presents music, concerts, children's theater, and performing and visual arts from July through October.

Nightlife

Barnaby's (North Conway, tel. 603/356–5781) has "real music for real people" every night.

Red Parka Pub (Glen, tel. 603/383–4344) is a hangout for the under-thirties crowd. Barbecued spare ribs are the house specialty.

Thunderbird Lounge (Indian Head Resort, North Lincoln, tel. 603/745–8000) has nightly entertainment year-round.

Wildcat Inn & Tavern (Jackson, tel. 603/383–4245) is a lively hangout for the après-ski set.

Western and Central New Hampshire

The countryside lying east of the Connecticut River from the Massachusetts border to the foothills of the White Mountains is as varied as it is beautiful. The Upper Connecticut River runs past Dartmouth College, an enclave of high culture and red brick in a land of calendar-page villages. Go eastward a few miles to the Lake Sunapee area for a total recreation package with boating, hiking, skiing, fairs, and events worth any family's special trip.

Farther south is the Monadnock Region, named for its singular peak, the second-most-climbed mountain (after Fuji) in the world. Hardwood forests and more than 200 fishable lakes compete for attention with clutches of covered bridges and antiques shops. Thoreau, Emerson, James, and Cather wrote here; writers and artists still come here to live unpretentiously and practice their craft.

Along Route 93 are New Hampshire's three major cities: Nashua, Manchester, and Concord, the state's capital. Don't be deterred by the sometimes bleak industrial landscapes associated with these three cities: What may appear as work-a-day urban centers are actually monuments to the 19th-century Industrial Revolution, which flourished along this stretch of the Merrimack River. Nowadays, despite the smokestacks and development, these urban outcrops offer worthwhile cultural opportunities. This tour will bypass Nashua and instead take you through Amherst, a town with one of the prettiest village greens in New England, then proceed north through Concord. From here you may go on to the Lakes Region or angle west and then return south along pastoral back roads where little appears to have changed in more than a century.

Important Addresses and Numbers

Visitor Information

Concord Chamber of Commerce (244 N. Main St., Concord 03301, tel. 603/224–2508).

Hanover Chamber of Commerce (Box A–105, Hanover 03755, tel. 603/643–3115).

Lake Sunapee Business Association (Box 400, Sunapee 03782, tel. 603/763–2495 or 800/258–3530 in New England).

Manchester Chamber of Commerce (889 Elm St., Manchester 03101, tel. 603/666–6600).

Monadnock Travel Council (8 Central Sq., Keene 03431, tel. 603/352–1303).

Peterborough Chamber of Commerce (Box 401, Peterborough 03458, tel. 603/924–7234).

Southern New Hampshire Visitor & Convention Bureau (Box 115, Windham 03087, tel. 800/932–4282).

Emergencies

State Police (tel. 800/852–3411).

Poison Center (tel. 800/562–8236).

Dartmouth Hitchcock Medical Center (Hanover, tel. 603/646–5000).

Cheshire Medical Center (580 Court St., Keene, tel. 603/352–4111).

Monadnock Community Hospital (Old Street Rd., Peterborough, tel. 603/924–7191).

New London Hospital (County Rd., New London, tel. 603/526–2911).

Valley Regional Hospital (Elm St., Claremont, tel. 603/542–7771).

Catholic Medical Center (100 McGregor St., Manchester, tel. 603/668–3545 or 800/437–9666).

Elliot Hospital (955 Auburn St., Manchester, tel. 603/669–5300 or 800/235–5468).

Concord Hospital (250 Pleasant St., Concord, tel. 603/225–2711).

Monadnock Mutual Aid (tel. 603/352–1100) responds to any emergency, from a medical problem to a car fire.

Getting Around Western and Central New Hampshire

By Car

I–89 bisects the region from southeast to northwest and continues into Vermont. North–south I–91 follows the Vermont side of the Connecticut River. On the New Hampshire side, Routes 12 and 12A are picturesque but slow back roads with frequent speed zones. Route 4 crosses the region, winding between Lebanon and the seacoast. Route 119 crosses southwestern New Hampshire before heading south into Massachusetts. I-93 provides fast and often scenic north–south travel. Once you leave I-89 and I-91, all roads are back roads.

By Bus **Concord Trailways** (tel. 800/639-3317).

Advance Transit (tel. 603/448-2815) provides public transportation for the upper valley.

Exploring Western and Central New Hampshire

Numbers in the margin correspond to points of interest on the Dartmouth–Lake Sunapee map.

The first leg of our tour of the region takes a slow road of particular beauty, Route 4, to a junction with Route 11, which the tour follows west in the direction of Lake Sunapee.

❶ **Andover,** on Route 4, 8 miles west of Franklin and 20 miles northeast of Concord, and the home of Proctor Academy, is a village of early Federal to late-Victorian period homes. Its free museum, open weekends from June through October, occupies a railway station built in 1874 in the neighboring hamlet of Potter Place.

❷ Colby-Sawyer College (1837) is the heartbeat of **New London** (on Route 114, 2 miles northwest of its junction with Route 11), but the inn and meeting house on Main Street show the visitor the face of an idealized American town.

Time Out **Peter Christian's Tavern,** in the Edgewood Inn on Main Street, is a hangout for youth where the soups are homemade and the hearty stews are available by the mug. "Peter's Father's Favorite Sandwich" is roast beef, cheese, onion, tomato, spinach, and horseradish; and there are more-basic combos as well.

❸ Not far away, beach, mountains, and state parkland set off **Lake Sunapee,** a jewel of water in the western highlands of New Hampshire. You can cruise it on the MV *Mt. Sunapee II* (tel. 603/763-4030), rise above it on chair lift, or picnic along its beach or in the park. The Craftsmen's Fair, the Antique and Classic Boat Parade, and the Gem and Mineral Festival all take place here (Lake Sunapee Association, Box 400, Sunapee 03782, tel. 603/763-2495).

❹ Head northwest on I-89 and exit at Lebanon to visit **Hanover** and the Dartmouth College campus. **Dartmouth** was founded in 1769 to educate "Youth of the Indian Tribes," but local boys could come, too. The handsome campus around the green is the northernmost Ivy League college and the cultural center of the region. Among the buildings to visit are **Hopkins Center** (tel. 603/646-2422), a prototype for the Metropolitan Opera House at Lincoln Center, New York City; and, across the green from the Baker Library, the Hood Museum.

The 10 permanent galleries of the **Hood Museum of Art** house works from Africa, Asia, Europe, and America. Assyrian reliefs from the 5th century BC and an amphora from ancient Greece are among the most venerable pieces. The American collections include silver by Paul Revere, paintings by Winslow Homer, and works by Native Americans. The award-winning

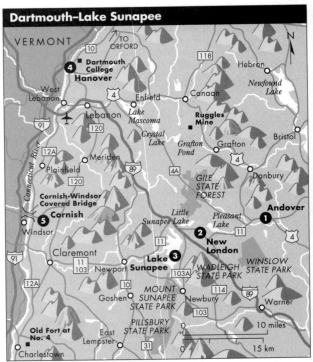

Dartmouth–Lake Sunapee

VERMONT

TO ORFORD

Hebron

Dartmouth College
Hanover

West Lebanon

Enfield

Canaan

Newfound Lake

Lebanon

Lake Mascoma

Ruggles Mine

Bristol

Crystal Lake

Grafton Pond

Grafton

Plainfield

Meriden

Danbury

GILE STATE FOREST

Cornish-Windsor Covered Bridge

Little Sunapee Lake

Pleasant Lake

Andover

Cornish

Windsor

New London

Claremont

Lake Sunapee

WADLEIGH STATE PARK

WINSLOW STATE PARK

Newport

Goshen

MOUNT SUNAPEE STATE PARK

Newbury

Warner

Old Fort at No. 4

PILLSBURY STATE PARK

East Lempster

Charlestown

10 miles

15 km

contemporary building was designed by Charles Moore. Free guided tours are given on weekend afternoons. *Wheelock St., tel. 603/646–2808. Admission free. Open Tues.–Fri. 11–5, weekends 9:30–5.*

It's a slow but pleasant back-road drive on Route 12A to the modest village of **Cornish,** with its brace of four covered bridges. Cornish was an unlikely host of the 19th-century American Renaissance, yet the American novelist Winston Churchill and the painter Maxfield Parrish lived and worked here, and it was here that the sculptor Augustus Saint-Gaudens (1848–1907) set up his studio and created the heroic, sensitive bronzes that would ensure his fame. Today you may tour Saint-Gaudens's house, studio, gallery, and gardens. Of particular interest are the full-size copies of the sculptor's famous pieces, as well as sketches and casting molds. At 2 on Sunday afternoons in summer, everyone is invited to bring a picnic lunch and enjoy a chamber-music concert on the lawn. *Saint-Gaudens National Historic Site, off Rte. 12A, Cornish, tel. 603/675–2175. Admission: $1 ages 17–62. Open mid-May–Oct., daily 8:30–4:30; grounds open until dusk.*

The **Cornish-Windsor covered bridge,** the longest covered bridge in the United States, was built in 1866 and rebuttressed in 1988–89. It spans the Connecticut River, connecting New Hampshire and Vermont.

When the Connecticut River was the Colonial frontier, a ragged **Old Fort at No. 4** was an outpost on the lonely periphery of Colonial civilization. What you see now is a re-creation, a living history museum whose costumed interpreters tell what went on in and outside the stockade in the 1740s. Although there are 13 buildings (where you will see demonstrations of weaving, cooking, and candlemaking) and a small museum, the fort is not comparable to Old Sturbridge Village in Massachusetts or to Old Mystic in Connecticut. During the year there are frequent reenactments of militia musters and training exercises from the French and Indian War era. *Rte. 11, Springfield Rd., Charlestown, tel. 603/826–5700. Admission: $4.75 adults, $3.25 children. Open late May–Oct., Wed.–Mon.*

Numbers in the margin correspond to points of interest on the Monadnock Region and Central New Hampshire map.

Covered bridges and 18th-century villages give the next part of our tour a Currier & Ives look, yet there are patches of real forest here, such as the undeveloped Pisgah State Forest, home to wolves, foxes, deer, and moose. From Cornish, return to Route 12A at Claremont. Continue south along the Connecticut River ❻ and follow Route 12 to **Keene.** The cultural and market center of the Monadnock is an interesting blend of the progressive and the nostalgic. The Arts Center on Brickyard Pond (tel. 603/358–2168) of Keene State College has three theaters, eight art studios, and a dance studio as well as the Thorne-Sagendorph Art Gallery, which regularly exhibits traveling shows from museums around the country and is a showcase for New England artists. Indoor and outdoor concerts are given here by nationally known rock and folk stars as well as local contemporary and chamber groups. The Putnam Art Lecture Hall (tel. 603/352–1909) offers an arts and international film series.

The 900-seat **Colonial Theater** (Main St., tel. 603/352–2033) is a 70-year-old concert house and movie theater where major acts (B. B. King, Taj Mahal, Bonnie Raitt, Judy Collins) appear and new films are shown. The theater has brass ticket-booths and near-perfect acoustics.

Keene has been recognized for its large number of trees and the width of its main street, where stately homes of 19th-century mill owners sit beside still older historic houses.

Time Out   **Lindy's Diner,** across from the bus station on Gilbo Avenue, is where you'll see the presidential candidates if you're here in February of an election year. The menu is most likely to feature liver and onions, pot roast, or meat loaf.

❼ Turn north off Route 101 for **Harrisville,** once called Twitchell Village. A preserved town (Historic Harrisville, Inc., Church Hill, Harrisville 03450, tel. 603/827–3722), it dates from the early years of the Industrial Revolution. It is perhaps the only mill town in America to have survived in its original form. Here are factories that once produced woodenware and woolens; the **Weaving Center** (tel. 603/827–3996), a shop of yarns and looms on Main Street, will teach you to weave a scarf in a day.

❽ Beyond Harrisville is the prosperous hill town of **Dublin,** the highest town in the state and the longtime home of the *Old Farmer's Almanac.* One of the entrances to Monadnock State Park is here, as well as **Friendly Farm** (tel. 603/563–8444), where children can see chickens hatching and play pat-the-goat.

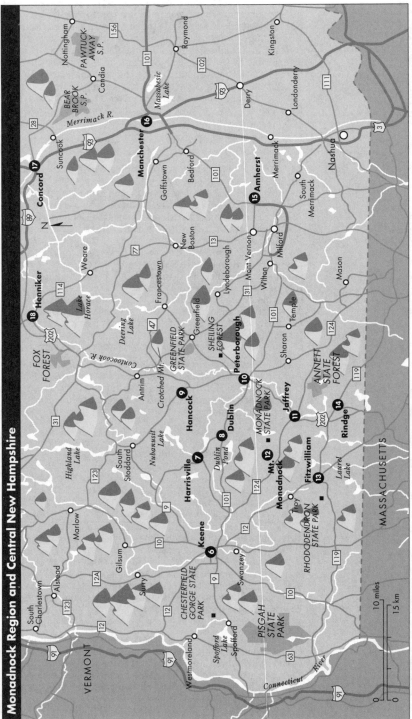

Monadnock Region and Central New Hampshire

❾ Just off Route 202, **Hancock** was founded (and named for the statesman John Hancock) when George Washington was president. Now preserved in its entirety as an historic district, it has a bandstand on the green and New Hampshire's oldest inn, the Hancock Inn of 1789. South of town, on Cavender Road, is a covered bridge across the Contoocook River.

❿ Farther south, **Peterborough** was the model for Thornton Wilder's *Our Town*. Main Street has not been overly updated, yet the town is now known as a publishing center for computer magazines.

Peterborough's Free Public Library was the nation's first, and the Historical Society's **Museum of Americana** (19 Grove St., tel. 603/924–3235) contains a circa-1840 millworker's house, a country store, and a Colonial kitchen, plus changing exhibits.

The **MacDowell Colony** (tel. 603/924–3886 or 212/966–4860), established by the composer Edward MacDowell in 1907, offers artistic seclusion to painters, writers, sculptors, composers, and filmmakers, among others. Only a small part is open to the public.

Time Out | **Peterborough Diner,** at 10 Depot Street, is a hangout for young professionals and anyone else who wants a quick bite to eat or a long dawdle over coffee. Choose a booth or a counter seat in a railroad-car setting. The spinach pie and occasional quiche are perhaps out of sync with the decor, but you can also have a cheeseburger or even franks and beans.

⓫ The drive south to **Jaffrey** on Route 202 gives you a momentary sense of an earlier time, when this was virgin territory. In the hillside cemetery of Jaffrey Center (the old part of town), the novelist Willa Cather is buried not far from Amos Fortune, the freed slave who became Jaffrey's town philanthropist. Cather, a perennial summer visitor, wrote *My Antonia* in a tent pitched in a local meadow. The **Amos Fortune Forum** (tel. 603/532–1303) brings nationally known speakers to the 1773 Meeting House on summer evenings.

⓬ You are now at the foot of **Mt. Monadnock,** a National Natural Landmark, which rises 3,165 feet above the plain. It is the most climbed mountain in America and second in the world only to Japan's Mt. Fuji. More than 20 trails of varying difficulty lead to the bald stone top, and park rangers redirect climbers if one route becomes overcrowded. The Monadnock Ecocenter has guided walks, a lecture room, and a small museum. Here you can identify the birds and plants you see on your climb. Allow at least three hours to go up and down the mountain. **Monadnock State Park** (tel. 603/532–8035) has picnic grounds and some tent campsites. On a clear day the view from the summit is of three states. The park entrance is 4 miles north of Jaffrey; turn right off Route 124.

⓭ A well-preserved historic district set around an oval common has made the town of **Fitzwilliam,** on Route 119, a textbook of Early American village architecture. The Meeting House (1817) now houses town offices; the **Historical Society** (tel. 603/585–3134) maintains a museum and country store in the Amos J. Blake House, a 19th-century law office. On a hillock at one end of the green is the church, at the other, the Fitzwilliam Inn (1796). Grouped about the common are well-preserved Colonial and Federal houses that are now antiques stores, a clock shop, and the public library.

Rhododendron State Park, 2½ miles northwest of the common, has picnic tables in a pine grove and marked footpaths. Sixteen of its 294 acres are solidly *rhododendron maximum*, the largest concentration north of the Alleghenies and well worth seeing at their peak, early to mid-July. Just at the entrance to the park is a wildflower trail that blooms somewhat earlier.

Time Out Just off Route 12, on Marlborough Road in Troy, the **Monadnock Mountainview Restaurant** offers uncomplicated food and a great view of the mountain from the Village Gathering Mall. Soup and half a sandwich (roast beef, tuna, or ham and Swiss cheese) are a bargain, and the children's menu includes peanut butter and jelly sandwiches.

⑭ The village of **Rindge,** 8 miles east of Fitzwilliam on Route 119, chartered in the middle of the 18th century, is a picturesque spot that becomes busy when the summer people arrive at the nearby lakes. During the academic year there are concerts and lectures at Franklin Pierce College (tel. 603/899–5111).

Cathedral of the Pines, an outdoor hall of worship, has an inspiring view of Mt. Monadnock from its Altar of the Nation. Services are held here by all faiths (no solicitations take place); the simple rectangular altar is composed of rock from every state and territory. Organ meditations can be heard at midday, Monday through Thursday. The Memorial Bell Tower, with its carillon of international bells, is dedicated to the American women, military and civilian, who sacrificed their lives in service to their country. The tower is built of native stone; the bronze tablets over the four arches are by Norman Rockwell. Flower gardens, an indoor chapel, and a museum of military memorabilia share the hilltop. Opposite the entrance, the Wayside Park of Annett State Forest has picnic sites. The turn off Route 119 is well marked. *Rindge 03461, tel. 603/899–3300. Open May–Oct., dawn–sunset.*

⑮ Return via Route 202 to Peterborough, and head east on Route 101. You'll pass **Miller State Park,** with an auto road that takes you almost 2,300 feet up Mount Pack Monadnock. Continue east on Route 101 (bypassing Milford) to reach **Amherst,** a bedroom community for the cities along I–93 that still retains its rural flavor. The village green, with its antique homes (all on the National Historic Register), is one of the prettiest in New England. Today, however, Amherst is almost better known for its dawn-to-dusk weekend flea market, on the western outskirts of town. The flea market, which operates May through October, attracts dealers and decorators from all over New England.

⑯ Farther on Route 101 is **Manchester,** New Hampshire's largest city. The mile-long redbrick **Amoskeag** textile mill, on the Monadnock's eastern bank, churned out 4 million yards of cloth per week at its production peak. Descendants of a work force of 17,000 immigrants and displaced rural Yankees still populate the area. The schedule for tours of the Amoskeag mills is irregular. Contact the Manchester Historic Association (129 Amherst St., tel. 603/622–7531).

The **Currier Gallery of Art,** a gem of a small museum in a downtown Beaux-Arts building, has a permanent collection of paintings, sculpture, and decorative arts from the 13th to 20th centuries. There's also the Zimmerman House, a 1950 Usonian home by Frank Lloyd Wright that you reach via museum bus. *192 Orange St., Manchester 03104, tel. 603/669-6144. Open Tues., Wed., Fri., and Sat. 10-4; Thur. 10-10, Sun. 2-5. Closed holidays. Reservations required for Zimmerman house.*

Time Out For riverside dining on the site of an old gristmill, the **Grist Mill Restaurant** (520 South St., tel. 603/226-1922) is inexpensive and informal, ideal for families. The menu lists everything from barbecue sandwiches to cream puffs drenched in chocolate fudge. The house specialty are its bread-bowl meals: turkey pot pie, seafood chowder, and broccoli-cheddar soup, among others, all served in very edible bowls made entirely of bread.

You can continue on I–93 north to the Lakes Region or get off at the second exit west (Boscawen) and proceed on bucolic Route 4 to Salisbury. If you stay on Route 4, you will be on a low-traffic back road that joins the Sunapee–Dartmouth tour. Otherwise, turn south on Route 127, skirting Black Water Reservoir, and continue to **Hopkinton,** known for its antiques shops and mansion-lined Main Street.

17 Head north on I–93 to **Concord,** the state's capital. The **Coach and Eagle Trail** is a free walking tour (maps are available at the Chamber of Commerce at 244 North Main Street, as well as in stores along the way). The route includes the Statehouse (the oldest state capitol still in use), the Colonial Revival City Hall (built as an intended contrast to the "preponderance of entire granite buildings"), and Franklin Pierce's Greek Revival home. While the **New Hampshire Historical Society Museum** (30 Park St., tel. 603/225-3381) boasts a Concord Coach, state-of-the-art transportation centuries ago, the **Christa McAuliffe Planetarium** on the campus of the New Hampshire Technical Institute allows the mind to travel far into the future. A fitting memorial to the country's first "Teacher in Space," killed in the *Challenger* explosion, the planetarium is the most advanced in the world. Reservations are strongly advised for the 92-seat space show, combining advanced computer graphics and sound equipment with views from the 40-foot dome telescope. There are hands-on activities for children. *3 Institute Dr., tel. 603/271–STAR Admission: $5 adults, $3 children over 3 and senior citizens. Closed Mon. and holidays.*

18 Head west on Route 9 and then south on Route 114 to **Henniker,** a lovely white-clapboard town that bills itself as "the world's only Henniker." It's home to New England College, site of the first Elderhostel and still host to Elderhostel programs during college vacations year-round. Stroll or picnic along the banks of the Contoocook River (one of the few New England rivers that flows north—its headwaters are at the foot of Mt. Monadnock), or look in at the college art gallery next to the administration building, home to a stagecoach tavern in the 1800s. The single-span covered bridge dates back only a few decades.

Western New Hampshire for Free

Cathedral of the Pines, Rindge

Currier Gallery of Art, Manchester
Harris Center for Conservation Education, Hancock
Hood Museum of Art, Dartmouth College, Hanover
Hopkins Center, Dartmouth College, Hanover (free tours)
Sharon Arts Center, Peterborough
Thorne-Sagendorph Art Gallery, Keene

What to See and Do with Children

Christa McAuliffe Planetarium, Concord
Fort at No. 4, Charlestown
Friendly Farm, Dublin
Lawrence L. Lee Scouting Museum, Camp Carpenter, Concord.
Maple sugarhouses, Alstead and Mason
Monadnock Children's Museum, Keene
The Ruggles Mine, Grafton

Off the Beaten Track

Mount Kearsage Indian Museum is a monument to Native American culture and a display of choice artifacts. You don't just wander through peering at labels; you are educated as you go. You'll find a birch canoe, moose-hair embroidery, a tepee, quillwork, and basketry, and you'll learn about lifestyles and attitudes. Self-guided walks lead through an early variety vegetable garden laid out the Native American way (the "Three Sisters" who always stay together are beans, corn, and squash) and into the "Medicine Woods" of herbs and healing plants. Tours begin on the hour (also on the half-hour midsummer–foliage season). *Kearsage Mountain Rd., Warner, tel. 603/456–2600. Open Mon.–Sat. 10–5, Sun. 1–5.*

The Ruggles Mine. More than 150 minerals are found here on top of Isinglass Mountain in the oldest mica, feldspar, beryl, and uranium mine in the United States. Primarily an open-pit pegmatite mine, now out of use, the space has giant caverns, winding passageways, and arched-ceiling tunnels to explore. The 19th-century owner, Sam Ruggles, was so afraid someone would usurp his claim that he mined only at night and sold his ore secretly in England. Watch for signs directing you from Route 4; the mine is about 2 miles from Grafton Center. Collecting is permitted. *Rte. 4, Grafton, tel. 603/448–6911. Admission: $9 adults, $3 children 5–12. Open May–mid-June, weekends 9–5; mid-June–mid-Oct., daily 9–5.*

Maple sugarhouses answer the question "Is there joy in mudtime?" When the days begin to warm, but the nights are still freezing—that is, sometime in late February or early March—the sap starts flowing from the maple trees. Visitors can watch the tapping process, including demonstrations of old methods. Then comes the cooking-down, followed by the reward: tasting the syrup. You can try it with unsweetened doughnuts and maybe a pickle, or taste sugar-on-snow, the confection that results when hot syrup is poured upon snow. Always telephone first to see if the sugaring-off is under way. Open to the public are: **Bacon's Sugar House** (Dublin Rd., Jaffrey Center, tel. 603/532–8836); **Bascom's** (Mt. Kingsbury, Rte. 123A, Alstead, tel. 603/835–2230); **Clark's Sugar House** (off Rte. 123A, Alstead, tel. 603/835–6863); **Old Brick Sugar House** (Summit Rd., Keene, tel. 603/352–6812); **Parker's Maple Barn** (Brookline Rd., Mason, tel. 603/878–2308), where a restaurant serves a whole-grain pancake breakfast any time of day along with a regular menu; and **Stuart & John's Sugar House & Pancake Restaurant** (Jct. Rtes. 12 and 63, Westmoreland, tel. 603/399–4486).

Shopping

There are galleries aplenty throughout the region, and the open studios of many artisans are marked along the roads by neat New Hampshire state signs. An occasional enclave of shops is the local equivalent of a mall, but don't expect a cluster of large discount or department stores. Fairs like the League of New Hampshire Craftsmen's at Mt. Sunapee State Park and Hospital Day in New London offer excellent shopping opportunities. Small-town fairs on church lawns offer bargains and occasional treasures of all kinds. The absence of a state sales tax regularly brings Vermonters across the Connecticut River.

Keene is the market town for the region, with enormous supermarkets in its own malls and, in its heart, an exceptional upscale mall in a restored mill. Peterborough has the headquarters and retail outlets of two top-of-the-line companies: the national, mostly mail-order **Brookstone** (Rte. 202N, tel. 603/924–7181) for tools and gadgets; and **Eastern Mountain Sports** (Vose Farm Rd., tel. 603/924–7231), known for rugged outdoor sportswear and equipment.

Antiquing is a major preoccupation for visitors to the Monadnocks, and you will find dealers in barns and home-stores that are strung along back roads and "open by chance or by appointment"; in well-stocked shops around village greens; and in clusters of stores along heavily traveled strips. Route 119 from Fitzwilliam to Hinsdale is a good stretch, as is Route 101 from Marlborough to Wilton. Hopkinton, Hollis, and Amherst are also good antiquing towns.

Shopping hours in Keene are generally Monday–Saturday 10–9, Sunday 11–6. Small towns are more likely to roll up the sidewalks at 5.

Antiques   **Antiques Center** (Main St., Charlestown, tel. 603/826–3639) has a wide inventory but specializes in fine china, glass, primitives, and fine furniture. It also carries ephemera.
Bell Hill Antiques (Rte. 101 at Bell Hill Rd., Bedford, tel. 603/472–5580).
Fitzwilliam Antique Center (Jct. Rtes. 12 and 119, Fitzwilliam, tel. 603/585–9092).
The New Hampshire Antiquarian Society (Main St., Hopkinton, tel. 603/746–3825).
Peterborough Antiques (76 Grove St., Peterborough, tel. 603/924–7297).
The Antique Shops (Rte. 12, Westmoreland, tel. 603/399–7039).

Crafts   **League of New Hampshire Craftsmen** (headquarters, 205 N. Main St., Concord, tel. 603/224–1471; shop, 36 N. Main St., tel. 603/228–8171). Juried crafts in many media are for sale in this headquarter shop and in branches throughout the state. A free map details shops and workshops open to visitors.
Artisan's Workshop. Most of the gifts, jewelry, handblown glass and other handcrafts available here are made by local artists and craftspeople. The workshop is next to Peter Christian's

Tavern in the 1847 Edgewood Inn. *Main St., New London, tel. 603/526–4227. Open daily and evenings.*

Dorr Mill Store (Rte. 103, Guild, tel. 603/863–1197). Fabrics, yarns, rug wools, and sweaters are sold in this famous store located between Newport and Sunapee. The remnants are especially tempting.

Mouse Menagerie of Fine Crafts (Rte. 120, Cornish, tel. 603/542–9691). If cats could shop, this store would be filled with them. There is a pricey collector's series of more than 50 mice, or you can choose more mundane creatures that wouldn't break a kitty's bank.

Galleries **North Gallery at Tewksbury's** (Rte. 101E, Peterborough, tel. 603/924–3224) has a wide selection of gifts and local handcrafts.
Sharon Arts Center (Rte. 123, Sharon, tel. 603/924–7256) is affiliated with the League of New Hampshire Craftsmen. Classes, shows, gallery, and a large shop are located on a pretty back road south of Peterborough.

Jewelry **Designer Gold** (68 S. Main St., Hanover, tel. 603/643–3864). Paul Gross, goldsmith, makes one-of-a-kind and limited-edition gold jewelry. You can commission whatever you want but don't see.
Mark Knipe Goldsmiths (13 S. State St., Concord, tel. 603/224–2920). Browse or buy custom work in this gallery and studio.

Malls **Colony Mill Marketplace** (West St., Keene, tel. 603/357–1240) is a warren of boutiques, specialty stores, galleries, and cafés a few steps from the center of town. The shops include **Country Artisans** (tel. 603/352–6980), which carries art and handcrafts including stoneware, textiles, prints, and baskets. **Autumn Woods** (tel. 603/352–5023) is the place for those who like the look but not the wobble of antiques. No kitsch here; just fine reproductions of Shaker and Colonial wood furniture in birch, maple, and pine. **Joe Jones Ski & Sport Shop** (tel. 603/352–5266) has sports gear as well as outdoor sportswear for men and women. **Toadstool Bookshop** (tel. 603/352–8815) has a particularly strong selection of children's books, but offers a variety of good reading material and art books. Frequent book signings introduce such authors as Ken Burns, a longtime Walpole resident. **Ye Goodie Shoppe** (tel. 603/352–0326) was founded in 1931 and has been handmaking chocolates ever since.
The Powerhouse (Rte. 12A, 1 mi n. of I–89 Exit 20, West Lebanon, tel. 603/448–1010). A onetime power station and three adjacent buildings on the riverfront have become a retail complex with 40 stores, boutiques, and restaurants. Free-standing sculpture and windows that overlook the Mascoma River make visiting almost as much fun as shopping.

Sports and Outdoor Activities

In addition to the normal outdoor activities in the hills, forests and mountains, horse-drawn sleigh and hay rides are seasonal pleasures hereabouts. Two providers are **Stonewall Farm** (Keene, tel. 603/357–7278) and **Silver Ranch, Inc.** (Jaffrey, tel. 603/532–7363).

Biking Low-traffic roads both along the river and elsewhere are ideal for biking. Try Route 12A north from Charlestown to Cornish; Route 4 from West Andover to Enfield; Route 10 from Hanover to Orford; and Routes 11, 103, and 103A around Sunapee Lake.

Farther south, the 45-mile **Covered Bridge Loop** is especially suited to biking. From Keene, follow Route 10 south to Swanzey, then take back roads, seeking out the six covered bridges (*see* Exploring Western New Hampshire, *above*). For planned routes throughout the Monadnocks, contact the **Greater Keene Chamber of Commerce** (8 Central Sq., Keene 03431, tel. 603/352–1303). For organized bike rides in southern New Hampshire contact the **Granite State Wheelmen** (16 Clinton St., Salem 03079, tel. 603/898–9926). For inn-to-inn biking in the Monadnock region contact **Monadnock Bicycle Touring** (Box 19, Keene Rd., Harrisville 03450, tel. 603/827–3925).

Camping   **Crow's Nest Campground** (Rte. 10, Newport 03773, tel. 603/863–6170).

Northstar Campground (278 Coonbrook Rd., Newport 03773, tel. 603/863–4001).

Otter Lake Camping Area (Otterville Rd., New London 03257, tel. 603/763–5600).

Rand's Pond Campground (Rand Pond Rd., Goshen 03752, tel. 603/863–3350).

Forest Lake Campground (Rte. 10, Winchester 03470, tel. 603/239–4267).

Greenfield, Mt. Monadnock, and Surry Mountain Dam state parks also have campsites.

Canoeing   The Connecticut River is considered generally safe after June 15, but canoeists should always proceed with caution. The river is not for beginners at any time of year. Canoe rentals are available from May to November at **North Star Canoe & Mountain Bike Rentals** (Rte. 12A, Balloch's Crossing, Cornish, tel. 603/542–5802).

Hannah's Paddles, Inc. (RFD 11, Box 260A–32, Concord 03301, tel. 603/753–6695) rents canoes for use on the Merrimack and Contoocook rivers, daily in July and August, weekends only during spring and fall.

Ledyard Canoe Club of Dartmouth (on the Connecticut River, Hanover 03755, tel. 603/643–6709) has rentals, classes, and shuttles.

Fishing   In Lake Sunapee there are brook and lake trout, salmon, smallmouth bass, and pickerel. Lake Mascoma has rainbow trout, pickerel, and horned pout.

There are more than 200 lakes and ponds in the Monadnock region. Dublin Pond, Dublin, has lake trout. Goose Pond, West Canaan, has smallmouth bass and white perch. Rainbow and golden trout, pickerel, and horned pout are found in Laurel Lake, Fitzwilliam; and there are rainbow and brown trout in the Ashuelot River. For word on what's biting and where, contact the Department of Fish and Game (tel. 603/271–3421).

Hiking   Hikes in the state parks include a steep, mile-long trail to the summit of **Mt. Kearsage** in Winslow State Park; a network of trails on **Mt. Sunapee;** rugged hiking in **Pillsbury State Park,** a wilderness area in Washington; and trails to the 3,121-foot summit of **Mt. Cardigan.** Trails may also be found at **Crotched Mountain** (Francestown and Greenfield), **Drummer Hill Preserve** (Keene), **Fox State Forest** (Hillsboro), **Horatio Colony Trust** (Keene), **Sheiling Forest** (Peterborough), and **Wapack**

Reservation (Greenfield). The **Harris Center for Conservation Education** (Hancock, tel. 603/525–3394) and the **Monadnock Ecocenter** (Jaffrey, tel. 603/532–8035) sponsor guided walks.

Rafting White-water rafting is a springtime thrill, as you chase the runoff of melting snow in a canoe or rubber raft. For the Contoocook River, regular trips start at the **White Birch Community Center** in Henniker.

State Parks

Mt. Sunapee State Park in Newbury has a tram up the mountain and is the site of a summerlong series of special events including the annual August Craftsmen's Fair. Consider **Bear Den Geological Park** (Gilsum), a 19th-century mining town surrounded by more than 50 abandoned mines; **Curtiss Dogwood State Reservation** (Lyndeborough, off Rte. 31), where the namesake blossoms are out in early May; **Pisgah State Park** (off Rte. 63 or Rte. 119), a 13,000-acre wilderness area full of wild game; and **Rhododendron State Park** (north of Fitzwilliam), with the largest stand of *rhododendron maximum* north of the Alleghenies.

Dining and Lodging

The **Lodging Reservation Service, Sunapee Region** (tel. 603/763–2495 or 800/258–3530), will find accommodations for you. The basic lodging of Monadnock remains the village inn, often the best place to eat as well. Chain hotels and motels dominate the lodging scene in Manchester and Concord, but bed-and-breakfasts flourish along the back roads.

Andover
Lodging

English House Bed & Breakfast. An English couple owns this Edwardian-period inn, and guests are naturally served tea and homemade cookies at 4 PM. Large, sunny rooms furnished with English and American antiques are hung with watercolors by the owner's mother and uncle, both well-known British artists. *Main St., Andover 03216, tel. 603/735–5987. 7 rooms with bath. Facilities: cable TV, cross-country ski trails. No pets. No smoking. MC, V. Rates include full breakfast, afternoon tea. Moderate.*

Bedford
Lodging
★

Bedford Village Inn. Within minutes of Manchester, this luxury inn was once a working farm, complete with horse-nuzzle marks on old beams. But antique four-poster beds (recrafted to hold king-size mattresses), Italian marble in the whirlpool baths, and 2,000 bottles in the wine cellar bespeak up-to-date elegance. Some suites have fireplaces. *2 Old Bedford Rd., Bedford 03110, tel. 603/472–2602 or 800/852–1166. 12 rooms with bath. Facilities: restaurant, cable TV, banquet hall, conference facilities, movies. No pets. AE, DC, MC, V. Moderate–Expensive.*

Canaan
Lodging

Inn on Canaan Street. Situated 2½ miles north of Canaan town, the inn is part of the preserved historical district on a street laid out in the 1700s. There is stenciling on the walls, and decorations in each room are based on a different flower. "Forget-me-not" has a working fireplace and can be combined with "Aster" to make a suite. *Box 92, Canaan St., Canaan 03741, tel. 603/523–7310. 4 rooms, 3 with bath. Facilities: cable TV, canoes. No pets. No smoking. MC, V. Rates include full buffet breakfast. Moderate.*

Concord
Dining
★

Hermanos Cocina Mexicana. Expect a wait, but you can browse in the *mercado* (market) next door until you're seated. The nachos supreme come with blue corn chips; taquitos or sopa de frijoles with cornbread are equally appetizing first courses. Avocado quesadillas, chimichangas, and salads are popular entrées, but desserts such as Miguel's dream (chocolate chips, cinnamon, pecans, and honey inside a warm tortilla) and the Kahlua pie are worth a little prior restraint. *6 Pleasant St. Ext., Concord, tel. 603/224-5669. Dress: casual. No reservations. MC, V. Inexpensive-Moderate.*

Cornish
Lodging
★

Chase House Bed & Breakfast. This is the former home of Samuel P. Chase, who was Abraham Lincoln's secretary of the treasury, a chief justice of the United States, and the founder of the Republican Party. A few years ago it was rescued from derelict obscurity and restored to 19th-century elegance. Some rooms have settees and canopied beds; some look out onto meadows and others across to the Connecticut River. The B&B is on Route 12A, just north of the Cornish-Windsor covered bridge. *RR 2, Box 909, Cornish 03745, tel. 603/675-5391. 6 rooms with bath. Facilities: canoes. MC, V. Rates include full breakfast. Moderate.*

Fitzwilliam
Lodging

Hannah Davis House. A Federal village house updated from its 1820 beginnings, this bed-and-breakfast opened in 1989 has lost none of its original elegance and charm. Much of the old glass has been saved along with the beehive oven and working fireplaces. Just steps from the green are antiques shops and the historical museum. *186 Depot Rd., Fitzwilliam 03447, tel. 603/585-3344. 5 rooms with bath. Facilities: cable TV, VCR. No pets. No smoking in bedrooms. No credit cards. Rates include full breakfast. Moderate.*

★

Amos Parker House. The original structure (now the great room and kitchen) must have been one of the earliest in the village. Now six fireplaces spread warmth in winter; a deck and spectacular flower garden make the most of summer. Wide pine-board floors show around the edges of Oriental rugs. *Rte. 119, Box 202, Fitzwilliam 03447, tel. 603/585-6540. 6 rooms, 4 with bath. No pets. No smoking. No credit cards. Rates include full breakfast and all taxes. Inexpensive-Moderate.*

Fitzwilliam Inn. Vermont Transit buses from Boston's Logan Airport stop at the door, just as the stagecoach once did. Indoors, too, much remains as it was in 1796. Local residents dally in the tavern, and the restaurant serves Yankee cooking. Upstairs in the rooms the furniture is a hodgepodge of early and late hand-me-downs. The imperfections suggest that this is how inns really were in bygone times. *The Green, Fitzwilliam 03447, tel. 603/585-9000. 20 rooms, 17 with bath. Facilities: restaurant, bar, pool, cross-country ski trail. AE, DC, MC, V. Inexpensive.*

Francestown
Dining
★

Maitre Jacq. The building is putty-colored and plain; the food provincial French; and the chef, is likely to ask whether you're enjoying your meal. The bouillabaisse contains lobster, monkfish, shrimp, mussels, clams, and more than a dozen other ingredients. Five-course, prix-fixe dinners seem an illusion in an isolated setting where even Francestown is 2 miles away. *Mountain Rd. at Rte. 47, Francestown, tel. 603/588-6655. Reservations advised. Dress: neat but casual. D, MC, V. Closed Mon., Sun. in winter. Moderate.*

Hancock
Lodging

John Hancock Inn. The oldest operating inn in New Hampshire dates from 1789 and is the pride of its historically preserved town. The dining room serves Yankee fare by candlelight, and the rubbed natural woodwork throughout the house is a tribute to centuries past. *Main St., Hancock 03447, tel. 603/525-3318. 10 rooms with bath. Facilities: restaurant, lounge. MC, V. Moderate.*

Hanover
Dining

Daniel Webster Room. The classic New England fare of this inn owned and operated by Dartmouth College is appropriate to the setting. An appetizer of house-smoked scallops with a cider-rosemary mayonnaise might be followed by saddle of lamb served with winter squash and celery root. The contemporary Ivy Grill serves lighter, faster food. Both restaurants are in the Hanover Inn, on the College Green. *Main and Wheelock Sts., Hanover, tel. 603/643-4300. Reservations advised. Dress: neat but casual. AE, D, DC, MC, V. Moderate-Expensive.*

Lodging
★

Hanover Inn. The inn's three stories of Georgian brick trimmed with white are the embodiment of American traditional architecture. This is the oldest continuously operating business in New Hampshire and is now a part of Dartmouth College. The building was converted from home to tavern in 1780, and subsequent additions brought it to its present size in 1924. Recent renovation has reduced the number of rooms to enlarge their space and create 16 junior suites. Furnishings include 19th-century antiques and reproductions. *The Green, Box 151, Hanover 03755, tel. 603/643-4300 or 800/443-7024, fax 603/646-3744. 92 rooms with bath. Facilities: 2 restaurants. AE, D, DC, MC, V. Expensive-Very Expensive.*

Henniker
Lodging

Henniker House. This vintage Victorian inn may open onto a sometimes busy residential corner, but step inside and you will have a keen view of the tumbling Contoocook River, a preferred meeting place amongst frogs and dragon flies come summer. The lavish array of breakfast food served in the river-view dining room is worthy of the most extravagant New England inns: soufflé roulade with béchamel sauce and toasted pine nuts; cottage-cheese crepes with fresh strawberries and pecans; and a sumptuous sausage-and-apple bake. Weekenders who arrive early on Friday or stay over until Monday receive a complimentary supper, too. *Box 191, Henniker 03242, tel. 603/428-3198. 5 rooms, 3 with bath. Facilities: Jacuzzi, kitchenette in suite. No pets. MC, V. Rates include full breakfast. Moderate.*

Keene
Dining
★

Henry David's. The restaurant is a tribute to its namesake, Henry David Thoreau, who never dined here but who would have enjoyed the greenery and the simple but well-prepared food. Crab bisque is a frequent soup of the day, and tomato cheddar is a regular. Scrod with lemon-thyme crumbs; baked chicken with apple-brandy sauce; and full-meal-size salads are usually on the menu. Choose from a long list of sandwiches; try a cup of chili served with honey-wheat bread and butter; or sample a boursin cheese and fresh-fruit board with sweet bread and crackers. *81 Main St., Keene, tel. 603/352-0608. Reservations accepted for 5 or more. Dress: casual. DC, MC, V. Inexpensive-Moderate.*

Lodging

Carriage Barn Guest House. The location, on Main Street across from Keene State College, puts everything within walking distance. The barn-cum-house is furnished with antiques mostly from this area, and the operational word is "comfortable." *358 Main St., Keene 03431, tel. 603/357–3812. 4 rooms with bath. Facilities: cable TV in sitting room. No pets. No smoking. No credit cards. Rates include breakfast. Inexpensive.*

Lyme **D'Artagnan.** The food is country-French nouvelle in this 18th-
Dining century public house. Summer dining is on a stone terrace over-
★ looking a brook, and the indoor dining area has wide-plank pine
floors and exposed beams. A four-course prix-fixe menu may
offer pâté of rabbit with hazelnuts on watercress; Scottish
smoked salmon; or poached golden bass with mushrooms and
leeks in vermouth sauce. The desserts include fresh pear almond cream tartelette; and apricot vacherin with apricot-al-
mond-rum ice cream. The flavors of Cool Moose brand ice
cream were devised here by the owner and chef. *13 Dartmouth
College Hwy. (Rte. 10), Lyme, tel. 603/795–2137. Reservations
required. Dress: neat but casual. AE, DC, MC, V. Closed
Mon.–Tues. No dinner Sun. Expensive.*

New London **Millstone.** A country cottage is now a small, homey restaurant
Dining serving new American cuisine in the center of New London.
There's a variation of roast duckling, a rosemary-chicken sau-
té, and a special such as veal del sol (sun-dried tomatoes, shallots, garlic, lemon, and wine sauce) every day. *Newport Rd.,
New London, tel. 603/526–4201. Reservations advised. Dress:
casual. AE, DC, MC, V. Moderate.*

Lodging **New London Inn.** A rambling 1792 country inn in the center of
town has an inviting porch with rocking chairs overseeing Main
Street. The owners' son is chef in the dining room, and the cuisine is more California than New Hampshire with specials like
grilled fresh tuna with braised sweet and hot peppers; breast of
chicken stuffed with goat cheese and basil; and a frozen white
chocolate and Bailey's mousse. *Main St., New London 03257,
tel. 603/526–2791 or 800/526–2791. 30 rooms with bath. Facilities: restaurant. AE, MC, V. Rates include full breakfast.
Moderate.*

Peterborough **The Boilerhouse Restaurant.** This contemporary restoration of-
Dining fers views of Noone Falls (lighted at night), first-rate food, and
a carefully selected wine list. Dinner entrées include gravlax of
Norwegian salmon (cured on the premises with spices and vodka, then served with horseradish and caviar); ranch-raised venison with apricots and red currants; poached salmon; and veal
with forest mushrooms in a brandy-Madeira cream sauce. Popular lunch entrées are scallops and tricolor tortelli; lemon
chicken with pine nuts and capers. While "Death by Chocolate"
is one way to go, the chef's original daily ice cream is also worth
sampling. Fortunately there's also spa cuisine, carefully for-
mulated to be fewer than 500 calories. *Rte. 202 S, Peterborough, tel. 603/924–9486. Reservations advised. Dress: neat but
casual. D, MC, V. Moderate–Expensive.*

Latacarta. Put a New Age restaurant in an old movie theater
and you get the essence of Peterborough. Offered here are
chicken, fish, and a pasta of the day in addition to classic vegetarian dishes. A small indoor café serves late lunches, light dinners, and between-meal bites. Everything is fresh and organic;
salt-free and reduced-calorie dishes are available on request.
You can read the Thoreau quotes on the menu while you wait. *6
School St., Peterborough, tel. 603/924–6878. Reservations advised. Dress: neat but casual. AE, MC, V. Closed Mon. Inexpensive–Moderate.*

Plainfield **Home Hill Country Inn.** A restored 1800 mansion set back from
Lodging the river on 25 acres of meadow and woods, this is a tranquil
★ place. The chef-owner is from Brittany, so there's more than a
touch of French in the 19th-century patrician antiques and collectibles. A suite in the guest house is a romantic hideaway.
The dining room serves classic and nouvelle French cuisine.
River Rd., Plainfield 03781, tel. 603/675–6165. 9 rooms with
bath. Facilities: pool, tennis court, cross-country ski trails.
French spoken. No pets. AE, MC, V. Closed early Nov. Rates
include Continental breakfast. Moderate–Expensive.

Temple **Birchwood Inn.** She-crab soup and roast duckling are two Sat-
Dining urday-night specials, and if you're really lucky you might find
cream-cheese pecan pie on the blackboard dessert menu.
Everything is cooked to order, so allow time for lingering. *Rte.*
45, Temple, tel. 603/878–3285. Reservations required. Dress:
casual. No credit cards. BYOB. No lunch. Closed Sun.–Mon.
spring–fall, Sun.–Thurs. in winter. Moderate.

Lodging **Birchwood Inn.** Thoreau slept here, probably on his way to
climb Monadnock or to visit Jaffrey or Peterborough. In 1825
Rufus Porter painted the mural in the dining room. Country
furniture and handmade quilts outfit the bedrooms, as they did
in 1775 when the house was new and no one dreamed it would
someday be listed in the National Register of Historic Places.
Rte. 45, Temple 03084, tel. 603/878–3285. 7 rooms with bath.
Facilities: restaurant, cable TV in sitting room, piano. No
pets. No credit cards. Rates include full breakfast. Moderate.

Troy **Inn at East Hill Farm.** It could be called a farm-resort, and it is
Lodging definitely a family affair. The owners met here as working college students and have owned the 1830 inn for 30 years. Children are not only welcome, they are planned for; the chef will
cook the eggs they gather. Finicky eaters can always order a
hamburger or hot dog if they don't like what's on the menu. Hay
rides or sleigh rides are offered once a week. Picnic lunches are
available on request—or how about a cookout? Almost anything you want in an easygoing family vacation is available
here. *Mountain Rd., Troy 03465, tel. 603/242–6495 or 800/242–*
6495. 42 rooms with bath. Facilities: restaurant, boating, cable
TV in common room, farm activities, fishing, indoor pool, 2
outdoor pools, sauna, indoor and outdoor whirlpools, tennis.
MC, V. Rates include 3 meals. Moderate.

West Chesterfield **Chesterfield Inn.** This upstairs dining room is candlelit and ro-
Dining mantic, the fare somewhere between Continental and new
American—that is, light. *Rte. 9, West Chesterfield, tel. 603/*
256–3211. Reservations advised. Dress: neat but casual. AE,
DC, MC, V. Closed Sun. and Mon. Moderate–Expensive.

Lodging **Chesterfield Inn.** The Federal period in American domestic ar-
★ chitecture was more than a touch elegant, as this 1781 home
well illustrates. The inn sits on a rise above the main Brat-
tleboro-Keene road, surrounded by rose, herb, and wildflower
gardens. Rooms have been appropriately furnished with armoires, fine antiques, and period-style fabrics. You may ask for
a fireplace or a balcony and have your wish granted. *Rte. 9,*
West Chesterfield 03466, tel. 603/256–3211 or 800/365–5515. 11
rooms with bath; 2 suites. Facilities: restaurant, some whirl-
pool baths. AE, DC, MC, V. Buffet breakfast included. Expen-
sive.

Wilton
Dining
The Ram in the Thicket. Either of the small, intimate dining areas in this formal Federal house lends romance to the international menu. The appetizer of the day might be sautéed olives, onion, and tomatoes. The filet mignon is prepared to order, and the lamb is cooked to a slightly pink, French turn. *Off Rte. 101 near Wilton, tel. 603/654–6440. Reservations advised. Dress: neat but casual. AE, MC, V. No lunch. Moderate.*

The Arts

The Arts Center at Brickyard Pond (Keene, tel. 603/358–2168) is the Monadnocks' center for music, theater, and dance, with performances year-round in a modern facility.

Claremont Opera House (Claremont, tel. 603/542–4433) is a restored 19th-century opera house with year-round performances of drama, music, and film.

Hopkins Center (Hanover, tel. 603/646–2422) also has year-round programs of dance, music, theater, and film.

Music   **Monadnock Music** (Box 255, Peterborough 03458, tel. 603/924–7610) produces concerts by the Temple Town Band (founded in 1799 and considered the oldest band in the United States), the Apple Hill Chamber Players, and other groups in summer.

Theater   **American Stage Festival** (Rte. 13 N, Milford, tel. 603/673–4005) encompasses the state's largest professional theater, offering Broadway plays and new works, as well as children's theater and concert series from early May through October.

New London Barn Playhouse. A converted barn on Main Street houses Non-Equity productions of musicals, comedies, and children's theater. *Box 285, New London 03257, tel. 603/526–6570. Season: mid-June–Aug.*

Palace Theatre (80 Hanover St., Manchester, tel. 603/668–5588), the state's performing arts center, is home to both the symphony and the opera and also hosts national touring companies.

Summer Theater at Brickyard Pond (Keene, tel. 603/357–4041) and the **Peterborough Players** (Stearns Farm, Middle Hancock Rd., Peterborough, tel. 603/924–7585) perform in summer.

Nightlife

Colonial Theater (95 Main St., Keene, tel. 603/352–2033) has the largest movie screen in town plus folk, rock, and jazz acts like k.d. Lang, the Clancy Brothers, and Phish.

Del Rossi's Trattoria (Junction 137 and 101, Dublin, tel. 603/563–7195) has big names in jazz, bluegrass, folk, and blues in an unpretentious country-Italian restaurant Friday and Saturday nights. Reservations advised. Best seats are saved for those who have dinner, too.

The Folkway (85 Grove St., Peterborough, tel. 603/924–7484) is an institution in the northeast. A coffee house, café, bar, and crafts shop, this restaurant has entertainment beginning at 9 PM Wednesday–Saturday. You'll see and hear Lucy Blue Tremblay, Greg Brown, among others with international reputations.

Rynborn (Main St., Antrim, tel. 603/588–6162) specializes in Chicago blues on Saturday night.

Sheraton North Country Inn Lounge (Airport Rd., West Lebanon, tel. 603/298–5906) hosts dancing Wednesday–Saturday, with a band on Friday.

Peter Christian's Tavern (39 S. Main St., Hanover, tel. 603/643–2345) has folk, jazz, or light rock Tuesday and Thursday.

Index

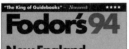

Fodor's Travel Guides

Available at bookstores everywhere, or call 1–800–533–6478, 24 hours a day.

U.S. Guides

Alaska

Arizona

Boston

California

Cape Cod, Martha's Vineyard, Nantucket

The Carolinas & the Georgia Coast

Chicago

Colorado

Florida

Hawaii

Las Vegas, Reno, Tahoe

Los Angeles

Maine, Vermont, New Hampshire

Maui

Miami & the Keys

New England

New Orleans

New York City

Pacific North Coast

Philadelphia & the Pennsylvania Dutch Country

The Rockies

San Diego

San Francisco

Santa Fe, Taos, Albuquerque

Seattle & Vancouver

The South

The U.S. & British Virgin Islands

The Upper Great Lakes Region

USA

Vacations in New York State

Vacations on the Jersey Shore

Virginia & Maryland

Waikiki

Walt Disney World and the Orlando Area

Washington, D.C.

Foreign Guides

Acapulco, Ixtapa, Zihuatanejo

Australia & New Zealand

Austria

The Bahamas

Baja & Mexico's Pacific Coast Resorts

Barbados

Berlin

Bermuda

Brazil

Brittany & Normandy

Budapest

Canada

Cancun, Cozumel, Yucatan Peninsula

Caribbean

China

Costa Rica, Belize, Guatemala

The Czech Republic & Slovakia

Eastern Europe

Egypt

Euro Disney

Europe

Europe's Great Cities

Florence & Tuscany

France

Germany

Great Britain

Greece

The Himalayan Countries

Hong Kong

India

Ireland

Israel

Italy

Japan

Kenya & Tanzania

Korea

London

Madrid & Barcelona

Mexico

Montreal & Quebec City

Morocco

Moscow & St. Petersburg

The Netherlands, Belgium & Luxembourg

New Zealand

Norway

Nova Scotia, Prince Edward Island & New Brunswick

Paris

Portugal

Provence & the Riviera

Rome

Russia & the Baltic Countries

Scandinavia

Scotland

Singapore

South America

Southeast Asia

Spain

Sweden

Switzerland

Thailand

Tokyo

Toronto

Turkey

Vienna & the Danube Valley

Yugoslavia

Special Series

Fodor's Affordables

Caribbean

Europe

Florida

France

Germany

Great Britain

London

Italy

Paris

Fodor's Bed & Breakfast and Country Inns Guides

Canada's Great Country Inns

California

Cottages, B&Bs and Country Inns of England and Wales

Mid-Atlantic Region

New England

The Pacific Northwest

The South

The Southwest

The Upper Great Lakes Region

The West Coast

The Berkeley Guides

California

Central America

Eastern Europe

France

Germany

Great Britain & Ireland

Mexico

Pacific Northwest & Alaska

San Francisco

Fodor's Exploring Guides

Australia

Britain

California

The Caribbean

Florida

France

Germany

Ireland

Italy

London

New York City

Paris

Rome

Singapore & Malaysia

Spain

Thailand

Fodor's Flashmaps

New York

Washington, D.C.

Fodor's Pocket Guides

Bahamas

Barbados

Jamaica

London

New York City

Paris

Puerto Rico

San Francisco

Washington, D.C.

Fodor's Sports

Cycling

Hiking

Running

Sailing

The Insider's Guide to the Best Canadian Skiing

Skiing in the USA & Canada

Fodor's Three-In-Ones (guidebook, language cassette, and phrase book)

France

Germany

Italy

Mexico

Spain

Fodor's Special-Interest Guides

Accessible USA

Cruises and Ports of Call

Euro Disney

Halliday's New England Food Explorer

Healthy Escapes

London Companion

Shadow Traffic's New York Shortcuts and Traffic Tips

Sunday in New York

Walt Disney World and the Orlando Area

Walt Disney World for Adults

Fodor's Touring Guides

Touring Europe

Touring USA: Eastern Edition

Fodor's Vacation Planners

Great American Vacations

National Parks of the East

National Parks of the West

The Wall Street Journal Guides to Business Travel

Europe

International Cities

Pacific Rim

USA & Canada

WHEREVER YOU TRAVEL, *H*ELP IS NEVER FAR AWAY.

From planning your trip to providing travel assistance along the way, American Express® Travel Service Offices* are always there to help.

MAINE
Yankee Tour & Travel
378 Western Avenue
Augusta
207-621-0055

Yankee Tour & Travel
475 Congress Street
Portland
207-775-6763

NEW HAMPSHIRE
Masiello Travel Services, Inc.
69A Island Street
Keene
603-352-8005

Griffin Travel Service, Inc.
323 Franklin Street
Manchester
603-668-3730

Milne Travel Agency
24 Airport Road
West Lebanon
603-298-5997

VERMONT
Milne Travel Agency
325 N. Main Street
Barre
802-479-0541

Milne Travel of Brattleboro
41 Main Street
Brattleboro
802-254-8844

American-International
Travel Service
114 Church Street
Burlington
802-864-9827

American-International
Travel Service
12 Main Street
Essex Junction
802-878-5326

For the office nearest you, call **1-800-YES-AMEX**.